Sophie Green i[illegible]ho lives in Sydney. She has written several fiction and non-fiction books, some under other names. In her spare time she writes about country music on her blog, *Jolene*. She grew up by the water in Sydney and will holiday by the ocean in preference to anywhere else. Her first novel *The Inaugural Meeting of the Fairvale Ladies Book Club*, a Top Ten bestseller in Australia, was shortlisted for the Australian Book Industry Awards for General Fiction Book of the Year 2018, longlisted for the Matt Richell Award for New Writer of the Year and longlisted for the Indie Book Award for Debut Fiction 2018.

ALSO BY SOPHIE GREEN

The Inaugural Meeting of the Fairvale Ladies Book Club
The Shelly Bay Ladies Swimming Circle

THURSDAYS at ORANGE BLOSSOM HOUSE

SOPHIE GREEN

SPHERE

First published in Australia in 2021 by Hachette Australia
First published in Great Britain in 2021 by Sphere in ebook
This paperback edition published by Sphere in 2022

1 3 5 7 9 10 8 6 4 2

All characters and events in this publication, other than those clearly in the public domain, are fictitious and any resemblance to real persons, living or dead, is purely coincidental.

A CIP catalogue record for this book is available from the British Library.

ISBN 978-0-7515-8517-9

Papers used by Sphere are from well-managed forests and other responsible sources.

Sphere
An imprint of
Little, Brown Book Group
Carmelite House
50 Victoria Embankment
London EC4Y 0DZ

An Hachette UK Company
www.hachette.co.uk

www.littlebrown.co.uk

O friend, understand: the body
is like an ocean,
rich with hidden treasures.

Open your innermost chamber and light its lamp.

Mirabai

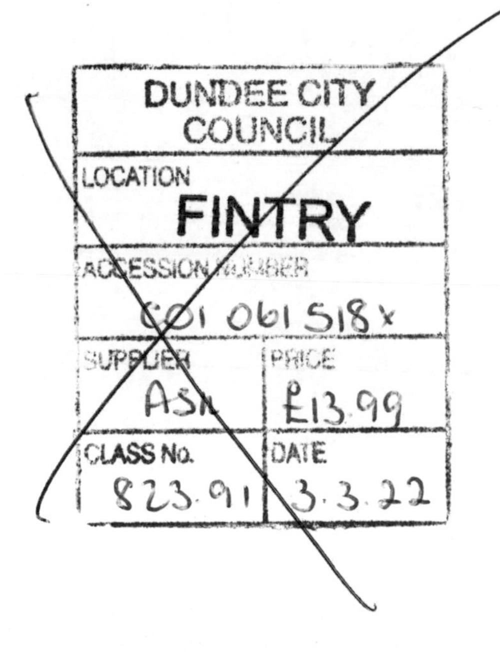

WINTER 1993

Sleepless in Seattle, starring Tom Hanks and Meg Ryan, is released in Australia.

A new British television series called *Absolutely Fabulous* debuts on the ABC.

The Piano, starring the young Anna Paquin, is released.

In the wake of the 1992 publication of *Diana: Her True Story* by Andrew Morton, TRH The Prince and Princess of Wales are now living separately.

Meat Loaf's 'I'd Do Anything for Love (But I Won't Do That)' tops the Australian singles chart for eight weeks.

U2 releases the album *Zooropa*.

CHAPTER ONE

The house looks the same as it always has. As it looked when she was a wife here. When she was a child here, growing up in these sugar cane fields near Atherton that were once her whole world.

The house probably looked like this when her father built it, replacing the more ramshackle dwelling his own father had constructed. Given how flimsy the wooden structure is, she is regularly surprised that it hasn't fallen down. A house on stilts, like all the other Queenslanders around here. Ridiculous, really, that such a thing should exist. But it is still here. Like her.

From this position she has a view of the cane, and the hills behind it. Emerald green they are, all year round; right now they're the backdrop to the dark orange of the flames turning the sea of cane from green to black and brown. When she was a child Grace Maud thought the burnt fields were dead. She still wonders how nature can haul itself out of such wreckage and renew.

'Can I get you anything, Mum?'

Tom appears in front of her, lines streaking out from the corners of his eyes, grey strands in his hat-flattened hair. He looks like he has more years on him than he ever has when she thinks about him. In her mind he's always young. Maybe that just means she's too old and her brain is stuck in gear somewhere around the 1970s, because he hasn't been young since then.

'What are you doing in here?' she says, then sniffs the air. There's a smell that takes her back to childhood, and flashes her forwards through her life. It's the smell of family and familiarity, of promising futures and hopes dashed. 'That cane's still burning. Aren't you meant to be watching it?'

'Are you telling me off?' he says, and while there's a little of the tone of the wounded child in there she can hear mischief too. He's always been cheeky.

'Yes, I believe I am,' she says. 'You're the boss now. You're meant to be keeping an eye on things.'

'Now?' He snorts.

She knows why he's snorting. In truth, he's been the boss since she decided to step back nine years ago at the grand old age of sixty-five. No brothers to inherit the place after her father died – the war took care of that. No husband to help her either – she took care of that. So she'd been running it mostly on her own for a while. Then Tom said he'd leave the city and come back to help her. Luckily for him his wife, Vivien, wanted to come too. That was the only reason Grace Maud felt she could step back: Tom had someone to take care of him while he was taking care of the farm, and the business, and the workers, and everything else that comes with growing cane and burning cane and cutting cane and shipping it off to be made into sugar and molasses and all the other things that a country needs to stay sweet.

'Grace Maud,' says Viv as she enters the room, bending down to kiss her mother-in-law's cheek. 'Have you been sitting in here alone all this time? Tom didn't tell me.' She glares quickly at her husband. 'I would have come to keep you company. Has he even offered you a drink? Cup of tea?'

'Course I have,' Tom says tersely, then his face relaxes.

Grace Maud recognises that particular quickstep: you say something mean to the one you love then remember you're not cross with them in particular, but it's too late to take back what you've said. She and Tom do it to each other as well.

'I just haven't got around to telling him if I want one or not,' Grace Maud says, squeezing Viv's hand.

Every day of her life, she's grateful that Tom found this girl. A tall, broad-shouldered city lass who has no problem tucking her hair into a hat, pulling on her boots and rolling up her sleeves to get out there and do whatever's necessary to keep the farm going. When Tom met her he called her the 'New Farm princess' because she'd barely been out of Brisbane and she liked the comforts of city life. People can change, that's for sure. Or maybe they don't change so much as adapt.

'So would you? Like a drink?' Tom says, scratching the back of his head.

She smiles at him. 'No, thank you, love, I'm fine.'

As she's grown older her eyesight has become less than perfect, so to her Tom looks more and more like her father and her youngest brother, Frank.

Frank was the brother who returned from the war in 1945, but he was never strong enough to work the cane. Grace Maud doesn't know what happened to him while he was in New Guinea – he would never speak of it. He only made it to thirty-nine. Their older brother's name was the last word out of his mouth, and Grace Maud has always wondered if William appeared to Frank right then, as he passed between worlds. She likes to think so. It gives her hope that one of them, or both, will come for her when it's her time.

On the mantelpiece are the other Llewellyn family photographs. Her brothers are handsome in their uniforms, and in other photos they're rugged in their working gear, their hair plastered to their heads in the Queensland humidity. Next to them is a photo of Grace Maud and Ellie Maud. Their father thought it was a good idea to give his twin girls the same middle name, and always insisted on people using both names. It was his way of honouring his mother, he would say when anyone asked.

He didn't point out that it annoyed his daughters no end and led to much teasing at school. And by the time the girls worked out they didn't have to use the Maud part, it was too late and they'd grown accustomed to it. Besides, it bound them together. They were Grace Maud and Ellie Maud, the Llewellyn twins of Atherton. Even after Ellie Maud moved to Melbourne, married a Hungarian man and took his name she was still Ellie Maud. Still Grace Maud's most beloved person.

When Tom was a baby Grace Maud would sit in this same spot, nursing him, gazing at the photos and the view. The panorama of her life and lifelines. She never tires of any of it. That's not why she moved into town. She moved because Tom and Viv needed to have their own home, even though they said they wanted her to stay. Their daughters, Felicity and Edwina, were grown by then and living elsewhere, but they come home occasionally and Grace Maud knows the place would be too crowded with her here too.

Besides, her great-nephew, Luca, needs his own space – as Grace Maud is reminded when he ducks his head to walk in the side door and only takes a couple of strides to reach her. Ellie Maud's husband was a giant and their grandson is six feet four.

'GM,' Luca says, bending in half to kiss her cheek. That's what he's always called her, partly because 'Great Aunt' doesn't appeal to her – or 'Aunt', for that matter – because it has a hint of dowager about it and she'd like to think she's not old enough for that, and also because he's young and the young seem to enjoy adapting their elders' names.

'Luca, darling,' she says. 'Is Tom being nice to you?' She glances at her son, who rolls his eyes.

'Kid gloves, Mum. Like you told me.'

'I did not!' Grace Maud says, but her indignation is fake: she did ask Tom to go gently on Luca in his first weeks on the farm. He is helping them out, after all; it isn't his dream to be a cane farmer. Just because university didn't turn out to be right for him and he left after one semester, that doesn't mean he's going to stay with them forever. Luca has never spent more than a few days in a Far North Queensland summer, or spring, and once he realises what it's like to live in humidity for months on end he might head for Cairns airport with nary a backwards glance.

'It's fine, GM,' Luca says, grinning. His dark-brown curls fringe his face, and Grace Maud can see that his already olive skin has taken on that look of baked-in dirt that is the result of layers of suntan. 'Uncle Tom hasn't got me doing anything dangerous.'

'Tom, mate,' says Tom, who is not Luca's uncle but his second cousin. 'Just Tom.'

Luca nods. 'Sorry. Forgot. Um, Tom, they're asking for you. Something about the plough?'

'Sure, mate. Mum, you staying for dinner?'

Grace Maud looks from her son's expectant face to Viv's. She knows they genuinely want her to stay, but being in this house that is no longer her home has made her more nostalgic than is good for her. It's why she doesn't visit often. She's only here today because it's the first day of burning and Tom insisted she come, as if it's a ritual that she has to take part in every year. It's nice that he still thinks of her as being part of the business. It's her name on the title, so she supposes it remains her business too.

'No, I think I'll get back,' she says. 'While it's still light.'

What she really means is: *while it's still light enough for you to not tell me that I'm too old to drive myself home.* That's been their one battleground lately: the fact she won't give up her licence. Why should she? Not being able to drive would sentence her to a life stuck in her house, and she can't bear the idea.

Tom looks disappointed and she's caught off guard. She forgets, sometimes, that he loves her. It's so easy to forget when it's never said, even when she knows that he's like her in that respect: they use actions, not words, to convey what they feel.

'Thank you for having me,' she says, pushing herself up from the chair with great effort. She sits too much these days and it's made getting up more difficult than it should be. All those years of riding horses when she was younger have made for stiff hips now, and they complain as she half-waddles towards her handbag.

Tom, Viv and Luca follow her down the stairs to her car.

'See you, Mum.' Tom bends and kisses her on the cheek, then Viv does the same.

'GM,' Luca says as he wraps his long arms around her. She squeezes him briefly then turns and lowers herself into the driver's seat.

The air is heavy with the cane smoke and she looks towards the fields that are on fire. No matter how many times she sees it, she wonders at the majesty and brutality of it: growing those verdant crops then setting them ablaze to prepare them for cutting.

She's seen that pattern in her own life: allowing something to grow, then doing something dramatic to pare it back. Or to destroy it. Perhaps it suggests that she's heartless. Or perhaps it's all she knows. After a childhood spent observing the pattern, it's in her blood and her marrow and the very gristle of her. She has known for a long time now that the way we grow up leaves an imprint on us that is both profound and invisible. Our own individual system of ley lines. And she has spent her lifetime wondering if all we do is follow those lines without knowing why, our course plotted before we are even conscious of it.

CHAPTER TWO

'Pat, have you seen the sugar?'

Patricia winces as, yet again, Gordon calls her by the nickname she can't stand. *Pat* is something you do to a dog. Or something you call a boozy old bloke at the local pub who stopped being Patrick when he left school.

'No, Gordon, I haven't,' she says, smiling with the bottom half of her face but not with her eyes. Never with her eyes if she's smiling in Gordon's direction. She's learnt – as have all the other women who work here, from the cleaner to the secretary in the admin office to the French teacher, even a senior English teacher like Patricia – that he takes a real smile as an invitation to familiarity. But if they don't smile, he tells them they're stuck-up – and as he's the school principal they can't afford to not be on his good side. Which he knows.

'I'm sure you used it at lunchtime,' Gordon says, standing a little too close.

She takes a step sideways.

'Lunchtime was a long time ago,' she trills, wondering if he watches her making tea so that he knows when she has sugar. 'I think I saw Dennis having a cuppa not long ago.'

She doesn't want to dob in the PE teacher but she's also desperate for Gordon to leave her alone so she can depart.

Honestly, she has no idea why he keeps trying to crack onto her, apart from the fact that he tries to crack onto every human with XX chromosomes who looks within reasonable reach of legal age. He's quite persistent with her, though, and has been ever since he started here a year ago.

The first day she met him he'd looked at her feet, shod in her favourite flat, brown work shoes, then at her face and said, 'Please don't tell me you're a *woman in sensible shoes*. Because that'd be no fun.' He'd winked slowly, as if she was supposed to know what he meant.

She didn't, but she's since found out: he wanted to know if she was a lesbian. Apparently that's what 'woman in sensible shoes' was code for, although she's never heard the phrase before or since.

At the time she had laughed nervously and said, 'Well, I *am* wearing sensible shoes, so . . .' Which was her version of fighting fire with fire.

'Dennis!' Gordon bellows now across the staffroom. 'Where's the bloody sugar?'

Patricia mouths *sorry* in Dennis's direction, but she knows he understands. The female teachers regularly use him as a means of deflecting Gordon's attention because Dennis is half a foot taller than Gordon, which seems to keep the older man in line.

Dennis nods in a resigned fashion and stands up to his full height. 'Dunno, Gordon,' he booms. 'Let's look together.'

Patricia exhales, then jumps as she feels a tap on her shoulder.

'Sorry!' squeaks Marjorie, the science teacher who joined them at the start of the year. 'Didn't mean to scare you.'

'That's okay,' Patricia says, but as she turns her head to talk to Marjorie she feels a twinge running down the side of her neck and towards her shoulder. That same twinge she's had for a few weeks now. It started after she helped her father into the car and he had suddenly gripped her shoulder, pulling her into a twist.

'What is it?' Marjorie says, looking concerned.

'Nothing. Just a . . . It's nothing.' Patricia doesn't need to share her woes. Maybe because if she started, she might not stop.

Marjorie nods. 'Aches and pains,' she says knowingly. 'It's all that marking. Bending over the papers.' She makes a claw out of her right hand. 'My hand gets *so tight*! I feel like my fingers will never straighten!'

Her high-pitched laugh makes Patricia jump again, although she should be used to it by now. Marjorie can often be heard before she's seen, no matter where she is in the school. Patricia wonders if the laugh is covering for something. No one can be that genuinely ebullient all the time.

Now Marjorie is poking her in the arm and nodding again. 'I went to this class. *Amazing* stretches. Yoga. You should try it! We could go together!'

'Yoga?' Patricia has heard the term but thought it was something to do with The Beatles visiting India.

'There's a teacher – Sandrine. She's French. She has a class on Saturday mornings. It used to be in the Presbo church hall.'

Patricia blinks, wondering what her Presbyterian mother would think of that particular nickname. Probably nothing, actually, given that her mother's fine brain is starting to disintegrate at the edges, and sometimes in the middle.

'But now it's in this *amazing* little house,' Marjorie continues. 'Orange Blossom House. She likes orange blossom orchids. That's what she told us. She's really lovely!' Marjorie frowns. 'And sometimes a bit mean. But yoga's *really* good for you. The stretches are *really* deep. And there's breathing.'

'Breathing?' Why would anyone need to learn breathing when we're all breathing all the time anyway?

'I know, it sounds funny! But it's great. *Trust me.*' Marjorie sighs. 'It really helps me cope, you know?'

Patricia knows she should ask Marjorie what she's coping with – in her experience no one drops a word like that into conversation without wanting to be asked about it – but Gordon reappears, triumphantly bearing the sugar.

'Found it!' he says redundantly.

'Wonderful,' Patricia offers. 'We'll give Dennis a medal.'

She glances in Dennis's direction and he gives her a half salute and a friendly smile as he walks out the door.

'I'll leave you to your hot beverage, Gordon,' Patricia says. She's confident that Marjorie will also leave him to it, because she knows not to be alone with him.

'You don't want one?' He looks slightly wounded.

'I have a *tonne* of marking,' Patricia says, hoping her uncharacteristic use of emphasis will convince him that she's far too busy to stay. The truth is that she has no marking today, but Gordon wouldn't know that because he doesn't care about the teachers' workloads.

'Me too!' Marjorie says, almost sprinting to her handbag and hoisting it onto her shoulder.

They trot out the door and along the long corridor, only slowing their pace when they reach the street. Patricia's red Ford station wagon is parked under a pathetic tree that offers hardly any shade against the clear blue Queensland sky. Even in winter it's best to avoid leaving your car in sunlight all day if you don't want your fingers burnt on the steering wheel, but she was running late this morning and it was the best she could get.

'Oh,' Marjorie says, making a face. 'You got the bad spot.' Her olive-green Toyota is parked beside abundant foliage.

'Someone has to,' Patricia says cheerfully. She doesn't want to tell Marjorie why she was late. None of her colleagues knows that she lives in her parents' home – the house she grew up in – because those parents need looking after, and of course the unmarried daughter was the obvious choice.

Patricia's two brothers have wives and children, which means their roles are now husband, father and provider. Son is no longer on the list. Not in the way it counts when their parents need it to count. Patricia's sister also has her own family and obligations that make her too busy to visit much, and she lives in another state anyway.

Patricia isn't bitter about it. Just slightly resentful. And weary. Between her father's physical ailments – of the sort that ageing people usually have, but which require regular attention nonetheless – and her mother's fading mental capacity, she feels like she's on alert the whole time. Which is probably how her sister, Annette, feels with her children. Patricia wouldn't know. She doesn't have children, and there's never been a glimmer of a chance of them.

'That's what you get for being too smart,' her mother once told her. 'It never does a woman good to be too smart for a man.'

Not that Patricia's resentful about that. It's life. She knows it. A person just has to make the best of their lot. That's what she tells herself every day, and she tries to do it with love. Her parents are her lot, and she loves them. They don't necessarily understand her, or she them. They're not her friends. But they're the only set of parents she has and she's not ungrateful for them.

As she turns to put her key in her car door she feels that twinge in her neck again, and gasps.

'Bye, Marjorie,' she says quickly, wanting to get in the

car and hide her pain. Except Marjorie is looking at her with sympathy, so clearly that didn't work.

'I think you should come to that yoga class with me,' she says, and this time her tone is firm. 'Seriously.'

'Okay,' Patricia says, still wincing with pain, because in that moment she can't think of an excuse and maybe, just maybe, it will help her with that twinge.

Marjorie nods slowly. 'Good. I'll give you the details tomorrow.'

'Thanks, bye.' Patricia hops into the car, closes the door and immediately winds down the window to let the heat escape.

Knowing she can't touch the steering wheel for a few minutes, she sits and waves to Marjorie as she departs. Then, gingerly, she puts the key in the ignition, lightly touches the steering wheel, and drives off to deal with whatever is waiting for her at home.

CHAPTER THREE

The café door is shut after the last of the customers and Dorothy wants nothing more than to pull out one of the chairs and collapse into it. Maybe Frederick could bring her a nice glass of wine. Or not. She's not meant to be drinking alcohol. The doctor told her that if she wants to give herself the best chance of holding a pregnancy she should eliminate a few things. Like wine. And coffee. And cigarettes. All the things she likes.

'Will that really help?' she'd asked him, wondering how she was meant to manage the stress of all this without her indulgences to fall back on.

'It won't harm,' he'd said, peering over half-moon glasses. 'And given that you've had three miscarriages it's advisable to do something different, don't you think? You're old to be trying to have a baby. Thirty-four is, well . . .' More peering. 'Not youn-g.' He enunciated the 'g' as if it was a separate syllable. For emphasis, of course.

What would you know? she'd wanted to say to him. *You'll never get pregnant. You don't know what this feels like.*

Nobody knows what this feels like. Dorothy hasn't met any woman who's had one miscarriage, let alone three. When she enquired – as gently as possible – if it'd ever happened to any of the women she knows well enough to ask, they all said, 'Of course not!' So she's the defective breeder. Four years of trying, three babies lost.

She feels Frederick's hands on her shoulders, kneading the knots that have been there for longer than she's been trying to become a mother. His willingness to massage her shoulders wasn't the main reason she married him, but it was a factor.

'You carry the weight of the world here,' he had told her once, and she couldn't disagree. Dorothy tends to worry about things – worrying is, as her mother says, her natural habitat – and the worries take up residence in her body, to make room for new worries in her mind. If she understood better how all that works, she might be inclined to think that because she's so full of worries there's no room for a baby. But that's nonsense.

'You're being irrational, Dorothy.' That's what the same doctor had told her when she mentioned that she was feeling overwhelmed by her life: running the café, paying the bills, managing the housework, all the things she has to do as well as trying to get a pregnancy to last longer than a few weeks. So overwhelmed that she felt like she could never be a good mother, so maybe it was just as well that she wasn't any kind of mother.

And that's what she tells herself every day now, when the worries start: *You're being irrational, Dorothy.* It doesn't really work, though.

'That was a busy day, my darling,' Frederick says as he continues to massage her shoulders, his strong fingers causing pain, just the way she likes it. She wants to feel that something has moved. Changed.

'Mmm,' she says, closing her eyes and leaning back towards him. 'Where did all those people come from?'

A large tour group had appeared just before midday, saying they'd heard there was proper German food to be had here. They'd asked her name and immediately said, 'But you must be a Dorothea, not a Dorothy.'

She'd wondered how they knew. Her family had moved to Cairns from Germany when she was a child and she was sure there were no traces of her German accent left. Of course, her thick blonde plait makes her look like a poster child for the Third Reich – something she has wrestled with – but it's her natural hair colour so she is loath to change it. Maybe the tourists were just guessing. It made her feel uneasy, though.

Dorothy likes to think of herself as a proper Aussie. Her parents left their country and their past and the Second World War behind when they came here, wanting their children to be Australians, not Germans. Australia had its problems, but they didn't include two wars being fought on its soil. Then she had to go and marry a German.

Frederick had been travelling around Australia, a backpacker with strong, tanned German legs and a rough beard. He'd stopped in Cairns because he wanted to see the Daintree Rainforest. Instead, he'd seen Dorothy wiping tables in a little café with a view of the water and, he told her later, he knew he wasn't going to travel any further. 'I found home,' he'd said.

She hadn't understood that, really, because she didn't know how a person could feel like home. But once they married she did. Frederick belongs with her, and she belongs with him. In the whole wide world, they managed to find each other. He is the one thing she doesn't worry about, because she knows she loves him and he loves her.

'You haven't been sleeping very well, have you?' he murmurs as he digs his thumb into the persistent knot near her right shoulder blade.

'How do you know?'

'I know,' he says. 'I can feel it when you wake.'

'I'm sorry,' she says, because she doesn't want to inconvenience him.

'There is nothing to be sorry for. But I don't want you to lie awake worrying the way you do.'

'How do you know I'm worrying?' she says, trying to keep her voice light. 'Perhaps I'm going over a Mozart piano concerto in my mind.'

'That Austrian!' Frederick teases. 'I don't believe it.'

It's their ongoing joke: Mozart versus Beethoven, and why Mozart can never be considered superior because of his nationality.

'Believe it, *Liebling*.' Dorothy may have left her accent behind, but marriage to Frederick has brought her back to her mother tongue. She sighs, more heavily than she meant to.

Frederick's hands still. 'I know you're worrying about whether or not you want to try again.'

'Of course,' she says. 'Aren't you?'

'No,' he says firmly. 'I want whatever you want.'

She knows that's not true. Even before they married he'd talked about the children they would have, and always with excitement. He's done well to hide how upset he's been that he's not yet a father, and she knows he's done it to protect her. It would be better, though, if he were honest – because when she believes he's hiding things from her, it's just one more thing to worry about.

'I believe you,' she says, even though she doesn't.

What she really wants, she supposes, is for the doctor to tell her whether she can or can't have children. Telling her to stay hopeful, to keep trying, to not give up – these are all platitudes rather than useful statements. Dorothy can handle a concrete truth, if only she were given it. If only she could give it to herself.

Frederick pats her lightly. 'Come. I will make you some lunch.'

Lunch at four o'clock is what they're used to by now, because they can't eat until all their customers no longer wish to.

'Thank you,' she says, picking up his hand and kissing it, before she pushes herself up from the chair.

CHAPTER FOUR

Tom pushes a ledger book across the table. 'Do you mind taking a look at these, Mum?'

It's the same kind of ledger book Grace Maud used, which wasn't much updated from the kind her father used. Figures remain the same no matter where they're written, so there was never a good reason to change the sort of stationery they used to record them.

The accounting books have always been kept in the old dresser that flanks one side of the dining room; Grace Maud's grandfather commissioned the piece from a local furniture maker, and through four generations there has never been a reason to get rid of it. Aside from a few dents and scratches, it has trustily stood sentinel over the dining table, which is not the same piece Grace Maud grew up with. Once it became clear she was only going to have one child and no husband, there was no point keeping a table meant for a much larger family.

The sitting room, too, has changed its permutation of furniture to accommodate the ebb and flow of inhabitants in the house. Viv wanted to remove her daughters' favourite chairs when they removed themselves to Brisbane but the girls protested. So they're still clumped together next to an old couch covered in a damask material that has never been suitable for the climate but which Viv loved at first sight.

'You know the business well enough by now to not need my help, surely?' Grace Maud says as she peers at the ledger, her tone indicating that she's gently teasing him.

'Yeah, well . . .' He scratches behind his left ear; he's been doing that since he was a little boy when something concerns him. 'You know I wasn't that good at maths at school.'

She nods, although it isn't true. She nods because he wants her to endorse the line he's been telling himself all these years, and sometimes a mother has to do what makes her child happy instead of correcting misinformation. Besides, his lack of belief in his mathematical ability has never stopped him being interested in how the business of running the farm works, although Grace Maud knows that Viv helps him with the bookkeeping. Which means Viv should be sitting at this table instead of washing up the plates they used for lunch, as Grace Maud can hear her doing in the kitchen.

'Vivien, would you like to join us?' she calls. 'You probably know more about these numbers than both of us put together.'

Tom looks tense.

'Did I say the wrong thing?' Grace Maud murmurs.

'No – just . . . I didn't want her to think I thought she'd made a mistake. Because I don't.' He screws up his face. 'I just want to try to understand them a bit better.'

Grace Maud looks at him and remembers the boy who had trouble sorting out his Bs from his Ds and was rapped over the knuckles with a ruler by his teacher because of it. He got the cane when he couldn't recite 'The Man from Snowy River' in the correct stanza order, and the belt when his third-form history essay was full of unfinished sentences. All of it without Grace Maud's knowledge. Once she found out, each new incident led her to ring the headmaster to issue a rebuke for the punishment of her son for something he couldn't change.

'Thomas needs to work harder, Mrs Clifford,' the headmaster would say each time, drawing out the 'Mrs' so she would know that he knew she was no longer a Mrs.

'He does work hard,' she would also say each time. 'Very hard. And it doesn't help.'

She remembered the nights they'd sat up when he was home from boarding school for the holidays, going over and over his homework – her bone-tired from a day in the cane, him exhausted and weeping because his brain simply wouldn't work the way the school wanted it to. Nothing made him recognise that a B wasn't a D, or that 'dog' wasn't 'god'. It still doesn't. There was no point trying to make the headmaster or his teachers understand that, however. Combined with the fact that Tom was left-handed, they had decided he was incorrigible, and possibly cursed, and the only remedy was for him to work harder. Not that any of them would assist him in the endeavour.

Grace Maud has long considered it a profound act of bravery that Tom finished school. She'd offered to withdraw him before his final year but he was determined to finish. However, those years left him with no confidence about anything he learnt there, including figures. He didn't have as big a problem with numbers as he had with letters – by some miracle, he could mostly read numbers straight – but her tender-hearted boy didn't extend the same kindness to himself that he did to others. Hence Viv doing the books and Tom semi-regularly asking Grace Maud to explain them to him.

Viv comes back to the table. 'Have I miscounted something, darling?' she says, laughing softly.

He grins. 'You know you haven't. Nah, I just want to ask Mum if she thinks we're making enough profit.'

'Enough for what?' Grace Maud says, and notices Tom and Viv exchanging glances.

Tom shifts in his seat. 'We're thinking of diversifying.'

'Oh?' Grace Maud sits back in her chair, feeling her spine become rigid. Her father always said only fools don't stick to what they know best. Cane is what this family knows best, and she has no intention of becoming a fool.

'Some of the farms around here are putting on cattle. Or more cattle,' Viv says.

Which suggests that she knew what Tom was going to say to his mother today. Grace Maud isn't surprised – Tom and Viv are running the business together now – but she can't help feeling put out. And left out.

'We think we could spread our risk better if we have something other than cane,' says Tom.

'Spread your risk?' Grace Maud frowns. What a ridiculous phrase. 'That sounds like you're dealing in diseases rather than livestock.'

Tom's face looks pinched then it relaxes. 'Ha! Good one, Mum.' He grins.

Grace Maud wants to tell him that she wasn't joking; she resists the urge. 'So you'd want to destroy some of the cane to make way for cattle?' she says instead.

'That's the idea.'

'We worry about something happening to the cane,' Viv adds. 'People might stop liking sugar as much as they do now. Or we might lose a crop due to something we can't control.'

'In all these decades we never have,' Grace Maud says firmly. 'Cane has always been a good crop.'

'And it still is,' Tom says.

Another glance between husband and wife.

'It's just an idea, Mum.'

Grace Maud breathes slowly. She recalls that saying: the first generation creates the wealth, the second generation keeps it, the third loses it. Although technically Tom is the fourth generation, Grace Maud and her father could probably be counted as one long second generation. She thinks of the family who used to have the property next door and how Angelo, the third-generation farmer, mismanaged the place and ended up selling. He gave Grace Maud the first opportunity to buy, but she couldn't afford it. Or, rather, she wasn't willing to take on debt to buy it. She was keeping the wealth, believing she could protect it forever. But she can't.

Tom is the next generation. Once she's gone, he can do what he wants with the wealth. Perhaps he'll lose it all. Perhaps she's a fool to try to stop him. She doesn't know if any family has escaped the third-generation curse, and she's hardly in a position to conduct a survey.

'I'm not sure, Tom,' she says, instead of giving him the hard 'no' she wants to. 'You don't know anything about cattle.'

'I can learn,' he says. 'We can learn.'

Grace Maud looks at Viv, who is smiling reassuringly. 'It could be interesting,' Viv says. 'I like animals.'

They're not animals, Grace Maud thinks. *They're cattle. And not knowing the difference is a problem.* She's not going to debate this now, though. Tom is her son, Viv is his wife, and she doesn't want to stand in the way of their ambitions. They're the ones doing all the work.

'Why don't you find out more about it?' she says. 'How much you'll need to buy the stock, how much land is required. That sort of thing.' She tries to sound encouraging. The way a mother should when her son shows her his dreams.

Tom exhales noisily. 'Sounds good, Mum.' He leans over to peck her cheek. 'Thanks.'

‘Thanks, Grace Maud,’ Viv says, tilting her head and smiling. ‘We really appreciate it.’

Grace Maud gestures to the ledger. ‘Do you still want me to look at the figures?’

‘Um . . . yeah, if that’s all right.’ Tom looks bashful. ‘I always appreciate you checking our work.’

‘And I never mind doing so,’ she says as she pulls the book towards her, picks up her reading glasses from the table and bends her head over the figures, just as she’s done for decades.

CHAPTER FIVE

Yorkeys Knob is a strange name for any kind of place. Patricia has always thought so, even though she grew up here. Except she knows why it's called that – there is, indeed, a knob of land with the calm Half Moon Bay on one side and the surf beach on the other. And there was a Yorkshireman, apparently, who inspired the Yorkeys part. Or maybe there wasn't. No one has ever had persuasive proof.

Fishermen used to populate this place – if she counts her father, they still do. Although he hasn't been to sea for many years now; he gave that up when Patricia was about to enter her teens, and her mother decided he should be settling down. So he bought the local newsagency and settled, all right. He hasn't been on a boat since. Patricia knows he misses it. Sometimes he'll be gone from the house and she'll find him on the beach, staring out past the reef, towards the horizon.

Once he stopped fishing he started having dreams, her mother said. 'He cries like he's missing someone,' she told Patricia once, looking perplexed. But Patricia knew what it was. She also thinks he misses the ocean so much that he can't bear to go out again: there's no guarantee that what happens in the present will match what happens in your memories. Living in the past can be safer. Less turbulent.

Patricia's brothers never had designs on the sea. They knew what kind of life it was for fishermen; and besides, their adoring mother had encouraged them to believe that Earth was too small for the great talents she was sure they had. By the time their father bought the newsagency, John and Peter had gone away to university in Brisbane, and Annette was married and planning to move to New South Wales, leaving Patricia to deal with her mother alone.

Their relationship has never been good. Patricia was the 'accident' her mother didn't quite get over, just as she didn't quite recover from having to give up her job after the war finished. Nora had never wanted to stay at home and raise children. Her own mother had looked after the children while Nora was at work, but once the men started returning from overseas the working women soon discovered their jobs were gone and they'd have to go back to unpaid housework. Somewhere in that postwar time – in the middle of her mother's rage – Patricia was conceived.

Her father never resented her arrival, but, then again, he wasn't the one who had to look after her. Not when he was at sea so often.

Patricia has long tried to make sense of why her mother has disliked her for so long – Patricia, after all, having done everything she could to be the 'good girl' she was meant to be – but it wasn't until her mother's mind started to fail, until she really needed her daughter in a way she hadn't before, that there was any kind of détente.

As Patricia turns around to head north on the beach, back towards the house, a breeze moves over her, carrying with it the scent of salt. Salty water, to be exact. What was it Isak Dinesen wrote once? The cure for everything is salt water: sweat, tears, or the sea. For Patricia the latter is always far more regularly the cure, which is why she's down here every single day of the week, regardless of the weather.

She sees the knob ahead of her, with its densely packed trees and its few neat rows of houses. Between here and the main part of Cairns there is a lot of uninhabited land, a couple of beaches and the airport. When she was growing up this place seemed like it was cut off from everything. Now, with the planes coming in – with tourists from the rest of Australia and the rest of the world arriving to see Port Douglas and the Great Barrier Reef, the Daintree Rainforest and Cape Tribulation, or go even further north to Cooktown and Cape York – she would like to have a little of that isolation back.

Mind you, she too should be wary of living in the past. She felt stuck here, as a kid. Her imagination was vast and wild; she read books and listened to her parents' jazz records and the classical music her grandmother loved, and the Frank Sinatra her grandfather favoured, and she dreamed of being anywhere but here. She even moved away for a while to find out if elsewhere was better. It's taken her over four decades to appreciate that here she is surrounded by beauty.

'Good morning, Patricia!' says the school's retired headmistress, Mrs Dampier, as she marches past. Patricia never worked with her but certainly knew what it was like to be a student under her command.

'Good morning, Mrs Dampier,' she says. She knows the woman's first name but would never dare use it.

'Chilly this morning, isn't it?' Mrs Dampier calls, but it's a rhetorical question because she's going at such a pace that she won't hear Patricia's answer.

It *is* chilly for Cairns: eighteen degrees Celsius at this hour of the morning. Patricia almost pulled on a woollen jumper before leaving the house, then decided that would be an extreme gesture.

'Pat,' huffs Mr Dampier in acknowledgement as he passes her, trying to catch up to his wife, as he does every morning.

'Mr D,' she says cheerily. For some reason she never minds him shortening her name, probably because he lets her do it in return.

Patricia folds her arms against her chest to hold in some warmth as she moves up towards the soft sand. Every time she walks on the hard sand she thinks she's being lazy. Soft sand is so much more difficult. So much better for developing strength in the lower legs. That's what Dennis told her. Right before he told her that she was a bit of all right and perhaps she'd like to have dinner with him at the club.

It wasn't really a question. Dennis is used to women wanting to have dinner with him, no doubt, and she was immensely flattered – and unnerved, just a little – but she's sure she's almost twice his age, so she told him she didn't think it was appropriate for them to go to the club. Even though she has found him attractive since the day he started working at the school.

He'd smiled at her in a sphinx-like way. 'Suit yourself,' he'd said. 'But I don't care about your age.'

Since then, they've been fine at work – because they're both adults and he didn't take it as a rejection, so that was nice. Because it wasn't a rejection. How could it have been when she's daydreamed about it ever since? She was wanting a man to notice her, because they barely seemed to. Not that she has been giving them a reason to notice her, for years now. She has what she considers to be a nondescript face; what she knows to be lank, shapeless hair because she can't be bothered styling it; functional clothes; sensible shoes. Yet there he was – handsome Dennis with his slightly too-big biceps – noticing her, and she'd panicked.

No, it wasn't a rejection, it was a correction. Back to the natural order of things. Dennis should be asking the younger staff members to go to the club. Patricia's polite refusal of his invitation would allow him to do just that.

She's almost back to the part of the beach where she can peel off and head up a path to the house when she sees one of the neighbours, Mrs Kovacs. Mrs Kovacs likes to tell Patricia about her fertile daughters and the children they just can't stop having, and she always ends by saying, 'It is such a shame you didn't have children, Patricia.' Her head will tilt to the side and she'll slowly blink. 'So pretty. Such a waste.'

There's never a good response to something like that, and Patricia doesn't want to try to think of one today. She picks up her pace, as hard as that is in the softer sand, and makes for the track that will take her off the beach and onto the road. Behind her, the waves are softly crashing on the shore. In front of her lie all of her responsibilities.

She sets her face against the day and walks towards the house.

CHAPTER SIX

'You know, Mrs Clifford, you really should do those exercises the doctor gave you.' Cecilia follows her gentle admonishment with a gently raised eyebrow.

Grace Maud scowls. For a year Cecilia has been helping her out around the place and now she thinks she's a nurse or something. If Grace Maud didn't like her so much she'd be annoyed. Which won't stop her pretending to be annoyed, because she has a façade to keep up. The farm workers all thought she was a tough old bird and that reputation did her no harm. It pays, she has found, to appear stern as a means of protecting a soft heart. Only Ellie Maud really knew what she was like; with her sole witness gone, Grace Maud can keep her tenderness to herself.

'I don't like them,' she says with deliberate peevishness. 'Their very existence suggests that I'm somehow decrepit. And we both know I'm not.'

Cecilia tsk-tsks, which she is quite fond of doing. 'But if the doctor thinks they're good for you, surely they're worth doing? You said just the other day that your hips hurt.'

'They're seventy-four years old! Of course they hurt. Yours are going to hurt when they're that old.'

Now Cecilia makes a noise that sounds like grumbling.

Grace Maud narrows her eyes. 'What are you doing here with an old thing like me?' she says. 'You're young. You're pretty. You should be running around with a beau rather than bothering with my aches and pains.'

'This again?' Cecilia rolls her eyes – another favourite thing to do.

They have their own little routine: Grace Maud tells Cecilia to get lost, and Cecilia sighs and flicks her hair or rolls her eyes and resists. It's entertaining, in its own way. Something Grace Maud would have done with her daughter, if she'd had one. But she never did, and she'd stopped being sad about it decades ago. Or tried to stop.

After her sister left for good, she was desperate for another female presence in her life. She thought she'd have a daughter. Two. Three. Instead she has a son. A good one, but it's not the same. Any mother would tell you. The boys distance themselves once they reach a certain age and they never close that gap. Girls stay close. Not in every case, obviously, but in most cases. They understand that their mothers need them – that they can't ever really let them go.

Thankfully Cecilia puts up with Grace Maud being stroppy from time to time, and while she's not a daughter she's like a granddaughter in many ways.

'I'm here, Mrs Clifford, because you pay me,' Cecilia says. She turns back to the sink and keeps washing the dishes. 'And because I like being here. Except when you refuse to do things that are good for you. Then I get cross.' She sniffs in a schoolmarmish way.

'I've never seen you cross in your life, Cecilia.'

'If you keep refusing to do things that are good for you, you might.'

'What would you have me do, then?'

Cecilia stops moving and looks out the window. It's a nice view: in the garden Grace Maud has installed an array of suitably tropical plants – two hibiscus, some clivias and a banana palm that refuses to grow fruit – that she pays a young man to keep in check once a month. He's a student at the university; a nice fellow whose parents Tom knows through the Lions Club. Jeremy, she thinks his name is, although she doesn't really use it so she can't be sure. She leaves cash out for him, so they rarely speak. The cash comes from Tom, as it does for Cecilia. Once Grace Maud decided to move from the farm into town, Tom insisted on paying for people to look after her, the house and garden – it's a point of pride for him to do so.

'I can't get into town that often,' he'd said when he suggested that she have some help in the garden. 'And I don't want you doing the mowing.'

She'd started to say that she had no intention of mowing, but he'd snorted and said, 'Don't even try to tell me that you won't do the mowing, because you and I know that you will. It's not that I think you're not capable of it, Mum – I just think you deserve to, y'know, *not work*. You've been working all your life.'

That was a rationale she couldn't contest, and she was, in truth, relieved not to have to worry about keeping the garden tidy. She was also relieved that Tom offered to pay because she doesn't have that much cash; she never has. Everything has always been tied up in the farm. Any extra money that wasn't spent on school fees for Tom went into improving the property and the business. And the school fees were necessary because in those days that's just what you did with a country kid: off to boarding school as soon as the parents could afford it.

Tom also said that Grace Maud shouldn't have to do housework any more, which is why Cecilia was hired, despite the fact that Grace Maud doesn't believe she needs looking after. She enjoys Cecilia's company, though – and it's entirely possible that this is the function Tom hired her for in the first place.

Grace Maud doesn't think Cecilia is admiring Jeremy's handiwork as she stares into the garden, although she can't tell if the girl's annoyed or simply thinking about something.

'There's a class,' Cecilia says slowly, half turning, hands still in the sink. 'At a place down the road. My mother tells me it's good for stretching.'

'Your mother the former star ballet student?' Grace Maud says disbelievingly.

Whatever Cecilia's lissom dancer mother calls stretching is probably what Grace Maud calls Olympic-level gymnastics. Not that Grace Maud has never danced. She used to enjoy it, long ago. She met her husband at a dance. That was one of the things she'd liked about him: he was smooth and light on his feet, yet able to keep a firm hand on her back when they moved around the dance floor.

Cecilia makes a face. 'She hasn't danced for years. Not since she left Argentina. She needs a good stretch as much as you do.'

As improbable as that sounds to Grace Maud, she appreciates that Cecilia is trying to help. 'And what happens in this class?'

'Yoga,' Cecilia says, giving the sink her full attention.

'Yoga?' Grace Maud searches her memory for anything she can associate with the word. 'Don't you have to be a vegetarian Hindu to do that? I don't want to give up steak.'

Cecilia laughs. 'I think you'll find that my mother is still a Catholic who likes eating meat. She says the yoga helps keep her young.'

Grace Maud considers the idea of placing herself in the company of women like Cecilia's mother and doesn't like it. She will be so much older, she's sure of it – wherever she goes she's the oldest person there. And if the other people in the class are younger, trimmer, more flexible, she will feel old. And she has no interest in feeling old. That's for old people. And she never intends to be one of them. So maybe this yoga business could be useful if it keeps her joints and muscles moving.

'I'll go with you,' Cecilia says gamely.

'No!' Grace Maud doesn't want a witness to her attempts to unfurl her body into odd shapes. 'Sorry, I didn't mean to say that so loudly,' she adds after Cecilia turns and frowns. 'I just . . . Well, you know me. I like to do things well. I don't want you to see me not do this well.'

'But I can drive you.'

Grace Maud stops herself from exclaiming again. She knows that Tom has told Cecilia to drive her around. He hasn't been able to stop his mother driving to the farm, but he wants to stop her going other places. He says her eyesight is failing – and of course it is, because things wear out. But it's only failing at activities like reading the newspaper, and she has glasses for that. She can see street signs and pedestrian crossings. She can see lights change from red to green to amber. She can still navigate herself around town without needing any kind of map. If Tom wanted to test her, he'd find she could drive to Sydney and back without a map, because she was brought up to store useful information in her head and to be resourceful.

There are a lot of things Grace Maud can still do that Tom has no idea about because he's never asked. But she knows she can do them. Part of the trick of getting older is to keep reminding herself of that. The instant she believes she can't do something, shouldn't go somewhere, she may as well buy her own coffin. So that's why, yes, she should give this yoga thing a try. Neither brain nor body should atrophy just because she might have to become a vegetarian Hindu for a while. Cecilia is not going to drive her, though, and that's that.

'Which class does your mother go to?' Grace Maud asks.

'Tuesday morning.' Cecilia pulls the plug and takes off the rubber gloves.

'Is there another?'

Cecilia gives her a look – an I-can't-believe-you'd-be-this-ridiculous look.

'Yes. Saturday morning. Eight o'clock.'

'You've done your research. It's almost as if you planned to tell me about this yoga thing.'

'I might have,' Cecilia says lightly as she folds the tea towel and places it on the bench. 'Now, I'm going to the shop. Shall we make a list? And don't tell me Scotch finger biscuits because you know they're bad for your heart.'

'But good for my *joie de vivre*,' Grace Maud says, then pauses for dramatic effect. 'All right. No Scotch fingers. How about cream wafers?'

'Maybe.' Cecilia picks up the notepad near the telephone, sits down next to Grace Maud and starts to write the list.

Grace Maud can't help smiling. Cecilia is a well-meaning girl; a lovely person to have in her life, even if she needs to keep her on her toes. Grace Maud may grumble about Tom molly-coddling her now she's older but she will always be grateful that he brought Cecilia to her. Although after she goes to that yoga class, she may change her mind.

CHAPTER SEVEN

Some days really are too much to handle. They start hard and only become harder as the minutes tick by. Dorothy tried to be hopeful about today, but as soon as they opened for breakfast service she knew that hope was misplaced.

Two of the regulars – young men who ran a plumbing business together – put in their usual order then started complaining to her about one of their customers, obviously thinking they knew Dorothy well enough by now to whinge about their lives. Then the kitchen hand sliced his thumb while he was dicing an onion and blood went all over the benchtop.

'*Gott im Himmel!*' she heard Frederick yell when it happened.

He's not a yeller, so she knew it was something serious. And it unsettled the patrons who were in for morning tea.

Lunch service was slow to start with, then several large groups came in and they all wanted variations to the menu. Dorothy knew that would be tricky for Frederick without help in the kitchen, so she'd jumped in to assist, in full knowledge that they always get on each other's nerves when they try to cook together. It's the only time they do.

In the olden days – when Dorothy was the previous version of herself – none of this would have rattled her. She has always been a worrier but right up until the time she had her second miscarriage she was an optimist too, for the most part. She hadn't been a great student, but she was sure she'd find a job when she left school – and she did. She wasn't the best-looking girl around, but she was sure she'd find a nice husband – and she did. She wasn't the most charming individual in Cairns, but she was determined to make friends – and she did. She *believed* that all these things would happen because she trusted that life was kind. Her parents had left Germany knowing, deep in their marrow, that the opposite was true, but Dorothy knew she couldn't carry on as they did. She had to really, truly believe that everything would work out for the best, otherwise there was no chance of stopping bad things happening. Of course little bad things happened, but if you took the attitude that they were a blip and could be corrected, you lessened the chance of really big bad things happening – like a whole country going wrong.

It took vigilance, because so many people were pessimists. Optimists had to be alert to all the naysaying and apathy; to the people who say, 'That's life,' and shrug their shoulders and never do anything to effect positive change. It was exhausting being an optimist, but Dorothy had committed herself to the cause and remained vigilant throughout her life.

Until a year and a half ago, after she lost that second baby. She just couldn't find a reason to keep being hopeful, despite days, then weeks, of searching her conscience and her soul and her immediate surroundings. She and Frederick had done all the right things. They'd kept themselves healthy, exercised regularly and eaten properly. Because she'd already lost one baby, when Dorothy found out she was pregnant she didn't run around town the way she usually did. With the first pregnancy she'd carried on as usual, because that's what the doctor said to do. After the miscarriage, the doctor told her she'd pushed herself too hard and that's why the pregnancy didn't last. So with the second pregnancy, Dorothy would go to the café, work, go home, let Frederick cook her dinner, then she'd literally put her feet up. She was quiet and calm – and hopeful. And still it hadn't worked.

After that she decided that being an optimist was for idiots who weren't alert to the realities of life. Which was a shock to Frederick, who said one of the things he loved about her most was that she was always positive. She told him that he'd just have to focus on the other things he loved, because that version of Dorothy was gone. It was too hard to maintain hope. If they were to try for a baby again, she needed to be realistic and believe that she could very well lose that baby too. Which she did. After that one she told Frederick she was glad she hadn't wasted energy wishing for the best. She felt mean doing it, because he was distraught, but she had to look after herself.

She suspects that secretly she's still an optimist, though, because every twenty-six days or so, when her period arrives – never on a regular schedule – she feels as though the soles of her feet have dropped away and she is being pulled into the centre of the Earth. Which means that some part of her keeps believing she'll fall pregnant again.

She's tried to see each bout of bleeding as a sign that she has another chance, so she's not so upset. It hasn't worked, though. That's why today is really too hard. She's bleeding, she's bloated, and she wants to lie down and moan quietly, then perhaps segue to a bout of crying. Instead she's at the café, writing cheques to pay bills and every now and then lifting her head to watch the world go by.

She can see the ocean, and knows the reef is just beyond her line of sight. The harbour is to her right with its backdrop of green hills. She finds Cairns dramatic and beautiful, even though she knows it so well. Or perhaps *because* she does. There are colours she couldn't find on another continent; there's the glittering promise of the ocean and the cruelty of knowing you can't swim in it for months at a time because of the stingers. To the west are the tablelands and a lushness she can hardly believe. To the north is the rainforest with its millennia of mysteries, its perfect, people-free beaches and the tangle of the jungle.

This isn't her land by rights, but it's her land by love and faith. She doesn't belong here – no one with white skin does, she firmly believes, because the sun can be so savage to those whose skin isn't made for it. Yet she can't imagine being anywhere else. When she has felt at her most desperate – when she has believed that God has deserted her, that her body has failed her, that she has disappointed her husband, that she will never, ever get this right – she has sought the solace of the land. She has stood next to trees that grew before Europeans arrived and pressed her head against their trunks, feeling them giving her some kind of life force, because she always feels renewed afterwards.

She jerks at the sound of the café's door being pushed open.

'Hello?' says a small voice, coming from a fine-featured face looking around the edge of the door.

'Yes?' Dorothy replies and hopes she doesn't sound irritated. She should have locked the door once lunch service was over.

'Are you open?' the young woman says, pushing the door a little bit more.

'No, we're not. Lunch service finished at three.' A glance at the clock tells her it's almost an hour past that.

'Oh.' The woman doesn't move. 'I just wanted a coffee.'

'I'm very sorry,' Dorothy says. 'We don't have any coffee ready.'

She grits her teeth as she realises what she's said – the opening she's given. The espresso machine has already been cleaned and turned off. She doesn't have time – or the will – to start it up.

'I can wait!' the woman says brightly.

'Dorothea,' Frederick says loudly as he walks from the kitchen, wiping his hands, 'are you ready to go home?'

She tries not to beam. It isn't the first time he's rescued her from this kind of circumstance – although he was so quiet after lunch that she thought he was having a nap.

'Oh,' he says, looking at the woman in the door, then looking at Dorothy, arching an eyebrow only she can see. 'What's going on here?'

'This young lady wants coffee.'

'That's too bad,' he says, dropping his hands by his sides. 'I'm sorry, but we are closed.'

The woman meekly nods, mutters 'Okay,' and retreats, closing the door.

This happens every single time: people will listen to Frederick but not to Dorothy. Yes, he's tall and broad-shouldered and that confers some kind of natural authority, but she's the one at front of house. She's the one whose word should be final. If only she were male, it would be.

If only she were male, a lot of things would be different. She wouldn't have problems getting pregnant, for one thing. She could leave that to someone else. Someone whose body is better equipped for it. Someone who doesn't feel like all her youthful hope and promise have been sucked away by the realities of life.

And here she is again, getting trapped in a spiral of thoughts about the ways she is failing herself and Frederick and the baby they are meant to have, and the future they dreamt of.

'What happened?' Frederick is saying, lightly touching her arm.

Dorothy blinks at him. 'What? She . . . she wanted coffee.'

'Not her. What happened just then?' He's frowning at her, concern crisscrossing his brow. 'The woman walks out, then you get this . . . this look on your face and you can't hear a word I say.'

She can't tell if he's guessed how distressed she is these days. She thought she was doing a good job of hiding it, but clearly she lapsed just now. They're both upset that she isn't pregnant, but she hasn't wanted him to know that his pang of upset is her chasm of something far beyond that. It's not pain; it's fear. She is terrified that what she wants most will never happen, and then she won't know who she is. Or be who Frederick wants her to be. Who they both want her to be.

What's worst is that she's starting to wonder if the fear isn't so much about not being pregnant but about becoming a mother. She's gone this long without a child – what if she really doesn't want one after all? That fear is something she can never tell Frederick.

'*Entschuldigung*,' she says – sorry. She doesn't want to say it in English because it sounds more pathetic that way. 'My monthly started today. I feel a little faint.' It's partly the truth, and enough to convince him.

He runs his hand over her hair and kisses her. 'Let's go home. You have done more than enough for today.'

She should probably express gratitude that they're not staying until absolutely every last thing is done, but it's her business too. The bills will still be there to pay tomorrow, and they will both be in early; it won't hurt them to leave today while there's still daylight.

She knows Frederick will have already done all he needs to before tomorrow. He's organised like that. The kitchen will be clean and ordered, and he'll have his to-do list for the morning, ready to check off each item as they complete it.

Dorothy thinks from time to time that she'd like to have that kind of list for her life, to help her feel more in control of it. But how does that joke go? *How do you make God laugh? Tell Him your plans.*

Once upon a time, when she was a girl, she didn't understand that. She does now.

CHAPTER EIGHT

It seems to Grace Maud that Cecilia was right: one doesn't have to be a vegetarian Hindu to go to a yoga class. But one does need to be younger than seventy-four. The other women – and they're all women – are several decades short of Grace Maud's age.

A young woman with frizzy hair is writhing around doing a version of what could be called calisthenics – even though the class hasn't started – and a middle-aged woman with the worst haircut Grace Maud has seen since the 1960s and a gloriously beautiful, completely bare face is sitting quietly, legs crossed, looking as bewildered as Grace Maud feels. Next to her, a sparrow of a woman chirps about someone called Gordon. Two other women are wearing ballet leotards and tights, and they certainly have the figures for them, even if one looks to have a scoliosis.

Ellie Maud had a scoliosis that was never corrected. A doctor told her she wouldn't have children because of it. Ridiculous notion. And thank goodness that doctor was wrong, otherwise they wouldn't have Luca now. Grace Maud smiles whenever she thinks of him. For all her longing for daughters, she isn't actually that fond of her granddaughters. How two young women with such sensible parents ended up with such flighty notions about life she'll never know. Imagine saying that you 'just want to be happy' and that's your reason for leaving your family and the places you know? Happiness has never been the barometer in Grace Maud's life. *Duty* is by far the sturdier concept.

Luca may not be her grandson but she considers him such, since Ellie Maud isn't around to be his grandmother. Grace Maud likes to think she's taking care of him for her sister. In reality he's probably taking care of her.

'Where would you like to go?' Cecilia whispers in her ear. 'There's a spot by the window.'

She gestures to a gap close to the front of the class, and Grace Maud feels immediately self-conscious. She won't know how to do this yoga thing and she doesn't want other people to see. She has her pride. It's one of the few things she has left since old age has taken away her straight spine and moderately uplifted bosom. But the back of the room won't be easy to wedge into.

When Cecilia told Grace Maud about the class she'd imagined it being in a hall of some kind, not in a house. Admittedly a quite large house – low-roofed, and made of stone and boards. They're in what looks to have once been a combined living and dining room surrounded by garden.

Orange Blossom House the sign out the front read, next to a path that curled between crowded banana bushes – which will look and smell lovely when their small white flowers bloom in spring – with the odd fern and some other plants that Grace Maud should know from years of living on the land but doesn't. She did, however, recognise the orange blossom orchids that form a small, almost devotional cluster nearer to the house, and the Atherton palms that flank the front door, which is actually at the side.

It opens into a short hallway hung with paintings of local scenes; maidenhair ferns sit on a low table next to an area where shoes are discarded.

'Am I meant to leave my shoes here too?' Grace Maud had asked. She always wore shoes in her own home, and was a firm advocate of wearing them in other people's.

Cecilia nodded. 'No shoes in the studio.'

'Why not?'

'You can't do yoga in shoes, or socks. And it's a sacred space.'

'A what?'

Cecilia rolled her eyes. 'A *sacred space*. You'll see.'

The studio itself – the old living/dining room – is painted white and has polished floorboards and large windows that let in the light and the greenery outside. And Cecilia was right: it does feel sacred. Everyone is quiet, and the space just inside the door is decorated with small statues and candles. But it isn't a large room, and feels smaller the longer they stand here and hesitate.

'Yes, let's go by the window,' Grace Maud says.

Cecilia pitter-patters quickly to the spot and drops the two foam camping mats she's brought with them.

The woman sitting on a mat at the front of the class, whom Grace Maud presumes is the teacher, frowns.

''Allo,' she says, then gestures to the mats. 'Is that all you have?'

Grace Maud recognises straightaway that her accent is French.

'Yes – this is what my mother brings,' Cecilia says, looking like a scolded child.

'Who is your mother?'

'Eva. She comes on Tuesday mornings.'

'Ah yes.' The woman nods vigorously, her tightly cropped curls bobbing.

Grace Maud thinks she looks like a soignée version of Shirley Temple with her curls and that upturned nose. But Shirley is frozen in time, and this woman, Grace Maud sees now, isn't as young as she'd feared and exudes the sort of self-confidence that comes from weathering hard, long experience.

The teacher smiles at Cecilia, her eyes almost disappearing. 'But probably Eva did not tell you that she really just uses the floor and forgets about the mat. No matter, they will do for now.' Her eyes turn to Grace Maud. 'Who is your friend?'

'This is Mrs Clifford,' Cecilia says, looking quite pleased with herself – as she should, given that this morning Grace Maud decided she was too old and too inflexible after all. But Cecilia wasn't having any of it.

'Does Mrs Clifford have a first name?'

The teacher's eyebrow arches and Grace Maud sees mischief in it. She's half impressed. She was expecting this woman to be more like Felicity and Edwina's ballet teacher – a Soviet with no discernible sense of humour and a work ethic she might have learnt in a gulag.

'Grace Maud,' says the owner of that name clearly.

'How . . . un-us-u-al. Are you very attached to both names?'

'Yes.'

'Fine.' A tight smile. 'I shall use them both. My name is Sandrine. And I know you are Cecilia. Your mother has told me about you.'

Cecilia looks surprised, and Grace Maud knows why: her relationship with Eva isn't that warm.

'Grace Maud,' Sandrine says in a tone that suggests command, 'this class is not very energetic – I like it to be a place of refuge not a . . . a . . . an *aerobics* class, you see?'

Sandrine's accent is more pronounced, Grace Maud notices, when she is searching for a word, but her English is perfect.

Even with her old-age hearing deficit, Grace Maud knows she'll understand it.

'I do,' she says.

'Still, we move. We *must* move otherwise the body . . . pfft!' Sandrine gestures with her hands to indicate a collapsing mound. 'But I will tell you if there is something you should not do. And maybe you will surprise yourself with what you *can* do.'

Grace Maud doubts it – she hasn't surprised herself in many years – but she decides to humour this Frenchwoman with her curls and her mascara and red lipstick and her leotard and noisy bracelets. She's the most interesting person Grace Maud has met this week.

'Okay, we shall begin,' Sandrine says.

Cecilia unrolls their mats, which stay curled up at the edges.

Looking down, Grace Maud realises it's a long way to the mat. She hasn't willingly been on a floor for quite some time, and she's not sure her hips will allow her to make it back up again. With help, yes; on her own, no.

She has a flash of realising the indignity of having to be helped to her feet in front of these strangers and the spry Frenchwoman, then immediately castigates herself for it. She has changed tyres on trucks and whacked machetes at cane. She has murdered snakes and accosted aggressive dogs. Her body has bent and folded and stretched and hauled and pushed for most of her life. Just because it has wrinkles on it now doesn't mean it's forgotten how to do all those things simply because she's withered a little since she moved into town. Somewhere inside this crepey-skinned shell is the warrior she used to be. And Grace Maud will need to find her again to get off this floor at the end of the class.

She takes a breath and props herself against the wall to help her lower to her knees, sure she can hear them groaning.

Cecilia looks at her expectantly and Grace Maud smiles in response. 'I'm fine,' she says, pulling her legs in front of her as she sits, only to see Sandrine getting to her feet.

'We will start with the *breathing*,' Sandrine says, catching Grace Maud's eye and giving her a wink. 'Everyone please find a comfortable position to sit in for a few minutes.'

Although Grace Maud isn't sure if a comfortable position is possible on this flimsy piece of foam on this hard wooden floor, she does the best she can to follow Sandrine's instructions. If it all gets too difficult, she thinks, she can just stay like this and breathe.

Grace Maud closes her eyes and, as Sandrine talks, realises how nice it is to have someone else take charge. Sandrine will tell her what to do. Grace Maud's only job is to listen and follow. The relief of it – after years of the pent-up worry that comes with taking responsibility for everyone else, for her family, for her workers and their livelihoods – feels temporarily enormous.

She pulls herself back from it, though, because there is nowhere for that relief to go in this room on this sunny Saturday morning amidst an assortment of a dozen different women and their different bodies and faces and hairstyles. It feels too big, and too old, and too scary, to be let out. So Grace Maud focuses only on her breathing, as Sandrine instructs, and waits for the rest of the class to unfold.

CHAPTER NINE

As Patricia puts the key in the car door she feels a pinch in her neck and shoulder. The slightest of movements and it's complaining. She feels like sighing, but that will just make her mother cross.

'Stop sighing,' she used to say when Patricia was practising piano and became upset each time she made a mistake. Which was often, because that's the nature of practising anything: one makes mistakes far more often than one gets it right. Sighing was an alternative to bashing the keys, which was what Patricia truly wanted to do. But that would be bad-tempered and she couldn't be that. She had to be polite. Controlled. Presentable. Just like her sister. Just like her mother. And her mother's mother. And every other woman they knew. Nice girls didn't lose their tempers, no matter how badly they played Chopin's nocturnes.

Once sighing wasn't an option, Patricia took to biting the inside of her cheek, which is what she finds herself doing now as she unlocks the door, stows her handbag behind the driver's seat, then walks around to the passenger side.

'Are you sure you want to come, Dad?' she says, hoping she doesn't sound irritated.

It's her mother who needs to go to the doctor – her mother is the reason Patricia's missing the staff meeting after the last lesson – and her father could easily stay at home watching *The Price is Right*. Except these days he doesn't seem to ever want to be alone, and that's starting to worry Patricia as much as her mother's changeable moods, forgetfulness and, now, rattly chest.

'Oh, yeah,' her father says vaguely as he sits heavily on the back seat, newspaper clutched to his chest. For the crosswords, he told her. He's going to do them while they wait for her mother to see the doctor. Crosswords he could have done at home, in front of *The Price is Right*.

'In you get, Mum,' Patricia says as brightly as she can, half tempted to buckle her mother in like her mother did her many years ago. Because that's what's starting to happen: she's becoming her parents' parent. Telling them to watch as they cross the road. Offering to cut up their food. Making sure they're not catching a chill. It's not the life she imagined for herself but it's the one she has, and she's trying to do it with love instead of nails-pressed-into-her-palms tolerance.

'Work without expectation of reward is karma yoga,' that teacher, Sandrine, had said in yoga class the other day. Because it was Patricia's first class she hadn't been sure she wanted to hear about philosophy or whatever that concept was. It had stuck, though. Work without expectation of reward – it doesn't apply to her teaching job, because she does expect the reward of being paid, and of her students managing to move on to their next year of schooling, or leaving school with at least a pass mark. It describes her work at home, though: there's no expectation of reward here. So the yoga class gave her something, at least, even if it didn't fix her neck and shoulder.

'You have to go more than once for that!' Marjorie had said when Patricia had remarked on it. 'It's not magic!'

But I want it to be. That's what Patricia wished she could say out loud. She wants the quick solution to the pain in her body. She wants someone to wave a wand and say everything is going to be all right. She doesn't want that person to have to be her, even though that was something else Sandrine managed to slip in: 'No one can make you happy but yourself.'

At the time they were all holding a posture that Patricia wished would end immediately, and she thought Sandrine was a bit . . . well, cruel to say that. Marjorie had mentioned that Sandrine could be mean. Except Patricia remembers what was said. Almost as if the pain she was feeling in her body helped imprint the words on her mind. That's quite a trick. Perhaps she could use it on her own students.

With all the car doors closed, Patricia starts the engine and reverses onto the road just as their neighbours pull up, honking a hello.

'Wave, Mum,' Patricia urges.

'Hm?' Her mother blinks slowly.

'Dale and Peta – they're saying hello.'

'Oh.'

Her mother's face transforms into the mask Patricia recognises: the beatific smile that tells the world all is well, regardless of the truth. The smile they never saw at home but which, amidst other people, covered for her parents' loud arguments, her brother killing the neighbour's dog, her sister running away from home for a month, the money troubles that never went away. For normal family life, because that's what it was. Just like Tolstoy wrote: all happy families are the same, but every unhappy family is unhappy in its own way. *Anna Karenina.* A book Patricia knows she's meant to love but which she finds unbearably, overwhelmingly sad.

They head for the end of the street and Patricia puts on the blinker to turn left towards town.

Her father grunts.

'What's that, Dad?' she says. She can hear the newspaper crumpling. Her father is probably going to do the crossword in the car too.

'John called yesterday. Forgot to tell you.'

'Oh yes?'

'Says he can't come next weekend.'

Patricia feels a sag of disappointment in her shoulders. Her brother John was supposed to come up from Innisfail and take her parents to Chillagoe to stay overnight with their brother Peter and his family. Peter never comes to Cairns. He says it's because he's 'flat out' running his service station. John is usually 'flat out' too, being a solicitor in Innisfail, but Innisfail is closer so it's harder to make excuses not to drive an hour up the road. Patricia had asked John to take their parents to visit Peter as she has no interest in seeing her oldest brother – at family gatherings he likes to refer to her as 'the one we can't get rid of' because she's unmarried. But her parents think he's the bee's knees.

'Did he say when he might be able to come instead?'

'No.' The newspaper rustles. 'Says he's—'

'Flat out. Right. Yeah. I get it.' She sighs and doesn't care that her father can hear it.

'Did he call Peter and say you aren't coming?' she asks.

'I don't know.'

Patricia knows: John won't have done it. He'll leave that up to her, which means she and Peter will get into a sniping session about her being too lazy to drive their parents to Chillagoe and not understanding why he's too important to visit them in Cairns. It isn't that she's lazy, of course. Laziness has never been Patricia's problem. It's because she doesn't want to see him. Somewhat astonishingly, given that in their adulthood she's never been warm towards him, Peter doesn't appear to have figured that out.

She's not going to drive their parents to Chillagoe, though. Peter's their child too and he can make an effort. That's the righteous position she's taking for today and she's going to stick to it.

'Where are we going, Patricia?' her mother says, sounding worried.

'To the doctor's, Mum.'

Patricia used to say 'remember': *To the doctor's, Mum – remember?* But she stopped when she realised it sounded like a taunt. Her mother remembers sometimes, and oftentimes not. That's just the way things are now and there's no need to point it out.

'It's a lovely day,' her mother says, her head turning towards the window.

Patricia is glad that they ride the rest of the trip in silence. She can use the time to silently fume at her brothers. It's a grudge she developed a while ago, and one that she treats like a hardy indoor plant that needs only occasional watering. Given she can never outwardly express her frustration with them, the silent fume is all she has. And it's enough to keep her going all the way to the doctor's surgery.

CHAPTER TEN

The little house in Kuranda had so charmed Dorothy and Frederick when they first inspected it that they'd decided the thirty-kilometre drive into town each day was worth it to live amongst so many trees. They like to tell people they live in the rainforest, because it's almost true: the village is in the rainforest, even if their house is on a street with other dwellings.

Towards the end of the year the greenery can feel oppressive, as the humidity rises and they begin to long for rain to break it. But in the winter, as it is now, it's perfect. Bright and alive. Each tree reminds Dorothy that life goes on: she is here now, but these trees have been here longer, and will go on longer than her, no doubt. On the days when she feels things are hopeless, she finds that reassuring.

She daydreams about those trees while she's at work. Not often; just when her brain needs to take a little break. It's the weirdest sensation of being homesick for a place she'll be returning to very soon. This morning she's been homesick for it since she arrived at the café. Saturday mornings are usually fine – lots of customers, the time goes quickly. Frederick likes being busy; so does she. This morning, though, she's feeling agitated, like she doesn't want to be here. And maybe she doesn't, if only her sense of responsibility would step aside and let her indulge in such a desire.

'Table two,' Frederick calls from the kitchen and she sees the new waitress, Tina, pick up the food from the pass.

That's when she remembers why she possibly-maybe doesn't want to be here: she and Frederick had a disagreement on the drive in. Not a fight. They don't fight. They agreed early in their marriage that they don't like fighting. Frederick's parents liked to fight and he has no wish to live like that again.

'I went to see my doctor,' Dorothy informed him as they started down the road to town.

'Why didn't you tell me?'

She knew he'd say that. She always tells him where she goes. As soon as it was out of her mouth – before, even – she knew he'd want to know why she hadn't told him already. A second later he'd realise it was because she wanted to hold on to the information for a particular time: now. Which meant it was something significant. And that would make him feel tense. She saw it in his jaw. In his brow. She knew all of this would happen but still she chose to wait, because she wanted this story to be hers to tell.

They share most things, but lately – with the most recent miscarriage – Dorothy's become more conscious of the things they don't share. Can never share.

'I wanted to think about what he said,' she replied, which was also true.

'And what was that?' Frederick's 'w' sounds are still 'v' sounds.

'He says there is . . . help I can get. With pregnancy. In-vitro fertilisation.'

She'd heard about it – 'test-tube babies' used to make news. Now they don't because more and more people are having them, although it had never occurred to Dorothy that she might become one of those people. Because that would mean she's failed. Doctors had to come in and help her have a baby. Just because it is true – she *has* failed – doesn't make it sting less.

'*Was ist das?*'

She shouldn't have expected Frederick to know – he doesn't have a female body, so why would he have any cause to know what in-vitro fertilisation is? But she didn't want to explain its technicalities. To tell him that something they usually enjoy alone together – such a central part of their relationship – would be broken down to clinical rooms and vials and temperature checks and injections.

'It's a medical procedure. They take my eggs, they take your . . .' She cleared her throat; they knew each other so well but there were still things she could not say. 'They put them together in a laboratory to make embryos. Then any embryos that are growing, they put into me.'

He was silent. Thinking. She knew his thinking face.

'So we have a Frankenstein baby?' he said sadly.

'Frederick, no! Frankenstein was made out of parts of other people. The baby would be completely ours.'

'But it's not natural,' he said. 'A doctor makes our baby. We don't.'

'We don't make babies anyway,' she snapped. 'Something is going wrong! I keep losing them!' Her breathing was ragged. She gripped the handle of the car door.

'It's not your fault,' he said. That's what he always says. They both know it can't be true.

'I think we need to accept that doctors might know better,' she said, then looked out the window at the trees that were giving way to town dwellings. She was descending from her safe place to the real world.

'I don't want you suffering any more.' His voice was quiet but strong.

'I wouldn't suffer!' she said, but she couldn't know if that would be true.

Frederick hasn't said anything since then, not even when they arrived at work, and he hasn't been looking at her. Not that she's given him much chance. She's staying at the desk or greeting people at the door, trying to ignore the pressure building inside her. Her mother tells her that she's 'too emotional'. Maybe today it could be true.

Dorothy glances around. There aren't that many people in the café. She could leave for a little while. Go for a quick walk. She won't even tell Frederick.

'Tina,' she whispers as she moves past the waitress, 'I need to go out for a little while.'

The teenager's eyebrows raise in alarm.

'You'll be fine,' Dorothy says, squeezing her arm. 'Get Frederick to help if you need it.'

She doesn't wait for a response, and doesn't turn back as she slips out the half-closed door and almost jogs to the corner. She sees the Kombi van that's always parked in the same spot, with tie-dyed T-shirts hanging in the window, Greenpeace stickers on the side and the cloying waft of clove cigarettes from the back window. If she walks past, the hippies who live in it will talk to her, like they always do, and she doesn't want to discuss whale extinction today, so she turns around and goes swiftly past the café in the other direction, feeling ridiculous but also righteous. She can leave if she wants. It's her business too.

This street has more trees, so she feels calm straightaway. It's longer and has fewer cars. No one is on the footpath, so she slows, trying to get her breathing to match. She's breathing too hard; she knows this. If it continues she'll have one of those turns she used to have as a teenager when she was worried about how she'd go in exams, because she knew she wouldn't go well yet felt the responsibility of wanting to do well. Being an eldest child, responsibility is Dorothy's blood type. By her teens she had developed an all-consuming need to always do the right thing. Which meant doing well in exams even though she would never be academic. Fretting about this unsolvable situation made her breathe faster and think slower. At first her mother would chastise her about being too emotional, then rub her back and tell her to breathe slowly. The paradox was confusing yet reassuring – and, now, helpful.

Breathe, Dorothea, breathe, she hears, and obeys.

With her hands on her hips, she lowers her shoulders from their regular location near her ears. She doesn't so much carry the weight of the world on her shoulders as resist it. Or try to. Then she feels guilty about being so caught up in her own problems. They're nothing, really, when compared to others'. Even in her own family.

When her sister, Cornelia, was born deaf Dorothy was young enough to not understand the impact it would have on her parents. On her. She thought Cornelia was the cutest thing she'd ever seen and was delighted to have her own living doll to play with. It wasn't until Cornelia was walking that the directives started.

'Dorothea, look after your sister. She isn't like you.'

'Dorothea, you have to make sure Cornelia doesn't hurt herself.'

'Dorothea, we can't watch you all the time – I'm relying on you to take care of your sister.'

Her parents were trying to keep Cornelia safe – Dorothy understood that. They had to work hard to provide for Cornelia's future; they had to make sure they could afford special tutors for her, because going to the same school as Dorothy was not possible, and they had no family in Queensland, none in Australia at all, so they had to manage the best they could without that help. Dorothy understood that too, and knew she had a part to play in watching her sister after school while her parents worked.

Once Cornelia was old enough to want to begin talking, it was Dorothy who learnt sign language so she could be her sister's translator. Their parents learnt a little bit: signs for *hello* and *I love you* and *Are you all right?* But in order for Cornelia to properly express herself to their parents, and the rest of the world, she needed Dorothy.

At first learning sign was fun; by the time she was in high school Dorothy took a measure of pride in the fact that she spoke not only English and German but sign too. Or Auslan, as it became. It wasn't just about fluttering her hands around – it was a proper language. Just not one her parents had time to learn completely, and given that they preferred to speak in German perhaps that was no surprise. When she really wanted to make a point to them Cornelia would speak out loud; she chose her moments and everyone paid attention.

Despite that pride, Dorothy knew intrinsically from a young age that any needs and worries she had would now rank behind her sister's, but she could never say this to her parents because they weren't doing it consciously and would react badly if she pointed it out. They'd feel guilty, of course, and Dorothy didn't want that. She felt guilty enough herself every time she wanted to see her friends or even spend time alone, because that meant she was being a bad sister. It didn't seem to matter that her love for Cornelia was so enormous that it took up almost all the space in her heart; her guilt was never assuaged.

Somewhere in there Dorothy tried to keep a sense of herself and what she wanted for her own life, although there was no one she felt she could talk to about it until she met Frederick.

Dropping her hands from her hips, she's almost strolling now, through a sunny patch where no trees are planted, crossing a road, drifting away from something and towards who-knows-what. She can't remember the last time she played truant from her own life. Probably because she never has. She's the dutiful one, the list-keeper, the crease-folder. She doesn't run out on things. On work. On duty. It's how she's been trained.

There's laughter somewhere ahead, from more than one person. She briefly closes her eyes and takes it in, feels it as a balm on a pain that is indistinct yet sharp.

As she draws near the source of the sound she sees a house surrounded by a lush, dense garden, with large windows that face the street. The laughter is coming from inside. Stopping on the footpath so she can see through the window, Dorothy wonders if it's rude to watch. But no one is paying attention to her.

A lithe woman in a black leotard with a lively face and bright red lipstick, her blonde hair in small curls, gives a knowing wag of her finger before she puts her hands on another woman who is much older, adjusting her into a strange shape.

Other women are in that same shape, or variations of it, their legs making a triangle with the floor, one arm reaching for the sky.

One young woman wobbles and almost falls, then rights herself and giggles.

'Cecilia,' says the woman in the black leotard, 'do you *realllly* think that is a posture I wish to see here?'

She snorts, and the woman who must be Cecilia makes a show of straightening up then going back into position.

So that's why they're laughing: they're having fun. How glorious. How strange.

The woman in the black leotard catches Dorothy's eye. Dorothy's immediate instinct is to hide – except the woman smiles like they know each other, and dips her head almost as if she's bowing.

Dorothy looks away. Now that she's been caught she doesn't think she should stay. If she were in that group she'd feel uncomfortable being observed. But there must be a sign somewhere to tell her what the class is.

Turning, she sees it: *Orange Blossom House*. Beneath it hangs a wooden panel bearing the inscription: *Yoga, Saturdays at 8 am. Tuesdays at 10 am. Thursdays at 6 pm. All welcome. No experience necessary.*

Dorothy has heard of yoga but never seen it. And she's only heard of it because one of the waitresses at the café was keen on it. In fact, she used to not work Saturdays because she wanted to go to class. Probably *this* class.

The waitress is long gone – back to Canberra, to her degree and her accountant boyfriend – so Dorothy wouldn't have to worry about anyone she knows seeing her. Not that she will necessarily be able to do what these women are doing. But they're laughing, and she needs something light, a distraction, in her life. Plus the woman in the black leotard seemed to almost invite her in. Didn't she?

Dorothy believes in fate. Meeting a good, kind man like Frederick had to be fate, when such men are so hard to find. Living in this beautiful place had to be fate, because she loves it so much. Leaving the café today, walking down this street when she did – it wasn't an accident that she found this house with its charming name and its very own cradle of trees. She isn't religious but there are some signs she can't ignore.

Dorothy can make Thursdays at 6 pm. Frederick can stay behind at the café and wait for her. She knows he won't mind. Or if he does, she'll work something out.

Feeling lighter, her shoulders at least twenty per cent lower, Dorothy turns and walks back to her life.

CHAPTER ELEVEN

Patricia hadn't planned to come to this Thursday night class, but she couldn't stay at home. Not again. Not for the umpteenth night in a row.

She's aware that having her so-called leisure time divided between extracurricular school activities – such as the eternal challenge of creating a school debating team that lasts longer than one defeat – and sitting with her parents as they nod off in their armchairs or watch television or both means she's classified as a spinster. Possibly with an adjective in front of it. Old spinster, even though she's not old. Sad spinster, although she tries to be cheerful most of the time. Although, wait, being a spinster is inherently sad, isn't it, so 'sad spinster' is a tautology. So just 'old'. And let's not forget pathetic. Pathetic old spinster.

Not that anyone has called her that. They don't need to when she's doing it herself.

Once, in the 1960s, she bought a T-shirt that bore the slogan *Here comes trouble!* Her mother took one look at it and said, 'Why would anyone announce that about themselves before people have a chance to find out if it's true?' Patricia has never forgotten it, so she should know that applying labels to herself, even inside the throbbing roar of her own mind, is equivalent. She shouldn't think it lest someone picks up on it.

So she's not pathetic or old, but she'll be both within a few years if she doesn't shake up her non-routine of serving the school and serving her parents. That's why she stayed later at school this afternoon and drove straight to the yoga class. She's not sure yet if she completely likes yoga, but she likes the fact it gives her an excuse to not be at home or at school.

'Where are you off to?' Dennis asked as she was leaving the staffroom and he was returning to it after athletics training with the Year Tens.

'Um . . . yoga,' she said, not sure if she should admit it. If he hadn't heard of it he might think she'd said 'yoghurt'.

'Oh yeah?'

Dennis looked like he wanted to have a chat about it. Which Patricia didn't want. She doesn't want to encourage any remnants of a crush that he might still have. Or that she might still have.

'I've heard of that,' he went on. 'And I saw someone doing it on a TV show . . .' He grinned, then she thought she saw him blush. 'She put her legs behind her head. I'm pretty sure my hamstrings will never be that long.'

It was her turn to blush. 'Right. Well, I'm going to be late. Bye!'

'Have fun,' he called after her. 'Maybe I'll join you next time.'

Patricia felt mortified. It was bad enough Marjorie had seen her in a leotard. Dennis absolutely must never.

By the time she reaches class, she's almost talked herself out of going. She feels like a bad daughter, even though she'll make her parents dinner when she arrives home. But as soon as she sees Orange Blossom House she's glad she didn't succeed.

The long white weatherboard building up on its little brick stilts seems to welcome her: its large front windows are ajar, and a candle in each corner like a beacon shows her that she's heading for the right place. Soft exterior lights accentuate the tall frangipanis on each side so they look like friendly sentries, about to lower the drawbridge to her evening. With the sun setting behind the house, yellow light is changing the colour of the lawn as Patricia steps onto the winding footpath and feels, much to her surprise, the stresses of the day almost sliding out of her body.

She can smell the incense that Sandrine likes to burn just as she hears Sandrine's mellifluous voice and the soft laughter of one of the students. By the time she's rolled out her mat and flopped on the floor, she knows completely and absolutely that it's worth being here just for these short seconds of respite from herself.

'Excuse me,' says a voice next to her and Patricia turns towards it.

Its owner is a woman at least a decade or so younger than her, with thick yellow-blonde hair in a plait that makes her look like she should be collecting wildflowers in the Swiss Alps, a pinch between her eyebrows and the biggest, roundest brown eyes Patricia has ever seen.

'Yes?'

'Have I brought the right thing?' The woman gestures to her mat, which looks like a newer version of Patricia's own.

'Yes, you have.' Patricia sits up properly. 'It must be your first time. I'm pretty new too.'

The woman smiles nervously. 'I don't really know what to do.'

'I don't either. But that's okay. I'm Patricia.'

'Dorothy.' The nervous smile turns into a furrowed brow. 'I don't actually know what I'm doing here.'

'A colleague told me to come because it's a good stretch. And it is. But . . .' Patricia searches for the right words. 'I actually feel more calm when I leave here. The breathing is good.' She smiles. 'I had no idea there was a right and a wrong way to breathe, so I'm learning the right way. And with the poses, Sandrine doesn't push you to do anything you aren't ready for.'

Dorothy looks surprised and Patricia thinks she can guess why: she's just blurted out a whole lot of information that Dorothy might have no interest in hearing. Dorothy's not her student, after all.

'Sorry,' Patricia says, 'you didn't ask to hear all that.'

'No, it's wonderful,' Dorothy says. 'Thank you. Calm is what I need, so now I know I'm in the right place.' She smiles and radiance almost glimmers from her.

'We're starting,' Patricia says softly, nodding towards the front of the room where Sandrine has stepped onto her mat. 'Don't try to copy me because I don't know all the poses yet.'

Dorothy nods and they both lie down as Sandrine commands.

The class begins slowly, as it always does, with Sandrine wandering between the mats, sometimes putting a hand on someone to adjust them with a light touch, sometimes murmuring encouragement. Today she floats in Dorothy's direction a couple of times but has no words for Patricia, who feels mildly, strangely, disappointed.

There are words in Sanskrit, which Patricia had never heard spoken before coming to this class, names of poses – of asanas, as they are properly called – that no doubt make sense if you know the language. Only one pose is named in English: downward-facing dog. Patricia wonders if it's because the Sanskrit name is too difficult to say. Regardless, she's learning to like the pose even if her legs still shake a little.

Her shoulder and neck still aren't fixed – despite Marjorie asking her every day if they are – but she finds herself worrying less about them. When she's in these poses, in her body, following

Sandrine's instructions – *inhale*, *exhale*, *inhale*, *exhale* – she doesn't think of anything else. Especially when the pose is painful. When she's in a standing pose that forces her hips open, that makes her hold still inside that opening and try to breathe through the pain, she is right there.

Like now. Her left hip feels like it's being made to do something unnatural. She feels like she's going to fall. Like she can't support her own weight.

'Use your back leg, Patricia,' comes Sandrine's voice in her ear, so softly only Patricia would hear it. 'You are making your front leg work too hard. You have two legs, no? They both have to work.'

She feels Sandrine behind her as she attempts to do what she's asked but it feels like nothing changes. Her legs are wobbling. Her hip feels like it's on fire. Her spine doesn't seem to know where it is. The whole thing is wrong. And stupid. *She's* wrong and stupid. She can't even hold this silly—

'*Breathe*, Patricia.'

Sandrine's hands are on her shoulders now and Patricia gulps in a breath, embarrassed to have a witness to her inadequacy.

'Breathe *slowly*. Inhale and come up out of the posture.'

'But—'

'Up,' Sandrine commands, and her hands are still on Patricia's shoulders, almost like she's trying to comfort her.

Patricia wonders why, then realises tears are rolling down her face.

She gulps another breath.

'Oh,' she says, and wants to run from the room. People are *seeing her* like this. Crying. Because of a little pain in her hip. She's pathetic. Dorothy, the new student, will think she's loony.

'It's normal,' Sandrine whispers. 'I promise you. The body keeps our secrets for us and sometimes yoga brings them out.

To the light, where they belong. So we can manage them. You didn't think it would be easy, did you?' She smiles and wipes the tears from Patricia's cheeks. 'This is not a place for anyone who is not prepared to feel pain. I have sobbed. Believe me. You are not the first.'

Then she's gone, off to attend to someone else, and as Patricia glances around she sees that absolutely no one has noticed what just happened.

Except Dorothy.

'Are you all right?' she says quietly as they all shift to a different posture.

Normally Patricia would say, 'Yes, thank you,' quickly. As a dismissal. You can't let anyone know what you really feel. It's not polite. But she pauses and thinks about it. In this place, *lying* would be impolite. This room isn't quite a cocoon yet she feels that it's some kind of protected environment. There's no judgement here. She doesn't judge others for what they can and can't do; no one is judging her.

'I don't know,' she says. 'But I look forward to finding out.'

Dorothy stares at her for a couple of seconds, then her face relaxes. 'I know what you mean,' she says.

They don't talk again until the class ends, the spell is broken and they're walking out at the same time.

'So do you think you'll come back?' Patricia says once they're on the footpath. She's clutching her rolled-up mat to her chest like it's a teddy bear.

Dorothy nods slowly. 'Yes. I found it very interesting. And calming, like you said.' Her face changes, as if a thought is trying to write itself upon her. 'I think I need it. All of it. I just didn't know I did until I came here.'

'It's strange how that happens, isn't it?' Patricia pulls her car keys out of her handbag. 'I guess I'll see you next week.' Or maybe she won't, if she doesn't come to this class again.

'You will. Goodbye.' Dorothy gives her a funny little wave, then pivots and walks away.

Patricia sighs – long and heavy, as if she's still holding on to whatever was in that hip. Or maybe she's simply anticipating how the rest of her night will go. Cook dinner, try to manage whatever is going on in her mother's brain, let her father rant about Prime Minister Paul Keating and how everything would be better if the Liberals were in charge, but John Hewson was never going to win that March election and they should have let Andrew Peacock have another go.

As she drives home she thinks again about what happened in class. About her tears and how she didn't realise they'd erupted. About the place in her body they came from. The deep, dark well of her hips and whatever she's stuffed down there all these years.

Maybe that's what yoga will teach her: the mystery of herself and what to do about it. Or maybe she'll just have a good stretch and that will be that.

The latter is what she'll tell Marjorie. Anything else Patricia discovers will be hers alone.

CHAPTER TWELVE

It's not in Grace Maud's nature to be sneaky, but this evening she has been. After telling Cecilia that she planned to do 'nothing much', she has driven herself – *alone*, Heaven forfend – to Orange Blossom House for the yoga class. It's not that she minds going on Saturdays with Cecilia, but Grace Maud is still an independent person and she can still see at night, no matter what Tom thinks, so it's partly to prove to herself that she can do it that she's decided to attend the Thursday class.

Besides, it's a nice thing to do: she is winding down the day, and is sure she'll sleep better afterwards.

Sleep is something that becomes erratic as one ages; Grace Maud wishes one of her parents had told her that. She also wishes she had Ellie Maud to discuss it with. They could be crones together, moaning about waking up at four o'clock and turning on the wireless for company. Although if Ellie Maud were alive she likely wouldn't do that because she'd still have her husband.

The early evening air is cool as Grace Maud walks into Orange Blossom House – the first to arrive, for a change – and positions herself at the back of the studio. She likes being able to observe the room and to copy one of the younger women, even though Sandrine regularly admonishes them to 'not look at your neighbour – yes, Grace Maud, you too'. She rolls out her mat but won't sit down on it yet. Instead she leans against the wall, and watches the others arrive.

There's a hunched-over woman who Grace Maud suspects is younger than she looks; she always walks in slowly, as if her feet are getting caught in something.

Sandrine buzzes in and winks at Grace Maud.

Another 'oldie' walks heavily to a spot by the window. She's one of those women who thinks old age means short hair. Grace Maud is regularly surprised by the number of women who reach fifty and decide they want men's haircuts. Just because you're in the realm of menopause doesn't mean you stop being a woman. Grace Maud has kept her hair reasonably long, even if she likes to pin it up into a lazy chignon. Which is why she approves of the long blonde plait on a younger woman who looks around nervously as she enters.

When she sees Grace Maud she looks relieved and moves towards her. 'Hello,' she says. 'May I go next to you?'

'Of course,' Grace Maud says, but wonders why the young woman is so keen on the idea. Perhaps she thinks Grace Maud is unlikely to be able to do the poses and she'll look good by comparison. Well, she'll shortly find out that Grace Maud is, in fact, quite good at some things. Not that it's a competition. Sandrine keeps telling them that.

'I'm Dorothy,' says blondie, and the brightness of her smile is out of proportion to the tentativeness of her demeanour.

'Grace Maud.'

Dorothy frowns. 'Oh. That's—'

'Unusual – yes, I know.'

These younger people seem to have never heard the name Maud before. Cecilia was also surprised the first time they met.

'Hello, Dorothy,' says a woman now standing in front of them.

Grace Maud recognises this woman from her first class: beautiful face and such a terrible hairstyle that she can only presume the woman has no idea how beautiful she is – because why would anyone knowingly put a bad frame on a masterpiece?

'Hi, Patricia! How are you? Are you well? Are you going there?' Dorothy gestures in front of them. 'This is Grace Maud.'

Grace Maud is somewhat amused by the speed of Dorothy's speech. It's almost as if the girl is too tightly wound to stay still. Which should make the meditation portion of the class interesting for all of them.

'Hello,' Patricia says, smiling. 'I'm Patricia. I'm fairly new at all this.' She shrugs an apology.

'Not to worry. Just because I'm old doesn't mean I have any more experience than you,' Grace Maud says.

'Oh, I didn't mean that.' Patricia looks like she's chewing the inside of her cheek.

'I'm sure you didn't. I'm just not looking forward to getting down to the floor. My hips are creakier than they used to be.'

'I could . . .' Dorothy stops. 'I could . . . help you?'

Her face is a symphony of emotions: different movements playing themselves out all over the place. Grace Maud wonders if she gets herself into this much of a tangle every time she offers assistance, and also recognises what's going on. Dorothy wants to help but not to offend, and she has an abundance of sympathy – perhaps empathy too – which means she analyses everything she says as she says it. How exhausting. Grace Maud decides to make it easier for her.

'That would be lovely,' she says, holding out an elbow to give Dorothy some direction.

'Good!'

Dorothy takes her elbow and forearm with both hands, and they simultaneously sink, then lie on their backs with their knees bent and their feet on the floor, the way Sandrine often likes them to start.

Grace Maud looks up to see that Patricia is covertly checking on them, which she finds irritating – just because she's older doesn't mean she's hopeless – but also quite nice. Grace Maud doesn't know this woman from a bar of soap yet she's taking an interest. It's the most attention Grace Maud has had since nurses fussed over her when Tom was born.

'Hands beside your hips,' Sandrine says, 'hips' coming out as 'eeps' in that accent of hers. 'Inhale . . . exhale . . .'

Sandrine is a good teacher; Grace Maud is prepared to admit this. She is clear in her instructions and encouraging without being sycophantic, which means she's not interested in her students' approval. And that suits Grace Maud fine because she's not about to give it. She was brought up in a family that showed approval by not showing disapproval. But if Grace Maud had ever believed that this class would be completely calm and gentle, she would have been disappointed. It's like cadet camp for ladies with joints that are tighter than they used to be and spines that are developing kyphosis years ahead of schedule.

Grace Maud feels those joints as she moves from lying on the floor to standing up and moving through postures that seem like they were designed to pull a pelvis apart, even if Grace Maud can feel the benefit afterwards.

Like this one, with her feet wide apart and her head hanging towards the floor, the backs of her legs protesting the strong stretch.

'Inhale, exhale,' comes the exhortation – and after she's taken a few breaths, Grace Maud hears Sandrine asking them to roll up to a standing position, slowly.

Instead of heeding the instruction Grace Maud hinges herself upright, and is rewarded with the unusual sensation of blood rushing out of her head. Then dizziness. Then the feeling of not being able to see properly. Then a touch of mortification: silly old biddy, what did she think she was doing rushing like that?

'Patricia,' she hears Sandrine saying, only a slight edge to her voice, 'can you please take Grace Maud's arm? Dorothy, the other side, please.'

She feels firm hands on her upper arms and a shoulder pressing against her on the left, like half a brace.

'We've got you,' Patricia says softly, but Grace Maud is still unsteady.

She is reminded of what happened the other day when she attempted to crouch to pick up a stick in the garden: she made it down, but not up. Luckily Cecilia was nearby and could help her. But it's one of her frustrations about her age. In her mind her body works the way it always did, so crouching isn't something she stops to think about; and by the time she does think about it, she finds herself awkwardly dropping onto the grass and calling out to a much younger woman for assistance, hoping the neighbours don't interpret it as some kind of distress call that might lead them to ring for an ambulance.

'There's a seat outside,' Dorothy is saying. 'Perhaps you'd like to sit down?'

'I don't want to . . . want to keep you from the class,' Grace Maud says, trying to make her brain work at its usual speed now her blood all seems to have gone elsewhere.

'It's fine,' Dorothy says, gently pivoting Grace Maud towards the door with Patricia's assistance. 'I don't like this pose anyway. Too hard!'

Grace Maud doesn't know what the pose is because they have her almost to the door.

'Please, I'm all right,' she urges. 'Go back to class.'

But the others don't answer; instead, they guide her to a bench seat deeper in the garden of Orange Blossom House.

They ease her down, sitting on either side.

'I got a bit dizzy myself,' Patricia says, 'so I'm happy to take a break.'

She is, no doubt, lying but Grace Maud appreciates that she's trying to smooth over the situation. Neither woman knows Grace Maud; doesn't know that it would take more to embarrass her than this.

'And I have first-aid qualifications,' Patricia adds. 'Just in case – you know – you feel faint.'

'Why do you have those?' Dorothy asks. She has kept hold of Grace Maud's arm and it feels quite comforting.

'I'm a teacher,' Patricia says. 'At the high school down the road. They like us all to have them in case a student slices open a knee or something.'

'Has that ever happened?' Dorothy asks.

'Not yet.'

'I should probably learn first aid.'

'It's a good thing to do. Handy.'

'Yes, and – I work in a café. There are knives in the kitchen.' Dorothy laughs almost nervously, like she's envisaging what could happen with those knives.

'Are you trying to distract me?' Grace Maud says, now feeling more *compos mentis*.

'What's that?' says Patricia.

'Are you trying to distract me until I feel better?'

'Not really.' She has a loose, throaty laugh. 'I'm just chatting. Dorothy and I only met at the last class so I don't know anything about her.'

Dorothy smiles. 'Grace Maud, how are you feeling?'

'Improved.'

'Do you want to go back to the class or go home?' Patricia says, her brow furrowed.

'I think I can manage the class.' Grace Maud pushes herself up from the bench, Dorothy's hand still attached to her. 'But I will listen to instructions more closely in future.'

'In my first class I got so caught up trying to breathe the way she says that I forgot what we were meant to be doing.' Dorothy's laugh is different to Patricia's: more of a tinkle.

'It takes a bit of getting used to,' Patricia agrees, then she turns to Grace Maud. 'You're sure?'

'I am.'

'Then . . . lead on, Macduff.' Patricia gestures for Grace Maud to go ahead of her.

'*Macbeth* is my favourite,' Grace Maud says as they walk back to the studio.

'Mine too,' Patricia says, beaming. 'Perhaps we should compare notes one day.'

'Perhaps,' Grace Maud concedes as she steps inside first, leaving her helpers to trail in after her.

She meets the eyes of Sandrine, who looks more worried than Grace Maud would have anticipated. Grace Maud gives her a nod then returns to her mat, pleased to see the class has moved on to sitting poses. She can handle those. If she can get down there.

'Dorothy,' she whispers, 'would you give me a hand?'

'Of course!' Dorothy says, looking like it's the thing she most wants to do in the world.

It's quite a gift, Grace Maud thinks, to make other people feel like they're not bothering you in the slightest. It's not a gift Grace Maud has ever had.

She rejoins the group, and is thankful that the rest of the class doesn't involve any dropping of heads. Instead there is plenty of inhaling and exhaling, and as Grace Maud considers the younger women on either side of her she realises that while this class may not give her back the body she used to have, it is presenting her with enough of interest that she is prepared to keep coming.

CHAPTER THIRTEEN

'You didn't go to the class on Saturday,' Marjorie says, a note of remonstration in her voice.

She and Patricia are both rostered on playground duty, which tends to involve making sure the Year Nine boys don't antagonise the Year Tens, and that the Year Eight girls don't hike up their uniforms in an attempt to impress any boy within eyesight.

In Patricia's experience, boys tend to be impressed by that sort of thing momentarily, then they'll move on to the next impressive sight. She's tried to tell the girls they're wasting their time, but they all read *Dolly* magazine and are convinced that short skirts are what boys like. Patricia knows it's useless telling them that they should be more focused on what *they* like. She might have read Naomi Wolf's *The Beauty Myth* but she's sure none of the girls – or Marjorie, for that matter – has. Patricia doesn't count herself as a feminist but that book opened her eyes to a few things. That's when she stopped going to the hairdresser to have her hair coloured. Grey is fine. And less expensive.

'No, I went to the Thursday evening class instead,' she says, keeping an eye on a Year Nine boy the size of a fully grown man who's standing over a Year Seven who is telling him to 'rack off' repeatedly. 'I needed to unwind after work.'

'I could have gone with you!' Marjorie says quickly and Patricia sees her mistake: she shouldn't have given her reason for going. Of course Marjorie would think that she too needs to unwind after work and why couldn't they share the experience.

Patricia likes Marjorie but isn't sure they'd make good friends, despite Marjorie's fevered attempts to befriend her.

Maybe it's because Marjorie's life seems easy – she goes to movies with friends, plays netball in winter, and cheerfully admits that she buys lots of clothes she never wears because shopping is fun – and Patricia's life feels hard a lot of the time. Plus Marjorie thinks that Alex Dimitriades, playing a high school student in love with his teacher in *The Heartbreak Kid*, is 'hot' – a somewhat worrying opinion given where they work. No doubt she thinks that way because she's still young herself.

Age is another difference between them: Marjorie is at full speed and Patricia sometimes feels like she's grinding to a halt. But the idea of trying to explain that to someone as breezy as Marjorie is exhausting. So it's easier to politely refuse her invitations to movies, netball and shopping, always with a smile and a thank-you-for-asking-it's-so-kind-of-you.

'Sorry,' Patricia says to her colleague's disappointed face now. 'I wasn't thinking.'

It's not the truth – she *had* thought about telling Marjorie she wouldn't be at the Saturday class – but it's a story that saves Marjorie's feelings.

She has spent quite a bit of her life protecting other people's feelings. Sometimes it can feel disingenuous – but what's the alternative? She can't say, 'I just didn't want to go with you, Marjorie.' That would be hurtful.

'You're liking it then – the yoga?' Marjorie asks, sounding hopeful.

Patricia hesitates. 'Like' isn't the right verb, but she's not sure she wants to get into that. The classes have challenged her ego, for one thing. There are poses she was sure she'd do in a cinch, thanks to childhood years spent in ballet classes, but which have left her feeling weak and foolish. Not that anyone else there cares. Patricia likes to do things properly, though, and she can't believe that it's so hard to hold still in a shape for ten breaths without feeling like you're failing a test you didn't even know you'd been set. Then, at the end of it all, to lie down on the floor with such relief that you want to cry, and instead surrender to the low incantations of an eccentric Frenchwoman who will inflict it all on you again next week.

'It's interesting,' she says instead. 'I'd like to keep going, to see what happens.'

Marjorie looks delighted.

'I'm just not sure I can commit to one class time or the other,' Patricia adds quickly.

Although that's not true either. She likes being there in the evening, to decompress before she goes home. She also likes Dorothy, who is a mixture of front and vulnerability that makes her intriguing. And she doesn't know if she'll see Grace Maud again but there was a spark about her that Patricia found appealing.

'G'day, ladies,' says Dennis as he approaches. He's clad in his PE teacher's uniform of loose shorts and a T-shirt that's tight enough to show he's suitably fit for his job.

Marjorie greets him with her usual enthusiasm. 'Hi, Dennis!'

'Dennis,' Patricia says, nodding her acknowledgement. In return she gets his endearingly lopsided grin.

'Just thought I'd let you know that Gordon is heading this way,' he says, glancing over his shoulder. 'This is your one-minute warning.'

He gives them a thumbs-up and leaves. Marjorie and Patricia look at each other with mild alarm.

'I'll go and check the loos for smokers,' says Patricia.

'I think the side gate may be open,' says Marjorie, and they scatter.

CHAPTER FOURTEEN

Dorothy looks around the yoga room and sees that her usual spot is taken. How annoying. Or maybe it shouldn't be. This isn't school – she's not meant to be in the same spot each time. In fact, Sandrine told them that it's good to take a different spot each time, to 'change perspective'.

There's a spot in front of Sandrine's mat but there's risk involved: Sandrine will be able to watch her all the time, which means spotting her mistakes with greater frequency.

'Are you thinking of going down the front?' It's Patricia, smiling.

'Oh . . . I don't know. Why?'

'You were looking at that spot. Come on, I'll go with you. We'll be brave together!'

Patricia grins and walks swiftly to the space, plonking her mat down before Dorothy has a chance to object.

'Grace Maud is here.' Patricia waves towards the door.

'Oh good,' Dorothy says, beaming at Grace Maud, who walks slowly towards them, listing a bit from side to side.

'Hello, young ladies,' Grace Maud says, dropping her mat next to Patricia's.

'I'm not that young,' Patricia retorts.

'You're younger than me,' Grace Maud says briskly, then walks towards the back wall, where she places her handbag next to some others.

'I should do that,' Patricia says, leaving her mat on the floor next to Dorothy.

'Ladies, ladies! Do not lie down to start with, please,' Sandrine announces as she walks into the room, a bright pink sarong tied around her hips and bobby pins with flowers in her hair. 'We are going to do some breathing. Some *pranayama*. Please take some blankets to sit on.'

She gestures to the shelves at the back of the room where there's all manner of 'furniture', as she called it during the last class: wooden blocks, and belts with metal loops on them, and rough grey blankets.

'I'll get them for all of us,' Patricia says and Dorothy smiles her thanks.

'I'm interested to find out how blankets are going to help us breathe,' Grace Maud says, carefully making her way to the floor with Dorothy's help. 'Not that I'm convinced I need to *practise* breathing. I've been doing it for seventy-four years.' She makes a noise that sounds like 'hmph' just as Patricia returns with a stack of blankets and distributes them.

'Sandrine said something the other day about how if you can learn to control your breathing it's good for anxiety,' Dorothy says.

'Are you anxious?' Patricia stretches her legs out in front of her. Her tone is matter-of-fact, as if being anxious is no different to having long fingernails.

'Sometimes. Life can be stressful!' Dorothy laughs, and it sounds forced even to her.

'Yes,' Grace Maud says slowly. 'It certainly can be.'

Sandrine starts issuing instructions: make sure you sit with your hips higher than your knees; if you have trouble keeping your spine long, sit with your back to the wall.

Dorothy is tempted to sit against the wall – she tends to collapse a bit whenever they sit in meditation – but no one else moves and she doesn't want to be the only one.

The first five minutes are spent listening to Sandrine talking about how breathing practice helps connect a person to their 'centre', whatever that means, by increasing awareness of how their body works.

Dorothy isn't sure she has a centre. She's always been a fairly scattered person. Or that's what her teachers used to say: *Dorothy should learn to concentrate*; *Dorothy has talents but she will never develop them unless she learns to focus.* Her parents never used to worry, though. 'School is only taught one way,' her mother would tell her. 'And it is just one part of your life.'

She was glad, because there were other children at school whose parents would punish them if they didn't top the class. Dorothy was never going to be that child. Besides, Dorothy had other things on her mind, like Cornelia.

It wasn't until Dorothy was in high school, learning about World War II and all the things her parents would never tell her, that she realised her mother had a different perspective on what was important in life.

She's also discovered that when she finds a class she likes – such as yoga – she can turn up and be a diligent student. As she is being now: following Sandrine's instructions as they inhale – pause. Exhale – pause.

Dorothy is so busy concentrating on the pauses that after a while she becomes aware that she isn't thinking and worrying about anything. Maybe that's the point? She'll have to ask Sandrine later.

After some time has passed – Dorothy has lost track – Sandrine announces that they will have a break.

'This practice is strong,' she says. 'So take ten minutes. Then we will come back, and as a special treat we will do some nice stretches.' She smiles enigmatically. 'We may run a little late tonight. But it will be worth it.'

Dorothy turns to Patricia. 'Would you like to go outside? I think I need some fresh air to help me take a break from all this breathing.'

She laughs, so Patricia will know she's joking. It's always tricky when you haven't spent much time with someone and they don't know your sense of humour. Then she sees that Patricia's face looks pinched, her lips puckering. And her skin is paler than it was at the start of the class.

'Um . . .' she says.

'Are you all right?' Dorothy glances to Grace Maud on her other side, to check on her as well. The older woman is frowning in Patricia's direction.

'I'm . . . not sure.' Patricia inhales, then looks surprised.

'I'm getting Sandrine,' Dorothy says, standing up.

'No, that's okay. I'm fine.'

'You're not fine,' Grace Maud says and nods at Dorothy. 'Go.'

Dorothy scurries over to Sandrine and tells her what's wrong. They walk back to where Patricia is now sitting with one hand on her abdomen, the other over her mouth.

'Patricia,' Sandrine says, squatting, 'do you feel a little nauseated?'

Patricia nods quickly.

'That is normal.' Sandrine rubs Patricia's thigh. 'But I forgot to say it. I was carried away. So much to tell you all.' She pulls a face. 'I'm sorry.'

'It's all right,' Patricia says, scrambling to her feet. 'But I think I need the loo.' She's gone before any of them can reply.

'Poor thing,' Dorothy says.

'It happens quite a lot,' Sandrine says. 'Sometimes with the breathing, sometimes in the poses. Yoga reveals who we really are, and in order to do that sometimes we need to throw the rubbish out. Sometimes it comes out here,' she gestures to her mouth, 'sometimes here.' This time she pats her bottom, waggling her eyebrows, and Dorothy blushes while Grace Maud laughs. 'To-tal eva-cu-a-tion,' Sandrine says. 'And she will sleep well tonight.'

'Is it really necessary?' Grace Maud asks. 'Yoga seems to be . . . somewhat trying.'

'Everyone is different,' Sandrine says. 'And yoga . . . well, Grace Maud, I am sure you know that change is always hard. When we come to the practice we bring allll the junk of our lives, *non*? That is why we come a lot of the time – because we know we need to be rid of that junk. But it took years to build up, you see? It is not quick, or easy, to throw it out. We must throw it out, though, if we want to return to ourselves. If we want to be whole.' She smiles softly. 'Sometimes we may even become happy. Imagine!'

Dorothy considers what Sandrine has said: the work required and what may result. She thinks about the pain she's already put her body through and what may be to come if she tries again. With each miscarriage she felt herself becoming less and less Dorothy – like part of her was seeping away. If yoga can bring even some of that back to her, it's worth trying. And it's better that she knows it will be hard sometimes. She can prepare for that. The worst lessons are the ones you're not prepared for.

'Patricia will be a while,' Sandrine says, standing. 'You should have a walk outside. Enjoy the trees. Even at night they are lovely companions.'

Dorothy looks at Grace Maud.

'Shall we?' Grace Maud says.

Dorothy grins and helps the older woman to her feet.

They take their time to walk outside and move towards a pink bloodwood that looks oversized for the garden. The night air is cool but Dorothy doesn't mind. That breathing made her a little overheated at times so this is a respite.

'So what do you think about this yoga?' Grace Maud says, putting one hand to her lower back.

'Do you mean do I like it?'

'I think we all like it or we wouldn't be here,' Grace Maud says bluntly.

Dorothy isn't sure whether or not she should be offended, although Grace Maud doesn't look cross. 'Um,' is all she can think of to say.

'I mean, what is it doing for you?' Grace Maud peers at her. 'Have you had what she has?' She jerks her head in the direction of the toilet.

'Oh – no!' Dorothy titters. 'Not yet! But I . . .'

She stops to think about something that happened to her the other day, pondering whether or not to tell Grace Maud. But who else *would* she tell? Frederick isn't in this class. She can't share the experience with him.

'You know how Sandrine is always talking about how we're meant to feel bliss?' she says, and Grace Maud nods slowly. 'I thought she was making it up. To get us to keep coming back.

But last week when we came out of that posture – you know, the *vira*-something one? Like this.' She drops into a lunge with her arms out to her sides.

Grace Maud nods again, maintaining their eye contact.

'When I stood up,' Dorothy says, starting to smile at the memory, 'I felt . . . something. A wave of something. But it's hard to put a name to it. I want to say peace, but that doesn't seem entirely right. Warmth, maybe?' She closes her eyes as she tries to recapture it. 'I wanted to hold on to it but it was gone so quickly. Maybe I imagined it.'

'I don't think you did,' Grace Maud says. 'If you felt it, it was real. I can't say I've had that experience yet, but I've had it doing other things. Riding a horse, if you can believe that.'

Dorothy gasps with laughter – she's never ridden a horse and can't imagine finding peace on one.

'There are moments when everything feels like it's in its right place,' Grace Maud goes on. 'You're not ruminating on the past or worrying about the future. You're just . . . there.' She smiles serenely. 'I believe that's what you're talking about.'

'It is.' Dorothy nods her head so vigorously that her plait whacks her neck. 'That's it! How can I get it again?'

'By not trying. Ah, there's Patricia.'

Patricia walks towards them looking slightly less pale but no less uncomfortable.

'All done?' Grace Maud asks.

Patricia blows air out of her mouth. 'Everything including the kitchen sink,' she moans and puts a hand on her belly.

'I guess you're initiated now,' Grace Maud says. 'Come on, let's take a turn about the garden and get your blood moving.'

'Okay,' Patricia says meekly.

The three of them set off at a slow pace, Patricia huffing occasionally.

And as Grace Maud recounts the reasons why she still believes learning to breathe isn't necessary, for a few seconds Dorothy doesn't think of what's gone wrong in the past or what might not happen in the future. She is right there, breathing and being, and this time she holds on to it for just a bit longer than she thought she could.

CHAPTER FIFTEEN

Sundays used to be lovely – Patricia remembers that. All the housework was completed on the Saturday so she had the Sunday free to do nothing much. She would read the newspaper, visit with friends or have them over to lunch, listen to music, read books, go to the beach if it was the right time of year. She'd laze. That was it. What a luxury that was, and one she didn't truly appreciate.

She knew – because once her friends started having children, before they completely disappeared into the vortex of overwhelm that being a parent could become, they told her so – that she'd been lucky to have only herself to worry about. 'I wish I could be selfish like you,' one of them had said exasperatedly as she wrangled a child into a high chair, and Patricia had recognised the barb within the statement. She'd never thought of herself as selfish; she still doesn't think she was, so much as self-centred. That's what happens when you do, in fact, have only yourself to care for.

Those days are over now. In her new life, Sundays are definitely for housework: three people generate a lot more washing and cleaning than one. They're also for trying to sort herself out for the week ahead: meals planned with supplies bought on Saturday, before the shops shut for the weekend; clothes for work ironed and hanging in the wardrobe. Small acts of order that help her manage the chaos of her mother.

Now, as Patricia turns off the iron and pulls the plug from the wall, her father announces, 'Your mother wants to go out.'

'Oh?' Patricia responds vaguely. 'To where?' She coils the cord around the base of the iron and pushes it into the corner of the laundry bench.

'To the shops.'

'Did you tell her that most of the shops are shut on a Sunday?'

Patricia tries hard to keep the irritation out of her voice. If her father could head off some of her mother's requests at the pass, Patricia wouldn't have to so often be the bad guy.

'No,' he says.

'Why not?'

'I didn't know they'd be shut.'

He sounds miffed, as if she's somehow let him down. But, of course, the reason he doesn't know that they're shut is because he doesn't do the shopping. Never has, never will.

Patricia sighs, because that's the only form of protest she can lodge. 'Okay, Dad. I'll talk to her.'

She finds her mother sitting on the couch in the living room, knees and ankles pressed together, shoulders back, spine straight, handbag on her lap. In the time Patricia has taken to do the ironing her mother has managed to dress herself in a twin set that's more suited to a colder climate but which she's had in her wardrobe for aeons. Her eyes are sharp, alert, and staring at her daughter.

Patricia never knows which version of her mother she'll get but it looks like this morning's is more present than usual.

'I hear you want to go out, Mum,' she says.

'Don't talk to me as if I'm a child,' comes the rebuke.

Patricia flinches. This is her real mother, and she hasn't encountered her for a while. Immediately she is on guard, even though she knows she doesn't have the same weapons as those in the arsenal her mother's been drawing from all these years.

'Sorry, Mum, I didn't mean to.'

'Of course you did, you stupid girl.' Now her mother's eyes are flint, the dark grey colour of her rage that Patricia recalls so well. 'You always mean the ridiculous things you do.'

Patricia feels her breath leave her, and can't breathe in again because her lungs are full of fear and memories and a desperate desire to escape. She is fifteen again. Or nine. Or seventeen. Every age from birth to the time when she moved out to get away from this.

But she's forty-six now and shouldn't be so affected by an elderly woman who is no longer in control of her faculties. This version of her mother will disappear soon. Patricia just has to wait, and try to not condescend lest she provoke a similar response. She'll go with appeasement instead.

'I suppose I have done some ridiculous things,' she says mildly, glancing up to see her father watching from the doorway.

He never used to see his wife treating her youngest child differently to the others; never understood why Patricia didn't want to spend much time at the house. So he probably thinks this current performance is an aberration instead of a glimpse into who his wife really used to be.

Her mother sniffs and pulls her handbag closer. Almost as if she thinks Patricia is going to try to take it. 'Letting Bradley go – that was the most ridiculous,' she says snippily. 'A perfectly nice young man. All the prospects in the world. Wanted to marry you. But oh *no*, he wasn't good enough for you. You had to go to Sydney.'

Her mother's stare is cold, as it was the first time Patricia heard this speech over twenty years ago. Versions of it have been uttered since, but none since she moved back into the house. She knows that the best thing to do is let her mother say her piece, then change the subject. Her high-school boyfriend, Bradley, is the only boyfriend her parents know about so he's the one her mother fixates on as the man Patricia should have married. Bradley was sweet and dull; perfect in high school but not for adulthood. He married the girlfriend he took up with after Patricia and was a father by twenty-three. As far as Patricia knows, they're still married. Good for them.

'Bradley and I weren't well suited enough for marriage, Mum,' she says gently, as she always does.

'*Suited?*' Her mother purses her lips. 'All this nonsense people go on with. You don't wait for anyone who *suits you*. You take the first person who asks you or you *miss out*. And you have *missed out*.'

Patricia again glances at her father. He seems unbothered, even though her mother has basically admitted to marrying him because he was the first person who asked. Perhaps it works both ways. Perhaps her mother was the first woman to accept him.

Patricia didn't want to marry someone just because he was there, or be proposed to just because she happened to be there. Yes, she's missed out. And yes, she is reminded of that constantly when she sees women younger than her with their husbands and babies. She had chances with men who pursued her, men who promised the world, but the world never materialised. She's been told she's too picky. That her standards are too high. That's why she's committed the cardinal sin of ending up alone.

Her standards are hers, though, and she doesn't believe she has to explain them to anyone else. Being alone isn't the worst thing in the world. Being lonely is far more unbearable, and that can happen just as well inside a marriage as out of it.

'I guess I have, Mum,' she says. 'I can drive you past the shops to see if anything's open, but I can't guarantee that anything will be.'

Her mother's eyes shift focus, her brow furrows, and she looks down at her handbag as if she's never seen it before.

'Shops? Why are we going to the shops?'

Patricia hears a noise of dismay from her father and wants to make one herself. But she won't because it will achieve nothing.

'I just thought it would be nice to take a drive,' she says, because she doesn't want to confuse things further. The story her mother knows is ever changing but Patricia likes to keep it on some sort of track.

'All right.' Her mother puts her handbag aside and slowly gets to her feet. 'Let's go and visit Annette.'

If only they could. If only Patricia could drive her mother all the way to New South Wales and let her sister take care of things for a change.

'Annette's busy today, Mum,' she says, taking her arm. 'But we'll go for a drive anyway.'

She hands her mother off to her father, picks up her own handbag and the keys from the kitchen bench, and follows them out the door.

CHAPTER SIXTEEN

Grace Maud's father liked to say that his children had never known a winter. While not technically true – there are seasons here in the far north just as there are in all other parts of the world – it wasn't until Grace Maud went south to visit Ellie Maud in Melbourne one July that she truly understood what he meant. Atherton – the whole region, actually, once you draw the line at Townsville – can be hot and wet and close, turning through seasons that southerners have no idea about. Sometimes Grace Maud feels like the tropics make your cells change. You learn how to breathe in water, the air is so thick with it.

Her father used to say that the line from Townsville should run all the way to the west coast, and that should make a new state taking in parts of the Northern Territory and Western Australia. Only those who live in this climate can possibly understand each other, he believed. In his eyes, Brisbane was as far from their affairs as Canberra was.

'It's looking good, eh, Mum?'

As Tom comes up beside her, he takes off his hat and brushes his fringe forwards.

She nods. 'Yes, a big year. Good rains.'

He grins down at her. 'You can take the farmer off the land but not the land out of the farmer.'

'I always know what's going on with the weather and the crops, Tom.'

If it sounds like a warning it's because she means it to. She still has an interest in this place – she gets an income from it, after all. Tom runs it but Grace Maud owns it. By the terms of their financial arrangement she doesn't get to take a hundred per cent of the cream, but the paperwork still has her name on it.

'I know you do, Mum.' He glances behind her. 'D'you want to come back to the house? I thought we could have a chat about . . .' He pauses, doesn't look at her. 'Next season.'

Grace Maud feels a thud in her solar plexus – a sign that this is going to be a chat she won't like.

Sandrine said something the other day about the body knowing what's coming before the mind does and it made sense to Grace Maud. She hasn't always heeded the thuds in her middle, the rumbles in her belly and constrictions of her chest, but has learnt that she should have. Each time she's had that kind of feeling, something has occurred after it. She will always remember the day Ellie Maud called and told her that she had a cough she couldn't shake and she was going to the doctor. Grace Maud's heart seemed to pull everything in towards it; even the air around her felt like it was being sucked into her chest. She knew: Ellie Maud was going to die from this. And six months later, lung cancer claimed her.

So when Grace Maud walks into the house with Tom and sees Viv sitting with tea and cake on the table, smiling brightly, she knows it's an ambush.

'Take a seat, Mum.'

Tom gestures to the couch, but Grace Maud chooses the chair. He can't make her get cosy with whatever's coming.

'Tea, Grace Maud?' Viv's smile now appears to be fixed.

'Thank you.'

'We wanted to talk to you, Mum.'

'I can see that.'

Tom's face drops a little but he recovers quickly. 'We're, uh . . .' He waits while Viv hands Grace Maud her tea and a slice of cake. 'We've been thinking about the future. And what we want to achieve.'

Grace Maud almost laughs. What they want to *achieve*? In her day you covered the bills and kept people fed. That was achievement. But she knows the past few years have changed how the younger generations view life and what it means. In this part of the world, she blames that Christopher Skase for opening the resort down the road in Port Douglas, letting everyone think they should be living like that all the time. Then there was that movie *Wall Street* and those wretched television shows – what were they? *Dynasty. Dallas.* Examples of people with too much money spending even more money than they had, and that was meant to be success. Greed is what Grace Maud calls it, but that isn't the popular opinion. Tom is right in the age group that would look at all of that and think that success – *achievement* – means having more. So she knows what he's about to say and she knows how she feels about it.

'Oh, yes?' she murmurs, folding her hands in her lap.

'A few weeks ago we talked about putting cattle on here,' he says, then he and Viv glance at each other. 'We've decided we want to expand. Buy another property.'

'With what money?' Grace Maud says sharply.

'We'd borrow,' Viv says, almost gushing, like borrowing is a good thing.

'Borrow? The interest rates are through the roof!'

'And they may always be,' Tom says. 'Mum, we need to grow.'

His eyes are pleading with her, just like they used to when he was a little boy wanting to drive the truck and his legs were too short for him to reach the pedals.

'Why?' she says, trying to remember that he hasn't been that little boy for a long time. 'What's wrong with what you have?'

'Nothing! But what's wrong with wanting more?'

'Because it's greedy. You make a living here. You don't want for anything. The land supports you. If you buy more land, you may find *you're* supporting *it*. And that's never a good position to be in.'

'You sound like Granddad,' Tom says softly.

'He knew what he was doing,' Grace Maud says, her blood rising. 'He wasn't the world's most adventurous man but he kept us all for years.'

She stops short of calling her son ungrateful but she feels that he is, because it's almost as if he's saying everything her father and she worked for over the years isn't enough. To work hard and have a good life – to feel at the end of the day that you've taken care of the people you love – aren't enough. There has to be *more*. More land, more money. Will they bring more happiness, if that is the goal? Grace Maud has yet to see the evidence.

'We thought you wouldn't like the idea,' Tom says.

'So why did you tell me?'

'Because we've already spoken to the Pontis about buying their place.' He says it quietly and firmly, as if it's final. 'And I didn't want you to hear it from anyone else before you heard it from me. From us.'

This time Grace Maud feels it in her lungs: a sharp intake of breath that goes nowhere, like she's stopped inside time. The seconds, the minutes, the hours are moving on without her and she's still, not breathing, not thinking. It's shock. She's felt it before. The shock of betrayal.

'Mum?'

Finally she exhales and turns to look past the kitchen, out the window that shows her the road that leaves the property. The road that will take her the hour and a half back to Cairns. Back home, she supposes. Her home is there now.

'How could you?' she says, her voice quiet but steely. She can barely look at Tom.

'What do you mean?' He frowns.

'How could you involve . . . *strangers* in our business before you've even spoken to me?'

He blinks. Viv appears to be holding her breath.

'Because I wanted to find out if they were interested first,' he says, almost sarcastically, as if she should know this. 'No point talking to you about it if they weren't.'

'Have you told anyone else?' She doesn't really have words to describe why she's feeling so let down. Perhaps it isn't logical. Except it feels logical to her.

Tom shifts in his seat and glances at Viv. 'The bank,' he mumbles.

'The bank? Our bank? *My* bank?'

Grace Maud stares at him. She's had an account at that bank since she was a child. Her father did all of his banking there. That bank knows all the financial details of their lives, yet clearly whomever Tom spoke with didn't feel the need to ask him if his mother should be part of their conversation. The mother whose name is still on the title of the property. Tom has power of attorney – a practical necessity – but everything remains in her name.

She glances down at her hands, which are shaking. It's not old age causing it. They've never shaken before.

'We worked this place together for years, Tom,' she says, wishing she didn't have to look him in the eye but it would be cowardly not to. 'You and me. We made decisions together.'

'I know.'

'So . . . what? Now that I'm old and you've sectioned me off to town, I'm not the first person you should talk to about something like this?'

'What are you really upset about, Mum?'

He sounds terse. Angry, perhaps. Angry with his own mother who has always tried to support him. Who will always love him.

'It's still my place, Tom,' she says, her volume going up. 'It's still my family's farm. My father's. His father's. It's still *my business*. And the *neighbours* and the *bank* know more about it than I do?' She puts her cup and saucer on the table, and pushes herself out of her chair. 'I think I should leave.'

'Come on, Mum,' Tom says, irritated. 'It's not that big a deal.'

'You are not the one to decide whether or not I think something is a big deal.'

Tom is on his feet too, moving towards her, so she puts up a hand.

'Mum, please, we just need to talk it through,' he says.

'I have no wish to talk any more today.'

She stares at him. Her only child. She made sure this place would be something he could rely on after she dies, and now he's decided he's going to borrow money, buy the neighbours' land, put cattle on the place, and she is the last to know. It's almost as if he doesn't trust her. He didn't want to tell her because he didn't think she'd be on his side. But by not trusting her, he has, indeed, put her off side. She's hurt. It feels petty. But it's real.

'Hi, GM.'

Luca steps in from the kitchen. He must have come up the front stairs, and probably heard every word.

'Hello, Luca,' Grace Maud says, trying to sound happy to see him.

'I didn't know you were coming.' He bends over to give her a hug.

'The day is full of surprises.' She smiles, a flash, then looks around for her handbag. 'And I'm leaving.'

'Really?' Luca says. 'I was planning to go to town tonight. See a couple of mates. Maybe I could come back with you?'

Grace Maud glances from Tom to Luca, wondering if this whole thing has been arranged: Tom drops the bombshell, then Luca smooths it over. But Luca doesn't strike her as a devious person so she doesn't think he'd be complicit in such a thing.

'I have to run into town tomorrow so I could pick you up,' Tom says. 'Maybe he could stay with you, Mum?'

Grace Maud keeps her eyes on Luca. 'Maybe he could.'

'Great.' Luca's face relaxes, his cheekbones growing sharper as he smiles. 'I'll grab some stuff.'

As he goes to his room Tom moves closer to Grace Maud. 'I'm not trying to hurt you, Mum,' he says, putting his hand on her arm – and she lets him, because he's still her son and she can't help loving him.

'Well, you have,' she says, and walks away so his hand has to drop. 'Tell Luca I'll see him in the car.'

Picking up her bag from the kitchen bench, she doesn't look back as she opens the door and walks down the stairs as quickly as her legs let her.

CHAPTER SEVENTEEN

'Miss! Miss! Look! I'm just like Boonie!'

Patricia turns to see one of her Year Nine students catching a cricket ball thrown by another. A cricket ball that is not an item permitted on school excursions.

'Damien, you know you're not meant to have that ball while we're off school grounds,' she says to the wannabe Test cricketer, holding out her hand for the ball.

'But miss—'

'The form your mother signed clearly stated no projectiles,' Patricia says, smiling in a way that she hopes indicates that she doesn't make the rules, she just has to enforce them. It's hard enough to get the boys interested in English; harder still when they don't like their teacher.

'What's a projectile?' Damien says.

'A ball, mate.' Dennis walks up next to Patricia and also holds out his hand. 'Especially a cricket ball.'

'But siiiirrr . . .' Damien whines.

Dennis opens and closes his hand. 'You'll get it back when we're back at school.'

'But this is a zoo, sir. The animals aren't going to care if I have a ball.'

'No projectiles, Damien,' Dennis says firmly.

With a sigh Damien hands over the ball, and Dennis puts it in a backpack that also contains a confiscated slingshot and two yoyos that were used on the bus. Patricia, sitting at the front, didn't find out about those until all the students had alighted.

'At least he wasn't trying to be Shane Warne,' Dennis mutters.

Patricia laughs. 'Fair point. And thanks for volunteering to do this with me. When I thought it would be a good idea to bring them here to write compositions about animals, I forgot how much testosterone Year Nine boys can have. I don't want to lose anyone in a lion enclosure just because they decided to be brave.'

'No worries.' Dennis looks at her curiously. 'Although I'm pretty sure you could've handled it.'

She smiles and shrugs. 'I don't know. My brothers are a few years older than me so I wasn't really aware of what they were like as teenagers. I was in those blissful years when little girls are still talking to dolls.'

He nods. 'I remember them.'

Patricia gives him a quizzical look. 'Really?'

'Two sisters,' he says.

Before Patricia can respond she hears music coming from the cluster of girls walking ahead of them. The unmistakable sound of Whitney Houston singing 'I Will Always Love You', as she has been on every radio station at every hour of the day for, it seems, most of the year. Patricia has tried to be sick of the song, but she finds something intriguing within it: the idea of giving up someone you love not just for their sake but your own. Not that she's ever been in a position to do that. But it doesn't stop her wondering what it would be like.

'Girls, turn that off!' she calls.

'Great song,' Dennis murmurs.

'I know, but I don't think the animals would agree.' She glances at him and is surprised to find him looking at her meaningfully before he quickly glances away.

The music stops and Patricia appreciates the fact that her female students rarely try to bargain with her the way the boys do. She'd spend her whole day negotiating if they did.

'All right, everyone, time to find your animal!' she calls more loudly to the rapidly dispersing students. 'You have one hour. Write a poem or a short piece of prose. ONE HOUR! MEET BACK AT THIS SPOT!'

Most of them are too far away to hear and she throws her hands in the air.

'We're going to lose some of them, aren't we,' she says to Dennis.

He laughs. 'It's not that big a place. We'll be right. So did you see the movie?'

'Hmm?' She looks around, trying to count how many students are within eyesight.

'*The Bodyguard* – did you see it?'

'Oh.' She turns back towards him. 'Yes.'

She saw it on her own – not that she'll tell him that – because she didn't manage to reconnect with any of her old friends in Cairns when she returned two years ago after a quarter-century away. They have their own lives now; it was naive of her to expect that some of them would want to pick up where they'd left off. She'd only been in touch with a couple of them in all that time, and only then by way of Christmas cards. Now it's her Sydney friends who receive Christmas cards.

'Did you?' she asks, figuring Dennis probably only asked her so she would reciprocate. That seems to be the reason most people ask personal questions. 'What are you doing on the weekend?' is code for 'Please ask me what *I'm* doing on the weekend.'

'Yep,' Dennis says. 'It was pretty good. Bit dramatic with the shooting and whatnot. Do you like movies?'

'I don't mind them,' she says vaguely, moving towards a seat and gesturing for him to sit beside her.

'I suppose you prefer books,' he says, sitting and angling his body towards her.

'I suppose I do,' she says with a small laugh. 'Although a great movie is a wonderful thing.'

'I saw *Sleepless in Seattle*. I thought it was pretty good. Interesting story.' He smiles at her. 'Romantic.'

She blinks in surprise, then thinks that he probably saw it with a lady friend. 'Right,' she says. 'I didn't.'

'Not your speed?' He looks genuinely interested in what she might say.

It's not the sort of conversation they usually have. Up until now they've mainly talked about how to avoid Gordon, whether or not the stingers have arrived at the Cairns beaches, and when they think the wet season will start.

'Too schmaltzy,' she murmurs. '*Top Gun* is more my thing. I like to be entertained.'

Music starts up again – this time a quite different, more aggressive song that she doesn't recognise.

'What is that?' she asks.

'Rage Against the Machine,' Dennis says quickly. 'Listen, would you—'

'Girls! Off!' she yells and the music stops.

Dennis swallows. 'Would you like to—'

'Miiiisss.' Damien appears with a cut over his eye and a streak of blood heading for his cheek.

'Damien – what happened?' Patricia says crossly and stands.

Dennis is slow to follow. 'Had another ball, didn't you, mate,' he says, raising his eyebrows.

Damien looks sheepish.

'I'll take him to get a band-aid,' Dennis tells Patricia.

'Thank you,' she says.

As he trails off behind the sorry-looking student Dennis holds her gaze for a few seconds, then Patricia turns away. She heads in the direction of a group of students who wanted to observe the monkeys. As nice as it was chatting to Dennis, she really shouldn't let the children roam the zoo unchaperoned. She could trust most to return at the allotted time but some of them may decide to jump into a snake enclosure instead and she doesn't want to have to explain fang marks to their parents.

She trails from one group to the next but doesn't see Dennis again until they all meet at their spot.

'You survived?' he says, smiling in that knowing way teachers have with each other.

'Yes. You?'

He holds up two tennis balls.

'It's been a lucrative visit as far as the ball cupboard is concerned. The owners of these are repeat offenders so they're not getting them back.'

Patricia laughs. 'I only managed to confiscate some bubble gum. Not so lucrative for me.'

She turns to the students amassing beside her. 'Okay, the bus is up there at the gates. Let's go.'

'I'll go ahead with them, if you don't mind being at the tail,' Dennis says. She nods her assent, and he gives her a thumbs-up, and they don't speak again for the rest of the day.

CHAPTER EIGHTEEN

'Meditation is not empty mind,' Sandrine intones. 'Focus on the pause that comes after your exhalation has ended. That's when the mind is naturally empty. That is your meditation.'

Not that Dorothy's mind empties right then. Oh, no – her thoughts rush to fill every moment they can. Every crevice of her mind is crammed full of what-ifs and what-abouts and if-onlys and I-should-never-haves, and they're all louder and more insistent than usual. Because that's the nature of worries, isn't it? They grow louder and ruder, until they topple you over.

Dorothy feels tears on her cheeks. She cried in last week's class too. Not loud sobs, just tears flowing out of her eyes without any prompting. Last time she was surprised. This time she feels embarrassed. What if someone sees her?

She feels something rising in her chest – a sob, it seems – and is *mortified*. This can't be normal. It's not as though she's in pain. The class was fine; challenging, but she managed.

Sandrine asks them all to roll to their right-hand side and sit up with their eyes closed, so Dorothy has to swallow the sob. But that makes it stick in her throat and she feels like she's going to choke.

Now Sandrine is telling them to open their eyes. As Dorothy does, she sees Sandrine standing in front of her, one hand on her hip and an eyebrow arched.

'You are struggling,' she says, just like that, like it's the most natural thing to say in the world.

Dorothy sees Patricia shuffle over so she's sitting nearby, and she can feel Grace Maud over her shoulder. She knows she should feel self-conscious but they probably heard her making that noise anyway. Great. Witnesses to her falling-apart.

'The tears flow when the body starts to open,' Sandrine continues. 'It is often part of the yoga practice. It is good for you. But it is also happening every time for you.'

She squats and puts her hands on Dorothy's shins. 'We don't want the distress to become overwhelming,' she says, in such a soothing tone that Dorothy wants to curl up and go to sleep. Instead she glances at Patricia – who doesn't look pitying, thank goodness.

'I have been this way,' Sandrine says. 'So I know. Not long after I started this practice I was crying all the time.' She flops a hand around. 'Hopeless. Rideee-culous. I did not know why. But I found out.' She shrugs. 'I did not want to be married any more. My body knew before my mind did. That is part of the mystery of this work we are doing here. I know not to question it now.'

She cups her hands around Dorothy's face. 'What is it your body is telling you?'

Dorothy opens her mouth and Sandrine holds up a finger. '*Non*. It is not for us to know. You do not have to share. But I would like you to think about this.'

'What did you do?' Dorothy asks.

'I left my husband,' Sandrine says with another shrug. 'I have never regretted it. My body knew and I trusted it. Why shouldn't I?'

She glances around at Patricia and Grace Maud. 'The same might apply to you ladies, but that is none of my business, of course. All I will say is that once you start on this path it will take you back to yourself, if you let it. There are so many ways to get lost. So many years to spend away from yourself. Yoga is the way home. This I know.' As she stands up her hand goes back on her hip, which she then juts out. 'And it keeps you young!' she trills. 'I do not mind if that is the reason you come.'

Patricia gets to her feet and holds out a hand to Dorothy. 'Up you get,' she says, then turns to Grace Maud. 'You too.'

Dorothy takes Grace Maud's other arm and they both pull her up.

'Keeps me young, you say?' Grace Maud looks sceptically at Sandrine.

'Yes, but it does not work miracles,' Sandrine says with a laugh, then she twinkles her fingers at them and Dorothy half expects her to be like Tinkerbell and vanish. Instead she makes her way to another student who looks as though she too has been crying.

Grace Maud regards Dorothy with curiosity. 'Would you like to talk at all,' she starts, 'about why you're crying? It's none of my business, of course, but I, ah . . .' She makes a face. 'Think it would be rude to not ask. Since it's happening here, and we have come to know each other a little. And I can be a good listener, on occasion.'

Grace Maud looks disinterested in a polite way, Dorothy thinks: not bored, not turning away like she has somewhere else to be, yet not burning with curiosity either.

Patricia is frowning the way Dorothy knows she frowns at Cornelia – like a big sister. 'You don't have to say anything,' Patricia adds quickly. 'I mean, unless you want to.'

'Do . . .' Dorothy stops and wonders how to start again. 'Do you ever cry at the end, like that?'

She asks Patricia, because she's fairly sure Grace Maud hasn't shed a tear since childhood.

'Not yet,' Patricia says carefully. 'But I have in one of the poses.'

'Because it hurts?' Dorothy asks.

'Yes, but . . . no.' Patricia shakes her head like she's trying to remove something from it. 'It's strange. It hurts my muscles but it also feels like some gate opens in my hips and something comes out. Some . . . emotion, I guess. Maybe it's the same sort of thing?'

Grace Maud raises her eyebrows. 'How intriguing. What comes out of the gate, exactly?'

'Stuff,' Patricia says and lowers her eyes. When she lifts them again, she smiles encouragingly at Dorothy. 'I think we all have things we've stashed away. So crying is to be expected.'

It had felt brave to Dorothy to come to this class when she didn't know anyone. So it probably felt brave for the others too. Braver still for Patricia to try to ease the way for her, because that's what she's doing, and for Grace Maud to offer to hear her troubles when they hardly know each other.

Except maybe they do. They're having this rather odd experience together, and no one else Dorothy knows is there. Why shouldn't she tell them why she's been so upset?

'I keep having miscarriages,' she says, then lets out a long, slow exhalation. She's never announced it to anyone before. 'And no one can tell me why. And I—'

She stops as she feels the shock of it; the same way she felt when she lost the first baby. The sensation is as sharp each time.

'That's a very hard road to travel,' Grace Maud murmurs as Patricia bites her bottom lip.

'But I *know* I make too much of a fuss about it!' Dorothy goes on. 'They're just miscarriages. No one has said I'll never have a baby. I just—'

'They're not "just miscarriages",' Grace Maud says almost sternly. 'I knew someone who had two and the worst part was that her doctor used to tell her to "just get back on the horse", as if she even felt like doing that.' She smiles reassuringly. 'But she had a baby in the end.'

Patricia reaches towards Dorothy as if to hug her, then stops and puts a hand on her shoulder. 'I'm so sorry, Dorothy. No wonder you cry at the end. Sandrine puts us through all that, and as soon as your body has a chance to rest it lets you know that it's been in the wars.'

'Maybe,' Dorothy says. It's a reasonable explanation, except she knows that's only part of it. The tears come from a place that isn't made of muscle and bone. There's a cave inside of her where she keeps all her wishes and hopes and dreams, and all her hurts. When her body is open at the end of the class she feels like the tears are coming from that cave, and they may be made of dreams or of misery. There's no way to tell.

'Sometimes babies just don't stick,' Grace Maud says. 'You're not doing anything wrong. You just haven't had one that's stuck yet. I'm an old duck, so you can believe me.'

Dorothy isn't sure whether Grace Maud is right, but she doesn't want to offend her by disagreeing.

'They can do all sorts of things these days, can't they?' Grace Maud continues. 'Test-tube babies and so on. Perhaps your doctor can tell you more about that?'

'Perhaps,' Dorothy agrees quietly. She's not ready to admit that she's talked about IVF with her doctor.

'I don't think the crying is a bad thing,' Patricia says. 'And it doesn't bother me. Just in case, you know, it happens again – don't worry about it.'

'Thank you.' Dorothy smiles quickly but still wishes she hadn't disturbed the others. It's one thing to talk to these two about why she's upset; it's another to cry so that everyone can hear it.

'I'm sorry, I have to go,' Patricia says, looking at her watch. 'Sorry to rush off.' She picks up her mat and handbag. 'See you next week?'

Dorothy and Grace Maud both nod and Patricia heads for the door.

'I'll walk you out,' Grace Maud says, taking Dorothy's arm.

It feels reassuring, almost grandmotherly – not that Dorothy remembers what that feels like. Her grandparents never voyaged from Germany to visit them. Letters were all she knew, and the occasional Christmas package of stollen and her mother's favourite marzipan carefully wrapped inside a sturdy box.

As they step out into the night, Dorothy feels her body let go of something and she sighs involuntarily.

'It's better to talk about things like that,' Grace Maud says. 'There's no benefit in keeping it to yourself. Other people have experiences that can help you.'

'No one I've asked has had a miscarriage,' Dorothy says glumly.

Grace Maud stops. 'Of course they have,' she says, sounding indignant. 'They're just not telling you. But miscarriages aren't at all uncommon.' She pauses. 'It was my sister who had two. She was upset, but she got through it. As you will.'

Her tone is so reassuring that Dorothy almost believes her.

'Now, I'll walk you to your car. Where is it?' Grace Maud seems to pull her a little closer, and their arms remain entwined until she's tucked Dorothy inside her car like she's tucking her into bed.

By the time Dorothy is driving up the hill towards Kuranda, she has forgotten her tears.

CHAPTER NINETEEN

Patricia hears the television go on in the living room as she puts on rubber gloves and starts the washing up. She knows it will be *Sale of the Century*: her father tries not to miss it. That's why dinner is usually on the table early in the evening, except for the night she goes to yoga. What a rebel she is.

'How does Mum seem to you?' Annette says as she picks up a tea towel.

Patricia's sister has deigned to fly up from Newcastle for exactly two days to see their parents. Thankfully she's staying at a hotel.

Patricia wants to flick dishwater at her and point out that it's a ridiculous question. She's the one who lives here so their mother doesn't *seem* anything – she *is* many things. Annette visits rarely and when she calls to say hello she never wants to talk to their parents. Just wants an update. 'Give me an update, Patricia,' she says each time. As if their parents are a weather report.

'What do you mean?' is what Patricia chooses to say, although she knows the answer.

'You know . . . is she a bit . . . *vague*?'

Annette picks up a plate and wipes it before looking around as if she has no idea where the plates go, except she used to live here and the crockery arrangements have never changed.

'Do you mean is she losing her marbles?' Patricia says, out of patience.

Annette laughs nervously. 'That's a bit much.'

'Is it?'

'Come on, Patricia, don't be short with me. I was just asking a question.'

'A rhetorical question.'

'Honestly, Patricia, just because you're an English teacher doesn't mean you get to play word games with me.'

Annette sounds like the whiny girl she used to be. Maybe still is. Except Patricia knows she's taken the bait again. Annette loves a passive-aggressive, slightly vague question, and Patricia loves being precise. So when Patricia comes roaring back with precision, Annette always gets to say her sister is trying to make her feel dumb, or just-because-you-have-a-degree-doesn't-mean-you're-smarter-than-the-rest-of-us.

Sisters. Who'd have one? Brothers are more straightforward. They use single syllables – when they're not grunting – and they're not vaguely interested in parents so there's never a passive-aggressive conversation to be had. Instead there's a dull throb of resentment that they get away with being hopeless because they're male and their lives are expected to be elsewhere. Patricia and Annette were always meant to be the ones who stuck around and helped. Then Annette worked out that she could get away too.

It's as if their parents are remnants of a life they all used to have, instead of living, breathing people who need the same sort of care and attention they gave their children. Patricia may not be enthralled with her life as it's currently lived, but she refuses to think that her parents are flotsam and jetsam.

'Just say what you mean, Annette. I live with Mum so I know what's going on. But I want to hear what you think is going on.'

She clangs the cutlery into the drying rack and Annette glares at her as if she did it on purpose, when really it's what Patricia does every night. She loathes washing up. Always has. Always will. She dreams of having a dishwasher but her father won't countenance the expense.

'Fine,' Annette huffs. 'She's all over the place. Forgetting things.'

'Yes, she is.'

'So what are you doing about it?'

Patricia tries counting to ten but only makes it to four.

'What am *I* doing about it?' She picks up a glass and tries not to smash it into the sink. 'Mum has four children. Shouldn't your question be, "What are *we* doing about it?"'

There's silence as Patricia washes the glass and puts it gently onto the tea towel that she laid out for the purpose. Glasses don't go anywhere near the cutlery; they always have their own flat area.

'Look, you're the one who chose to live here, so I think it's your responsibility.' Annette picks up a knife to dry.

There's so much that Patricia wants to say, but she knows there's no point. Annette is telling herself a story, the way she always has. It used to be the story that Patricia was more favoured by the teachers, by their brothers, by their parents, even though it was never the case – it just suited Annette's narrative better. If Patricia was the golden child, Annette could have tantrums about life being so unfair, even though she saw – just as their brothers saw – their mother tearing strips off Patricia fairly regularly.

'Just because you're the pretty one and you can play piano – it's not FAIR!' Annette would rage, throwing books off shelves, burying dolls in the garden. And this when she was in her teens. The payoff was that people – their grandparents, for example – would tell her that no, it wasn't true, Patricia wasn't so special. Annette was lovely and wonderful.

It got worse once it became clear that Patricia was also athletic and good at it, which meant she won prizes and went off to compete in state titles. Annette would also then say that it 'wasn't fair' that Patricia got to be the sporty one.

Patricia, for her part, never said that it wasn't fair that Annette was the graceful one, because she learnt young that Annette wasn't saying these things to start a debate but, rather, to end one.

On her wedding day, a giddy Annette drew Patricia aside and said, 'So I got there first for once!' She'd laughed, almost jumping up and down.

'What do you mean?' Patricia asked, her hair in a ghastly bouffant, her body squeezed into an unflattering blue taffeta number that all the bridesmaids were forced to wear.

'I got married before you did!' Annette said in a high-pitched, singsong way. 'Somebody wanted me before somebody wanted *yoooou*!'

Patricia was so shocked that her sister's childhood resentments had clearly been in the pack ice all along, that the thaw that seemed to take place during her adolescence had been a ruse, that she didn't answer. Just let Annette skip off back to the reception. She's never forgotten it, although she imagines Annette thinks she has. And her sister hasn't ever said anything like it again, although when Annette's husband once said that he couldn't believe 'a good-looking sheila like you hasn't been snapped up, Pat', Annette's glare was so fierce that Patricia was surprised her brother-in-law wasn't knifed in the night.

The thing is: it's such a ridiculous situation. Annette has always been the literal golden-haired girl. She was the cute one, the sweet one, the one their mother dressed like a doll and paraded around to the admiration of others, until she reached puberty. Patricia was the smart one, the bookish one, the one who was meant to leave Cairns and find her way somewhere that had more universities and better jobs. Now Annette flies overseas for holidays, and Patricia has returned to the family home.

'The doctor is checking her regularly,' Patricia says more calmly than she feels, pulling the plug and taking off the rubber gloves. 'There's not much else to be done. There's no cure for dementia.'

'Dementia!' Annette almost shouts it.

'What did you think it was?'

'I thought maybe she needed to eat some more meat!' Annette puts down her tea towel, half the dishes not yet dried. 'God – dementia? So . . . what do you do?'

'Nothing. I just told you.'

'There must be *something*.'

In Annette's world there's always something: a trip to a specialist in Sydney; or a weekend away in Melbourne for a pick-me-up shopping spree; or a little trip to the Whitsundays to rejuvenate.

She sniffs. 'It's Mum. There has to be something. I can't bear . . .'

'It's fine, Annette, I'm handling it,' Patricia says wearily.

'Well, they can't come and live with me if Mum goes funny,' Annette says.

'I didn't say they would.'

'I'm too busy for that.'

'Of course.'

'So are John and Peter. I mean, they're *busy*. You know?'

'Right.'

'I have a child who I *swear* will end up in juvenile detention if he doesn't stop hanging out with those dreadful friends. We're beside ourselves. I just can't cope with anything else.'

Ah yes, the naughty nephew. First he was kicking the babysitter and now he's off to jail. Apparently. Patricia's interpretation is that he's a bright kid who's bored at school – she's seen his type before, over and over again. He really needs to take up a hobby or three, but no one has asked what she thinks about the matter.

'And it's not as if *you* have much going on,' Annette adds quietly.

There it is.

'So it's perfect, really,' she continues. 'You being here.'

Patricia considers that word: 'perfect'. Sandrine said something the other day about how no one's postures are perfect, so they're all perfect. Patricia tried to understand the idea then and failed, because it bespoke a need to think of the universe as benign – to believe that everything we do is as it's meant to be and all is just so. That we are complete beings. Whole. That our imperfections are perfect and vice versa. She wasn't ready to believe that she's imperfectly perfect. It seemed too easy. But then Sandrine said something else: that a certain phase of life could be a hard *sadhana*. A hard practice. And that this, too, is meant to be.

So perhaps Patricia being here *is* perfect. Perhaps she is perfect, and so is Annette. If only she could believe that, she might be able to let go of so much ancient angst. But she's not ready to do that.

Instead of answering her sister, she strolls into the living room. 'Everything all right, Dad?'

'Right as rain,' he says, keeping his eyes on Glenn Ridge.

Patricia nods and walks back into the kitchen.

'Just let me know if you need anything. With them,' Annette says, her eyes shifting around the room.

It sounds like a conciliatory statement but Patricia isn't sure she can trust it. Their past is still in that pack ice, and spring may never come.

'Sure I will,' she says, then picks up the tea towel to dry the rest of the washing-up.

CHAPTER TWENTY

The version of Cecilia sitting in front of Grace Maud isn't one she's encountered before. She's used to Cecilia being calm and competent; sunny of temperament and willing to ignore Grace Maud when she's not as pleasant. This Cecilia is almost incapable of speech. She's wringing her hands, her dress, her hair – anything she can grab hold of – and cry-hiccuping at the same time.

When Grace Maud had opened the door not even five minutes ago, not sure who could be knocking so loudly on a Sunday morning, she almost hadn't registered that it was Cecilia and for a second thought a stranger was pushing her way into the house.

'I'm sorry,' Cecilia says through her tears, her face splotchy, the corners of her mouth turned down.

'For what?'

'For coming here.' Sniff, sniff.

'Did I say I don't want you here?'

Cecilia frowns. 'No.'

'Then why are you apologising? If there's something to be sorry for, I'll let you know.'

Cecilia nods, blinks, looks towards the living room window that has a view of the front garden and the street.

'Now, why don't you tell me what's happened?' Grace Maud says as gently as she can.

She's never been a person given to eliciting confessions from people. As a teenager she didn't sit around with other girls and gossip; she had Ellie Maud, so she'd had no need for anyone else. She didn't have a daughter to practise on, and her granddaughters were never interested in spending time with her – probably because they lived with her and certainly because they thought she was part of the furniture.

Grace Maud used to think about telling Tom that he was spoiling his children and that they would never learn to appreciate the value of the hard work their parents put into things. But she thinks they know it now, living in Brisbane and constantly calling and asking for money that Tom has finally stopped giving them.

'You can live for free here,' Grace Maud heard him say once, when he was on the receiving end of one of those calls. 'Right. Well, you've made your choices, Edwina. I can't keep paying for them.'

Grace Maud thought at the time that Edwina was lucky it wasn't her on the phone, otherwise she'd have given her unsolicited opinion of both girls. She also wanted to tell Tom that it was too late to turn off the tap when he'd kept the rivers of cash flowing all his daughters' lives. He'd trained them to depend on him; he shouldn't have been surprised that they continued to do so.

Cecilia, on the other hand, is a resourceful young woman who is managing her studies alongside her work for Grace Maud, and never complains about anything. Although today she has clearly blown a gasket, as Grace Maud's father might have said.

'It's my mother,' Cecilia says, still sniffing.

Grace Maud looks around for a tissue, then remembers she has a clean one in her pants pocket and hands it over. 'Is she all right?' she asks, thinking something terrible must have happened to prompt these tears.

'Yes!' Cecilia says exasperatedly. 'She's fine! But I'm not!' She dabs at her eyes.

Grace Maud sits and waits for her to go on. Cecilia needs her to listen more than speak.

'She said I need to stop going to university.'

Cecilia looks at Grace Maud expectantly. Clearly she wants some kind of response.

'Why?' Grace Maud obliges.

'Because I won't find a husband if I have a degree. She says men don't like educated women. And anyway, I won't need a degree because I'll be a housewife and there's no degree in that. How can she say that? How!' Cecilia starts crying again.

'I know this may not be what you want to hear, but it's not necessarily her fault,' Grace Maud says.

Cecilia frowns and looks, briefly, furious.

'Your mother's generation – mine – quite a few of us, really, were told that. Or it was made clear in other ways.'

Grace Maud stops, not sure how much she should reveal of her own life. Cecilia isn't her friend, even if both of them know that the real reason Tom hired her was to keep Grace Maud company.

She recalls going to the shops one day before Cecilia arrived, and returning just in time for Cecilia to see her carrying several heavy bags into the house.

'You don't really need my help, do you?' Cecilia had said, nonetheless trying to take one of the bags.

'I think we both know that,' Grace Maud had said. 'But that doesn't mean I don't appreciate you being here.'

They'd stood in the kitchen staring at each other.

'I don't want to do things you'd rather do yourself,' Cecilia had said at last, tentatively.

'I can assure you that I have no burning desire to clean the house,' Grace Maud told her. 'I'm thrilled you're doing it. And I enjoy having you here.'

For a second Cecilia had looked as if she might cry, so Grace Maud had clucked her tongue and said, 'Now you're here, you can help me unpack the groceries.'

After that they hadn't exactly started exchanging confidences but had relaxed around each other more. So while it isn't a friendship – yet – Grace Maud feels affection for the young woman. And she also feels the responsibility of having lived a long time and being able to offer some insight that Cecilia lacks simply because she hasn't been alive as long. If Grace Maud had known an older woman who could have given her the right advice, she might have made different decisions and saved herself a lot of mess.

'I got married because I thought I should,' she says now, 'not because I really wanted to. I had my son, and I'm happy to have him. But I wish I'd known I could manage very well without a husband.'

'So you were married a long time?'

'No. I asked him to leave. And it cost me a lot of pain and my parents a lot of money. I would rather have done without both.'

Cecilia looks mildly shocked.

'Your mother may have her own regrets, Cecilia,' Grace Maud says carefully. 'And some women deal with that by trying to make the other women in their lives follow the same path. A sort of philosophy that if one has suffered, all should. Or she may genuinely believe what she says. But you don't have to go along with it.'

'I'm not saying I don't want to ever get married,' Cecilia says defensively.

'And I'm not saying that you shouldn't. Just that you can make up your own mind.'

'But my mother . . .' Cecilia looks to the window again, almost as if she's trying to work out if she can escape that way. 'She says I can't stay at home if I keep doing my degree.'

'Did she act like this when you started university?'

'She complained about it. That's why I didn't go straight out of school. I worked at that fish shop at the marina for a couple of years. Mum thought the owner's son might be interested in me.' She snorts. 'He was. But I wasn't interested in him. I wasn't going to marry him and have babies! I'm only twenty years old!'

'So what prompted the fight this morning?'

Cecilia sighs and pulls at her dress again. 'We went to mass. Mum has friends at church. They have a son. The mother . . . told Mum that their son thinks I'm pretty but he could never marry a girl who has a degree. She said he only likes traditional girls. This was *in front of me*. And in front of him! It was so embarrassing. But Mum said *I* embarrassed *her*. We had a fight on the way home. Once we got there I left.'

Grace Maud knows that Cecilia's mother will have no idea where her daughter has gone and is probably worried about her, even if Cecilia wouldn't believe that. She also knows that her loyalty is with Cecilia, and she wants to help her.

'How long ago did your father die?' she asks.

'Two years. Why?'

Grace Maud nods slowly. 'Do you think your mother is worrying about how she can afford to keep paying for you and your brother to live at home? Perhaps she thinks that if she marries you off it will be one less concern.' She holds up a hand. 'I'm not saying it's right. I'm just trying to understand her.'

'I pay her rent,' Cecilia says tersely.

'It may not be enough. She may wish to sell the house, for example, and buy something smaller.'

Cecilia shrugs. 'Maybe.'

Grace Maud thinks for a few seconds. 'I'm sure your mother loves you. But clearly something is going on. Would you like to move in here for a little while? I have the space. And I'll keep paying you for the two days you do for me.'

Cecilia's mouth opens and closes, then opens again. 'Would that be okay?'

'I wouldn't offer if it weren't.' Grace Maud smiles. 'This is the first time I've lived alone in my entire life. I'm not the most sociable person in the world but I'm not sure I like being alone. You'd be doing me a favour.'

This isn't quite true – Grace Maud has adapted well to living alone and being able to do what she pleases when she pleases – but she knows it wouldn't require much more adaptation on her part to introduce Cecilia to the household. Besides, the girl pretty much runs the place as it is.

'Only if you're sure,' Grace Maud adds. 'And if it doesn't cause even more problems with your mother.'

'I think she'll be relieved,' Cecilia says, with a touch of sadness.

'You possibly both need a bit of time apart to think. And I'll enjoy having your company.'

'Are you sure?'

'I am. And don't ask me again or I'll change my mind.' Grace Maud arches an eyebrow. 'I only do these things if I want to. As you shall discover when you spend more time with me.'

'Thank you,' Cecilia says, and there's that sadness again. It's to be expected. Only a person with no conscience would be immune to a family member who is upset.

Cecilia will learn, as the years go on, that a family is an ever-evolving collection of upsets occasionally punctuated by joys. This is, no doubt, why so much is made of weddings and babies: everyone can agree, usually, that they are worthy of celebration. And the times in between are negotiations of niggles and disagreements and opinions and trade-offs.

'You're welcome.' Grace Maud pushes off her chair. 'Now – shall we organise to retrieve some of your belongings?'

'I'll do it,' Cecilia says, standing up. 'I'll go now.'

Grace Maud sees her out the door, then retreats to her kitchen and puts on the kettle. One last lonely cup of tea before her life changes, again.

CHAPTER TWENTY-ONE

'Can I get you anything else, darling?' Frederick puts her pot of tea on the table and a hand on the back of Dorothy's neck.

'No, thank you.' Dorothy smiles up at him, then across to her friend Ruth.

One advantage of having your own café is that when you invite friends to morning tea, there's always somewhere to go. Dorothy just hasn't had time to do it lately – certainly not at the café – but Frederick insisted when she mentioned she hadn't seen Ruth in months.

'We can manage,' he'd said.

Ruth had suggested they meet at her place, but Dorothy knew she couldn't take that much time away from the café. The only real break she has is at night, but Ruth can never see her then – she has a two-year-old son and a four-year-old daughter, and night-times are for baths and dinner and stories.

'I'm sorry it's been so long,' Dorothy says to Ruth. 'The weeks have been . . .' She sighs.

'Busy?' Ruth smiles sympathetically.

'Fast. I thought I saw you a month ago, but it was . . . when? February?'

Ruth nods and licks the cappuccino foam off her spoon. Frederick is one of the few people in Cairns who can make a decent coffee – if only they could find a way to tell the tourists that.

'We've both had a lot on,' says Ruth, picking up her cup. 'I barely know what day it is. Sandy wants me to go back to work, but really . . .' She shakes her head. 'I *am* at work. What does he think having two kids is like?'

Dorothy feels that little stab in her heart that happens each time someone talks about their children like she understands about motherhood. She supposes it's a compliment – *you're one of us* – but it never feels like it.

'I guess he's finding out right now?' she says, trying to imagine Ruth's burly rugby-playing husband caring for two small humans.

'If he doesn't drop them on their heads I'll say it's a good day.'

Ruth says it with affection, but Dorothy has heard this before so never really knows if Ruth is actually worried about Sandy being alone with the children or not. Dorothy likes to think that Frederick would be a kind, gentle father but she has no way of knowing until it happens. If it happens.

'I thought you were going to tell me you're pregnant!' Ruth says brightly. 'When you called, I mean. Not yet, hey?'

Another stab. She knows that Ruth isn't trying to hurt her – no doubt she thinks Dorothy getting pregnant is just a matter of time. She doesn't know about the miscarriages; Dorothy is too ashamed to tell her.

'No.' Dorothy pours a cup of tea, although it's probably stewed by now. The darkness of the liquid confirms it, and to offset the bitterness she tips two spoonfuls of sugar into the cup and stirs.

'Dorothy?'

'Hm?' She glances up to see Ruth frowning at her.

'Did I say the wrong thing? You went quiet.'

How much should Dorothy tell her? They have known each other since school, but Dorothy was one of those girls who longed to confess her secrets yet was scared she'd be laughed at. Ruth had told her everything, and Dorothy was able to get away with a facsimile of confession: talking about boys she liked, whingeing about teachers, speculating about formal dresses. She never revealed the real stuff; she never said *I want* or *I need* or *I dream*. Even though Ruth said those things to her. Dorothy had never said that she loved Cornelia and felt shackled to her at the same time. How could Ruth understand? How could anyone?

It's possible that not sharing confidences is a German thing. Her parents can be austere and remote; and from what she remembers of her grandparents they were much the same. Dorothy has no idea if they were always that way or if the remoteness developed in the wake of the war – no one wanted to speak about the unspeakable so they didn't speak about anything much at all.

So Dorothy never learnt to confess from her parents, and as she wasn't brought up Catholic she didn't learn it at church. Her parents pretended to be Lutherans but they didn't go to church. She'd once heard her mother tell her father that she was too ashamed to face God, and he'd said he understood, that he felt it too. Shame, therefore, might be all that Dorothy has learnt from her parents, and it too is a powerful reason to never tell anyone anything. It makes a person so lonely, though, to not confide.

She tells Frederick things, of course, but her mother once told her that you should never rely on a man for emotional support – they're just no good at it, she had said – so Dorothy tends to stick to the facts with Frederick: she can't get pregnant, so needs to look into ways of changing that situation. As opposed to: *I'm a hormonal, emotional mess and I need you to prop me up.*

Ruth has been her friend for years, though – couldn't she trust her now? Is Dorothy not being a proper friend if she doesn't trust Ruth with the problem that's occupying so much of her time and energy?

'You didn't say the wrong thing,' she says, looking into her friend's eyes. 'I just . . . don't know how much to tell you.'

Ruth holds her gaze. 'You can tell me anything, you know that. Haven't I told you things?'

Dorothy nods. She remembers Ruth, in tears, telling her that their father had beaten her younger brother. Then that her brother had left home, joined the army and hadn't been seen since. Another time, when a boy in their class had stopped Ruth after school one day and grabbed at her breasts, tearing her singlet, telling her she shouldn't go around dressed like that if she didn't want that sort of thing to happen. The singlet was part of their school sports uniform. Yes, Ruth has told her things. And Dorothy has told her nothing.

'I've been having trouble,' Dorothy starts, 'holding a pregnancy.' She takes a sharp breath in and follows it with a long sip of tea.

'Oh, darl,' Ruth says, but there's no pity in it, just understanding.

'There have been a few . . .' This time Dorothy's inhalation is ragged and she knows she can't say the word.

She's relieved when Ruth nods, knows she doesn't have to say more.

'That's tough,' Ruth murmurs. 'I'm sorry you had to go through that.'

'Me too.' Dorothy smiles, even though she doesn't know why. Is she trying to make herself feel better? Trying to signal to Ruth that she shouldn't feel bad for her? It's a reflex and Dorothy wishes she didn't do it. Wishes she wasn't always smiling through her pain like it doesn't matter.

'But I have a plan. I think,' she continues. 'There's a clinic in Brisbane. For in-vitro fertilisation. Have you heard of it?'

'Test-tube babies?'

'Yes.'

They're both silent as they take sips of their beverages.

'That's a long way to go,' Ruth says. 'How long do you have to stay?'

'I don't know yet. I haven't told my doctor that I want to do it.'

'What about Frederick? Does he go too?'

'He's still not convinced it's the right thing,' Dorothy says, remembering their latest 'discussion' that had bordered on an argument.

Frederick had reiterated his concerns that the process would be too hard on her body. Yet it was also the first time he'd said, 'I think it is our best shot.'

Dorothy sighs. 'And it's tough, because we . . . This place. I'm not sure how to manage the time away. Frederick probably wouldn't be away for that long, but I might be.'

Ruth looks down into her coffee, then up at Dorothy, a slight smile on her face. 'Well, I told you Sandy wants me to go back to work.' She raises her eyebrows.

It takes Dorothy a few seconds to realise what she means, and she lets her hopes rise – then fall.

'I don't think we could afford to pay you much,' she says.

Ruth presses her lips together and glances to the side, like she's thinking. 'Could you pay me in meals? As in, meals I can take home for Sandy and the kids?'

Right then, Dorothy lets herself hope. It's dangerous, but she can't help it.

'Yes,' she says, 'I think we could.'

'Honestly, that would probably be better than a wage. At least the taxman can't take meals!' Ruth laughs, her eyes wide, like she's discovered something wonderful.

'Would you really like to work here?' Dorothy asks.

'The reason I don't love Sandy telling me to go back to work,' Ruth says, 'is because for him it's about the money. I think the hours would be okay, though. Mum can watch the kids, and I'd be home after lunch, wouldn't I?'

Dorothy nods.

'And it's not forever, right? It's just while you're away.'

Another nod. Although Dorothy wonders if Ruth could be available if she does end up having a baby . . . No, that's too far ahead. She can't let herself think it or she'll jinx herself. Again.

'Then I reckon we have a plan,' Ruth says.

They sit there grinning at each other, two old friends who have seen those grins change through lost teeth and badly applied lipliner, and Dorothy thinks this is the best day she's had in a long time.

'Thank you,' she says, and the words don't sound enough for what she feels.

'Don't thank me yet,' Ruth says with a snort. 'I may be hopeless. But it's the least I can do. You've helped me out of a jam so many times. You're a good friend to me. I hope I can be to you too.'

'You are,' Dorothy says quickly, before the tears that are in her throat move up to her eyes. 'I'm lucky.'

'We both are,' Ruth says, reaching across to squeeze her hand. 'It's just that sometimes we forget to say it.'

SPRING 1993

Jurassic Park, starring Sam Neill and directed by Steven Spielberg, is released.

A new American comedy show called *Seinfeld* debuts on the Nine Network.

The hit Australian TV drama *A Country Practice* nears its end on the Seven Network.

Ray Martin finishes his role as host of *Midday*.

Madonna embarks on her Girlie Show tour.

Crowded House releases the album *Together Alone*.

CHAPTER TWENTY-TWO

Patricia pulls a cardigan around her shoulders as she leaves Orange Blossom House. Even though spring has arrived there's still enough winter in the air to cause her to cover up at night. She dreams of the warmer season ahead, when she can embrace her inner lizard and bask in the sun.

'That was a tough one tonight,' Dorothy says behind her.

'Yes.' Patricia stops to wait.

'I'm a little slower than usual,' Grace Maud says, almost creeping along the path.

'So am I,' Patricia says. 'I thought my hip joints were going to pop at one point.' She winces at the memory of a standing pose held for so long she actually thought she might yell an obscenity.

'I really feel like a little old lady tonight,' Grace Maud says, patting her thigh. 'These feel like they don't want to work.'

'Seriously, Grace Maud, we're all feeling it. I'm not just saying that.' Patricia turns and keeps walking to the street. 'And I hardly think we could ever call you a little old lady. You're bendier than half the women in there!'

'How ridiculous,' Grace Maud says, but she looks quite pleased.

Dorothy sighs. 'You're more flexible than me. My body feels like it just wants to stay curled up no matter how many times I try to force it open.'

It's true that Dorothy is stiff – surprisingly so for a young person. But Patricia can see that there's also a form of armour there: Dorothy is protecting herself against something. Or someone. Maybe against the class? Or herself.

Patricia has seen it before, in students. The ones who feel like they have the most to lose – for whom the stakes of mere existence are the highest – are the ones who hold themselves, and walk, rigid. Shoulders hunched, heart protected. She just didn't have the vocabulary for it until she came to yoga and heard Sandrine talking about 'not putting your heart in a cave'.

Once Sandrine even walked up to a student who was standing upright, feet together, hands by her sides, and said, 'Dear, dear – don't you think it's time to drop your weapons?' Sandrine saw something Patricia couldn't see, but immediately the student's shoulders lowered – then she started to sniffle. This turn of events intrigued Patricia enough that she has started observing others. In a casual way only – anything else might be considered creepy.

So in her casual way she has observed that Dorothy has armour, and weapons, but without knowing her better Patricia won't be able to discern what she's protecting.

'Don't force it, then,' Grace Maud is telling Dorothy. 'You'll do yourself an injury.'

Dorothy appears to consider the advice as they step out onto the footpath.

'Here's my car,' she says, turning towards them with a smile that seems a bit too bright for the occasion. Another weapon.

'See you next week,' Patricia says. 'That's if we can walk properly by then.'

'Goodbye,' Grace Maud says, and heads in the same direction Patricia is walking.

'You must be parked near me,' Patricia says – a safe statement given there are only two cars in this part of the street.

'Is that yours?' Grace Maud gestures to the vehicles as they cross towards them.

'The big red beast? It is.'

'What do you need a car that size for?' There's amusement in Grace Maud's eyes, if not her voice.

'I need to drive my parents to places.' Patricia smiles in such a way that she hopes indicates she'll take no further questions on this subject. Her own form of armour.

'I see.' Grace Maud opens her car door. 'Well, cheerio.'

Patricia gives her a wave as she unlocks her own car door, smiling as she thinks of how abrupt Grace Maud can be. Sometimes she doesn't even say goodbye. Tonight both Patricia and Dorothy received a farewell. Maybe they're getting under her skin.

As Patricia puts her handbag on the passenger seat she hears Grace Maud's engine turn over. And over. And over.

She pushes open her door and walks to Grace Maud's. 'I think your battery's flat.'

Grace Maud looks up with irritation. 'I'm aware of that. I was simply hoping that if I kept trying, the engine might decide to change its mind.'

Patricia can't help laughing, although that will probably irritate Grace Maud more. 'Can I call the RACQ?' she says. 'Sandrine will have a phone.'

'Oh, they'll take hours at this time of night,' Grace Maud says, although she makes no move to do anything else.

'I could drive you home,' Patricia offers tentatively. 'You could come back for the car tomorrow.'

It's the right thing to do, of course, but she and Grace Maud aren't friends and she's quite mindful of the fact that Grace Maud may not want them to become so.

Grace Maud makes a noise that sounds like satisfaction, then withdraws the keys and puts them in her bag. 'That's a plan,' she says and, in a sequence of movements that are quite fluid for someone who was complaining not long ago that her legs weren't working properly, she locks up her car and is at Patricia's passenger door in seconds.

'I'm not far,' she says once their seatbelts are done up and Patricia is pulling away from the kerb. 'Left at the T-intersection then keep going.'

Patricia smiles her thanks for the directions.

There's no one else on the street – no humans, no cars. Cairns at night can still be like a country town, particularly in these residential areas full of shade-giving trees and architecture that's a mix between climate-friendly dwellings of old and boastful dwellings built by people who made a lot of money in the 1980s.

'So why are you driving your parents around?' Grace Maud asks. 'They're probably the same age as me. *I'm* still driving.'

It's no surprise that Grace Maud is being direct – it's something of a trademark – but Patricia is still taken aback. Mainly because this is the first time she's been asked the question. The first time she's had to explain the reality of her life now. Her siblings know what it is and barely care; her colleagues don't know. Her friends are so distant from her that there's no one to enquire.

'I don't know your exact age, obviously,' Patricia starts, 'but—'

'Seventy-four.'

‘You’re not far off them. And Dad’s still all right to drive. But Mum—’

‘Cross over at the next intersection.’

‘Thanks. Mum wanders off.’

‘In the car?’

‘In her head.’

‘I see.’

‘So I drive them where they need to go,’ Patricia says, even though Grace Maud has no doubt figured that out for herself.

‘Then they’re . . .’ Grace Maud takes an audible breath. ‘Very fortunate to have a daughter who cares so much. Right at the second street.’

‘Thanks. And thanks.’ Patricia laughs but it’s a half-hearted sound. ‘Most days I don’t feel like I care enough.’

‘That’s what it’s like when you’re in the thick of it. You’re so wrapped up in all the things you have to do that you feel like you don’t have enough time to care. But the doing is the caring. I’m just up here on the left. Where the palm tree is.’

Patricia pulls up outside a sweet little house that’s on its way to being a cottage.

‘Thank you for the lift,’ Grace Maud says as she opens the car door.

‘Can I walk you to the house?’

‘No, that’s fine, thank you. I’m not worried about robbers or hooligans in this neighbourhood.’

‘What about your car? I could pick you up tomorrow morning.’

‘I have a girl who comes on Fridays. She’ll take me. Thanks again.’ Grace Maud gets out of the vehicle, walks slowly to her gate, then up the short path to her house.

Patricia may not be seeing her to the door, but there’s no reason why she can’t sit and make sure that Grace Maud’s key works, and that she turns on a light once she's inside. The doing is the caring, after all.

Now she'll go home to do things for her parents, and she'll try to remind herself that it's out of care, not duty, even as she grits her teeth from time to time. Because she realises that implicit in Grace Maud's statement that she has a girl who comes on Fridays is the admission that there's no one else to take her to her car. And while Patricia doesn't know the state of Grace Maud's relationships, she knows that she herself is going home to two people who depend on her, and probably love her even if they don't say it. And while that may not be the family life her peers have, it's the one she has, and the one she'll re-dedicate herself to each and every day.

She dropped her weapons when it came to her parents, and she has no plans to pick them up again.

CHAPTER TWENTY-THREE

With her feet as wide apart as she can get them and her hands on her hips, Grace Maud attempts to bend forwards from the waist as smoothly as the women around her.

Suddenly Sandrine is in front of her holding a chair. 'I think your hands are better on this than on the floor,' she says with a quick smile before she's off to help someone else. Before Grace Maud can tell her that she might be inflexible but she doesn't need a bloody chair.

Sandrine has a habit of mind-reading. Whenever Grace Maud is in a pose and wanting to give up, Sandrine will say something like, 'Giving up is the easiest thing in the world but I don't recommend it.' And there will go Grace Maud's thoughts of playing the little old lady and saying the pose is too hard. Or that life is too hard, which is sometimes how she feels. Especially lately. After her last visit to the farm. Which she's trying not to think about as she's promised herself that these ninety minutes in Orange Blossom House will be her respite from worry.

Instead her mind wanders to Cecilia. A little while ago, after another fight with her mother, the girl was talking about leaving Cairns. Grace Maud hates the idea. As much as she doesn't really need anyone at home, she enjoys Cecilia's company. Then Luca came home with Grace Maud from the farm that day and Cecilia was there. Grace Maud saw the look that passed between them and knew she'd get to keep Cecilia for a while longer. Luca too – not that she knows if he's planning to leave.

They had a bashful chat, then Luca slipped away to see his friends and Cecilia tried very hard not to ask questions about him, but not hard enough. Grace Maud pretended not to know what was going on – it can be quite fun to play dumb sometimes – but she's pleased. Luca has lovely qualities, and so does Cecilia. Worse matches could happen. As she should know.

'Are you with us, Grace Maud?' Sandrine's voice intrudes on her thoughts.

Grace Maud looks up suddenly to see that the others have moved on to a different pose. It takes her a few seconds to feel the pain in her neck, like a rebuke, and a few more to scowl because of it.

'Breathe,' Sandrine says as she approaches. 'Breathe and push down through your feet to roll up slowly.'

Grace Maud starts to nod her assent and feels the pain again.

'Enough for you for now,' Sandrine says and guides her to the wall. 'Please sit. Soles of the feet together. *Baddha konasana.* It will be good for your hips too, yes?'

She's gone again, and Grace Maud feels the relief of having the wall behind her, holding her up. She presses her skull against it and closes her eyes. Why can't she do this every class? It's nicer than a lot of the other poses.

It doesn't take long for the rest of the students to take the same pose, albeit on their mats, and Grace Maud wonders if it's more of Sandrine's sleight of hand, whereby she makes invisible adjustments to the class to accommodate everyone's idiosyncrasies. It's not the first time Grace Maud has noticed her doing it, but it's the first time she's really appreciated it.

When the class moves on to other sitting postures Grace Maud joins them, her neck feeling less vulnerable.

'Are you all right?' Patricia asks when class is over and she's rolling up her mat.

'Oh, yes.' Grace Maud smiles her reassurance. 'I was too hasty to move, that's all. It'll be fine.'

'Or perhaps someone is being a pain in the neck?' Patricia says, smiling mysteriously.

'What do you mean?' The thought of her troubles with Tom makes Grace Maud sound sharper than she intends.

'Oh. Nothing.' Patricia looks confused. 'Only that, um, Sandrine said something last week about how things can manifest in the body. You know how we say someone is being a pain in the neck? Well, sometimes they . . . are.' A quick smile, like she's testing the waters.

Grace Maud stares at her. She knows too well – and too recently – how the body throws up its warning signs. She just never thought anyone else would understand.

'I agree,' she says, and Patricia looks relieved.

'Hello,' Dorothy says meekly, clutching her handbag against her chest.

Grace Maud recognises what it is: Dorothy is, consciously or not, putting up a barrier. She probably doesn't want to talk to them at all but she's too polite not to.

Grace Maud long ago gave up caring if others think she's being rude. She and Patricia and Dorothy have watched each other make strange shapes with their bodies for several weeks now. If that's not an entrée to inquisitive conversation, she doesn't know what is.

'What's going on with you?' she says.

Dorothy looks startled. 'Nothing.'

Grace Maud replies with a sceptical look. '*Really.*'

'No.' Dorothy looks at Patricia, who is clearly trying to keep her face in neutral.

'You're holding that handbag like you're concealing the code to the world's most guarded safe,' Grace Maud goes on.

'Oh, that!' Dorothy's laugh is artificial. 'I didn't even think about it.'

Around them the other students are starting to leave, calling goodbye to Sandrine.

'Let's go,' Grace Maud says, smiling gratefully as Patricia picks up her bag and mat from the floor, carrying them with her own. 'You can tell us on the way out.'

That tightness in her hips makes her waddle a bit as they walk and Grace Maud envies – as she has before – the easy gait of the younger women. Perhaps she never walked like that; years of riding horses gave her a certain way of moving that could never be called graceful. But she likes to think it felt more fluid than it does now. Not that she'll ever get that back, no matter how much yoga she does. The body she had is gone, and in exchange she has experience and wisdom. Which is why she's determined to find out what's bothering Dorothy, because she can probably fish something out of her past that will help.

'Honestly, it's nothing,' Dorothy says again.

'Liar!' Grace Maud says cheerfully, and is rewarded with slightly shocked expressions on the younger women's faces.

'Dorothy, you've seen me crawling around the floor like an infant,' Grace Maud adds as they step off the path outside the house so they're not blocking the others. 'And last week you had my *derrière* in your face when we did that ridiculous hip stretch. I think we're past the point of pretending not to know each other well. And you aren't very good at hiding emotions on your face, so I can see that it's not nothing.'

Patricia, standing beside them, gives an encouraging nod.

Dorothy looks up at the night sky, breathing through her mouth. 'I have to make a decision,' she says. 'And I am really . . . stuck.'

'You know, I'm a believer in the idea that we can overthink things,' Grace Maud says. 'Because I do it often. I also believe that we are better off if we learn to trust what we feel.' She smiles. 'One benefit of being a senior citizen is that I get to make statements like this.'

Dorothy sighs. 'I want a baby. But I think I have to accept that I need help.' She pauses. 'It's been . . .' She swallows. 'Hard. For my husband. For me.'

'I can only imagine,' Patricia murmurs.

Dorothy looks from one of them to the other, as if she's deciding what to say next.

Grace Maud knows not to push at a moment like this. But she also knows that it's a privilege when a person tells you something painful, so the best thing she can do is bear witness.

'The help is in Brisbane,' Dorothy continues at last. 'And it's expensive. And time-consuming. And for all I know . . .' She sighs again, loudly. 'For all I know, it won't do any good. My husband isn't sure either.'

Grace Maud takes Dorothy's free hand. 'You've wanted a baby for a while.' It's an acknowledgement, not a question.

Dorothy nods. 'But . . . maybe I shouldn't. Maybe it's not meant to be.'

'There's no such thing as "meant to be",' Grace Maud says. 'That's a nice phrase people trot out to stop themselves getting upset. If you feel something is right for you, you must do your best to *make* it be.'

They stand in silence for a few seconds.

'I wanted children,' Patricia says softly. 'I was going to say it wasn't meant to be,' she glances at Grace Maud, 'but I don't think that's true. It just didn't happen. For whatever reason. I never met the right man.' She laughs, but it's the laugh of someone who is trying not to cry. 'Or I never made it happen.'

A wistfulness settles on Patricia's face and Grace Maud recognises it: the mixture of regret and relief that arises when you know you've become the person you want to be only because some of the things you thought you wanted never happened.

'If it's what you want, I think you should do it, Dorothy,' Patricia continues. 'I don't know you very well but I completely support you. And I think Grace Maud does too.'

'Would I be standing out here in this old leotard if I didn't?' Grace Maud smiles archly at them both.

Patricia gives her a funny look. 'You know that I support you too, don't you?'

'What's that supposed to mean?' Grace Maud hears the snap in her tone; she doesn't like being caught off guard.

'In there,' Patricia nods towards the house, 'we were talking about someone being a pain in the neck. That's your chance, you know? To actually talk about that pain-in-the-neck person. It might help you.'

Grace Maud considers this. 'Help me with what?'

'To lessen the pain.' Patricia shakes her head and laughs softly. 'Are you always this difficult?'

'Yes.'

Grace Maud glances at Dorothy, whose eyes are wide. Just like her heart. Dorothy has trusted her almost from day dot. Patricia is a clear-eyed, clear-minded sort of person. Perhaps

Grace Maud wouldn't be burdening them if she identifies that pain in the neck by name.

'It's my son,' she says, shifting her weight from one foot to the other. She can hear Sandrine telling her to *stop leaning, you are throwing out your pelvis!* 'Tom. He, uh . . .'

She feels the whole story sitting in her chest, over her heart, forcing its way up into her neck, her jaw, her head. She feels her disappointment in him, her anger that things have gone so awry, her inability to articulate this clearly even when she has a willing audience, because to say it out loud feels enormous, like she'd be letting it escape into the ether and there would be no chance of containing it. Controlling it. And oh, how controlling she's had to be all these years, to keep things together.

'Go on,' Patricia urges kindly.

Grace Maud's sigh is freighted. 'He wants to buy another property. Expand the business. Which is fine in principle. But he didn't tell me. He told the bank manager. He told the *neighbours*. Before he told me. And I'm the one whose name is on the title.'

She stops, not wanting to remember what Tom said that day but knowing she has to, because she can't avoid the truth or the past.

'This is my history. My father worked the property. His father. It would have gone to my brothers, but they . . .' She looks at each woman in turn and sees only receptivity. 'Died. World War II. Or thereabouts. And my sister is gone too. So it's mine. Tom started working with me when he was in his twenties.'

She thinks of the scrappy young man so lean that his jeans fell off his hips, and the sturdier, middle-aged proposition he's become. Her son. Grown up. In charge.

'We worked it together,' she continues. 'Then I backed off. I was past retirement age. It's his now, although I still own it. But he wants to build an empire, I guess, and he needs to borrow to do it. It's just easier to do it when he doesn't consult me.'

Patricia presses her lips together. 'You feel like you're not useful any more,' she says. 'Or, rather, that he doesn't see any use for you.'

Grace Maud holds her gaze. 'That might be it. Or maybe I think he doesn't respect what his forebears built. Doesn't think it's enough.'

'Do you wish you hadn't let him run it?' Dorothy asks. 'I mean – do you think he's doing a bad job?'

'No,' Grace Maud says quickly, because she knows it's the truth. 'He's doing a fine job. But I suppose . . .' She winces. 'I'm his mother. I guess part of me thinks I should be able to tell him what to do, except he's not a little boy any more and I can't control him any more than I can control the moon. And even though I wanted the place to be his to do with as he wishes, I still have my loyalties to my father. To my grandfather.'

Suddenly she is a child again, standing next to Ellie Maud as they watch the cane burn, hearing her father giving instructions to their brothers, passing on the knowledge his father gave him.

'Their ghosts are watching me,' she says. 'And I'm letting them down if I give up on the place.'

'You could feel that way,' says Patricia. 'Or you could see it as passing the farm on the way it was passed on to you, just differently. Not to take sides,' she adds, holding up a hand in peace. 'Just to offer a perspective.'

'I'm sorry this is so hard for you,' Dorothy says. 'I wish I had a solution to suggest. But I don't know anything about farms.'

Grace Maud smiles wanly. 'You don't want to. They're

more complicated than they seem.' She shifts her weight again and sees the light in the studio go out. 'We should move on.'

'Okay,' Dorothy says meekly, stepping back onto the path.

'Let us know what you decide,' Grace Maud adds, and Dorothy looks quizzical.

'About your options,' Grace Maud explains. 'For a baby.'

'Oh.' A pinch appears on Dorothy's brow, then disappears. 'I will.'

'Whatever you decide, it will be the right thing,' Patricia says, then she glances at Grace Maud. 'Not that I can say the same thing to you. I don't think you like having that pain in your neck.'

'I'll sort it out,' Grace Maud replies. 'But not tonight.'

She can tell that answer doesn't satisfy Patricia at all, but sensibly the other woman doesn't mention the subject again as they head to their cars.

CHAPTER TWENTY-FOUR

The drive to John's house is only going to take them an hour or so, but Patricia wishes she hadn't agreed to do it. It should really be John coming to them from Innisfail.

'Sorry, mate,' he'd said when he called yesterday. 'Footy match in the morning.'

'You don't play football,' Patricia said, the trip-wire on her temper starting to hum.

'I train a local team. Kids.' She heard him drag on his cigarette.

Patricia has been dreading her brother's visit because of this habit. The only thing that weaned her mother off the smokes was the fact that she couldn't remember she had a nicotine addiction, but if she sees John with them she might remember. Patricia has spied her with a longing look on her face whenever they're in the garden and the neighbour's smoke wafts across the back fence.

The problem has been avoided thus far because John so rarely visits. Except a week ago he'd called and said he was going to come north and wouldn't that be ace? They could have a family barbecue, he said. No prizes for guessing who'd be making the coleslaw, the salad and handing him the tongs to turn the snags.

'Presumably you were aware of that when you arranged to visit this weekend,' Patricia says flatly.

She knows not to use emotion on John: he'll say she's being irrational, and that will be the *sine qua non* for him to declare himself the victor of every argument. He's been doing it to her since she was a child.

The worst part of it is that she doesn't even think he's a bad bloke – just a product of hanging out with friends who called their mothers, sisters and assorted other women in their lives 'hysterical' on a regular basis. Small-child Patricia wasn't immune from this assessment, even though it was also John who met her after school when her mother was otherwise occupied, and watched her while she climbed the monkey bars in the local park, picking her up if she fell. She misses that John; she hasn't seen him for a while.

'Forgot, mate. I've been flat out here.' Another drag.

Patricia doesn't know how his secretary stands it. As a solicitor in a small town John is mainly confined to his desk doing conveyancing and wills, which means anyone else in the office has to put up with his smoking. When they finally get to see him, he'll reek of Marlboros and the smell will give Patricia a headache.

So she has that to look forward to as she tries to keep her eyes on the road and not glance around at scenery she hasn't sighted for years. It's hard to resist these surroundings, though: thick with cane, the plants thriving in the rainfall – more rain than in most parts of Australia – along with the banana palms. It's lush in a way that parts further north may not be.

Not that Patricia has seen much of what lies beyond Port Douglas. She's only been to Cooktown once, since the unsealed road forms a barrier to all those who don't have an appropriately outfitted vehicle. When she was in her twenties, she and a friend and the friend's boyfriend borrowed a Land Rover Discovery with bench seats in the back and enough room to transport a platoon. They took their time driving north, absorbing the scenes of red dirt and epic vistas, before the wet season started early and forced them south to Cairns.

Now that Patricia has no friends with Land Rovers, Innisfail is as far as she's likely to travel. But the desire to leave Cairns doesn't take hold of her any more – although it's taken hold of Marjorie.

'I want to go to Japan!' she'd announced as they left the assembly hall on Tuesday morning. 'They have all those direct flights now.'

'That's nice,' Patricia said absent-mindedly, thinking of the load of washing she'd forgotten to hang out before she left the house.

'Don't you think it would be great? So much fun!'

'Do you speak Japanese?'

'No,' Marjorie said. 'Should I?'

'I guess not. I'm sure a lot of Japanese people can speak a little bit of English.'

Patricia has no idea if that's true but it seemed like the kindest thing to say. Marjorie can be known to fret if she thinks she's misstepped.

They turned for the staffroom and Marjorie glanced over her shoulder. 'Don't look now,' she said quietly, 'but Dennis is following us.'

'We're going to the staffroom, Marj,' Patricia said, amused. 'I think *everyone* is following us.'

'But not *everyone* was looking over at you all the time in assembly!'

Patricia laughed and shook her head, mainly to hide the fact that she was pleased by this news if it was true.

'Do you have a thing going on?' Marjorie asked in a conspiratorial whisper.

'No. We have no things.'

'Are you sure? He's always coming into the staffroom after school when he knows you're there.'

'I think you'll find that's because he always has some extra session on after school. Running. Jumping. Whatever those kids do.' Patricia had flapped a hand dismissively. 'Anyway, I'm not the only one in there after school. You are too.' She gave Marjorie a look.

'Oh, he's not interested in me,' Marjorie said with a tinkling laugh. 'Besides, I think I'm seeing someone.'

'You think?'

'I'm waiting for him to ask me out,' she said demurely, and Patricia knew who it was: the recently arrived maths teacher, Mr Li, whose muscles are distractingly large for someone who spends most of his time with a calculator.

On his first day Marjorie could barely contain herself, and she's been fluttering around him ever since.

'Nearly there, love,' Patricia's father says and she realises she's let herself drive on autopilot. Not the most conscientious thing to do, but they're still safely on the road.

'Yes, Dad,' she says, seeing the outskirts of the town ahead. Five minutes away. Possibly ten. She's no good at judging distances.

She sees her father's head is turned towards the half-open window. Beyond him are rows and rows of mango trees, their leaves vibrant, their fruit still several weeks away.

'I thought that farm was cane,' she murmurs.

'It was.' Her father nods slowly. 'They sold. New owners put in mangoes.' He glances in her direction. 'It's been a while since you've driven this way.'

'Yes, I guess it has.'

She hasn't been to Innisfail since she moved back in with her parents. And John wasn't living there when Patricia moved away, so it's been decades. Still, not many people around here change their crops. They like to keep what the soil's been used to. She understands – she's been the same way – even as she knows that change is not only desirable but necessary if fields are to stay fertile.

'It'll be good to see the boy,' her father says, turning to the window again.

'Yes, Dad.'

She looks in the rear-view mirror at her mother: she's sitting silently, staring back at her with eyes Patricia no longer recognises.

'Not long to go, Mum,' she says, although she has no way of knowing if her mother is even really there.

She probably won't find out until John starts smoking and her mother wants to join him. How strange to realise now that it might be a good thing: a sign that part of her mother is still with them, even if they don't see it often.

'Turn off up here,' her father says.

John lives on a small property out of town. Ever since he bought it seven years ago he's been talking about growing some exotic fruit on it, although there's nary a new tree to be seen.

'There they are,' John says as Patricia puts on the brakes and rolls down the window at the end of his long driveway.

She wants to correct him: he's not talking to a bystander so he should have said, 'There *you* are'. But he hates it when she points out that he's wrong about something. Everyone hates to be wrong, she supposes, except no one stops to consider that her job means she hates it when people can't use the language properly.

'G'day, Dad,' John says, and they shake hands.

'Mum.' Peck on the cheek.

'Patricia.' Another peck.

Patricia refrains from flinching as she inhales the stench of cigarette smoke embedded in John's hair and clothes. She notices that his paunch is bigger and his jaw slacker than they were the last time she saw him. And his hairline has receded further too. Ooh, she bets he doesn't like that. He used to have quite a mane. It was his trademark, along with the anchor tattoo he acquired during a mysteriously brief stint in the navy and which their mother abhorred, declaring that tattoos were for people who'd been to jail. Then she forgave him, because he brought her a bottle of 4711 and a bunch of flowers and said he'd wear long-sleeved shirts from then on. He's wearing one today, although the sleeves are rolled up just to the point where the tattoo starts to be visible.

'Come in,' he says, striding ahead. 'The barbie's on.'

Patricia pulls the bowl of coleslaw out of the back seat of the car and looks up to see her mother standing still, her fists clenched and her feet planted at an odd angle, like she's a toddler about to have a tantrum.

'Mum?'

Her mother's head swivels towards her. 'Where are we?' she says.

'We're at John's, Mum. We're going to have lunch.'

Patricia can see that John has stopped at his front door. Their father is still walking towards it; he's so used to his wife being confused that he probably hasn't registered what's happening.

'What's going on?' John calls.

'Nothing,' Patricia responds. 'We'll be there in a second.'

She catches up to her mother, the coleslaw tucked under her arm. 'Mum? It's all right. We're at John's.'

Sometimes, when her mother is hovering between remembering and forgetting, her face looks like a blank slate: no expression, no light in her eyes, everything still. Sometimes she isn't recognisable. That's how she looks now, with her fists still clenched by her sides.

'I don't know him!' she shrieks. 'Who is he!'

John strides towards them. 'What's going on, Patricia?' he says as he blows past their mother. 'Get her inside.'

'I can't get her to do anything,' Patricia says softly. 'She's an adult.'

'She's bloody well not behaving like one!' John makes a face like a disgruntled handyman who's been told the hardware store doesn't have the screwdriver he wants. 'How have you let it get like this?'

'I didn't let it get like anything, John. Her brain is doing whatever it's doing. We can't control it. And why is it my responsibility anyway?'

'You're the one living with her.' He juts his close-to-nonexistent chin in her direction.

'So is Dad.'

'He shouldn't have to worry about this.'

'Why not?'

'Because it's a . . .' He rolls his neck like a fighter limbering up. 'It's a . . .'

'Oh, you were so close to saying it's a woman's job, weren't you?' Patricia can feel her top lip curling while she keeps an eye on her mother, who now appears less tense. 'How convenient for you all that it's the women who have to do everything.'

'Stop whingeing – you're living rent-free.'

Is that what it is, she wants to say. Because it certainly feels like she's paying some kind of price. Instead, she takes a breath, as she does when confronted by an angry teenage boy in one of her classes.

'When did we stop being friends, John?' she murmurs so their mother can't hear. 'Was it when you became a selfish moron? Or were you always like that and I just had to grow up in order to realise it?'

She can see the surprise in his eyes. She can feel the surprise on her own face. It's unlikely that many people call him on his bullshit, but today she's in the mood for it.

'I, uh . . .' He frowns. And swallows. 'What's the real problem, Patricia?'

What's the real problem? How can he not know? Maybe because she hasn't told him. But why should she have to tell him? Why can't he *see* that it's hard to take care of two adults as well as yourself?

She straightens her shoulders and stares at him. 'The real problem is that I'm exhausted. It's not just the housework. It's the worry. I worry about them all the time, John – about Mum especially.'

His frown deepens. 'But I thought you wanted—'

'John?' their mother says, holding out a hand like she's about to lead him across a busy road.

His gaze moves away. 'Yeah, Mum. I'm here.'

Their mother takes hold of his arm, and Patricia turns back to retrieve the mayonnaise from the Esky in the boot.

CHAPTER TWENTY-FIVE

'Honestly, Cecilia, there is really nothing more for you to do.' Grace Maud gestures to the spotless kitchen bench that matches her spotless floor, cupboards – and the rest of the house, for that matter.

'Oh, are you sure?' Cecilia says, eyes wide.

'You've wiped that benchtop five times,' Grace Maud says, amused because she knows exactly why Cecilia wiped it that many times, why she's delaying her departure to the shops.

'It was really dirty!' Cecilia flaps the tea towel she's holding, as if it contains the answers as to why there was so much alleged dirt.

'It wasn't.' Grace Maud pulls out a chair from the kitchen table and gestures to the one opposite. 'You'd better take a seat. He could be a while yet.'

'Who?' Eyes still wide.

Grace Maud has no idea why Cecilia's playing this game when she knows that Grace Maud knows that she overheard the phone call earlier during which Luca said he was coming over to visit. He didn't specify whom he was visiting but they all knew it would be Cecilia. Grace Maud is fond of her great-nephew but there's no reason for him to visit her so regularly.

This will be the second time this week. The first time Cecilia wasn't here.

'You should have called first and saved yourself a trip,' Grace Maud had said to him then.

'What do you mean?' He'd bent his head towards her then brushed his hair out of his eyes. Handsome kid. Just like his grandfather. Grace Maud knew exactly what Cecilia saw in him.

'She's not here,' Grace Maud had said with a laugh.

Luca had tried to hide his disappointment, bless him, but Grace Maud's eyesight wasn't yet so bad that she didn't catch it.

So she wasn't at all surprised when he called an hour or so ago saying he was thinking of coming to town, and would Grace Maud mind if he popped over? Of course she wouldn't.

'And I'm sure Cecilia will be happy to see you,' she added because she knew she had an eavesdropper.

An eavesdropper who is now looking at her with faux innocence. Grace Maud smiles as she realises that Cecilia probably thinks she disapproves of their mutual interest, which she most certainly does not.

'Luca,' she says. 'As you well know, Luca is about to arrive.'

'It will be nice to see him again,' Cecilia says, a little breathlessly.

'I'm sure he'll be thinking that of you. And I won't be hanging around when he gets here.'

'Are you going out?' Cecilia looks almost hopeful.

'No – I'll be going to my bedroom. That way you two can pretend I'm not home.'

It's only then that Cecilia looks nervous. 'I don't really know what to say to him. I haven't talked to a lot of boys.'

'Well, boys are humans too, so you can talk to him about human things. Work. Hobbies.'

Grace Maud tries to remember her courtship with Clark: it had consisted of a few dances in a local hall and some polite chitchat. Dances were such a good way to meet young men. She knew several women who'd met their husbands that way. But the dances don't exist any more, not the way they used to, and going to a nightclub to dance in a circle with your friends just isn't the same thing.

'Let him do the work,' Grace Maud continues. 'And he will, if he likes you. It's one way of finding out – if he doesn't ask any questions about you, he's not interested. It hurts, but at least you'll know.'

Cecilia's face falls.

'That's unlikely to happen,' Grace Maud says. 'But you mustn't get so wrapped up in one boy you hardly know – and I say that with love for him, obviously. A pretty thing like you will have many suitors, if you want them.'

'I'm not pretty!' Cecilia says with such conviction that Grace Maud starts to laugh.

'I'm afraid to tell you that you're wrong,' she says with equal force. 'Why ever would you think you're not?'

Cecilia screws up her mouth. 'My mother's always telling me to stand up straight and change my hair and put on lipstick so I look better. I had my hair in a ponytail the other day and she said I looked ugly and I had to take it out. She said men like long hair.'

'I doubt she thinks you're ugly. But I do think she's saying things she was probably told herself. It can be very hard to let go of fixed ideas. As I've mentioned. If we don't question them when we hear them the first time, before we know it they've taken hold and we're stuck with them.' Grace Maud smiles benevolently. 'Your mother may not know any better. That doesn't mean you can't.'

There's a knock at the back door and a called 'hello' followed by heavy footsteps.

'Hi!' Cecilia says, jumping up as Luca ducks to fit under the doorframe.

'Hi.'

Luca looks genuinely delighted to see Cecilia, and Grace Maud is glad that he's not in the 'treat 'em mean' camp. As opposed to the man walking in behind him.

'Tom,' Grace Maud says tersely, standing.

She may be shorter than her son but she wants to at least attempt to be on eye level. They haven't seen each other since she was at the farm, and she's been ignoring most phone calls in case it's him. She knew a lot of them would be, because he wants her to agree to his idea and he won't let it go. That's his personality.

'Mum,' he says, holding his hat in his hand.

They stare at each other.

Grace Maud is barely aware of Luca and Cecilia chatting away together, but aware enough that she doesn't want them to witness whatever she and Tom have to say.

'Cecilia, why don't you and Luca go into the sitting room?' she says. At least that room has a door that can be closed so no one can hear anything.

Luca looks from Grace Maud to Tom and back again. 'Or maybe we could go for a walk?' he says.

Grace Maud hadn't realised he was so astute but she's grateful for it now. 'Lovely,' she says, and barely notices them leaving.

'Mum—'

'If you say "We need to talk", I'm going to ask your school to pay back all that money I spent on your education,' she says, her voice cold. 'Don't be so lazy.'

Tom blanches momentarily, then he looks steely, and she feels almost proud because he gets that steel from her.

She can't recall ever being angry at Tom before. Frustrated, of course – she's a mother and he's a son. Annoyed – yes, that's a given too. Confused, ignored, irritated – all of them. But never angry the way she is now. The way she has been ever since they last spoke.

They've always had a fairly good relationship, as much as any mother and son can when they work together as well as live together. It was just the two of them for a while, before he went to the city, before Viv arrived. They had their disagreements. They resolved them. Now, though, because Tom's been acting as if she's no longer relevant – as if the farm is no longer her concern – that is an altogether different sensation. It makes her feel like he's a stranger – and she can get mad at strangers. Enraged, actually.

The people Grace Maud loves have never been the objects of the blowtorch she has been known to turn on underperforming workers or sleazy passers-by. She knows what people used to say about her in town, before she became too old to be noticed. The word most commonly used was bitch, and she didn't mind that at all. If people were calling her a bitch it saved her some effort, because all she had to do was meet their expectations. But she has never been a bitch to Tom – she's never needed to be. Now she thinks bitchiness would be too mild for what she's feeling.

'I was going to say I'm sorry,' Tom tells her, although he could have made that up on the spot.

How strange, she thinks, to be so distrustful of her son all of a sudden. To find herself unable to believe a word he says. The only person she could ever trust completely was Ellie

Maud; perhaps she should never have believed there would be anyone else.

'Sorry for upsetting me,' she says. 'Rather than sorry for going behind my back in the first place.'

Tom sighs, looks down and shakes his head. 'Mum, we have to think about the future.'

'And by "the future", I presume you mean what happens once I'm dead? Given that you're acting as if I already am.'

He doesn't disagree.

'I can't imagine,' Grace Maud goes on, 'that you have any idea what it's like to work your whole life, then have your only child attempt to disconnect you from that work and all it has brought simply to feather his own nest.' She tries hard not to let her voice grow louder, but doesn't believe she succeeded.

He stares at her, still silent.

'So let me tell you how it feels, Thomas – it's awful.' Her breath catches as she inhales and she has the horrible suspicion that she may cry.

'Mum, we never meant to hurt you.'

'Yet you didn't consider that you might.'

'When are you going to let this go?'

He sounds more amused than cross, which makes her even more furious. Does he think she's not allowed to have an opinion? Or that she's so close to death she no longer has an interest in the place that has been her lifelong home?

She grips the back of her chair. 'Why would you think I have any intention of doing that?'

'We're just trying to set things up for the future,' he says. 'For the girls.'

'The girls couldn't care less about the farm, so I don't see what they've got to do with it.'

He sighs again. Another shake of his head. 'Mum, what are you so upset about? As I said, I'm just planning for the future. The way you and Granddad did.'

Grace Maud has no intention of backing down; Tom just hasn't realised it yet. But that's because he's never put her in this kind of position before. They've never really had a conversation, just the two of them, about the things that matter to them. They've never needed to; most families don't, she guesses. You spend your whole life with someone and it's either presumed you share the same values, or you infer what each other's values are from the way each person behaves. That's how a mother can be seventy-four years of age and find herself with a son who has no idea about what matters to her. Although she is now very clear about what matters to him.

'It's my home,' she says. 'And my parents' home. My grand-parents' home. My brothers' home. My sister's home. You're making me feel like I've already relinquished that home when I'm the very reason you have a right to it in the first place. Me, and my forebears. It is *still my property.*'

She doesn't expect him to understand. A person who under-stood would never have behaved this way in the first place. She has to say it, though. This is the only opportunity she's likely to have.

'I can see you're going to need a little more time to think about it,' Tom says. He scrapes some of his hair behind his ears and puts his hat on. He never puts his hat on inside. 'So I'll leave you alone for a while.'

Then he nods, and he's gone; and although Grace Maud has never been one of those people who minds being alone, right now she feels more alone than she ever has in her life. The distance between her and all the people she has loved and lost feels as vast as a galaxy and as unbridgeable as time itself, and there is nothing for her to do but to walk out into the garden and look to the heavens and hope that somewhere up there, out there, is a place she can go one day and never have to be so heartbroken ever again.

CHAPTER TWENTY-SIX

There is nothing to be gained by sitting in the car wringing her hands, but Dorothy can't seem to stop herself.

'We don't have to do this,' Frederick says, his warm hand on her shoulder, his lips pressing against her temple. 'We can find another way.'

'How?' she gasps.

She's already worked herself into a state for no good reason. Certainly there is nothing to gain from it apart from making her short-tempered with her husband and angry at herself for allowing it to happen.

Her mother used to tell her to 'stop those little tornado tantrums' and she did for a while, at least while her mother was watching. They'd still happen in her bedroom. Or when she was walking down the street. Histrionics, that's what they're called, but they're part of her. Frederick's always accepted that. He knows they're over as quickly as they arrive – except for today. This one has lasted as long as the drive to her parents' house, and Dorothy knows she can't go inside like this and show her mother that those tornado tantrums never really went away.

'I can get a loan,' Frederick says.

'If you get a loan it will be to help the business, not for us to have a baby.'

Dorothy closes her eyes. This was a bad idea, thinking her parents would be the ones to help them. They have no idea about the miscarriages. They don't even ask when Dorothy and Frederick are going to have a baby. At least they're respectful like that. Or disinterested.

There's that little thought darting in from the back of her brain: is she trying to sabotage this on purpose? Is she carrying on, acting like it's the hardest thing in the world, because she actually doesn't want to try to get pregnant any more? Which is different to not wanting a baby. She wants a baby. Her conversation with Patricia and Grace Maud after yoga the other night clarified that for her.

When Patricia said, 'If it's what you want', it was the 'if' that mattered. Patricia didn't tell her she *should* want a baby, that it's the only thing that's important for a woman. There's Patricia without any babies: a strong, intelligent woman who seems quite content with herself. So content that she doesn't make any judgements about Dorothy and her life. *If it's what you want.*

In that moment Dorothy felt freed – and certain. It was what she wanted. It *is* what she wants. She just doesn't want to have to go through more blood and pain and pressure to get it. But she called the government to ask about adoption and they said it would take years. So many years that by the time the child turned up she and Frederick might be too old to be eligible for it, which seems like bureaucratic cruelty at its finest. How can you know you want a baby before you want one? How are you meant to guess that you might want one at a certain time and put your name on a list to get one? Dorothy's still young and she's still too old for that list.

Frederick sighs. '*Liebling*, I've said this before, I know, but I'll say it again. You don't have to do this. *We* don't have to do this. I don't think that you becoming this upset is good for you.'

His hand is still on her shoulder and she concentrates on it to try to calm her mind. He is here with her, she is here with him, and they can do this together.

'I think . . .' She stops. 'I think not trying will make me more upset.'

She turns to look at him and sees how worry has changed his face. Cupping her hands around his cheeks, she kisses him. 'You know me. I always make a drama.'

'Only your mother says that.' His face relaxes a little.

'Yes, well, now she's going to have the chance to say it again.'

They look into each other's eyes. Dorothy doesn't know why she trusted this man as quickly as she did, but he's never given her cause to doubt him, and she hopes she hasn't given him cause to doubt her. Even when she doubts herself.

'Time to go in?' he says, and she nods.

As they approach the front door it opens, and her parents greet them in their restrained way.

'We saw you sitting in the car,' her mother says. 'We thought maybe you had changed your mind about visiting! Hello, Friedrich.'

'Clara,' Frederick says, bending to kiss her on the cheek and accepting, as he always does, that she uses the German form of his name. He shakes Dorothy's father's hand. 'Dieter.'

Dorothy receives a peck on the cheek from each of her parents, then follows them down the hall to their sitting room with its rows of books and LPs and its absence of a television. They've never had one and Dorothy doesn't imagine they ever will.

Dorothy feels a pinch on her upper arm and turns, knowing that Cornelia will be standing there.

Hello, Dorothy signs. *Still living at home, I see?*

It's their running joke even though it stopped being funny a while ago. Cornelia is still living with their parents, even though she's in her late twenties, because there's no job she can do in Cairns. That is, there's no workplace that will accept someone whose lip-reading is excellent but whose spoken voice is not. It's easier, their parents decided long ago, for Cornelia to continue to be supported by them. Which means living at home and doing the housework in exchange. She reads voraciously; she's one of the most educated people Dorothy knows. If they lived in a city maybe there'd be somewhere she could work, or more that she could do, but not here.

When Cornelia was young her paediatrician said that there were homes for 'children like her'.

'It will make it easier on you,' he'd told their parents, but her parents' response was unanimous: the hardest thing in the world would be separation from their daughter. That's when they'd hired a tutor to teach sign to both Cornelia and Dorothy. That's when Dorothy started being the family translator.

She was in danger of staying at home forever herself, wondering if she'd ever be able to leave Cornelia to try to communicate on her own, until her father had sat her down one day.

'You must have your own life,' he said. 'If you want to live elsewhere, of course you should.' Dorothy wanted to ask him why, therefore, had he put such a responsibility on her at a young age, to be Cornelia's voice in the world.

Instead, she said, 'What about Cornelia?'

'We'll manage,' he said firmly.

Her parents had learnt some sign over the years and it was enough, it seems, for them all to get by.

Once she'd moved out Dorothy thought she'd revel in the freedom; instead she missed Cornelia's silent-yet-noisy presence.

She'd become so attuned to knowing where Cornelia was just from the sound of her footsteps, the way she swallowed saliva, her loud mouth-breathing whenever she was upset about something. Her sister, it turned out, was a symphony and she hadn't realised it.

She couldn't go back, though, because her father was right: she did need to make her own life. And Cornelia needed to make hers. There was every chance they'd live together again, one day, once their parents were gone, because Cornelia would be no more able to work in a 'normal' job then than she is now.

Cornelia was one of the first things Dorothy told Frederick about when it became clear that they were serious about each other. It's one of the reasons they are trying to create a successful business for themselves: so they can buy a bigger house one day, with room for Cornelia in case they need it. Frederick didn't waver when Dorothy told him about the extra responsibilities that could come with marrying her. Just as her father has never wavered in his commitment to them all.

'So unlike you to have the afternoon free,' her father says now, gesturing for them to take a seat. 'We thought it must be something important that you would come here.'

Dorothy feels guilt that she doesn't think her father meant to cause. It's true that she doesn't visit often – because she rarely has time. It's also true that she could make arrangements to see them at night. But she's always so tired. Yoga is the only thing she does at night apart from going home, and that's because it gives her far more than it takes. She knows that if she were to see her parents for dinner the conversation alone would drain her. They're intellectuals who have demands. She doesn't listen to enough different recordings of Beethoven's piano concertos to be able to say which conductor is best, and she can't readily come up with anything else to talk about that will satisfy them.

'I know I haven't visited for a while,' Dorothy says meekly, wishing she could take Frederick's hand – for strength or protection, she's not sure which. 'I'm sorry for that.'

Her mother shakes her head. 'You have a business. It is fine. We understand.'

But I miss you, Cornelia signs.

I know you do, Dorothy replies, and this time she knows the guilt was instilled on purpose. *I miss you too.*

Dorothy wants to say more but she knows it's equivalent to talking in a language no one else understands – Frederick knows fewer signs than her parents do – so instead she squeezes Cornelia's hand and smiles.

Cornelia sits on her favourite chair and Dorothy knows she'll pick up most of the conversation through lip-reading. Sometimes Cornelia's ability makes Dorothy self-conscious, like she can't hide anything, but today she doesn't want to: there's no reason to exclude her sister from this conversation.

'It is something important, yes,' Dorothy says, looking at Frederick for encouragement, which she receives in the form of a small smile.

'I've – we've – been trying to have a baby for a while. It, uh . . .' She feels her face crumple a little. 'It hasn't worked. I have – I have, uh . . . *problems*.'

She risks a glance at her mother and sees the tiny indication of concern she used to see occasionally when she was a child. If she fell over and skinned her knee, her mother would always tell her to get up and stop crying, but there would be a moment – sometimes more than one – when Dorothy would see that she was genuinely worried. She held onto those moments, because it meant her mama really cared, and sometimes Dorothy needed to remind herself of that.

'There's a place in Brisbane,' she continues. 'A clinic. We think they can help us.' She catches Frederick's nod in the corner of her eye and takes courage from it. 'But it's going to be expensive. To go there. To stay there. I may need to be away for a while.'

She doesn't want to say the next part. She hopes they won't make her. This is not something she ever wanted to ask them for.

Not that she thinks they wouldn't be generous, but just as her mother wanted her to stand on her own feet in childhood, Dorothy has been trying as hard as she can to do that her whole adult life. So she doesn't expect to feel her father's hand patting her knee. That's why she flinches. And regrets it, because to him it must seem like she's scared of him. She's not. She never has been. But how delicate this dance of family is, when the people who know you so well are the ones whose feelings you want to protect so vociferously, whose opinions you worry the most about.

'Dorothea,' her father says softly – that low tone that lulled her to sleep on the rare nights he wasn't working late. That sang to her and let her know she was safe. Dorothy may be able to look after herself, she may now have a husband to care for her too, but she will never stop being a little girl who simply wants to be reassured that her father will keep the monsters away.

'Your mother and I always hoped you would ask us for help,' he says. 'But you two . . .' He pats her again, then withdraws his hand and sits up straight. 'So independent.' He smiles kindly.

'Whatever you need, just tell us,' her mother says. 'You have never asked for anything. She would not even let us help her buy her first car, Friedrich, did she tell you?'

Frederick laughs and shakes his head.

'So stubborn sometimes.' Her mother smiles but Dorothy sees that concern again, mingled with fear. Maybe one day, far in the future, she too will know what it's like to never stop worrying about her child.

'Just tell us how much you need and we will go to the bank,' her father says.

'And if you need . . .' Her mother stops, swallows. 'If you would like someone to come to Brisbane with you, well . . .' She shrugs. 'I will have the time.'

'Thank you, Mama,' Dorothy whispers. 'Thank you, Papa.'

She wants to put her head in their laps, like she used to. Usually after she'd been teased at school for her German accent and long hair. If the other kids weren't calling her 'Sauerkraut' they were calling her 'Rapunzel'.

Her mother would let Dorothy be upset for about ten seconds, then she had to put it behind her. It seemed heartless then. Now Dorothy sees that her parents were possibly trying to shield her from their own hurt. They had brought their daughter to this land where all she found was insults.

'I have cake for you,' her mother says, her eyes crinkling as she smiles. 'In the kitchen. Tea? Coffee?'

'I'll help you,' Frederick says, standing.

But it's all five of them who go into the kitchen to wait for the kettle to boil, making small talk about local news while Cornelia watches, her eyes flickering from mouth to mouth. And all the while, Dorothy lets herself feel what is rising from her toes to the crown of her head – an awareness she can almost hear Sandrine coaxing her into.

The past is gone. The future is unknowable. All she has is now. And her now is profoundly different from the past of even a few minutes ago. So perhaps her future will also be different to the past she has known.

Perhaps it's time to let that past go and believe that she deserves the future she wants. The one that waits for her in the clinic in Brisbane; and the one that is here, in this room, with the people who love her.

She feels a tap on her arm again and Cornelia starts signing so quickly she almost doesn't catch the start of her sentençe.

You will be a wonderful mother, she says. Then she glances at Clara and back to Dorothy. *You have been to me.*

Dorothy's breath catches. Cornelia rarely says anything sweet to her. They joke with each other. They stick to facts. Emotion is not something Cornelia enjoys. Dorothy will take it as it's offered, though.

Thank you, she says. *And I love you too.*

Cornelia rolls her eyes, pinches Dorothy's hip then picks up a piece of cake and takes far too big a bite.

CHAPTER TWENTY-SEVEN

'You're here late again.'

Patricia looks up from a pile of essays to see Dennis walking into the staffroom, a quizzical look on his face.

She smiles weakly. 'It's easier to do the marking here than at home.'

A look passes across his face but she can't read it.

'What about you?' she says. 'Cricket training?'

He shakes his head. 'Swimming. I just brought a bunch of them back from the pool.'

'I would have thought you could go home, then? No need to be in here.'

She glances down at the essays. She doesn't want to be rude, but the longer he talks to her the later she'll be leaving, and she told her father she'd be home by six.

'Thought I might see you,' Dennis says cheerily and she glances up sharply.

Does he mean that? Or is he like that odious maths teacher, Mr Blake, who tells every female teacher, regardless of her age or marital status, that she 'brightens my day each time you walk past in that skirt'. No point telling Gordon about it, of course, because Gordon is the one who made the rule that all female teachers have to wear skirts.

Dennis looks innocent enough, however.

'So it's, uh, noisy at home, is it?' he continues.

'Hm?'

'You said it's easier to mark here?' He pulls out the chair next to hers and sits.

Patricia tries to be annoyed that he's distracting her from work, but she's still wondering whether he really did come to the staffroom to see her.

'It's, um . . . yes, it's calmer.'

She doesn't know how much to tell him. If she says she lives with her parents, he'll know she's a washed-up spinster. Which is what she knows other people think she is. When her parents were still going to church regularly, the mother of one of Patricia's school friends said as much, which her mother relayed on one of their monthly phone calls with something distinctly resembling glee.

'Poor Patricia,' the woman had apparently said, 'isn't she married yet? Such a shame. What a waste. We all thought she'd be first. Oh well – all the good ones are taken now! She'll just have to lower her standards. No one wants to be an old maid.'

'The good ones?' Patricia had said when the conversation was reported to her. '*What* good ones? Almost every boy who went to my school was either as thick as two short planks, or as mean as Ebenezer Scrooge, or as useless as tits on a bull!'

'Patricia!' her mother had roared. 'How dare you use that word!'

'Which word – "bull"?' she'd said, furious but not entirely sure why. Was it because her own mother was gossiping about her instead of defending her? Because she'd been talked about in such unflattering terms? Or because what was said was true: it was a shame and a waste? She's still trying to work it out.

Patricia and her mother hadn't spoken for weeks after that. Later, Patricia would wonder if it was nascent dementia making her mother meaner than usual, but that day after church was the last time they'd had a substantial argument. Now they live together and barely speak because her mother can't. Life is impossible with its trade-offs and near-misses and almost-nearlys. Finally she has a rapprochement with the woman who gave birth to her and it's because that woman's mind is turning to dust.

Dennis is frowning at her; perhaps he said something and she missed it.

'Hm?' she offers.

'I asked if you have a lot of people at home.'

For some reason, she doesn't want him to think that she has a husband and children waiting for her either. Although her lack of a wedding ring has probably told him that already. But still . . . what will he think of her if he finds out she lives with elderly parents? And why does she care what he thinks?

She doesn't want to lie, though. Lies are difficult and time-consuming to maintain. She knows this because she had a colleague in Sydney who had an affair with another colleague, confided in Patricia and insisted that Patricia maintain the lie in front of her husband and the rest of the staff. Patricia did, but their friendship never recovered.

She takes a breath. 'Just my parents,' she says. 'But my mother has dementia and she can be a handful. So I do some work here after school and it means I can go home and look after her and my father.' She looks at her watch. 'Which I'll have to do in a little while.'

'I'm holding you up,' Dennis says, pushing away from the table.

'It's fine,' she replies, and means it. Not many people ask her about herself any more. She doesn't want to scare him off.

He nods slowly. 'If you don't mind me asking – have you always lived with them?'

'Oh, no!' she says quickly. 'I was in Sydney for a while. A long while. But when my mother became a, uh . . . a handful, shall we say, one of us had to look after her. And my brothers and sister were otherwise occupied. So I moved back to Cairns a couple of years ago. Then I moved in with them a few months ago.'

He nods slowly. 'My nana lived with us for a while. Until she died. Mum spent more time looking after her than us kids. It's tough when they get old. Tough for them, I mean.'

There's quiet for a few seconds.

'Must be hard for you, though,' he says, placing his hands on the table and spreading his fingers as if he's trying to resist something. 'Giving up your life.' His eyes meet hers. 'Your dreams.'

She considers what he's said. 'I guess it depends on how we define what our lives are,' she says softly. 'I'm not close to my parents, but I didn't want to leave them here with no one to keep an eye on them. That's not . . . fair on them, is it?'

He sighs. 'I guess not. But didn't you want to stay there?'

'Sure.' She shrugs. 'And I also wanted to move to Paris and smoke Gauloises and talk about Vincent van Gogh's short life and Simone de Beauvoir's writing and run off with Serge Gainsbourg.'

She blushes, because she's revealed more than she meant to, but Dennis is looking at her with something resembling wonder.

'I didn't, though,' she rushes on, 'because Paris was just a dream. And staying in Sydney was also just a dream, as it turns out.'

Dennis glances out the window, where daylight is waning, then turns back to her. 'It's not too late,' he says, his eyes alight.

She feels slightly nervous, like she's waiting for him to ask her something. 'For what?'

'To go to Paris.' He waves a hand. 'Do all that other stuff.'

Now it's her turn to look out the window. 'Maybe not,' she murmurs, 'but it feels like it.'

When their eyes meet again, his are still intense and bright.

'Do you have any dreams you didn't chase?' she asks, deciding it's only fair that he reciprocate.

He smiles ruefully. 'I was going to be a pro surfer.'

'Really? I mean, I can see it.'

Now it's his turn to blush.

'You look like you fit the bill,' Patricia adds hastily, gesturing towards his torso. 'You have a tan. And you're, um . . .'

Now she's done it: set herself up to comment on his physique when that's undoubtedly unprofessional and probably puts her in the same category as Mr Blake.

'I'm what?' Dennis says teasingly.

'Athletic.' She smiles tightly to show that she's not trying to be inappropriate.

'Thanks.' He puts his elbows on the table, which shortens the distance between them.

'So you never turned pro?'

He shakes his head. 'I wasn't good enough. When I was a grommet I was surfing with MP and those guys at Kirra.'

Patricia's confusion must show on her face.

'Michael Peterson,' he explains, although Patricia is still in the dark. 'He was a few years older but he was winning things. I guess I thought I was good enough to win tournaments too, and it sounded like a great idea – travelling the world to surf.'

'So did you win anything?'

'No.' He glances down, but when their eyes meet again he holds her gaze and doesn't break it. 'My dad died. Heart attack. Sudden.'

Patricia wants to say the usual things – *I'm sorry, that's awful* – but she senses he doesn't want to be interrupted and, besides, those things are trite.

'Mum couldn't handle the mortgage on her own.' He sits back in the chair. 'So I got a job pulling beers, went to teachers college because I needed a career that I couldn't easily be sacked from, and cut back my surfing to the occasional Sunday morning.'

'That was good of you,' Patricia says, 'to support her.'

Dennis gives her a funny look. 'It's no different to what you're doing.'

'I guess that's true.' They stare at each other for a few seconds. 'So . . . you didn't marry?'

There's no point pretending she doesn't know he's single. Marjorie knows the marital status of every teacher in the school and is not withholding of the information.

'Nah.' He smiles and shrugs. 'I think I grew up a bit when Dad died, and I find it hard to meet women I can talk to. Plus I'm picky.'

He looks at her with intent. If Patricia didn't know better she'd think he's trying to tell her something – although that's impossible. She is, most decidedly, too old for him.

'Anyway,' he says, standing up abruptly, 'I've held you up long enough.'

'I don't mind,' she says, and she really doesn't. He's more interesting than she'd presumed and she wouldn't mind talking to him further.

'Might catch you again some other afternoon,' he says, and as he passes her she feels his hand press her shoulder lightly.

CHAPTER TWENTY-EIGHT

The first day's driving was reasonable: they left Cairns in daylight and arrived at Mackay before the sun set. But the second day, to Brisbane, has Dorothy wishing she'd never left home.

She's never been in a car for this long. Her parents were used to crossing countries in less time than it took them to drive from Cairns to anywhere, so long drives were not an endeavour they endorsed. 'Why would we move all this way to be here, then get in a car and go somewhere else?' her father had said when Dorothy asked if they could please-please-please drive her to Townsville when one of her best friends from school moved there.

That friend was far from Dorothy's mind as she and Frederick went through Townsville the first day. She was surprised to see it was so different to Cairns: it looked wide open to the sky, where Cairns seemed coddled by rainforest. Townsville was ordered, as befitted a garrison town, and the sun covered it in a bright yellow blanket so different to the dappled tones of home.

Brisbane definitely feels like it's in another country; if they were in the northern hemisphere it would probably be in another continent. It's not just the distance: Brisbane is a city, and she's not used to that. There are so many people here, for one thing. For another, it's dominated by a river and she can't wrap her head around the geography of that.

'The river is a double M,' Ruth had said when Dorothy expressed her concern about being able to navigate her way around, but the explanation hadn't made any sense then and doesn't now. How can she orient herself around a letter of the alphabet when she's used to an ocean?

Luckily Frederick decided she should drive so he can navigate. Driving she can handle, even if she's slightly flustered by the amount of traffic and the number of traffic lights.

'Where are we staying?' she asks as they pass a sign for the airport.

'Ascot,' he says, which means nothing to her.

Frederick spent some time in Brisbane before he made his way to Cairns, where they met. He still has friends here, one of whom has offered them a room in his house. Dorothy was reluctant to take it, because she didn't want to tell a stranger what they're doing in town. That was until Frederick told her his friend didn't ask why they were visiting, and if he did Frederick would say they felt like a change from Cairns.

Brisbane certainly is a change – with a glance to her left Dorothy can see tall buildings in what she presumes is the business area of the city. So many buildings so close together. She could never live in a place like this, with all the concrete footpaths and people walking along them. She's only noticed one park, and there's certainly no ocean.

When she was growing up and reading novels set in New York and Paris and London – the usual glamorous places people dream about visiting – she thought they sounded wonderful. And exotic. So different to her own life. Sometimes she has to remind herself that she's European and that if her parents had stayed in Germany those very cities would be mostly easy for her to visit. Because she doesn't feel European. She feels Australian. And not just Australian: she's a Far North Queenslander. Brisbane may be a small city by world standards – even in Australian terms – but it's like it belongs to a different state to the one she lives in.

Her eyes flick to and from the rear-view mirror. People in the city like to drive close and it makes her nervous. What happens if she has to slam on the brakes? They'll smash right into her rear! She can't understand why they don't know that. What's so good about this place that they're all rushing to get to it? There's no beach. There's no rainforest. There's no reef. There's probably yoga. But not with Sandrine.

Dorothy smiles as she thinks of class last week. Patricia passed wind while they were in a posture with their legs over their heads, and Dorothy laughed so much she had to come out of the pose. Grace Maud was cackling away too, in the sitting posture she'd chosen instead of the shoulder stand.

'It is to-tal-ly nor-mal, Patricia, darling,' Sandrine said as she sashayed past.

'Oh god,' Patricia groaned. She was the colour of beetroot. 'Did everyone hear?'

'*Oui.* And why are you laughing, Dorothy?' Sandrine's eyebrow arched. 'It will happen to you too.'

'Then you can laugh at me,' Dorothy had said to Patricia.

'I look forward to it,' Patricia muttered, before joining Grace Maud on the floor.

There wouldn't be a teacher like Sandrine in Brisbane. Maybe not in the whole world. And there would be no Grace Maud or Patricia in the classes here either. Dorothy used to think it was the yoga that brought her back each week, then she thought it was Sandrine. Now she knows it's both of those things, and it's also Patricia and Grace Maud. They're all learning together, and that makes her feel less inept. None of them is pretending to be any better at it than they are. Dorothy has felt vulnerable in the class – because, as Sandrine tells them, the postures open them up in ways that aren't just physical – but she knows she's not alone. She and Patricia and Grace Maud may not feel vulnerable all at the same time yet they have such similar experiences that they don't need to explain anything.

If only they were also about to go through IVF – then Dorothy wouldn't feel so alone. Frederick is supporting her, but it's not as if he'll ever really understand what's going to happen to her body. She barely understands it herself; after her GP told her how many needles were involved she didn't hear the rest.

He'd assured her that the doctors in Brisbane would explain everything. Would that include explaining why she has to come this far for treatment? Cairns isn't a backwater. Not really. They have an airport.

'You could have the treatment here,' her doctor had said, 'but there's only one specialist and he's booked up for ages. I tried to get someone in two months ago, but the wait list was so long she went to Brisbane too. It's a sacrifice travelling so far, I know – but won't it be worth it when you get your baby?'

Dorothy wanted to ask him what he knew about the sacrifice it would take. It would never be his body being poked and prodded, his subterranean bits getting explored with cold steel instruments. All while in a strange place, with only a stranger's home to go back to each day. She has to stay in Brisbane to take the hormones, then wait for her eggs to be 'harvested'.

'Delightful term,' Grace Maud said when Dorothy told her and Patricia. 'We harvest sugar cane. I hardly think it's appropriate to apply the same terminology to you.'

'I suppose "collected" would be better,' said Patricia, then frowned. 'But "collecting eggs" is what you do to chickens.'

'How about "gathering"?' Grace Maud offered.

'That's a bit mild considering what the procedure sounds like,' Patricia said. 'I really think that when they come up with a new medical process like this they should come up with new words for all the different parts and leave the existing English language alone. Why should a word like "harvest" be used to describe something that's done to a woman's body?' She shuddered. 'It makes you sound less than human, Dorothy, and I don't like it.'

Dorothy didn't like it either. But there was no other word and that's what she is in Brisbane for: to be harvested. And Frederick will do his bit, and hopefully there will be an embryo on the other side.

Frederick will have gone home by that point – he can't leave the café for that long – and Dorothy's parents are paying for her to fly home. Once she's been implanted. Another delightful term that makes her sound like an experiment.

'There's a right-hand turn coming up,' Frederick says, bringing her back to the car and the busy Brisbane road.

'Okay,' she says, checking her rear-view mirror yet again before putting on the blinker.

One more shot, that's what she told Frederick this is. One more shot to have a baby and if it doesn't work she's giving up. Or maybe she won't. It's her prerogative to change her mind. For now, though, she's committed to the needles and the cold steel instruments and the prodding.

'We're almost there,' says Frederick as she makes the turn into a clearly marked Racecourse Road, which is busier than she's ever seen one of Cairns' busiest streets. There are people strolling on the footpaths, sitting in cafés, going in and out of a bottle shop. She can see it all because there are several cars cruising slowly on this road, so she has time to look.

'That's it – Kent Street,' Frederick says, gesturing to the right.

'Oh!' Dorothy becomes flustered as she misses the turn. He could have given her more notice – although she reminds herself that he's as unfamiliar with this place as she is.

'It's all right,' he says, flashing her a smile. 'We'll take the next right and go around the block.'

She nods and puts on her blinker.

'It's all going to be all right,' he says soothingly, patting her wrist.

Dorothy hopes that turns out to be true.

CHAPTER TWENTY-NINE

'This feels a bit strange, doesn't it? Being here on a Saturday?' Patricia squints up into the sky. 'I'm not used to coming out of relaxation into sunshine.'

'Thank you for changing,' Dorothy says. 'I wanted to come to the first class I could.'

'It's nice to do something different,' Grace Maud says, swinging her handbag onto her shoulder. 'How are you feeling?'

Dorothy's shoulders sag a little, then she straightens. 'As though I've been in a washing machine. I felt like I was getting into and out of a hospital gown more than I was changing underwear!' She laughs but it's the laugh of someone trying to find the good in a situation. 'The needles aren't pleasant. The anaesthetic.' She shakes her head as if trying to ward off a fly. 'After it was all over I felt like my body didn't really belong to me any more. Do you know what I mean?'

Grace Maud remembers all too vividly the day Tom was born. The shocking pain of it; her panic at being at the farm with everyone out in the cane. Then her mother arriving just in time to deliver the small human who had occupied her for forty weeks. Grace Maud had felt like her body had been taken away – that Tom was her, and she was a husk without him. It took her several months to feel as though she belonged completely to herself again.

Now she and Tom haven't spoken for weeks and Grace Maud has no intention of being the first to make contact. How strange, she thinks, that they were once in the same body and now they are so far apart.

'I do,' she says to Dorothy. 'It's good preparation for what you'll feel like after you give birth.'

Dorothy looks pleased. 'You think I'll give birth?'

'That's the point of all of this, isn't it?' Grace Maud smiles benignly. 'Of course you will.'

She knows there's no *of course* about it, but she also knows that belief is a powerful force, and she wants to encourage Dorothy to believe.

'How did your friend Ruth go at the café while you were away?' Patricia asks as they reach the footpath.

'She was great,' Dorothy says, still looking pleased. 'I couldn't have done it without her. I offered her some permanent shifts but she says her husband isn't that keen on her doing any more work. Which is funny because he was the one badgering her to work in the first place.'

'You mean, apart from the work of taking care of him?' Grace Maud says.

'Hm.' Dorothy stops. 'Do you think . . .' She has a funny expression on her face.

Patricia matches it with one of her own. 'What?'

'Would you like to come to our café for morning tea?' Dorothy says nervously. 'I'd really love for you to see it.'

Grace Maud considers the day full of nothing stretching ahead of her and can't think of a reason to refuse. Although the humidity is so intense that she's not sure a hot beverage is in order. It's around this time of year that she starts to count down towards the wet season and the rains that will break the thickness in the air.

'Sounds lovely,' she says, and turns to Patricia.

'Great. Yes.' Patricia's eyes flit from side to side.

'Out with it,' Grace Maud says.

'What?'

'That was hardly a rapturous response.'

'I just, uh . . .' Patricia puts a hand to the side of her head. 'Do you have a phone at the café that I could use? I'll need to let Dad know that I'll be late home.'

'Of course!' Dorothy says with a big smile. 'Should we see if Sandrine would like to join us? Are we allowed to do that kind of thing?'

'She's a person, Dorothy, not a demigod,' says Grace Maud. 'I think you can ask her to morning tea.'

Dorothy's smile widens. 'I'll just pop back in.'

Grace Maud turns to Patricia. 'You're a little old to be telling your parents where you are, so I presume when you said your mother's mind wanders a bit that it's perhaps more serious than that?'

Patricia's face crumples a little, then she rights herself. 'I don't think I can trust Dad to watch her unless I specifically remind him to.' She grimaces. 'Mum always used to say she couldn't trust Dad around us kids because fathers aren't as careful as mothers. And she was right: the only injuries we got were when he was watching us. Now I have to ask him to watch her and I—' Her breath catches.

Grace Maud steps closer and puts a hand on her arm. 'You do the best you can,' she says firmly. Sternly. 'If your heart is in the right place – and from what I've observed, it most certainly is – your best is all that can ever be asked of you. You're their daughter, not their jailer.'

Patricia nods quickly but she doesn't speak.

'Are you an only child?' Grace Maud continues.

'No. I have a sister and two brothers.'

'And where are they?'

'My sister's in New South Wales. Newcastle. My brothers aren't that far away, but it's not like they're rushing to be of assistance.'

'Couldn't your sister help with your parents?'

A hollow laugh. 'I don't think so. She's too *busy*.'

'And you're not?' Grace Maud grips Patricia's arm a little tighter, then lets go as she sees Dorothy returning with Sandrine. 'You're allowed to live your life, Patricia.'

'Am I?' Patricia's eyes are bright with tears, which she blinks away as the others arrive.

Dorothy walks with Sandrine to the café while Patricia drives Grace Maud – as she already has that morning. Patricia offered to drive Grace Maud when she called to say that Dorothy would like them all to go to class together, and Grace Maud hadn't felt inclined to refuse. As independent as she likes to be, she doesn't mind being taken care of, especially when there are no strings attached.

She looks back now over the past few years of Tom doing nice things for her and wonders if he was just trying to butter her up. If so, it failed. No doubt she will seem heartless if she tells anyone outside the family just how long she's gone without speaking to her son, but that's not the reason she hasn't mentioned it to Patricia or Dorothy. It's because it's none of their business.

As they enter the café Grace Maud is intrigued to see Dorothy's husband – a tall man with long arms, which he wraps around his wife. Dorothy looks proud, and leans into him as he hugs her to his side.

'Frederick, I'd like you to meet Grace Maud and Patricia, my friends from yoga class,' she says. 'And this is our teacher, Sandrine.'

'Dorothy talks about you a lot,' Frederick says. 'I am very pleased to meet you all.'

He takes their order then leaves them to it, disappearing into the kitchen. They take a table near the front with a view of the water, and Dorothy insists that Grace Maud has the best seat.

'What a lovely idea,' Sandrine says, smiling at each of them in turn. 'This is the first time any students have asked me to join them.'

'Really?' Dorothy says. 'But you're so . . .' She looks shy again. 'Friendly.'

'It is fine,' Sandrine says. 'I completely understand. They like me to be their teacher. I liked my teacher to be that way too.'

'Who was your teacher?' Patricia asks.

'A woman in Brisbane, where I lived. Her name was Prema.'

'Prema?'

'It means "love" in Sanskrit. I do not think,' Sandrine says with a wink, 'it was her original name. She was not Indian. But she had been to India, to study. That was a few years ago. Can you imagine? No women did this. Not even now. She was remarkable. So she inspired me to keep going to class. Then she told me to become a teacher. She trained me. That is how it goes: the teacher picks the next.'

'There was no school you could go to?' Patricia asks.

Sandrine laughs. 'That would be easy, no? But there was not. In India, one teacher chooses one student to carry on their work. So that is what she did.'

'And where is she now?' asks Grace Maud.

'Still in Brisbane.' Sandrine smiles. 'But she told me, "The student has three jobs: the first is to find the teacher, the second is to love them, the third is to leave them."' She pauses and looks down. 'She knew before I did that I needed to leave.'

'Leave Brisbane?' Dorothy asks.

'Leave everything. My husband, my life.' Sandrine throws her hands in the air. 'Even my children. They are adults – I have to say this.' She laughs. 'And I did not abandon them. My daughter has even moved up here. Although she does not come to class – she thinks yoga is *boring*.'

'That's a significant amount of change in one life,' says Grace Maud.

'It was. But it was necessary. And it happened in the right way. I kept going to yoga because I was in pain – physically. Or I thought it was just physical. I was a dancer for many years. I hurt my knee and I could not continue. I tried so many treatments, but only yoga healed that pain. Do you know why?'

She looks around the table and Patricia and Dorothy shake their heads.

'Because it comes from love, not punishment. Everything else was a punishment for having been injured in the first place. Yoga taught me to love myself. To love what my body can achieve. Also to know that there is no such thing as perfection. We are all perfect. And we are all imperfect. You see?'

Grace Maud doesn't see how an ageing body can be perfect when it restricts a person so much; when all it does is remind them that they're not young and agile any more. But she presumes Sandrine won't figure that out until she too is in her seventies, by which time Grace Maud will likely be in the ground. Or in ashes. She hasn't decided her preference.

'So – if you don't mind me asking – why did you leave your husband?' Patricia says.

'Ah, well – I was in pain there too,' Sandrine says, although she looks quite cheerful about it. 'My spirit was broken, just like my body. Once I healed the body, my spirit started to heal. And I knew I could not bear to stop it – which is what he demanded.' Her face clouds temporarily. 'Sometimes we are so scared of being alone we will put up with terrible things to avoid it. But it is not scary.' She looks directly at Patricia, who glances away.

'You've been alone since?' Dorothy enquires.

'Well, that is the funny thing – I moved here and met a dashing young man.'

'Young?' Patricia is quick on the draw.

'Younger than me.' Sandrine shimmies her shoulders. 'And quite delicious.'

'Oh!' says Dorothy, looking almost shocked.

'There is life out there to be grasped,' Sandrine continues, looking at each of them and stopping at Patricia. 'Our story is never over until we are. And yoga helps us write that story.'

Patricia colours, then picks up her coffee and holds the cup at her lips.

Grace Maud isn't sure that she personally needs a lecture about these things, nor is she a fan of this hippy type of mumbo-jumbo – but perhaps it helps the younger two. Therefore, she will keep her mouth shut, and keep going to yoga for the way it makes her feel in her body. Her spirit she can take care of herself.

CHAPTER THIRTY

'How's your yoga going?' Patricia asks Marjorie as they take up their station for lunchtime playground duty, knowing full well that Marjorie wasn't at the Saturday class Patricia attended. She's still feeling slightly guilty that Marjorie introduced her to yoga in the first place and then Patricia switched classes.

Marjorie shrugs and gazes at the students in their clumps of twos and threes and fours. 'I haven't been going.'

'Why not? I thought it was doing you good.'

'I find it hard to get motivated sometimes.' Marjorie lets out a *huhh* sound. 'I know it's good for me, but I need someone to keep the pressure on me to go.'

She glances at Patricia then looks away, and Patricia realises that Marjorie's motivation for inviting her to class might not have been friendship. How self-centred of her to think that it was about her; how selfish of her to not consider that her colleague might need help.

'I've always been like it,' Marjorie says in a rush. 'I was a really good runner at school. Then I stopped school and didn't run any more. My dad said it was because I was lazy, but I think it was because I didn't have a coach any more!' She laughs, high and forced. 'I really need a coach!'

Patricia feels herself stuck in the mire of a quandary. She's not averse to the idea of being Marjorie's conscience when it comes to yoga, but – still being selfish – she loves her little Thursday night trio with Dorothy and Grace Maud, and doesn't really want to change it. She could go to a second class on Saturday – Sandrine has mentioned that practising yoga more than once a week will speed progress – but she has a lot of housework to do.

'I can go with you on Saturday every now and again,' she tells Marjorie, wanting to be helpful without committing to something she will find hard to break if she needs to.

'What's on Saturdays?' asks Dennis.

He's managed to appear without either of them noticing, as he tends to do whenever Patricia is on playground duty. She saw Gordon glaring at them recently when they were chatting while two of the boys were pretending to be boxers, so she's been on alert about Dennis since then. But not so alert that she spotted him today.

'Yoga!' Marjorie says.

'Oh yeah?' Dennis folds his arms and looks across the playground. 'Oi, Kenneth – try that again and I'll take that tennis ball off you.'

Patricia turns and sees a disgruntled-looking Year Nine shoving the ball into his pants pocket.

'What was he doing?' she says, knowing she should have spotted it before Dennis did.

'Shaping up to brand that Year Seven over there.' He nods at a small cluster of not-quite-pubescent boys. 'No wonder they're usually in the library at lunch. Probably be back there tomorrow. Anyway – yoga.' He grins at her and for some reason she grins back. 'I've been doing a bit of reading about it.'

'What have you been reading?' she asks.

'Some book called *Light on Yoga*. My mum recommended it. Turns out she's started doing yoga. Marjorie was talking about yoga the other day' – at this Marjorie looks like a startled proud parent – 'and I was thinking of giving it a crack. Mum said it was invented by a bloke so I should do all right.' There's that grin again. 'Not sure I'd be as bendy as the bloke in the book, but it might be worth a shot. Good for the hammies, Mum says.' He puts a hand to the back of his thigh, just in case Patricia's in any doubt about what he means.

'Sandrine's a great teacher, isn't she, Patricia?' Marjorie says.

'She is. And I believe that Saturday class isn't too full.'

'Is that when you go?' Dennis says, glancing quickly at her as if he doesn't care about the answer.

'I've been going on Thursday nights.' Patricia pauses, thinking of what might happen if Dennis starts attending that class. While she has no objection per se to him being there, she's not wild about the idea of him seeing her in a downward-facing dog with her bum in the air. It's safer to send him to Saturdays.

After some initial shyness about how she looks in some of the postures, Patricia's relaxed now. She doesn't think about whether or not anyone's watching her, because they're not. It's freeing, and not something that's easy for her – or most women, she thinks – to replicate in the rest of their lives. Everywhere else they go, everything else they do, their bodies are being assessed and critiqued – and not just by men. Other women can be the worst offenders. Patricia's been guilty of it too and she doesn't even know why, apart from the fact that she grew up hearing her mother and sister do it to practically every woman they knew.

'We have athletics training on Thursday nights,' Dennis says, sounding disappointed. 'So you're, ah, safe for now.'

He looks at her as if she's hurt him, and she wonders what expression she had on her face.

'The Saturday class is just as good,' she says, just as Dennis looks away.

'*Kenneth!*' he shouts. 'Get over here now and give me that ball.'

The offending Kenneth takes his time wandering over and deposits the ball in Dennis's outstretched hand.

'Sorry, I should have been watching,' Patricia says when the boy's gone again. 'Marjorie, we'd better disperse. Check the other areas.'

'I'll head to the back playground,' Marjorie says. 'See you, Dennis.'

'*Ciao*,' he says and Patricia's eyes widen.

'I learnt Italian last year,' he explains.

'Why?'

'Because I was sick of pronouncing *cappuccino* incorrectly.'

She's not sure if he's joking and can't tell from the neutral expression on his face. 'Seriously?'

'Yep. And I want to go to Italy someday. I'd like to be able to talk to the locals. By the way . . .' He turns completely towards her. '*Sei una bella donna.*'

'I have no idea what that means,' says Patricia, who became an English teacher partly because no language has ever interested her as much as her own.

'Never mind. Maybe one day you will.'

She frowns. What does *that* mean?

'Gotta run,' he says, and grins. '*Ciao*.'

'*Ciao*.'

He tosses her the ball and she catches it just in time, giggling for no apparent reason.

CHAPTER THIRTY-ONE

'They didn't have your butter,' Cecilia says as she unpacks the shopping, placing items on the kitchen bench.

'That's outrageous,' says Grace Maud drily. 'I presume there was an alternative. And please do not say margarine.'

'No, not margarine.' Cecilia smiles as she pulls out a stick of another brand of butter and waves it at Grace Maud.

'Thank you for going to the shops.'

'You're welcome.'

The shopping is now something that is in Cecilia's domain alone. Grace Maud used to insist on going, as she thought that not going meant she was starting to resign from life. But she almost had a car accident the other day and it made her think that perhaps her eyesight isn't as good as it should be for driving after all. So instead of having it tested then possibly having her licence revoked, she's chosen to not drive. Patricia picks her up for yoga; Cecilia goes to the shops. And driving to the farm is no longer something she wishes to do, so she doesn't really need to drive and her life is less stressful without it.

'I like your dress,' she says, admiring the fine cotton number she hasn't seen on Cecilia before.

'Thanks. Mum hates it. She told me when I wore it to church last Sunday.'

'Then I presume you won't be wearing it to church again.'

'No.' Cecilia starts slamming items down on the countertop.

'I hope you're not going to do that to the eggs,' Grace Maud says.

'Sorry, what?' Cecilia turns towards her and there are tears in her eyes.

'My dear – are you this upset over a dress?'

'A dress and . . .' Cecilia sighs, then huffs and shakes her head. 'I haven't seen Luca for over a week.'

'Ah.'

Grace Maud doesn't really want to involve herself in this relationship, but she can hardly be uninvolved given the parties. And if she didn't expect Cecilia to keep her informed of events – or lack of them – she'd be fooling herself.

'That's farm life,' she explains. 'When the harvest is on, everyone has to work until it's done. You can have several days in a row where you work all day, sometimes into the night.'

'But he hasn't even called!'

'The phone's in the house,' Grace Maud says gently, 'and that's a long way from some of the paddocks. If he's working far from the house he wouldn't be back until very late at night. Too late to call. And before you say he should call you in the morning, they leave before dawn.' She smiles reassuringly. 'He will call you as soon as he can. I'm quite sure of it.'

The phone in the kitchen rings and they both raise their eyebrows at each other.

Cecilia picks it up. 'Hello? Cecilia speaking,' she says breathlessly.

She listens; her eyes go to Grace Maud's and she looks startled. 'It's Tom,' she says, her hand over the receiver.

'You know I'm not taking his calls,' says Grace Maud, cross for an instant. Cecilia has been running interference for her all this time, so why would she stop now?

'You have to take this one,' Cecilia says, and startle has given way to fear.

Grace Maud's heart speeds up – she can hear the strange, dull thud of it in her ears. Her brain races through the reasons why Tom might call and Cecilia might say she has to speak to him. She swallows and puts her hand out for the phone.

'Yes?' she says curtly, because she still doesn't want to cede any ground.

'Mum?' Tom's voice is fractured, almost as if he's crying. She can't help that tug towards him – her boy is in pain – yet also can't help wondering if this is a manipulation.

'Yes, Tom,' she says with less ice.

'It's—' Now he's definitely crying.

'Tom, take a breath,' she says, and she feels Cecilia's hand holding her other wrist. It doesn't calm her because now she is sure someone has died.

She can hear his breathing, which sounds like long hiccups.

'The farm, Mum,' he says with more control. 'It's gone.'

'Gone?'

She wants to say *Where has it gone to?* as it's such an improbable concept. How can it be gone?

'There was a fire. The wind came up. We . . . we—' More long hiccups.

Grace Maud remembers her father standing on the edge of the cane fields, sweeping his hand in a semicircle and telling her that burning was an art and not for amateurs. You had to know all the conditions. He'd stopped short of saying you had to read the runes too, but it wouldn't have surprised her if he'd had superstitions.

Only once did a fire get out of control, but it was near the road and it stopped there. That seems like yesterday, and like forever ago. Time has its own logic, and its own lessons. She has been standing here saying nothing for probably five seconds, but she has travelled decades into the past, and into the future, and she knows that recriminations can last far longer than the words it takes to utter them.

She's still the head of this family and she has a job to do – and that is to do what her father would have done in this circumstance.

'Is everyone all right?' she says.

'Wh-what?'

'Are you and Viv and Luca and the workers safe?'

At the mention of Luca's name Cecilia's grip tightens.

'Yes. Yes, Mum, we're safe.' She can hear relief in his voice – the relief of that little boy whose punishment isn't as bad as he feared. 'But the house,' he goes on. 'It's burnt. There's nothing—'

Now he sobs, and she can hear a voice in the background. Not Viv's. Perhaps Luca's. The boy whose own heritage is in that place.

Grace Maud thinks of the photos of her brothers on the mantelpiece, and is grateful for the photo albums she brought with her to town. She thinks of her brothers' graves, and their parents', in a nearby paddock. Perhaps their headstones are burnt too.

Sandrine has told them a little bit about Hinduism during class. Not that yoga is Hinduism, she stresses, but from time to time she talks about the gods and the goddesses. Grace Maud likes the idea of a religion that has so many goddesses. Imagine being able to choose which one you'd like to worship, and being able to change your mind? She remembers Sandrine talking about Shiva: the destroyer; the creator. She talked about the fire that burns everything which is not authentic. How this is the fire – the *tapas*, she called it – of the yoga practice, burning off what isn't needed, and how we shouldn't be afraid of it. It's an appealing, if dramatic, thought. But Grace Maud needed that farmhouse. She needed the fields around it. She's not sure that this destruction will lead to the creation of anything but pain and grief and remorse. There is no solace for her there.

But she has to be able to offer solace to others. There's no point living this long if you can't learn to be good in a crisis.

'It will be all right,' she says to her weeping son. 'We can rebuild.'

'But the crop – it's gone. The money, Mum.'

She considers what to say next; how much to reveal. Tom knows that when Ellie Maud died she left Grace Maud the money she'd inherited from their mother, which their mother had inherited from her parents. Grace Maud hadn't inherited any of that money because she had the benefit of living on the farm – their mother had made it clear. It turned out that Ellie Maud had used the money to buy a house – with her husband's cooperation, since she couldn't buy it in her own name – hung onto it for years, then sold it once she knew she was dying. She'd put the money into an account and made Bela the executor of the will, and he had ensured that Grace Maud received every cent. She'd bought her house in town, and she has money left over. Money she's living on, frugally, because even though Tom has been insisting on paying for Cecilia and the gardener, she doesn't want to rely on him for everything. That's not fair – the last thing she wants to be is a burden. But the farm is still her responsibility, and there is no point worrying about future financial burdens if they can't take care of their most pressing problem now.

'I have some money,' she says. 'We'll sort it out.'

He's silent, and she can hear that voice again in the background of his call but still can't work out who it is.

'Where are you?' she asks.

'At the place next door.'

Grace Maud doesn't know the neighbours any more. A young couple moved in after she moved to town, and Tom didn't seem to have much to do with them.

'I'll come to you,' she says.

'Mum, you can't drive while you're upset.'

'I'm not upset, Tom. I'm fine. But Cecilia will drive me.' She looks to the younger woman, who nods. 'We're on our way,' Grace Maud says and hangs up before he can respond.

She doesn't want him asking questions about how and why she has enough money to cover that year's crop. She also doesn't want to give herself the opportunity to feel slightly pleased that the fire means they won't be discussing the very issue that has kept them apart. For now.

Without a word between them, Cecilia picks up the car keys and her handbag, Grace Maud collects her own bag, and they leave the house, and the shopping on the bench.

CHAPTER THIRTY-TWO

If Dorothy didn't have all these customers to distract her, she knows she would fall apart. But she's not going to think about it. That's what she decided this morning: *no thinking*. Then the day makes it easy for her by sending tourist after tourist through the doors for breakfast or coffee or tea or all of it. Orders for eggs, orders for toast, chitchat about the spring humidity, questions about crocodiles, questions about stingers.

Dorothy spent a minute wondering if Ruth would be interested in coming back to the café to work a couple of shifts a week – since she'd enjoyed it so much, she said, while she was covering for Dorothy – then two new customers came through the door asking for lamb's fry, which she had to tell them they didn't serve.

'What kind of country is it when a man can't get lamb's fry for his breakfast?' the man of the pair huffed.

'Shut up, Ern,' muttered the woman beside him, then she gave Dorothy one of those smiles that doesn't quite reach a person's eyes. 'We've been to a few places looking for lamb's fry.'

'We have sausage,' Dorothy said helpfully.

'Blood sausage?' the man asked, narrowing his eyes.

'Any sausage will do, love, thanks.' The woman grabbed the man's wrist and yanked him towards a table. Then she ordered for both of them: sausage, bacon, eggs, tomatoes, four pieces of toast for him, one for her, a strong pot of tea and lots of milk, and did they have sugar cubes or was it just that loose stuff in the bowl? On any other day Dorothy would have found them mildly annoying but today they've been useful, keeping her busy.

'How many people is this for?' Frederick says, squinting at the docket.

'Two.'

He raises his eyebrows and glances towards the table. 'All right,' he says, then smiles at her. Not his usual smile. A slightly sad smile. A sympathetic smile. A smile that makes her want to scream.

'Dorothy?'

She turns around and there's Patricia. Dorothy notices she has her hair pulled back and remembers Patricia telling them she's growing it out, a decision she came to after Grace Maud made a slightly unkind, if true, remark about Patricia's choppy long bob not doing much for her face.

'Should I cut it all off, then?' Patricia had said with more good grace than Dorothy would have mustered in the circumstance.

'God, no!' Grace Maud had said. 'Grow it long.'

'Long?' Patricia had frowned. 'I've never had it long.'

'Why not?'

'I wasn't allowed.'

'When?'

'When I was . . . Mum didn't like it long.'

Grace Maud had looked at her as if she was slightly stupid. 'And how old are you?'

Patricia had blushed and said nothing.

That was a week and a half ago. Dorothy hasn't seen them since. Which is, no doubt, why Patricia is here now.

'Hello, Patricia,' Dorothy says as cheerfully as she can.

'I thought I'd come to see if you're all right,' Patricia says with similarly fake-sounding cheer. 'You've never missed a class unless you've been away. And you didn't say that you were going away.'

'Oh, yes!' Dorothy trills, turning to take a plate of fried eggs from the pass. 'I'm fine!'

'Grace Maud didn't come on Thursday either.'

'What?' Dorothy stops.

'She called and said she wasn't feeling well.'

'I'll, um . . .' Dorothy nods at the eggs then quickly takes them to their table. 'How did she sound?' she asks as she returns.

'Tired. So maybe she has a little bug. She has Cecilia there so if anything is really wrong, at least there's someone to check on her. And I don't want to . . . be nosy, you know?'

'I do.'

They stare at each other.

'You probably think I'm being nosy coming here to check on you,' Patricia adds, and laughs in a we-both-know-I'm-pretending-this-is-funny way.

Dorothy blinks a few times, because the prickle around her eyes tells her that crying is imminent, and it's ludicrous to feel so emotional about someone coming to see how she is. But Frederick has stopped asking – at Dorothy's request; and she doesn't want to tell Ruth because she's too embarrassed; and her parents would never pry like that. So Patricia is the first person to express concern today and Dorothy didn't realise she needed it so much.

'Dorothy?' Patricia is leaning closer. 'I'm so sorry – I didn't mean to upset you.'

The ding-ding of the bell at the pass tells Dorothy that more food is ready and she scurries away to pick it up and deliver it before coming back.

'Can we go outside for a couple of minutes?' Patricia asks gently.

Dorothy glances at Frederick, who half smiles and nods slowly. Thank goodness for the times when they can read each other's mind.

She pushes open the café door and leads Patricia around the corner. The Kombi van is long gone now and in its place is a rundown Mazda bearing a *Joh for PM* sticker. Dorothy is sure it's been abandoned. The air feels cloying and makes the stray hairs from her plait stick to her neck. It's hot in the café too, near the kitchen, but at least the fan is going. Out here she feels like the humidity is closing in on her, just like her mind is.

'What's happened?' Patricia asks, not standing too close.

Dorothy has noticed, more than once, that Patricia is very good at the choreography of social interaction. Perhaps it's because she's a teacher and she has to control students. Or perhaps she's simply considerate.

This time Dorothy gives in to the prickle around her eyes, and feels warm tears sliding down her cheeks. 'I'm bleeding,' she says, then shrugs and blows air out of her mouth, trying to make it sound like an accident. A slip-up. Not a big deal.

Why does she do that? Why do all the women she knows do that? They'll have something serious to say and their tears can be so thick that they're running down their necks, and still they'll smile in the middle of it all, maybe even laugh, trying to tell a different story. Although Dorothy's never sure who that story is for – the woman herself or the person watching? It's strange behaviour, but she's always done it. She wouldn't know how to cry in front of someone and actually give in to it. What might happen if women really succumb to their pain? To the anguish of not getting what they really want, either because they've been told they can't have it, or because nature is conspiring against them? Or sometimes because life just seems so hard that what they see is an unscalable peak, always in sight yet beyond their reach.

'Oh,' Patricia says, and there is anguish in it. She hugs Dorothy tightly and says into the side of her head, 'I'm so sorry. After everything you went through.'

Dorothy brings her arms up around Patricia's back and returns the hug. She feels something like a fracture in her chest and knows that she can't allow it to go further. She can't let go here, in public, with a woman she is very fond of but hasn't known for long. So she drops her arms and moves back.

Patricia looks surprised for a second.

'We'll try again,' Dorothy says, sniffing, bringing her wrist to the top of her cheeks to absorb the tears.

'In Brisbane?'

Dorothy nods vigorously. 'We have to.'

Patricia glances towards the water. Dorothy can hear seagulls and feels that crack in her chest again. Out there, life is easy and free – water laps in the harbour, birds live their bird life, fish swim, boats sail. In here, in her body, in her head, she feels trapped by the task she's set herself and has to keep remembering that she's doing it because she believes she will be free on the other side. She will become the mother she wants to be. She and Frederick will be the parents they have planned to be. She will have a child she can love always. That love will be her freedom. Her eternity.

'I don't want to be more nosy than I already am,' Patricia says, 'so I won't ask you how you are all the time. But you can always tell me.' Her gaze is direct and sincere. 'I am your friend, I hope. And you are mine.'

'Yes,' Dorothy says, and ducks her head to flick away more tears. It's her hormones; it must be.

'I know you may not feel like coming back to class, but I think Sandrine would say it could help you,' Patricia continues, her voice heavy with concern. 'I know it helps me when I'm feeling low. It's a distraction. I don't think about anything except the pain I'm in!' She laughs nervously.

'When do you feel low?' Dorothy asks. Patricia always seems so calm and in control of her life. She can't imagine her not being able to cope with anything.

'Only sometimes,' Patricia says airily. 'When I'm worrying about my parents getting frailer, or when my sister has said something mean. Nothing major. Nothing like you've experienced. But I think yoga can help in proportional ways, if you know what I mean.'

Dorothy nods. 'Yes. But sometimes it feels like it's ripping me apart.'

'Me too. Sandrine says that's normal. You can feel a bit pushed and pulled but there's no other method for really finding out what you're made of.' She stares at Dorothy for a few seconds. 'I know that you are made of strong stuff. You may not even realise that yourself.'

'I think . . .' Dorothy's breath catches in her chest. 'I feel like I'm made of mess at the moment.'

'Of course. I understand.'

And Dorothy can tell she does. Sometimes she thinks Patricia has worked out exactly who Dorothy is but she still wants to talk to her. To be her friend. It's a rare gift of acceptance, and Dorothy can only hope she offers it in return.

Patricia bends to kiss her on the cheek. 'I hope to see you in class on Thursday. But I'll be thinking of you in between.'

She turns and walks down the footpath, away from the water, and Dorothy realises her car is probably parked there.

The café door opens and Frederick sticks his head out, looking at her inquisitively.

'Coming,' Dorothy says, plucking her order pad and a pen out of her apron. She glances in Patricia's direction and sees her friend raise her hand to pull at her ponytail. How lucky, Dorothy thinks, that she knows someone who cares about her enough to come to check on her. To support her. That day Dorothy first wandered away from this café and towards that yoga class, she could not have known what Orange Blossom House would bring her. Now she does, and it gives her the strength to walk back inside, sniff back her tears and get on with her day.

CHAPTER THIRTY-THREE

'Thank you for driving me,' Grace Maud says as the car approaches the turn-off to the road she knows so well. The one that used to lead home and now leads to a sight she doesn't want to see, but has to.

'I'm glad I could come with you,' Cecilia says, putting on the blinker.

In silence, they pass fields that not so long ago were abundant with cane. Now they're the mangled landscape of a broken heritage: burnt plants, twisted out of shape; all the years of toil by the men in her family, and the men who worked with them, gone. All the care that Grace Maud put into sustaining the business to ensure it would be hers and Tom's, and no one else's, is sunk into that soil. Who knows how long it will take to remake what they've lost.

After Tom's phone call, Grace Maud had thought she wanted to head out immediately to see the damage. But then she considered what she would see when she got there, and realised that she wasn't ready to have her memories irrevocably altered. She wanted to remember the farm the way it was just a little bit longer.

It's the same reason she didn't want to see either of her parents dead. She wanted to remember them alive, and seeing them dead would mean she might only think of them dead. Ellie Maud had been different: she'd gone to the funeral home after their mother died, viewed the body, said her goodbyes. She wasn't here, though, when their mother died. So maybe she needed to check for herself.

Grace Maud didn't need to see for herself that the farm had been destroyed – she heard it in Tom's voice. So she went to see him at the neighbours' place instead, and held onto her memories for a few more days. Cecilia had brought her breakfast, lunch and dinner, and even stayed up late a couple of nights, too worried to go to sleep, but Grace Maud was too deep inside her grief to really know what was going on.

Then the time came – she felt it – when she needed to make the drive so familiar to her that she recognises each groove in the road. She needs to see her son again. Tom hasn't come to visit her, whether from shame or heartache or an acknowledgement that technically there's still a breach between them, Grace Maud doesn't know. She isn't angry at him – how can she be? The fire wasn't his fault. Or she doesn't think it was. He won't say exactly what happened. Won't tell her who was meant to be watching.

They burn that cane several times a year and the rules and the pattern are always the same; and they've had the same workers the past few harvests, so it wasn't as if someone didn't know what to do. Maybe they were complacent. Maybe it was Luca. Grace Maud doesn't want to think about that possibility. Not because she wouldn't forgive him – she would, because he's Ellie Maud's grandson – but because she wouldn't want him to carry the guilt. He's a sensitive boy, still figuring out his place in the world. Everyone makes mistakes. If this is his, despite the devastation it has wrought, they can work their way through it. Although she may never know.

When the car approaches the husk that used to be the house, Grace Maud hears Cecilia gasp. The girl has never been here before, but she doesn't need to know what was there to appreciate what has been lost.

Grace Maud keeps her gaze straight ahead, not daring to look at the fields closest to the house. At what's left of the scores of years of her father's work and her own after it. Those home paddocks were as familiar to her as her own body, because she used to gaze out at them each morning. Now they're empty.

She goes to open the car door but it's wrenched open before she gets the chance.

'Mum.' Tom puts out his hand to help her alight.

She thinks he might cry again and isn't sure she can endorse that kind of behaviour on a regular basis. Her father didn't cry when his sons died; nor did her mother. That means Grace Maud doesn't cry either. Tom has had his cry on the phone, and that was understandable, but they need to buck up now.

She feels something like satisfaction when she sees that he looks tired and a decade older, but he's not crying. 'Tom,' she says, accepting his kiss on her cheek. She'd considered being stern with him – perhaps even trying to talk about the matter that has come between them – but she can see that sternness wouldn't be appropriate. He's grieving too.

They walk together to stand next to the stilts that are all that's left of their old Queenslander. Grace Maud can smell smoke and wonders if this is how funeral pyres smell. Ellie Maud and Bela went to India once, to Varanasi, to stand beside the Ganges and watch as the burning pyres were put into the water. Ellie Maud had told her sister about the smell, how it was almost reassuring. The rituals of death and life, she'd said, were comforting. This doesn't smell like a ritual, though – it just smells like death. Death of history, of effort, of dreams, of money. Of family. Her family.

Then Grace Maud remembers about a very important part of the property.

'What happened to the graves?' she says, and Tom's face contorts.

'The stones got damaged.' He shakes his head. 'I'm so sorry, Mum.'

He turns to look to the west, across the expanse of their land, and she remembers the little boy who used to follow her around as she gave instructions to the workers and saddled up a horse to go and inspect the crops. This place is in his blood as much as her own blood is in him.

'It's not your fault, Tom,' she says. 'We've been lucky all these years not to have something like this happen. Wind changes . . .' She shakes her head. 'It's just luck.'

'Are you trying to make me feel better, Mum?' he says, glancing in her direction.

'Are you going to tell me that would be a first?'

He turns completely towards her and smiles. Probably the first smile he's made in days. 'Is that you making a joke?'

'Perhaps. Enjoy it while you can.'

Out of the corner of her eye she sees Luca and Cecilia standing together, their body language betraying their affection for each other. She has no idea if Tom knows about the relationship, and wasn't intending to say anything. Now she doesn't think she'll have to.

'Hi, Grace Maud.' It's Viv, her face puffy, her hair flying everywhere.

She pulls Grace Maud into a hug and Grace Maud pats her twice on the back.

'I'm so sorry that you don't have a home,' Grace Maud says once they've separated.

'I'm sorry *you* don't.' Viv sniffs and wipes her nose with the back of her hand.

Grace Maud almost smiles: when Viv first arrived she was quite the lady, and now she's become a bushie.

'The neighbours have been great,' Viv continues. 'They have workers' quarters that are empty so we've been staying there.' She pulls at her shirt. 'I just wish I had some other clothes to wear. I stink of smoke. Sorry.'

'Why are you apologising?' Grace Maud says. 'You haven't done anything to hurt me.'

Viv's eyes meet hers and widen. If Grace Maud were more suspicious by nature, she might think Viv had something to confess. But she's not, and she's never been a fan of whodunnits, so she doesn't want to know if Viv is trying to admit to something nefarious.

As much as she's not a fan of lying – it has a habit of complicating matters – Grace Maud has never been interested in rigour around the truth. Some people insist on it – live by it – but in her experience the truth is rarely what it's cracked up to be. The stories we tell ourselves are of more interest; and in time, of course, those stories can become the truth. So Grace Maud knows that the truth of what has happened to this farm is already changing, and if she were to insist on knowing it she may discover that it's both far more damaging and far less interesting than a story.

'I presume the insurance payments are up to date?' she murmurs to Tom. That's one of the jobs that now falls to him.

'Yes, but I don't expect to get anything from them.' His voice is hard. 'They'll find a way to make sure the cause of the fire is nothing we can claim on. Don't know why we pay those bloody premiums.'

'Just see how you go,' Grace Maud says.

She glances at the paddock opposite the house, then shuts her eyes. She doesn't want that image, that wreckage, in her mind. She wants to remember the lush, tall green plants she grew up with; the plants she used to hide in so her brothers had to come looking for her. The plants that sustained her financially throughout her adult life.

'It's hard to look at,' Tom says softly. 'I try to make myself, but I can't.'

'I understand,' Grace Maud says. 'I had to come, but . . .'

'Now you want to leave?' He puts a hand on her shoulder. 'We'll make it right, Mum, I promise.'

Grace Maud nods. 'We still have that other matter to resolve.'

'Not now, Mum,' he says, sounding irritated.

'Why not now? You have a blank slate.' She gestures to the burnt fields.

As soon as she says it, she knows she shouldn't have. It was a mean thing to do. But she couldn't not mention the issue that has been between them these past few weeks. She doesn't want to be in that limbo again, even if it was one of her own creation. It doesn't make sense to wait for everything to be rebuilt before they confront the fact that Tom's wishes for the future don't match her own.

'Grace Maud,' Viv says, looking shocked. 'It's too soon.'

'I'm sorry to upset you, Viv, but this is no time to stall over sentiment. This is still our family property. There's still a business here. And while you and Tom are rebuilding, it will surely factor into your thinking that you want to rebuild the way you want it to be. Just you. Not me.' Grace Maud looks at the stilts. 'But they were my family photos in that house. My memories. My brothers, gone. My parents, gone. My sister, gone. So you might appreciate that I have some interest in sorting out exactly what is to be done here.'

Viv makes a noise that suggests she's almost crying.

'Mum, please.' Tom wraps his arms around his wife.

Perhaps it *is* too soon. Perhaps she has been unkind. But what she sees here – the evidence that there aren't even remnants of her family members left – makes her realise that she is, most likely, profoundly alone in this world, and she needs to act fiercely to look after herself.

'I think I'll take myself home,' she says, although she knows that will upset Cecilia even as it pleases Tom and Viv.

She walks briskly to the car, buckles herself into the passenger seat, and waits for Cecilia to realise it's time to go.

CHAPTER THIRTY-FOUR

The knock on the door is firm and loud enough to be heard over the radio that Grace Maud has taken to keeping on all day. ABC Classic FM. Less vexing than talkback radio but with enough strident symphonies to keep her engaged with the day.

Another two taps. A pause. Three taps.

Grace Maud waits, hoping whoever it is will leave. This area isn't known for door-knockers of the religious or sales persuasion, but it doesn't pay to take chances. She doesn't want to be trapped into talking to someone whom only rudeness on her part will dislodge. Not that she objects to being rude on occasion, but she doesn't have the energy for it today.

Another two taps.

There's no way anyone can see her from outside: the pane of glass on the front door is at the top, over the head of all but the tallest people. So if she stays very still they'll eventually leave.

'Grace Maud!'

She sinks a little into the couch. It's not a door-knocker.

'Grace Maud, it's Patricia and Dorothy!'

Lovely. A double ambush. She had thought that neither of them would believe they knew her well enough to come looking for her when she didn't turn up to class. That way she wouldn't have to tell them what's happened.

It's so much easier to handle bad things when one doesn't have to talk about them. She knows the new fashion is to *talk about your feelings* – she blames Americans and their fondness for 'therapy', as popularised on television shows and in movies – but Grace Maud has survived very well by saying not much at all about her feelings. After Ellie Maud died, Tom wanted her to 'talk about it, Mum. Come on, don't bottle it up'. But Grace Maud wanted to bottle it up. Her grief was hers, and she wanted to keep it to herself. It would disperse if she talked about it, and she wanted to keep it close, because that meant keeping Ellie Maud close.

There is no evidence, Grace Maud thinks now, none at all, that talking about grief makes it any less intense. It just makes it shared. And a problem shared is not a problem halved. It's a problem shared.

'*Grace Maud!* I know you're home – your car's here!'

This is a trick statement, as the car is parked in the garage at the rear of the property. But she admires Patricia's pluck.

Her body betrays its lack of stretching as she pushes up from the couch, and her hips tell her that she needs to move them more as she slowly walks to the radio to turn it down.

Another two taps on the door.

'I'm here,' she says imperiously, hoping this will signify that she really doesn't want to be bothered and that they should leave as soon as possible.

As she opens the door she sees Patricia looking very much like the schoolteacher she is.

'I'm surprised you're not waving a finger at me and saying, "tsk tsk",' Grace Maud says. She turns and walks back towards the sitting room.

'No "hello" then?' Patricia says, and Grace Maud hears the door close quietly.

'Hello,' she says over her shoulder.

'We didn't want to bother you,' says Dorothy with that apologetic tone in her voice that drives Grace Maud mad on occasion. The girl is far too sorry for everything. If you give people excuses to blame you for things, they'll take them.

'Then why are you here?' Grace Maud glares at both of them as she sits heavily.

Patricia frowns. 'Grace Maud, I really don't think this is like you,' she says.

'Then you don't know me.'

'I've seen you in downward-facing dog every week for the past few months. I think I know you pretty well.'

She sits without being invited, directly opposite Grace Maud. Dorothy takes another chair and folds her hands in her lap, her plait resting on her shoulder.

'What's happened?' Patricia asks, more gently.

Grace Maud wants to say that she'd have told them already if she wanted them to know. But she can't blame them for being curious. The three of them have become fairly familiar with each other. She might have withheld details about herself, but Patricia has talked about the difficulties of managing her parents, and Dorothy has been completely honest about her challenges falling pregnant. They've indicated that they are including Grace Maud in their lives, but she's done nothing much to include them.

This is the first time she's thought about that, actually. She's taken lifts from Patricia, offered advice to them both when it's been asked for – and sometimes when it hasn't – and talked about yoga poses with them. They've chatted about Sandrine, discussed tourists in town and politicians in Canberra, and whether or not they still watch *A Country Practice* (Grace

Maud has never watched it but she reads about it in the newspaper) – the sorts of things that friends talk about. That *familiar* friends talk about. No wonder they've turned up at her doorstep.

Still, she's unsure of what will happen if she tells them; she doesn't know how this script will run, and at her age maybe it's too late to take those sorts of chances.

'Nothing you need to worry about,' she says, which is the truth. They can't unburn the farm.

'But we *are* worried,' says Dorothy, her face pinched. 'We've been very worried. It's not like you to just not come to class three times in a row.'

'Maybe I'm sick of it,' Grace Maud says, pursing her lips.

'We all know that's not true.' Patricia stares at her in an accusatory way. 'The last time you were there you said how much looser your back feels.'

'I really don't have to explain anything to you,' Grace Maud snaps.

Patricia glances at Dorothy, who looks upset.

'No, you don't,' Patricia says. 'But we'd like you to. We may not be able to help you. But maybe we can. Have you ever considered that?'

For so much of her life Grace Maud never considered if she needed help with anything. She had Ellie Maud on the end of the phone, always helpful and encouraging. They never unburdened themselves to each other; they never had to. They knew the nuances of each other's voices and that was enough. That shorthand they had – it took her a long time to realise that other people may never find that. After Ellie Maud died, Grace Maud missed it so much; missed knowing someone so intimately. She never wanted to know someone like that again, even if she could, because losing them was so hard.

Tom had told her once that she kept him at a distance because she was so used to having her sister to talk to. He said she didn't understand what it was like for him, knowing that his own mother chose her sister over him. Her response was to tell him that he was being selfish. But he wasn't – he was being honest. If she'd tried harder with him then, maybe they wouldn't be so far apart now.

If she tries harder with Patricia and Dorothy, maybe they could become . . . not replacements for Ellie Maud, but, at the least, a reconnection to the world around her.

She looks at Dorothy's worried face, then Patricia's more stern visage, and sniffs. 'Fine. The farm burned down.'

Dorothy gasps.

'How much of it?' Patricia asks.

'All of it.' Grace Maud closes her eyes briefly. 'Well, most of it. The house. Most of the fields. The wind picked it up . . .'

She closes her eyes again. Someone takes hold of her shoulder, and when she opens her eyes she sees Patricia.

'That's terrible.' Patricia's eyes fill with tears. 'I'm so very sorry that this happened to you.'

'Grace Maud, I had no idea.' Dorothy's hands are entwined, her knuckles white. 'I read in the paper about a fire near Atherton but I didn't know it was your place. They didn't say who owned it.'

'Was anyone hurt?' Patricia asks.

'No. Thankfully. Tom and his wife and my great-nephew are staying with their neighbours. They don't want to come to town. And I . . .' Grace Maud glances around. 'I don't have room for them anyway.'

'What will happen now? Will you rebuild?' Patricia has let go and Grace Maud misses the feeling of warmth on her skin.

She nods. 'They'll replant the cane. As for the house – I don't know.' She feels her resolve faltering and knows it will show on her face. 'I don't think they can ever replace what was there.'

'Did you lose much?' Dorothy says softly.

'Photos. Some letters. I brought a lot of it here but I left a few things there . . .' She laughs at herself. At the absurdity of thinking that everything would stay the same. That she could move from that place and keep it the way it was when she lived there. That Tom and Viv would never change it, or time would never alter it. That fate wouldn't have its hand in everything. 'I made it a shrine. To my family,' she says. 'How ridiculous.'

Her inhalation is ragged and Patricia's hand is back on her shoulder, squeezing gently.

'I feel as though my whole life has been lost,' Grace Maud whispers, and she bows her head because she feels it's true. 'That's why I haven't been to yoga.'

'I see.' Patricia squeezes Grace Maud's shoulder again before removing her hand. 'That's understandable. But you're coming back.'

'I don't feel like it,' Grace Maud says.

'I don't care.' Patricia stands up and puts her hands on her hips. 'It will be good for you.'

'I'm not interested in that.'

'Well, I am. And I think Dorothy is too.'

'I am!' Dorothy declares and stands up herself.

Grace Maud almost laughs because it looks as though she's being ganged up on by two slightly annoyed library monitors.

'You need yoga,' Dorothy says. 'Just like I do. It's good for you. And it's a distraction. I'm so busy thinking about what my body's doing that I always forget what I'm worrying about.'

'Same for me,' says Patricia. 'So I'll pick you up on Thursday night, and if you don't want to come I'll have to consider hiring a man to lift you into the car.'

'Do you know such a man?' Grace Maud says, and is amused to see a slightly guilty look on Patricia's face.

'Maybe,' she says meekly.

'Really?' Dorothy is agog.

'We're not discussing this,' Patricia says. 'We're going to leave you alone now, Grace Maud, but I'll be back on Thursday.'

'And I'll be waiting for you in class!' Dorothy says, before following Patricia to the door like a duckling chasing its mother.

The lack of ceremony in their departure and of sentiment in their statements reassures Grace Maud that perhaps these two women do understand her just a little.

Which doesn't mean she will acquiesce to Patricia's demand. But as the front door closes behind them, she starts to consider it.

SUMMER 1993/1994

Blue Heelers premieres on the Seven Network.

Mrs Doubtfire, starring Robin Williams, is released.

Whoopi Goldberg's *Sister Act 2* is
released in time for Christmas.

American TV series *The X Files* airs for
the first time on the Ten Network.

Heartbreak High has its debut on the ABC.

'All for Love', performed by Sting, Rod Stewart and Bryan
Adams, tops the Australian singles chart for two weeks.

Schindler's List, directed by Steven
Spielberg, is released in Australia.

CHAPTER THIRTY-FIVE

Another Christmas Day, another opportunity for the womenfolk to spend hours in the kitchen, sweating as they roast fowl in the oven and cook things on the stovetop, all in the name of preserving the traditions of a hemisphere many have never visited. Patricia used to think this when she was younger, and now she's cursing it, because these days she's the one in the kitchen. Her mother stopped cooking – or was stopped, rather – a couple of years ago, after Patricia realised she could no longer be trusted around anything that involved temperatures above twenty degrees. That's how Patricia's found herself having to uphold Christmas culinary practices she disparages because it's 'always been done this way' and who is she to question it?

She's the one doing all the work, that's who, but Annette and Peter and their families, in attendance at Christmas lunch this year, think it's outrageous that Patricia would suggest they have a cold meal. Peter, who can't even boil an egg. And Annette, who brings a salad – the one cold element she'll allow apart from the ham – and spends a considerable amount of time talking about how tedious it is to shred lettuce in a hotel room.

So Patricia finds herself in a sleeveless dress and an apron, her hair stuck to the sides of her head because the ceiling fan does nothing to dissipate the humidity, listening to her family members having a wonderful time as they drink and chat in the living room.

Annette wafts in at one point and cursorily asks if she can help, but Patricia knows this is a performance and her own part is to say, 'No, I'm fine'. She isn't fine – she's panicking about the timing of bringing everything together at the table – but she doesn't actually want Annette in here with her.

Patricia opens the oven door to check on the turkey. She hates turkey. Such a dry, tasteless bird. No one likes turkey, yet they persist in having it for Christmas lunch because they've always had it. There are so many things in this world that persist because they always have. She never used to question that practice as much as she does now. Thanks to yoga, probably. Specifically, to Sandrine asking them why they should hang onto their stiffness, their aches and pains, simply because they've always had them. Because they're safe.

When Patricia started to feel the tightness in her neck and shoulders release – when she unfurled, almost literally, from that cave she'd created with the top half of her body – it was terrifying, because she finally understood that she'd been hiding inside herself all that time, fearful of showing herself to anyone and not being loved for what is really there. So she understands how other people can be reluctant to let go of something that they believe has been in their interests for a long time. Yet she also knows what came on the other side of that release: not just freedom of movement but an epiphany. She held onto something that wasn't serving her for too long simply because she was unsure of what was on the other side, even though it had a very good chance of being better.

Since then, she's seen so many opportunities in the world around her for people to change, to improve, when they're holding onto something old. The teacher in her wants to share her knowledge, but the civilian part of her knows that's rude. All she can do is lead by example.

Except she's prevented from setting an example in her own family because none of them will let her lead. They're happy to load her up with all the responsibility – of cooking today, of looking after their parents – but they won't allow her to make the decisions that could alleviate her burden just a little.

'How far away is it?'

Patricia turns at her brother's voice. 'About half an hour,' she says, trying to fluff up her hair.

'Seriously?' Peter goes to the fridge, opens it, pulls out a tinny. 'I'm starving.'

'Well, if you'd deigned to help me, it could have moved faster.'

He looks at her as if she's said something disgusting, then starts laughing. 'Yeah, right. That's not my job.'

'What is your job, then?'

She hadn't meant to get into this today but she's hot, her dress is sticking to her legs with sweat, she's sick of doing everything and he's provoked her.

He grins and opens the tinny. 'To eat.'

She wants to slap him.

'Peter, would it occur to you for a moment that I have my hands full here? And I don't just mean Christmas lunch.'

A slurp of the beer. 'Jeez, now I know why John stayed away this year. Did you give him this lecture last year?'

'It's not a lecture,' she says quietly. 'It's a statement of fact.'

'Splitting hairs,' he says with the shorthand of siblings.

'They're your parents too. I shouldn't have to do everything on my own.'

'I have a wife and kids.' He says it so matter-of-factly, laying it down like the trump card he knows it is.

'So if I were married and had children and you were single, you'd be living here and looking after them?'

He stares at her, and she knows it's the first time this idea has been put to him.

'No point discussing that,' he says, 'because it's never gonna happen.'

She knows that he's referring to her being married with children more than the idea of him being the one to care for their parents.

'Do you need a hand?' Annette asks again as she enters the room.

'I'm not ready yet.'

'Still?' Annette makes a face. 'You've been in here for *hours*.'

'Because it *takes* hours, Annette,' Patricia snaps. 'When's the last time you cooked Christmas lunch all by yourself?'

Annette's mouth opens, then she too goes to the fridge and pulls out the salad.

'I'll put the dressing on,' she says.

'The lettuce will get soggy by the time everything else is ready,' Patricia says exasperatedly.

Annette shoves the salad back into the fridge. 'I'm just trying to *help*! Peter, why aren't you doing something to help?'

'You girls have it all worked out,' he says, then salutes them with his beer and leaves.

Patricia catches the sharp glance Annette sends her way. When they were younger they'd occasionally be in agreement about one thing: that Peter was skating through life, mainly because their parents thought the sun shone out of him.

'If you were really trying to help,' Patricia tells her sister, 'you'd come up here every now and again and give me a break.'

She stops and presses her hands on the kitchen bench. She

hadn't meant to say that, and she knows how it will be received. So there's only one thing to do now.

'Sorry,' she says. 'I'm just tired.'

Annette looks mildly triumphant for a second, then something else settles on her face. Something that looks almost like care, if not concern.

'It's school holidays now,' she says, 'so you shouldn't be as tired.'

Patricia keeps pressing her hands down to stop herself telling Annette that it isn't school that makes her tired. That it actually energises her to be around the students, because while some of them will never be interested in learning, several of them are, and each year she has the chance to encourage a young person to open their mind and dream and discover. The tiredness she feels now is a tiredness of spirit, not of body. It's the tiredness of defeat, of knowing that for all her efforts to look after her mother properly, she can't do it on her own. It's the tiredness of having no way out; of knowing that this is her life for the next however long.

The GP says her mother is in fine physical condition and could go on like this for years. Many years. But Patricia doesn't know if *she* can. When the road only has one destination, being stuck on it in a car with no change in gear and no way to unlock the doors is a deeply unpleasant sensation, made worse by the knowledge that part of you doesn't want to get off that road because it's duty that put you on it in the first place, and wanting to get off means you're failing in your commitment to the ones you love.

But there's something else Patricia's been learning: that she has to put herself first. Because she can't take care of her parents properly if she can't take care of herself. Yet so much in her life is preventing her from doing that. She can almost feel her breaking point coming, and desperately wants to stop herself before it does. Yet here are her sister and her brother, with no intention of helping her. And they will be the first to criticise if she can't adequately care for their parents.

They are never going to see her point of view, though. That wouldn't be in their interest. She's here, doing the job they should all be sharing; they have no incentive to change things. So it's up to her to work out how to look after herself while also continuing to take care of her responsibilities, and never mentioning the juggle to any of her siblings because they simply don't care. For now, seeming to agree with Annette would feel not like surrender but safeguarding her own wellbeing.

'You're right,' Patricia says. 'I shouldn't be tired.'

Annette gives a little nod of her head. 'I'll come back later to do the salad,' she says, turning away.

'Thank you.'

Alone again, Patricia puts her elbows on the counter and her head in her hands and lets herself cry for ten seconds, then goes back to what she was doing before she was interrupted.

CHAPTER THIRTY-SIX

Another trip south, another occasion to feel both wretched and hopeful. Except this time they drive the first stretch through torrential rain, thanks to the advent of the wet season in the far north. In the back seat, Dorothy clutches her abdomen and wishes she could fall into a hole instead of returning to a city that is still strange to her and will always be.

'Ovarian hyperstimulation,' her doctor in Cairns told her when she went to see him with a bloated belly and more pain than any period had ever given her. Apparently it's a not uncommon side effect of the hormones she's been injecting herself with to stimulate the follicles in her ovaries – as the name suggests.

Her doctor also told her that it can be quite dangerous and that perhaps she shouldn't go to Brisbane. But Dorothy said that would be a waste of her overstimulated ovaries, because if she doesn't go to Brisbane what point is there in taking all those hormones? The solution, her doctor said, was for Dorothy to lie on the back seat and to try not to 'agitate' herself.

However, being un-agitated isn't really an option when she feels like this: not so much as if she's a ripe watermelon as a fermenting one. She can almost feel her follicles popping out eggs – except the doctor said that was clearly a figment of her imagination and she could try being less fanciful.

Dorothy wanted to tell him to try being her for half an hour and see how much he likes it. Instead she smiled and thanked him and left. There was no prescription that could help her apart from 'stop taking the hormones', and having come this far that's not advice she's prepared to follow. This baby is a project now, and one she has to believe in.

Sandrine said the other day that if Dorothy couldn't believe in the baby no one else was going to do it for her. 'And you want the *bébé* to feel welcome, *non*?'

The simple way she said it – as if the baby's arrival is a matter of time, not chance – made Dorothy feel more confident than she has since the process started. Sandrine would no doubt say that Dorothy has taken control of her own mind and that has made the difference in her attitude. Perhaps it has. But she didn't arrive at this new awareness without doing all the work in yoga class, and trying to meditate outside it.

That's why she's brought some yoga books with her to keep her company while she's in Brisbane. She ordered a couple at the local bookshop after Sandrine recommended them, and ordered *Yoga Journal* from the newsagent, who seemed to think it was a magazine for nudists and 'those bloody vegetarians'. Obviously he believes that nudists and vegetarians are of a piece. Dorothy hasn't met a nudist and has barely met a vegetarian so she can't really say.

'How are you feeling, *Liebling*?' Frederick asks.

Dorothy hates that he has to sit in the front alone, like a chauffeur. She isn't very good company for him in her horizontal position across the back seat.

'The same,' she says, trying to make her voice sound strong. He's probably sick of her sounding weak; she certainly is. 'The doctor said it could last for a few days. I guess it will stop when they take the eggs.'

'I suppose you can't sleep lying like that,' he says sympathetically.

'Not easily. But I'm trying to doze.' She certainly needs to sleep. The pain has kept her awake the last couple of nights. 'I'm sorry that I'm so boring.'

He turns his head a little to smile at her. 'You never bore me.'

'Really? I bore myself.' Her eyes close even without her wanting them to.

'Ah, but you don't see you the way I see you. You know how you say I'm so handsome and strong?'

Her eyes open. 'You are!'

He laughs. 'I love that you think so, but I do not see myself that way. I think I am a little bit tubby and a little bit ugly.'

'Don't talk that way about my husband, please,' Dorothy says primly.

'This is what I mean. You see me as someone else.'

'I see you as you are.'

'And I see *you* as you are. So when I tell you that you cannot bore me, please believe it.' He's silent for a few moments, then adds, 'Every day with you is an adventure. It has been from the start.'

Dorothy thinks about her life, which doesn't seem that daring or interesting. She wakes up, she goes to work, she tries her best, she goes home, she tries her best there too. There are no adventures.

'I'm trying to work out what you mean,' she says. 'I don't think I can.'

He laughs. The sound is kind, reassuring. 'You embrace every day, my Dorothy. As if it is a chance to start over. Even when you are sad, you try to find the good in the day. You are . . . *einzigartig*.'

Unique; her German vocabulary is still good enough to remember that.

'That is what I mean,' Frederick goes on, 'when I say every day is an adventure: however it starts, there is no telling where it will end. You are not afraid of that. I think you even like it.'

'Hm.' Dorothy thinks about it some more, although she still doesn't really understand what he means. It's enough that he believes it, though.

'I saw your yoga books in the suitcase,' Frederick says. 'You are really interested in it, aren't you?'

'Yes – I've learnt a lot about my body. I know I've told you that, and how the breathing helps when I'm feeling stressed. But it's so strange . . . It just makes sense. Do you know what I mean? So I want to know more. Sandrine says yoga is thousands of years old. Maybe that's why it makes sense – because so many people have done it. It almost feels like I know it. Like I've always known it. It's helping me.'

She smiles, thinking of Sandrine's playful admonishment of her the other day for something she was doing completely wrong. Sandrine never makes any of them feel foolish. Instead, she encourages them to want to have the best experience they can.

'I can tell,' Frederick says. 'You do not get as down about things any more. Even with this problem,' he nods over his left shoulder, 'you are not letting it make you think you are doing something wrong. You always used to think it was your fault.' He pauses. 'It was never your fault, Dorothy. It was just something that happened. Those babies weren't meant to be.'

She knows he's right, but his words still register as a pain in her heart. They were her babies – their babies – and she has trouble thinking of them as beings who could never exist.

They are still real for her. She dreams about them sometimes. They don't have faces, but she hears the names she chose for them and wakes up in tears. Then she feels guilty that she is so upset about little people who never were, when some people never have the chance to have children, or even get married. Dorothy has no right to wail over miscarriages when the rest of her life has worked out just fine.

But Frederick didn't intend his words to hurt her, so she doesn't tell him any of that.

'I guess not,' she says.

'I still don't like that you have to go through this,' Frederick says softly.

'Hm?' She turns her head so she can see him.

'It's . . . barbaric.' His breath catches in his chest. 'You are in so much pain. And there are all those needles. It just doesn't seem right that you have to go through all of this. And I . . .' Another catch. 'My part is over in five minutes.' He laughs, but there's no mirth in it. 'It's not fair. To you.'

'But it will be worth it,' Dorothy says passionately. 'Once we have a baby, we'll forget that we ever had to do this.'

He's silent for a minute or so, then murmurs, 'What if there is no baby?'

'There will be,' Dorothy says confidently. She believes in this baby, now more than ever, and with that belief comes the pounding of something louder and more certain: her blood, her strength, her determination.

'But if there's not—'

'There will be, Frederick. I've decided. That's all there is to it.'

His face is angled in such a way that she can't see any expression he may be making. She watches him, but he doesn't move.

'You've been driving for a while,' she says at last. 'You must need a break.'

'We need petrol,' he says. 'I will stop at the next service station and we will both have a little break.'

Dorothy closes her eyes again and hears the road underneath the car and the rumble of the engine. The faint noise of the radio that Frederick keeps on low, even when there's a song she knows he likes.

'I love you,' she says.

'And I love you,' he replies.

She tries not to fall asleep before they reach the service station and almost succeeds.

CHAPTER THIRTY-SEVEN

Grace Maud didn't return to the yoga class exactly when Patricia and Dorothy wanted her to; not because she was inherently resistant to the idea but because she didn't want to go outside. Also, Sandrine took four weeks off over Christmas and the new year, and Grace Maud took advantage of them.

Cecilia kept scolding her. 'You can't stay inside all the time. Do you want me to get Luca to carry you to the car?'

They both knew that was an empty threat, but Cecilia was obviously concerned because her manner became more and more fake-cheerful each time she appeared. 'Beautiful day out there!' she'd say as she almost skipped down the hallway, shopping bags in her hands.

'Are you going to whistle while you work, Snow White?' Grace Maud said once. She knew she'd used too much snark when Cecilia looked as if she wanted to cry. Grace Maud felt ashamed but didn't apologise. That was probably her lowest day. After that she tried smiling more, and was rewarded with Cecilia's own lovely, bright smile.

When Grace Maud was ready to re-emerge, she called Patricia and said she would be attending the next class.

Now she is feeling regret in direct proportion to the difficulty of holding her downward-facing dog.

Sandrine warned her when she arrived. 'You have not been practising long enough to take a break like this, Grace Maud,' she said. 'You will feeeel it.'

Grace Maud's hamstrings are telling her that she's pushing them too far. She concentrates on her breathing, trying to distract herself.

The combination of a vacation from yoga and her age isn't one she's experienced before and she doesn't like it. She can't reverse the old age, so she'll just have to keep coming to class regularly, because she knows she felt better than this before. The weeks away have calcified her, but they're also the best advertisement for the postures she endures, and sometimes enjoys, in this class.

No, that's enough. Too hard.

She bends her knees and comes to the floor, into child's pose, to have a rest. Sandrine always says they can come into child's pose any time they need a break.

'Are you all right?' It's Patricia's voice in her ear and, presumably, her hand on Grace Maud's back.

'Yes. Just old,' Grace Maud says into her mat.

Patricia pats her, which makes Grace Maud sit up. 'I'm not a dog, Patricia.' Although she half smiles as she says it.

'Of course you are,' Patricia says. 'You're a downward dog.' And she pops back up into the pose herself.

'Oh, that's hilarious,' Grace Maud replies, smiling even though Patricia can't see it. But she doesn't rejoin her in the pose. They'll be finished soon enough and on to the next thing, so she'll wait.

She sits back on her heels and her thighs register their disapproval. Too bad. She has to try to stay here for a little while.

If she gives in to discomfort – to *sensation*, as Sandrine likes to call it – not only will she not progress, she'll go backwards.

'The body is designed to be moved,' Sandrine is always reminding them. 'If you do not move it you can expect that it will stop working.'

Like the Tin Man in *The Wizard of Oz*, one needs to keep oil in the joints, and yoga is that oil. Not that Sandrine's ever mentioned the Tin Man. That's Grace Maud's own association.

The rest of the class is, thankfully, sitting postures. These Grace Maud can handle, even if her joints bleat at her whenever she asks them to move.

'Open those eeeeps!' Sandrine commands.

'What if they don't want to open?' Grace Maud mutters, and Dorothy titters.

'Mine don't either!' she whispers.

'I can hear you ladies in the back,' Sandrine calls. 'I am coming to you.'

Patricia groans.

Within seconds, Sandrine has her knees on Dorothy's thighs while Dorothy presses the soles of her feet together, her face screwed up.

'I want you, Doro-tee, to do this *baddha konasana* at home with a bag of rice on each thigh. Two kilograms each bag. Hold for as many breaths as you can. Okay? It will help you when you give birth.'

The sudden stillness around them can only be caused, Grace Maud thinks, by her, Patricia and Dorothy holding their breath at the same time. Dorothy's most recent trip to Brisbane was only three weeks ago, and Grace Maud knows that she hasn't gone to her doctor yet for a blood test because she's scared it will show she's pregnant, and then she'll have to start her vigil all over again, waiting for the end.

'What makes you think there's a baby?' Dorothy says softly. She lets out an 'ah!' as Sandrine lifts her knees off her thighs.

'I can see it,' Sandrine says, and as she smiles her eyes disappear. 'In your body. In your face.'

'See what?'

'You are pregnant, no?'

'I, uh . . .' Dorothy inhales sharply and sits up.

Sandrine – always good at reading cues, Grace Maud has noticed – says nothing more and walks over to another student.

'She can't know,' Dorothy says.

'So you don't think you're pregnant?' Patricia asks as she pulls herself into the twist Sandrine has asked for.

A woman in front of them turns around and glares. Dorothy looks chastened. Patricia looks away. Grace Maud glares back, and the woman quickly turns her head.

'A trip to the doctor and a blood test are in order,' Grace Maud says, smiling. 'Then perhaps we'll have a celebration.'

Dorothy looks uncertain, but says nothing more.

For the rest of the class they all remain silent, and as they leave they don't mention the subject again.

But once Grace Maud is back in Patricia's car, she buckles her seatbelt and makes a noise of satisfaction. 'It's good to have some good news.'

'If it is good news.' Patricia turns the key in the ignition.

'I have a feeling it is. That it will continue to be.'

'Do you have many feelings, Grace Maud?' Patricia says cheekily.

'Too many to count,' Grace Maud replies as she looks out the window.

'I know what you mean.'

They look at each other briefly, then Patricia focuses on the road ahead.

The rest of the short drive is spent talking about Patricia's work, and by the time Grace Maud walks in her front door, the feelings she can count are the ones in her body telling her she's worked hard and needs to rest.

After a quick shower, she takes herself to bed and sleeps longer and more deeply than she has in weeks.

CHAPTER THIRTY-EIGHT

It takes Dorothy one more week to crack and go to the doctor for a blood test. One week of waking up every morning feeling like she's had far too much cheap wine even though she's had no alcohol at all. One week of the smell of the blue cheese that Frederick likes to eat after dinner making her want to vomit when previously she loved it. One week of Frederick looking at her curiously each time he leaves for work, not asking what she knows he wants to ask: *Are you pregnant?*

She owes him an answer. And she also owes herself one. If she really is pregnant she may as well know. And if she isn't, she needs to know that too.

She receives the results on the Thursday afternoon; too late to tell Frederick because he's already left work, but just in time to tell Patricia and Grace Maud. She will tell Frederick tonight.

However, Dorothy doesn't want to announce it at Orange Blossom House. Sandrine already knows, it seems, but she doesn't want anyone else overhearing.

'I'd like to talk to you both,' she announces to her friends as they prepare to leave at the end of class. 'But, um . . . not here.'

'Why don't you both come to my place for a chat?' Grace Maud says. 'Patricia is driving me home anyway.'

Now they're all sitting in Grace Maud's kitchen while she pours a brandy for herself and a gin for Patricia, and makes Dorothy a weak tea with lots of milk and sugar.

'This won't stop you sleeping,' Grace Maud promises as she puts the cup and saucer on the table. She sits, her own drink in front of her, and says, 'Well? Are you pregnant?'

'Yes,' Dorothy says weakly.

'And why do you sound like that?'

'Because I'm worried.'

'That's normal,' Patricia says.

'So this is a result of your . . . procedure?' Grace Maud sips her brandy.

Dorothy nods. 'But I . . .' She feels her bottom lip trembling and bites it.

Patricia pats her wrist. 'You don't have to say it.'

'But I want to.' She hiccups back the fear she's been carrying since she received the result. 'I've never had a problem *falling* pregnant. I've had a problem *staying* pregnant. The doctor thought if I had the IVF it would have a better result.'

'Because there are scientists involved?' Grace Maud says.

'Yes. I needed to try something different. Something that wasn't just . . . me.'

Dorothy bites the insides of her cheeks to try to stop crying. Because it's not straightforward; none of this is. She wants to be pregnant, yes, of course – but not pregnant *again*. She wants to be pregnant for the first time, so that all the fears she has learnt to have aren't there. And the tug of war in her mind about that – the fact that she is undoubtedly ungrateful to wish to be pregnant for the first time rather than the fourth – has made her feel like she's losing her grip on reason.

'Because you didn't want to risk another miscarriage,' Patricia says quietly, seriously. 'And now you think that even though the scientists were involved, this time it will be another miscarriage.'

Dorothy gasps out a cry, because she didn't expect anyone to understand. 'Yes,' she says. 'Am I crazy?'

'Oh, no,' says Grace Maud. 'I'd say you're rational.'

'Really?' Despite her best efforts, Dorothy can feel tears on her cheeks. 'Because I've been going round and round in my mind trying to work out why I'm not happier and thinking there's something wrong with me.'

'How long have you been doing that?' Grace Maud asks.

'For a few hours.'

Dorothy feels a wave rise inside her – more like ten waves, in quick succession, all crashing on different shores. She's been having this sensation since she started taking the hormones for the treatment and has been so good at not bothering anyone with it, but now she's worried about the baby, too, it's impossible to control it. Or them. The waves. The relentless waves.

So she doesn't. She lets out a loud sob and puts her head on her hands. 'I'm sorry,' she wails.

'For what?' says Grace Maud with a gentle tone they rarely hear.

'I'm such a mess.' Dorothy lifts her head to see two concerned faces, then puts it down again.

'That's understandable,' says Grace Maud, 'but this distress isn't doing you any good.'

'It's the hormones,' Dorothy says into her hands.

'What?' Patricia asks.

Dorothy looks up. 'The hormones.' She sniffs. 'First it was the ones I had to inject. Now I guess it's the ones that are happening naturally. And I . . . And I . . .' She hiccups back more tears.

Grace Maud shifts and puts an arm around her. 'Menopause was the best thing that ever happened to me,' she mutters.

'Hm?' Dorothy rests her head on Grace Maud's shoulder. It feels like a shelter from a storm.

'Menopause,' Grace Maud says more loudly. 'It's a blessing. People carry on about "the change" like it's more of a curse than the curse, but believe you me, my dear, not having to deal with all those hormones and all that . . . mess every month was an incredible relief. Still is.' She takes Dorothy's face in her hands. 'What happens every month to women is cruel, in my opinion. And you've had a huge dose of it all at once. Pregnancy is making things seem harder because it's all swirling inside you.'

Grace Maud pats Dorothy's cheek, removes her hands and smiles kindly, which makes Dorothy want to start wailing again. Sometimes – at the worst times in your life, usually – people being nice to you is really difficult to cope with.

'You're not crazy,' Grace Maud continues. 'It's the experience that's crazy. And the stress you're putting on yourself about whether or not this pregnancy will last is, in my non-medical opinion, exacerbating matters.' She pauses and looks intently into Dorothy's eyes. 'I'm old and I know a few more things than you. So please know I am saying this from experience, and with love. If you lose this baby, it will be terrible. But you will survive it. If you have this baby, that too may be terrible – as only children can be, because you love them so much – but you will survive it. And you will survive it because you are stronger than you believe you are.'

She sits back and Dorothy feels her eyes tighten with more tears.

'Also because I believe you have friends here.' Grace Maud looks at Patricia, who smiles. 'And if you have a problem, you can talk to us. It may not help. Or it may. But the offer is there.'

'Thank you,' Dorothy whispers.

'Would you consider talking about yourself more than you do, Grace Maud?' Patricia asks, her head to one side, her gaze frank, and Dorothy wonders what this is about.

'What do you mean?' The imperious version of Grace Maud has returned.

'You've told us about the farm. But you haven't said anything about that other matter with your son. About him wanting to buy more land. Or did the fire resolve that?'

Grace Maud blanches.

'Sorry, that was a clumsy way to put it,' Patricia says, sounding chastened. 'But I do really want to know. I think Dorothy does too.'

Dorothy nods vigorously.

Grace Maud presses her lips together. Her forehead furrows, then smooths. She has remarkably unlined skin for her age, and Dorothy has always wanted to know if she has a secret. Or maybe it's just her high forehead, her curved brow.

'It's not resolved,' Grace Maud says, so softly that Dorothy almost doesn't hear her. 'I tried to discuss it. My timing wasn't very good but I don't know when it would be. If we all waited for timing to be right for something we'd be waiting forever.'

'Do you miss him?' Patricia asks gently.

'Yes,' Grace Maud says quickly. 'But I'm also still cross at him. Perhaps that makes me a bad mother. I should feel only compassion for him at such a time.'

'I think that makes you normal,' Dorothy says. 'Sometimes I was so upset with my parents for making me look after my sister and then I'd think I was being a bad sister.' She shrugs. 'But I wasn't. I think it was just normal.'

'Does your sister need looking after?' Patricia is peering at her.

‘Um . . .’ Dorothy looks from Patricia to Grace Maud. She hasn’t told them much about her family because it’s never really come up. Mainly because all they ever seem to talk about is her trying to get pregnant and, now, actually being pregnant. But there’s no reason not to talk about Cornelia. Or anything. She feels bonded to these two in a way that is different although no less close than the way she feels about Ruth.

‘She’s deaf,’ Dorothy starts. ‘I learnt sign language with her. My parents didn’t learn as much. So I’m Cornelia’s translator, I guess you’d call it.’

‘How did you feel about that?’ says Patricia.

‘It was all right.’ That was Dorothy’s automatic response but she stops and considers whether it’s her real response. That line protects her parents; it does nothing to acknowledge what things were like for her or for Cornelia.

‘Really?’ Grace Maud prompts.

Dorothy looks down at her hands and thinks of how often she used them when she was still living with her sister. There’s a whole language in them that she’s always been glad she knows but which she does not miss when she’s not using it.

‘No,’ she says. ‘Actually it wasn’t. I loved being able to talk to Cornelia but it meant she had trouble talking to anyone else if I wasn’t there.’

‘Did she go to school?’ asks Patricia and Dorothy shakes her head.

‘She had a tutor at home,’ Dorothy explains. ‘The tutor could sign.’

‘Where is she now?’

‘Still at home. She can’t work. Hardly anyone can sign.’ Another shrug: *no one can do anything about it*. ‘She does the housework and she reads.’

‘Does she have any friends?’ Grace Maud says.

'No. I'm her friend.' That answer came out so quickly because it's true, yet the truth of it makes Dorothy so sad that she doesn't think about it often. When they were young she didn't think about it at all, because she was so wrapped up in herself; it's only now that she has a separate life that she realises everything Cornelia can't do and doesn't have, and feels the pain of it, and has to stop herself thinking about it because sometimes the pain is overwhelming. Besides, the pain is so close to pity and Cornelia has no tolerance for that.

'That's hard on both of you,' says Patricia.

'I guess it is.' Dorothy looks at her hands again then glances up in time to see Patricia and Grace Maud looking at each other.

'Anyway,' Dorothy continues, 'it's life, isn't it? We can't change it. I just have to make the most of everything I have, because I am really, really lucky. I get to have friends like you.'

She smiles at them both even if her breeziness is an act, because sometimes she does wish she could change it. Sometimes she thinks she'd swap what she has just to give Cornelia a chance of living a different life.

'I'm sure Cornelia thinks she's lucky to have you,' Patricia says kindly.

'Maybe.' Dorothy smiles. 'Sometimes she just says I'm a pain.'

Grace Maud laughs. 'We can all be pains when we choose to be. I think it's quite a useful trick to have up one's sleeve. Now, there's something I've been wanting to ask: Dorothy, why don't you tell us how you and Frederick met.'

Dorothy is surprised at the change of subject, but as she recounts the tale of the tall young tourist who swept her off her feet, she forgets to worry about anything that was bothering her before. By the time she departs an hour later – after a call to Frederick to tell him where she is – she feels lighter and also as if she's on more solid ground. She has anchors in this life – her parents, her sister, her husband, her friends – and for the first time she realises that they can hold her steady if anything goes wrong. And it may not this time. It's all right for her to start believing that.

CHAPTER THIRTY-NINE

'I would say "penny for your thoughts" but that's a bit of a cliché, isn't it?'

Patricia turns at the sound of Dennis's voice and it takes her a second to remember she's in the staffroom. She's been so caught up in the to-do list in her head that she's not even sure how long she's been there.

'The kettle's finished boiling,' he says, gesturing towards the rising steam.

'Thanks,' says Patricia; she'd completely forgotten she switched it on.

'Finished for the day?' he asks, pulling two mugs out of the cupboard.

'Ah . . . yes.'

'Not sure what day it is?' He grins.

She's noticed that Dennis likes grinning, but today she's not in the mood for relentless upbeatness.

'I guess not,' she snaps, and his grin falls.

She regrets her sharpness as soon as the words are out of her mouth. It's not fair to take out her bad mood on Dennis. It started this morning as she was in her usual rush out the door after preparing breakfast for her parents and trying to remember if she made herself lunch to take to work. Her mother had pursed her lips and said in a scolding tone, 'It's time you gave up that silly job. Men don't like their wives to have silly jobs.'

Patricia has no idea if her mother was talking to her or if she was thinking of an imaginary person with a silly job, but it certainly hadn't been a good way to start the day.

She reaches for one of the mugs, but Dennis puts his hand over hers.

'I'll make it,' he says. 'Strong black tea, one sugar. Right?'

'How did you know?'

'I've seen you make it before. Sometimes I pay attention in here.' The grin returns and she smiles back.

Dennis isn't a bad person. That's not the reason she wouldn't go out with him. Of course, he may not be a good person either but the signs point in that direction. He's capable of kindnesses, as she is witnessing now.

Many people are, she's realised. The world seems hard, and harsh, a lot of the time, but she believes most people want to make it better for themselves and each other. They don't always know the best way to do it – and sometimes they fumble in the trying – but most of the time they're all trying to do their best. Just as she is. Just as Dennis is.

'How have you been, Dennis?' she says. It's the first time she's ever asked him. No wonder he looks surprised.

'Fine.' A big grin this time. 'How are you?'

She wants to say 'fine' or 'good' or 'well' – they're the default answers. But they're not the truth, and at this particular moment she's not interested in lies. Plus she doesn't want him to think she only asked him how he is so he would ask her in turn.

'That's not much detail,' she says instead. 'How's work going? Are you enjoying it here?'

He looks momentarily confused. 'Um . . . yeah. Why?'

'Why what?'

'Why do you want to know?'

'Because I've never asked you. It's rude of me.' She smiles weakly. 'I was brought up to have better manners than that.'

Her parents weren't warm-hearted when she was growing up, but they were well mannered; qualities which, she's found, should never be confused for each other.

'All right.' He makes a funny face that she finds endearing. 'Yeah. I like it here. The kids are mostly okay. A couple of them are good athletes. If I do my job right maybe they'll get into state champs.'

'That's wonderful,' she says, and means it. 'I have to confess that I've never seen you teach so I don't really know what you do.'

'That's okay. I was never good at English, so . . .' He shrugs. 'I don't really get what you do either. But I'm not at school any more so I don't have to.'

He shifts closer to her. A tiny bit. So tiny she may be misinterpreting it.

Then he turns to pluck the teabags from the mugs, puts sugar into one of them and stirs before he presents it to her. 'Strong and black with one.'

'Thank you.' She takes a sip without thinking and burns her tongue, wincing.

'That looked painful,' he says, starting to laugh.

'That doesn't mean it's funny!' She winces again, then joins in his laughter.

'It's kind of funny,' he says. 'It's basic chemistry or something that the tea was going to be too hot to drink.'

'Which is why I'm not a science teacher,' she says, putting the mug on the benchtop.

'I reckon you could be. I reckon you could be anything you wanted to be.' He says it so casually, as if it isn't one of the kindest things anyone could say to a person.

There are few things more validating, Patricia believes, than being told you can do or be anything. Oh, it can have its disadvantages: there are some students whose parents should never have encouraged their darlings to believe such a thing because it means they think they don't have to work. So she revises her thoughts: said to an adult, it's a lovely compliment.

'Thank you,' she says, lowering her eyes briefly. When she lifts them again, it's to see him gazing at her.

Patricia looks away first. She checks her watch – unnecessary, but a good prop for a person who wants to make a getaway. And she needs to get away because Dennis is making her uneasy in a way she hasn't felt since she used to have intense crushes on boys in her teens, and that one time in her twenties on a man she would see on the bus to work. They never spoke, but she imagined a whole life with him.

'I have to go,' she says. 'I have a few things to do before I make my parents' dinner.'

He frowns. 'What about your tea?'

'Oh.' She realises the flaw in her logic and laughs nervously to cover it. 'Yes. I, uh, should have made it earlier.'

He puts his mug on the bench. 'Are you trying to avoid me?'

She can hear disappointment, maybe even sadness, in the way he says it, but there's no accusation there.

'What?' She laughs again, even though she's not the laughing type. Not at school anyway, where she has a serious job and a serious persona to match. 'No! Of course not. Why would I do that? I have no reason to avoid you.'

She picks up her tea and takes another scalding sip to stop herself babbling, but she can feel him looking at her.

'I don't want to scare you off,' he says. 'I mean . . . that's the opposite of what I want to do.'

She meets his eyes and he's looking at her in that way he has: like he's trying to see inside her mind.

'I know you didn't want to go out with me last time I asked,' he says slowly. 'But I hope you'll change your mind if I ask now.'

That fluttery feeling is back, and Patricia doesn't like it. Dennis is a colleague, and he's still younger than her, and while she knows him slightly better now and knows that he's good company, it's not appropriate for them to go out. It could end badly. He might hate her. She might hate him. They'd still have to work together.

'I think we should be friends,' she blurts without looking at him. She can hear her own breath – rapid and not at all under her control.

'I don't want to be your friend, Patricia,' he says, pushing away from the bench.

She dares to look at him again, thinking he might be angry with her. Instead there's something almost resembling pity in his eyes.

'I'm interested in a lot more than that,' he goes on. 'I always have been. But . . .' He sighs. 'I'm certainly not going to push you. I guess I just wanted to let you know that I haven't changed my mind about you.' He laughs softly. 'My mum told me you'd say no. This time.'

'You told your mother about me?' Patricia says, slightly shocked.

'Yeah. She has that sixth sense mothers get – knew something was going on. I told her I'd met someone amazing. But . . .' He shrugs. 'She doesn't think I'm amazing back.'

Patricia swallows, not sure what to think. Still, she's curious. 'What . . . what did your mother say?'

He laughs. 'She said, "Give it time." But I guess she would.

She's my mum.' He takes a gulp of tea, pours out the rest and puts his mug in the sink. 'Gotta run. Cricket training.'

When he reaches the door, he gives her one last, long look and this time Patricia can't hear herself breathing at all.

CHAPTER FORTY

'So this is my beach,' Patricia says as she places towels on the sand then begins to swivel the umbrella into the sand.

'I have been to Yorkeys Knob before, Patricia,' Grace Maud says, amused.

'I know you have! But I've never invited either of you here before.' She looks almost nervous and Grace Maud is touched that she cares so much.

'Frederick made us some sandwiches.' Dorothy puts her basket on a towel, then stretches her arms into the air and takes a big breath. 'It's so nice to be by the ocean! I hardly ever get the chance.'

'Once the stingers are gone you should come over for a swim,' Patricia suggests. 'Only, ooh, three months or so to wait.'

'I thought we might be getting together at your house,' Grace Maud says, glancing at the sky and seeing pillowy clouds that hold the promise of tropical rain. 'I'd like to meet your parents.'

'Mum's having a bad day.'

Patricia fusses around with serviettes and plates, not looking up, and Grace Maud understands that the topic is closed.

'I'll help you down,' Dorothy whispers in Grace Maud's ear, taking her elbow and assisting her to sit on a towel.

'Thank you. But I think you should stop doing that soon. Not that pregnancy makes you weak, but your ligaments loosen – activities you're used to can become more difficult.'

Dorothy nods and turns to help Patricia with the food.

Grace Maud stretches her legs out in front of her. She may still need help getting up and down but her legs aren't as crotchety as they used to be. She supposes she has Sandrine to thank for that. And these two young women with her now, since they made sure she returned to class.

'This was a lovely idea, Patricia,' she says. 'Thank you for suggesting it. And please thank Frederick, Dorothy, for allowing you out on a Sunday and for the sandwiches.'

'I will!' Dorothy's laugh floats on the air.

'Did you spent much time in Cairns, Grace Maud, when you were living on the farm?' Patricia asks as she sits down and pours them glasses of water.

Grace Maud gazes across the water and sees a small sailboat bobbing by. She remembers the one occasion her husband took her sailing, while they were still courting. He couldn't sail but told her he could. She was lucky that there was so little wind that day they barely made it out from shore. She was also lucky that she realised Clark probably lied about other things, such as how much he cared about her. All these years she has protected him. Or maybe it's herself she's been protecting, because she doesn't want anyone to know that she was unloved. The story she told everyone, including Tom, was that Clark missed his homeland so much he had to go back. It's a fiction she no longer has to maintain because no one cares. And she owes her friends the truth, if they are to really know her and her them.

'During the war, my sister and I came to Cairns quite a bit,' she says. 'There were American soldiers here. Protecting the north. As you may imagine, this was a romantic notion for us. We thought we might, you know, meet some dashing young men in uniform.'

She glances at the others. Dorothy looks like she's being told the most fascinating story ever.

'We had a friend whose family lived near the harbour and we stayed with them. We seemed to have so much time.' She smiles, thinking of Ellie Maud's arm looped through hers and how hopeless they were at playing coquettes. They only knew how to relate to men as they would their brothers; they had no idea how to charm and beguile. Not that it stopped them trying whenever they met a likely candidate.

'Our friend's parents invited us to a dance. All the officers in town were going to be there. Of course, Ellie Maud and I had to be there, although our father insisted on attending as well.'

'That must have been strange,' Patricia says. 'Wanting to meet men while your dad was watching!'

'It was the done thing to have a chaperone,' Grace Maud explains. 'And my father didn't think our mother should be subjected to Americans.' She makes a face. 'He wasn't a fan. Thought they had no business being here.'

'My parents love Americans,' Dorothy says. 'Without them, we don't know what would have happened. You know, at the end.'

Yes, Grace Maud knows. The end of the war. The liberation of Europe and the remaking that followed.

'Fair enough,' she says. 'Well, I met an American. Clark Clifford. From a farming family in the Midwest.'

'Was he handsome?' Dorothy asks breathlessly.

'He had a strong nose and a strong jaw, and when my mother met him she said they were indicators of good character.' Grace Maud raises her eyebrows. 'Just goes to show you that reading faces wasn't her strong suit.'

'Why?' Patricia frowns. 'What happened?'

'Nothing, at first.' Grace Maud remembers Clark telling her how much he loved the landscape around Cairns. She loved the fact that he appreciated her home region and never wondered if he was telling the truth. 'We had fun at the start. There were dances then – they were such a good way to interact with young men without pressure. It's a pity they don't happen any more.'

She can picture Ellie Maud laughing giddily the night she met her future husband and Grace Maud and Clark dancing next to them. The dances were something the twins shared; they couldn't know that this one dance, this one night, would eventually separate them.

'But then . . .' She closes her eyes, considering how much to tell them. What she considered cruelty, some women would simply call marriage. Perhaps Dorothy puts up with things that Grace Maud refused to tolerate. However, she doesn't want to lie. Her truth is hers; and if it's not acceptable to the others, she can't do anything about that.

'Clark changed after we married,' she says quietly. 'He wanted me to stop working the cane. My father had given him a job, and Clark wanted me to stay home and keep the house tidy for him.' She laughs caustically. 'He didn't like my argument that I could do both because I'd been doing both for years. Looking after the family home. Cooking. Doing the washing. And working. I was very capable. But he didn't care.

'After Tom was born, Clark said he wanted to move home. To the United States. He wanted Tom to grow up where he had, and farm the way his family farmed. None of this "cane nonsense", he said. Then he started refusing to cut cane, but wouldn't find other work off the farm. He said we had to go to the US and we could come back after my parents died.'

'Grace Maud, that's awful.' Patricia reaches over to place her hand on Grace Maud's. 'What did you do?'

Grace Maud feels the emotions of those times as if they're still happening to her. Everything is written on the body, Sandrine says, and Grace Maud's anger and pain have been stuffed down inside her for years. Waiting. Simmering. All because she wasn't allowed to say she was angry. Wasn't allowed to tell her husband she didn't want what he wanted. Dutiful wives didn't do that. Instead, she had to be devious.

'I knew Clark thought he could take whatever share of the farm I inherited, because as my husband what was mine would be his. My brother Frank was meant to take over, but Dad always said he wouldn't leave us girls out. Frank died later, so if I hadn't . . .' She swallows. 'I couldn't let that happen.

'I told my parents what Clark wanted to do. Mum said I had to stay with him; I'd made my bed, and so on. Dad was furious. He asked what I needed. I said I thought Clark was greedy and lazy, and if I could give him enough to make him go away he'd take it. Dad said he could give me the money but it would go against my inheritance. I didn't care about that. I just wanted to make sure the farm stayed in the family.'

There is a sensation in her chest as if her bones and ligaments are moving, separating. She's never talked about Clark to anyone outside of the family, which means it's been many years since she's talked about this.

'It worked,' she says. 'He took the money and went. We never divorced. It was so hard to do back then. Clark died in his forties – his sister sent me a letter with the news. So that was that.'

Dorothy sighs, and Patricia turns her head away to look at the water.

'You're very brave, Grace Maud,' she mutters, and when she turns back her eyes are bright with admiration.

Grace Maud smiles sadly. 'Only if you consider it brave that I valued what I wanted more than I valued what he wanted. There were several people who thought I was appalling.'

'They were idiots!' Dorothy declares.

Grace Maud laughs. 'I can't disagree.' She peers at Patricia. 'Have you ever found yourself in that sort of situation, Patricia?'

'Why do you ask?' Patricia says quickly.

'Because you're not married even though I'd think many men would have wanted to marry you. So either you're not the marrying kind. Or,' she raises an eyebrow, 'you perhaps told someone to get lost.'

Patricia snorts. 'I'm not a lesbian, if that's what you mean.'

A strangled noise comes from Dorothy's direction.

'Oh dear,' says Grace Maud. 'Here I was thinking I was being subtle.'

Laughing, Patricia says, 'I haven't told anyone to get lost either. It just . . .' She shrugs. 'Hasn't happened. So much of life is in the timing, don't you think? Like meeting you two – that's purely because we went to the same class.'

'I think it was fate,' Dorothy says dreamily. 'It can't just be luck.'

'Or perhaps we make our own luck,' Grace Maud says.

'As you did,' says Patricia with a nod of acknowledgement. 'You could have done what everyone thought was the right thing and stayed married.'

'True.' Grace Maud brushes her hands together, ready to change the subject. 'Let's have a sandwich. They look delicious, Dorothy.'

They eat in silence for a minute or so, then Dorothy asks if they really understand what the Sanskrit words in class mean;

and does anyone really meditate at the end or do their brains chatter like hers?

As Dorothy talks, Grace Maud contemplates that perhaps fate has played a role in her life by bringing her to this place at this time. But she also knows that most of her life has been forged in the fire of her determination. There was luck, yes, but more than that: the resolve to never let go of that luck once it arrived, and to make the best of her lot while doing so.

They're skills she passed on to Tom, so she can't blame him for trying to make the best of what he has, even if it involves change. Instead, she should be proud that he has learnt from her, and let him take his place in the same lineage of strength and hard work that has shaped her.

AUTUMN 1994

Four Weddings and a Funeral, starring Hugh Grant and Andie MacDowell, is released in Australia.

Philadelphia, starring Tom Hanks, is released.

East 17 top the Australian singles chart for seven weeks with the song 'It's Alright'.

Frontline, a satirical TV comedy starring Rob Sitch, begins on the ABC.

The final episode of *Mother and Son* airs on the ABC.

Kurt Cobain, lead singer of Nirvana, dies in Seattle, Washington.

CHAPTER FORTY-ONE

No. This can't be happening. Not again. Not now. She's in her second trimester. It's the furthest she's ever gone, and she's made it this far without any problems. The blood can't be real. There's hardly anything. *It's not real.*

But it is real, because it's on her fingers and it smells like iron. It's the smell of every month of disappointment she's experienced over the past few years.

While the others are in *savasana*, blissfully relaxing, Dorothy's slipped out to the funny old loo at the back of Orange Blossom House. It's the students' toilet – Sandrine must have her own inside the house – and Dorothy's only been here a couple of times before. She usually tries to avoid it, because its corners are full of daddy-long-legs and the toilet paper roll is always near its end. It's a necessary visit tonight, though. Once she felt the dampness in her underpants she knew she couldn't wait until she got home.

Her bag is still in the studio. With her car keys in it. How is she meant to get away from here without the car? If she goes back in, she knows Patricia and Grace Maud will want to know where she's been for . . . ten minutes? Fifteen? She's lost track. Sitting in here staring at her fingers, wanting the colour on them to be anything other than red.

'Dorothy?' She hears Patricia calling. So much for making an escape.

'Dorothy, are you in the toilet?'

'Y-yes,' she says hoarsely, then quickly stands and pulls up her underpants and tights before she flushes.

'Are you all right?'

She wants to scream, *No! I'm losing my baby! Again! AGAIN AGAIN AGAIN!*

Instead she clears her throat and opens the door to see Patricia holding her mat and bag.

'Thanks,' she says, reaching for them. Patricia hands them over slowly.

'What's going on?' It's Grace Maud, a few steps behind. 'You disappeared.' She stops and narrows her eyes. 'What is it?'

'It's nothing.' Dorothy shakes her head vigorously. She doesn't want to bother these two. They need to get home. As does she. Then she can ask Frederick what to do. He'll know. He's known every other time. She wishes she could remember what he said those three times, because then she would know too, but her memory is empty.

'It's something.' Grace Maud steps closer and takes her arm. 'Perhaps we can help.'

'Really, it's—'

'Why don't you let us decide if it's nothing?' Patricia says, her voice soothing, her face showing concern but not panic.

Good. That's what Dorothy needs to see. Someone who isn't panicking the way she is.

'I'm bleeding,' she says, then takes quick breaths, like she's trying to expel reality with each exhalation.

'How much?' asks Grace Maud.

To Dorothy, one drop is too much, but she says, 'I . . . I don't know how much is a lot.'

'Are your pants soaked?'

Dorothy shakes her head.

'Good.' Grace Maud nods twice, as if the matter is settled. 'It may be nothing, but you should have it checked.'

'Shall we take you to the hospital?' Patricia asks.

'Oh no – I don't want to bother anyone,' Dorothy says quickly.

'Dorothy,' Grace Maud says, 'doctors and nurses need patients otherwise they have nothing to do. It's not a bother. Besides, you pay taxes, I presume – and taxes pay for this hospital visit you're about to have. So you're going. That's that.'

They walk her slowly to the car, cheerfully farewelling Sandrine, who is standing by the door looking as if she wants to ask questions.

Luckily Casualty isn't busy and they take Dorothy through within a few minutes.

'I'll call Frederick,' Patricia tells her.

'Please don't. I don't want to worry him.'

'He'll be more worried if he doesn't know why you're not home on time,' Grace Maud says, and Dorothy relents.

On the bed, wearing a hospital gown, she gazes at the fluorescent lights as the doctor pokes around. She's been in this position before, so many times, and each time she feels the indignity of it. She could be anyone. Or no one. To the doctor she's a specimen, and her insides are a curiosity, and if he remembers her name once he withdraws his gloved fingers she'll feel mildly appeased. But in the end, the indignity will add to the pain of whatever the diagnosis is. Because it always does. Just once Dorothy would like to feel as if the small tragedy of her lost babies isn't being played out while there are other patients waiting to be seen, and nurses who turn away, discard their gloves, scrub up for the next patient and never think of her again.

This is my life, she wants to say to them. *This is my body. Why don't you care?*

Maybe they can't care. Maybe their job would be too hard if they cared about everyone. Maybe it would be impossible. But that doesn't mean she can't hold onto a small hope that today she'll be treated like a human going through something instead of just being the next name on their to-do list.

'Look, Dorothy,' the doctor says, pulling off his gloves and throwing them into a nearby bin, 'I know it's alarming to see blood, but I don't think you have anything to worry about.'

She stares at him. This isn't the outcome she's prepared for. 'What?'

He shrugs. 'It happens sometimes in the second trimester. If you're, um, active with your husband, sometimes that can cause it.'

Dorothy blushes. She was, in fact, 'active' with Frederick this morning, before they left for work. With the pressure off because she's pregnant, they've been enjoying each other a lot more.

'I see that may be the reason,' the doctor says cheerfully. 'No need to discontinue. Just be aware that this can be the result. But if there's a greater amount of blood than this, come back in straightaway. Otherwise you have a normally progressing pregnancy and you can go home.'

Almost throwing off the gown, Dorothy dresses as quickly as she can and makes for the waiting room, the rush of the news carrying her along. She's still pregnant. There's still a baby inside her with its little beating heart. She doesn't feel she can dare to hope yet that it will last all the way. But maybe soon. Maybe by the third trimester.

When she emerges, she sees that the waiting room is busier. Patricia is easy to spot, though, and Grace Maud is next to her, their heads bent towards each other, then turning towards . . . Frederick. He must have flown here. Or maybe more time has passed than she realised.

'*Liebling!*' he cries as he grabs her, hugging her.

'It's all right!' she says breathlessly. 'I'm all right!'

He pulls back, looking confused. 'Yes?'

She smiles and nods vigorously. 'Yes.'

'I'm so pleased,' Grace Maud says, patting her once on the arm.

'That's great,' says Patricia, kissing her cheek. 'Really great. So what happened?'

'It's just . . .' Dorothy glances at Frederick and blushes again. 'Something that happens.'

Frederick gives her a funny look. 'But there must be a reason?'

'I'll tell you on the way home,' she says quickly. 'We should let Patricia and Grace Maud go.'

'We'll leave you to it,' Patricia says, picking up her handbag. 'But if you need anything, give me a call.'

Dorothy waits for the other two to depart before she clutches Frederick's hand. 'Our baby is fine,' she says.

'That is the best news.' He kisses her forehead.

'But next time we, ah . . . you know.' She glances around to see if anyone is nearby. 'We may have to be a little more gentle.'

His eyes widen, then he smiles. 'I understand,' he says.

'I knew you would.'

She nudges him, and he puts an arm around her shoulders. As they walk to the car, Dorothy feels hope trying to flicker inside her again.

Maybe this baby really will last. Maybe this time her dream really will come true.

CHAPTER FORTY-TWO

'What happened?' Patricia says, breathless, as she almost throws her handbag onto the kitchen counter.

'It's all right, Patricia, she's back now.'

Her father sounds annoyed, as if he hadn't called her at work, in a panic because his wife was no longer in the house.

Patricia had to ask Gordon to cover her class, which means she owes him a favour and she knows he'll call her on it. Nothing is ever straightforward with a man like that.

'Dad, that's not the point! How long was she gone?'

He shrugs, and starts to leaf through the newspaper. 'I don't know.'

'Dad, stop! Stop reading the bloody paper!'

He looks up, surprised. Patricia doesn't swear. Not around him. Not around anyone. Years of teaching have trained her out of it. She can't afford to swear outside of school lest she slip up while she's at work.

'I don't see why you're so upset,' he says grumpily.

'Because Mum was missing, Dad. And I had to leave work.'

'She wasn't missing. She just wasn't here.'

'Or in the street. Because you looked. You told me.'

'No,' he concedes.

'So where was she?'

'I don't know. She just . . . came back.'

'After how long?'

He glances at her, then to one side, then the other. He's probably preparing to lie to her, which means her mother could have been gone for hours.

'Hard to say,' he mumbles.

'Where were you?'

'I'm not her jailer!' he replies, his voice raised.

Patricia has a moment of feeling like a naughty child – except it was never her father who disciplined her. That was her mother's job, because her father was so often at sea.

'Yes, you are, Dad. We both are.' She sighs. 'We talked about this when I moved back in. How I have to work so we can afford to stay here, which means you have to be the one to keep an eye on Mum when I'm not here. You said you would. You said—'

The catch in her throat takes her by surprise. She doesn't know if she's upset that her mother was roaming the streets, not in her right mind or any mind at all; or if she was more scared than she realised when she got that call, and now it's catching up to her. Or perhaps she's angry that this is her life now, that these are her responsibilities, and she can't even go to work without something going wrong.

The other day it was her mother burning her hand on the kettle when she checked to see if it had boiled. A few days before that she left the hose running for hours. Each time, her father wasn't paying attention. Not because his own mind is faltering, but because, as he told Patricia, he's still not used to his wife not being there. She was always the sharp one. The one who remembered all the names and birthdays and phone numbers. She could recite the names of all the prime ministers from Barton to Fraser.

That's when her memory started to become fuzzy – while Fraser was still in The Lodge. She thinks Bob Hawke was the compere on *Bandstand*, and Paul Keating is a used-car salesman whose ads run every night at 6 pm, when the news is on. 'Don't buy a Falcon,' she's taken to murmuring when she sees him, which Patricia tries not to take personally given that's the make of her car.

'Dad,' Patricia says, leaning on her elbows, dropping her head into her hands. It feels so heavy, like her brain is full and it's dragging her towards the earth.

'Yes?' he says in a more conciliatory tone.

'We have to think about a home.' She lifts her head and her neck pings.

Great. Yoga is two days away and she won't be able to stretch it out properly until then.

'No, we don't.'

'Well, you don't want to be her jailer, and I can't be here all the time. But if she wanders off again she might end up in the ocean, or hit by a car.' She throws up her hands. 'Or walking to Timbuk-bloody-tu.'

'I'll be more careful,' he says, and she sees something in his eyes she's never seen before: fear.

She doesn't know if it's fear that he'll be alone most of the day if her mother moves into a home, or that his marriage will be effectively over because his wife won't live here any more. Or maybe that the home might be his destiny too, one day.

Patricia hopes not. He's in solid shape, and his brain works fine. He has niggles and pains and other problems, but that's it . . . for now. There's no reason for him to need constant care. No more than Patricia herself needs it. No more than everyone needs it. Someone to love and cherish them. To care for and comfort them all the days of their life. In sickness and in health.

They're vows of marriage, but more than that: they're vows of love. They apply to everyone we love.

Patricia doesn't like her mother, but she loves her. So she will love and cherish her, care for and comfort her in sickness, as it's turned out, even if that care might take the form of finding someone else to tend to her on a daily basis. Because they can't properly care for her here. The mother she knew – her father's wife – is gone. It's tragic, and it's mundane. They're not special. They're just the latest family to have to make a tough decision in the name of love.

'Dad,' she says calmly, 'we've tried. We've both tried. But she's worse. She's a lot worse. We just don't see it because we see her every day. But she's barely speaking now. We haven't noticed because we talk all the time, or the TV's on. Her eyes are . . .'

She hears him sniff loudly and looks at him. Her father – the mostly silent, strapping man she grew up with – has his head in his hand, hiding the side of his face from her.

'She's not there any more,' he says gruffly. 'I know.'

'It won't get better, Dad. And do you really want to spend your life watching her?'

'But it's not right to put her in a home.'

'Not right for whom?' There's steel in her voice, but there needs to be. She has to be the parent now; it's her law to lay down.

'For your mother.'

His hand drops and she sees the tears clinging on under his eyes.

'Sorry to be tough, Dad, but there's one of her, and two of us, and no one else is coming to help us with this. We have to look after ourselves too, or we'll wear out. And we'd be no good for her like that.'

He rubs his hand over the table top, like he's trying to sand it. Concentric circles.

'Who would pay for it?' he says softly. 'Would we have to sell this house?'

'No,' she says, because she's been thinking about this for a while and she's formulated a plan. 'You need somewhere to live. I'll ask Peter and John to help with the cost of the home.'

'You can't ask them!'

'Why not?'

Although she knows the answer. It'll be the same answer as when she suggested a few years ago that her brothers could help pay for renovations to the house that they'd jointly inherit one day anyway. Her father's already told her that the house is being left to the boys, given that Annette has a husband and doesn't need the money. Patricia is to inherit any cash they have left in their bank account. Apparently she won't need more than that because she's just a single woman with no dependants.

'They have families to support.'

Patricia glares at him. 'You and Mum are their family too.'

Now they're glaring at each other.

'All right,' she says after a minute or so has passed. 'We'll take out a mortgage on the house.'

'That means they'll inherit a debt!'

'Dad, they're both richer than Croesus and they never help you out,' she almost spits. She's fed up to the eye teeth of her brothers being held up as the family paragons when they can't be bothered to phone more than once every few months and they visit on the twelfth of Never. 'Not one cent. It's about time, I'm afraid. I can't afford to pay for it, nor can I afford to stop working to be here full-time to look after her.'

In the silence that follows, she can almost hear the sound of them both fuming about their separate grievances.

'We'll get a mortgage,' her father says at last, so quietly she almost misses it.

A second of laughter escapes her. He'd rather go to the bank for the money than put out his precious sons.

'Sure, Dad,' she says.

She pushes off the countertop, feeling weary. Her neck is still hurting. She really wants to just lie down on her bed and sleep until it's time to go to yoga on Thursday. But she won't do that. It wouldn't be fair. It wouldn't be caring or comforting.

'I'll start making dinner,' she says, although it's much too early. 'Maybe you'd like to go for a walk? Mum probably won't wake up for a while, and I can keep an eye on her.'

He nods and pushes himself up to standing. Tucking the newspaper under his arm, he walks towards the back door without so much as looking in her direction. A punishment, probably, for forcing him to have a conversation he never wanted to have. It wasn't one she wanted to have either.

She wonders if that ever occurs to him. That none of this is what she really wants, but it's what she's prepared to do. Because she loves them. Even if she'll never be sure that they love her back.

CHAPTER FORTY-THREE

Meditation is the part of class that Dorothy likes the least, even though she really wants to be good at it. Sandrine is fond of saying that it's the whole reason yoga postures exist – to prepare the body for meditation – but Dorothy would rather do an hour of standing poses than five minutes of meditation. Each time she feels like she did as a small child pretending to have afternoon naps at kindergarten. She would lie down with the others and close her eyes. She'd hear the teacher walking around, then try to time it so she could open her eyes and see if everyone else was really asleep or if there was another child who was also awake. There never was. And if the teacher caught her she'd be in trouble. Which she could never understand, because she wasn't *trying* to stay awake, she just *was* awake and didn't know how to make herself fall asleep.

Sometimes in class, when she's sitting on a blanket with her legs crossed, trying to keep her spine long and straight and focus on her breathing, she worries that Sandrine is going to find out that she's not really focusing on her breathing but instead letting her brain whirr through a thousand things. Sometimes she thinks it's like having a mind full of mosquitoes with that irritating little whine going on all the time. The difference is that her mental mosquitoes never come in to land and draw blood. If they did, it would mean Dorothy could think about just one thing at a time. Like her breathing.

Today she's thinking about the fact that her ligaments are getting so loose with the pregnancy that it's more comfortable to sit than it used to be, but for a shorter period of time, because then things start to ache. And if the baby moves around that's an extra distraction.

It's so weird, having another person alive inside her. She's seen that movie *Alien* with Sigourney Weaver and now thinks the alien is a metaphor for childbirth. It incubates then it explodes out of its host. Lovely.

That's what going to happen to her: she's cooking this little person who is then going to emerge from her, probably destroying everything in its path, and her GP doesn't really want to talk about it because that's 'ladies business', and it's too expensive to see her obstetrician just because she wants to talk about her fears of being ripped open, and she doesn't know who else to ask about it. Even if she did, it's not something that's discussed a lot in chitchat between women. Not the women Dorothy knows anyway. It's as if none of them has ever had a period and none of them has ever given birth, just like none of them has ever had a miscarriage. Even with Ruth, there are some conversations they've simply never had.

Dorothy hasn't tried to talk to Grace Maud yet, but maybe she should, because Grace Maud is a sensible type of person and she might have some good advice.

She hasn't tried to talk to her mother about it either, but nor has her mother offered any advice. And shouldn't she? Isn't that what mothers are for? Isn't that what Dorothy will have to do one day?

Oh, great. Now she's breathing more quickly. It's because she's thinking too much. Thinking about becoming a mother. Not just the childbirth bit but the actual mothering bit.

Dorothy's going to have to be wise and composed and competent. She'll have to know how to guide her child's upbringing so they grow up to be responsible and caring and decent. How can she do that when there are plenty of days when she feels she's none of those things?

'Listen to your breathing,' she hears Sandrine say.

That's right. *Breathing. Focus. Listen.*

And what happens if her child is naughty? Are they born naughty? Do they become naughty? How's she going to cope with a naughty child?

And what if . . . what if . . . what if . . .

This is the thought she doesn't like to have, but she has it. She can't help it. What if the child has something wrong with it, like Cornelia? Would Dorothy manage as well as her parents have? She doesn't have a big sister or brother for this baby, the way Cornelia has her. Dorothy loved playing with Cornelia when they were little, because even if Cornelia was upset she tended not to cry. She was a little built-in audience for everything Dorothy wanted to do. That helped their parents manage, no doubt. But what if Dorothy finds herself in that situation and it's just her and the baby?

It will be all right, she hears Frederick saying in her head. He's been saying that to her a lot lately, when she has these little whirlwinds of worry.

'Become aware of your surroundings,' Sandrine is saying. 'Some of you whose thoughts have taken over, you may need some time.'

Is Sandrine talking to her? Does she know? Dorothy is a bad meditator. She can't do this one simple thing right. Bad meditator. Bad mother. That's her path. She doesn't know how to change it.

'Slowly open your eyes.'

Dorothy opens them, and sees others emerging as if they've had a restful sleep. Lucky them.

'I think I prefer a relaxation lying down,' says Grace Maud as they roll up their mats. 'Meditation isn't for me.'

'It isn't?' Dorothy feels not pleased exactly, but reassured.

'Oh god, I can't switch off in either one,' says Patricia. 'My brain just goes round and round and round.' She shakes her head. 'Hopeless.'

'You too?' Now Dorothy is relieved.

Patricia shrugs. 'I think it's normal. How are we meant to switch off our lives?'

'We're not,' Grace Maud says definitively. 'And it's not like anyone can make us.'

'I felt like Sandrine was talking to me when she said people's thoughts were taking over,' Dorothy says sheepishly.

'She's talking to everyone,' says Patricia.

'Really?'

'Why do you think she says it every week?'

'She does?'

Patricia laughs. 'Maybe you're usually more relaxed and you don't hear it.'

Dorothy considers this. 'No, I think mainly I'm worrying about so many things that my brain is too noisy to hear it.'

Grace Maud frowns, just a little. 'What's worrying you tonight?'

Dorothy feels the prick of tears. Why does Grace Maud have to be nice to her? It's so much easier when people aren't nice. She's much less likely to cry then.

'Everything!' she says, sniffing to hold back those tears. 'Nothing in particular!'

Grace Maud gives Sandrine a wave, and takes Dorothy's arm to guide her outside. 'It's normal to be nervous about your first baby,' she says softly as they walk behind some slow leavers.

'I know.' Dorothy sniffs again.

'I was terrified.'

'You were?' Dorothy stops walking and Patricia almost bumps into her.

'Don't forget I gave birth in the forties. Things were a little more brutal then when it came to childbirth. Women died not infrequently.'

Dorothy's mouth drops open. Dying hasn't occurred to her before now.

'And I can see I shouldn't have said that,' says Grace Maud, 'as you're going to add that to the list, aren't you?'

Dorothy goes to say 'no', but it wouldn't do much good because Grace Maud will just say she's lying.

'But you shouldn't,' Grace Maud continues, 'because the risk is much lower now. We have a hospital here and you'll be in excellent hands.'

'It's going to hurt, though,' Dorothy says.

'I'm afraid there's no way around that.' Grace Maud starts walking again. 'But the pain is temporary and you won't remember it.'

Dorothy looks disbelievingly at the older woman.

'You'll remember that you were in pain,' Grace Maud explains, 'but if you try to conjure that pain again, you can't. It's a blessing, and you'll think so too.'

'What if I'm no good at it?' Dorothy says, almost whispering.

'Childbirth?'

Dorothy shakes her head. 'Mothering.'

'None of us is good at it, really,' says Grace Maud matter-of-factly. 'Our children all think we've failed them in some way at some point. You probably think that of your own parents.'

Dorothy nods, and Patricia makes a face.

'But we do our best. That's really all we can ask of ourselves.'

They've reached the street, and move away from the gate so others can depart.

'You're a kind-hearted woman, Dorothy,' says Grace Maud. 'So you're one up on me.'

'That's not true!' Dorothy squawks.

Grace Maud waves a hand. 'It is, and that's fine. We can't all be lovely. But you are, and your child will be lucky to have you.'

'I completely agree,' says Patricia, smiling broadly.

Dorothy takes a moment to think about what Grace Maud has said. She doesn't know if she's kind-hearted, but she trusts Grace Maud. And Patricia. They seem to think she will manage motherhood, as does Frederick.

That may not stop her worrying about it the next time she's in meditation – probably before then – but she'll remember it when the time comes for her to take her baby home and start on the unfamiliar journey of raising it.

'Thank you,' she says, and kisses them each goodbye. 'See you next week.'

And she walks to her car slowly while her baby gives her a good, strong kick.

WINTER 1994

HRH The Prince of Wales reveals in a televised interview that he was unfaithful to his wife; that same night Diana wears a black 'revenge dress' to the Serpentine Gallery in London.

The band Wet Wet Wet has chart success in Australia with 'Love is All Around'.

The movie *Speed*, starring Keanu Reeves and Sandra Bullock, is released.

Kylie Minogue releases the single 'Confide in Me'.

The Sum of Us, starring Russell Crowe and Jack Thompson, is released.

American singer-songwriter Jeff Buckley releases his debut album, *Grace*.

CHAPTER FORTY-FOUR

Patricia feels more frantic this time than last time. Because it was never meant to happen again. Her mother is meant to be in a home. She's meant to be watched by professionals whose job it is to make sure she doesn't wander. But Patricia's father still hasn't told Peter and John that he's going to take out a mortgage to pay for the care, and until he does that he won't let Patricia start looking for a place for his wife. So he's still in charge during the day while Patricia's at work, and today he got chatting to the next-door neighbour over the back fence and didn't realise that his wife had walked out the front door. Which was open, because he likes to get some air through the house.

There's no point Patricia castigating her father. He feels guilty – she heard that in his voice when he reached her in the staffroom. Luckily, this time classes were finished for the day. And it's Friday, so the staffroom was almost empty.

Patricia was trying to catch up on some marking because the weekend would be taken up with housework. When the phone rang she knew it would be for her. It was an instinct, or a foreboding. There's no way to tell which.

Dennis picked it up. He was the only other person there, poking around in the fridge in what seemed to be an exercise in delaying his departure.

'Yes, she's here. Whom may I say is calling?'

She was impressed he said 'whom'. It made him seem old-fashioned in a good way. In the sort of way that an English teacher like her appreciates.

'Patricia, it's your father.' Dennis didn't smile, which was uncharacteristic. But she was already concerned anyway – by now, concern is her regular state of being.

It was concern that made her not pay attention in yoga class last night. Sandrine came over while they were in a standing pose and put her hands on Patricia's shoulders.

'These have been getting higher each time,' she said. 'Soon they will reach the ceiling. You are worrying. Trying to carry a weight. These shoulders, they're bracing against it. Try to relax them for me.'

Patricia tried. She failed.

But Sandrine – who never makes anyone feel bad for something they can't do – simply patted her and said, 'This is your homework.'

As Patricia took the phone from Dennis, she felt like her shoulders were so high they were around her ears.

'She's gone,' her father said, and Patricia felt her breathing become shallow and rapid.

'How long ago?'

'I, ah . . .'

'Dad – where were you?'

'Out the back.'

She wanted to yell. To scream, actually. She wanted to scream at her father and ask him how he could be so careless. Remind him that they'd talked about this, over and over. He just kept saying, 'I'll look after her.' But he didn't. He forgot. Or never thought of it in the first place. The other day Patricia came home and the front door was open, her father was in the kitchen and her mother could have been anywhere. Luckily she was in the back garden. But he wasn't watching her.

'I'm coming home now,' she said and hung up without saying goodbye because she was too furious.

'What's going on?' Dennis asked.

'I can't – I have to go,' she said, flustered, picking up her work, dropping it. The essays slid onto the floor. She wanted to be two years old again and entitled to sit down and have a tantrum.

'I'll get those,' Dennis said, collecting the papers and stacking them neatly before handing them to her. 'How about I come with you?'

'You don't need to,' she said, although having someone else in the car might help to keep her calm.

'Yeah, I think I do. I'll drive. We can come back for your car later.'

She'd hesitated, feeling as though he'd seen straight through her older self to that two year old; as though he knew that she was too unsteady right now to be of use to anyone. It was a relief.

'Okay,' she said.

Now, Dennis is driving them to Yorkeys Knob.

'Where would you like to go?' he says as they near the beach.

'Um . . .' Her mind is blank. How do you start searching for someone who won't be thinking about where they're going? It's not like her mother has a plan. She's not a teenager absconding to a shopping centre.

'I don't know,' she admits. 'She could be in someone's garden. She could be on the beach.'

She turns her head from one side to the other as Dennis drives slowly.

'Is the beach likely?' he asks.

'She's gone there before, so maybe. But she doesn't like sand that much. So maybe not.'

'She's done this before?'

'Yes. Um – let's . . . let's turn left here.'

Patricia tries to remember the houses her mother's friends used to live in. She had three friends close by she would meet for afternoons of gin rummy. Her addled brain might spirit her away to what used to be familiar.

'I think – yes, this street here, on the left.'

Dennis turns and slows to twenty kilometres an hour while Patricia keeps swivelling her head left to right. No sign of her mother.

'What if she's walked towards the main road?' she says, her voice strangled.

'She's pretty old, right?' Dennis says. 'Do you really think she'd make it that far?'

He has a point, although that doesn't stop her panicking.

'I don't know,' she says. 'I don't know anything.'

She's no longer a two year old; she's five, or eight, or ten. One of the ages when she was asked to make decisions for herself and became paralysed with the fear of saying the wrong thing, all the while knowing that for her mother there was no right thing. Whatever Patricia said was silly. She was a 'silly girl'. She's spent all the years since making herself into the opposite of a silly girl, but now the layers of her adult self are peeled back. Because whichever way they drive, it could be the wrong way. The only right way is the way that leads to her mother, and she won't know what that is until they find her.

'You know more than most people, Patricia,' Dennis says seriously, and his hand takes hers.

She accepts it, regardless of what he may think that means, because she's grateful for it. She takes a slow breath and her thoughts slow down with it.

'Let's go to the golf course,' she says, remembering that until a few years ago her mother liked to play nine holes from time to time.

'And that is . . . ?' Dennis lets go of her hand so he can take the wheel properly.

'Right up here.'

As they approach the entrance to the golf course, Patricia sees a small person who is, without doubt, her mother, standing on the side of the road, staring at a tree.

'There she is,' she says, more calmly than she thought she would.

Dennis stops the car a few metres away, and Patricia jumps out and almost jogs over.

'Mum?'

'Hello, Patricia.'

'I've been looking for you.'

Her mother's head turns and she looks at Patricia with softness in her eyes. She's been doing that lately, and it's one of the ways Patricia knows she's deteriorating. Softness is not in her mother's repertoire.

'I have a good handicap,' her mother says.

'I know, Mum. You're a great golfer,' Patricia says, taking her mother's elbow. She always talks to her mother about the past in the present tense; her mother becomes confused otherwise.

'Mum, we need to get home,' she adds. 'It will be dinner-time soon.'

There's no point admonishing her for disappearing. She doesn't know she's done anything wrong.

By now Dennis is at her mother's other side. 'Mrs McKinley,' he says, 'I smelled something really good in your kitchen. Any chance I could stay for dinner?'

Patricia frowns at him. She has no idea what he's on about.

But her mother looks at him and smiles. 'Of course,' she says, moving away from Patricia's grip and taking Dennis's offered arm.

Dennis raises his eyebrows at Patricia and nods towards the car.

'How did you know that would work?' she says quietly.

'My nana used to go walkabout. Food was always the thing that would get her home.'

Suddenly she wants to know more about the Dennis who went looking for his lost nana, who can be so kind to her mother when he doesn't know her, who offered to drive Patricia without her needing to say she herself was in no state to drive.

'We're having lamb chops,' her mother says as Dennis helps her into the back seat and carefully does up the belt.

They aren't having lamp chops, but they're her mother's favourite and Patricia is encouraged to hear that she wants to eat anything at all. Lately she's been refusing to eat. Or maybe she can't eat. Patricia isn't sure which, because she doesn't know if her mother has the capacity to decide not to do anything.

Last night Patricia fried chops and cooked vegetables – the sort of dinner her mother usually likes – and cut everything up into small pieces. Once the food's cut up, her mother is able to use a fork with no problem – her motor skills are intact. Patricia had left her parents to it while she made another dinner for herself – if she had her choice, she'd never see another chop again – and got back to the table to discover that her mother hadn't eaten anything. Patricia tried to feed her, like she was a toddler, but her mother wouldn't open her mouth. Perhaps she's finally forgotten how to eat. Or it's a form of hunger strike: she wants to die and that's her way of expressing it. If that is the case, Patricia can't blame her. Being trapped inside an able body with a disabled mind is a nightmare with no prospect of an end.

If her mother won't eat again tonight, Patricia will need to have yet another tough conversation with her father and try to make him talk to his sons.

For now, though, the immediate drama is over. Patricia feels her shoulders drop as she gets into the passenger seat, and listens as her mother tells Dennis about the day she almost won the golf club championship.

CHAPTER FORTY-FIVE

When Grace Maud's parents died, there was no discussion about where they would be buried. Each of them had declared it would be on the property, in the paddock one removed from the house, next to a stand of Burdekin plum trees that their mother had planted when the twins were children. When their mother went first, Grace Maud called Ellie Maud and asked if she still thought their mother should be buried on the property and not in a graveyard. Ellie Maud told her to talk to their father. He said they needed to stick to the plan. By the time their father died, Ellie Maud was ailing and Grace Maud didn't call to ask her anything. Instead she was glad that neither of their parents was alive to see another child die.

It's a strange thing, to be an orphan. Not just an orphan because your parents have died but because all your siblings have died too. And it's a strange thing to orphan your only child by cutting him out of your life. Which is what Grace Maud has been doing to Tom. That's why she asked him to meet her at the graves today; it's also why she knew he would agree.

She believes him when he says he didn't mean to hurt her, because he's never intentionally hurt her; and she knows she let her indignation about what he did run away with her. Something an old lady could allow herself, perhaps, except when she causes her son far more harm than he has caused her.

'I'm so sorry these were damaged by the fire,' Tom says as he crouches to brush dirt off his grandfather's headstone. 'They were the first . . .' He turns to look at her. 'The first things I checked on. Once the house was gone. I had to know these were still here.'

'And they are still here, even if they're a bit beaten up. Your grandfather could give any fire a run for its money.' Grace Maud smiles at the memory of the tall, reedy man who had command of this place for so long.

'That's what I figured.' Tom stands up, and winces, putting a hand to his hip. 'That's getting harder. Not as young as I used to be.'

'We never are.'

Grace Maud gazes around at the burnt fields and the new shoots of plant life. The birds are starting to come back now, with that peculiarly Australian cacophony that becomes background noise when you're used to it but is stunningly absent when it's gone. The return of the birds means returning seed and grubs too. The cycle of fire: ruin and renewal. Grace Maud just isn't sure she has enough gumption for the renewal phase. She's done it too many times with metaphorical fires in her life, and she doesn't want to become so tired of it that she can't start that forward motion each day. There's a point past which all humans go, when the body starts its inexorable process towards death, and it can be fast or slow. She doesn't want a slow death. She wants to be as alive as she can be until the very end.

'I've been thinking,' she announces, 'about this place.'

Tom turns to her with a curious look in his eyes. 'So you've finally decided to grow avocados instead of cane,' he says, his eyes crinkling as he smiles.

'The decision will be yours, Tom.' She looks towards the horizon, across the scope of everything her family has worked on for years, and the land that existed for millennia before that, and knows how insignificant her time here has been. This place is her home, and her parents' and grandparents' home, but it was someone else's home well before that – thousands of years before. It will be someone else's home after she's gone. So she doesn't really know any more why she's clinging on.

'I don't have any right to stop you doing what you want to do. This is your place now.' She smiles so he knows this isn't a decision she has made in defeat, but he seems perplexed.

'I know this seems like a dramatic turnabout,' she continues. 'But when the fire happened . . . You were as upset as I was. That didn't surprise me so much as remind me that just as I've been here since I was born, so have you. And what have I been working for all these years if not to give you the opportunity to look after this place the way I have?'

Tom gets a strange look on his face. 'Are you sure?' he says after a few moments have passed.

'Have you ever known me to make an announcement when I'm not sure?'

His forehead relaxes. 'No.'

She nods, satisfied, and glances down at the headstones bearing her parents' and brothers' names.

'A person can cling onto the past for too long. This place was never meant to be mine forever. It was always ours. My parents'. Their parents'. And before that . . .' She closes her eyes and shrugs. 'It doesn't belong to any of us really, does it? We took it. And we didn't ask nicely. My father believed in terra nullius, but it never sat right with me. We're here now, though. Although who knows? That Mabo decision could mean we're not here for long.'

'I'd fight it if anyone tried to take this place,' Tom says fiercely.

'You'd be fighting history. You may not win.' Grace Maud pokes the earth with her foot. 'I was upset, Tom, because you were treating me as if I was too old to matter any more.'

He opens his mouth, but she silences him with a look only a mother can give. 'You may not have meant to, but the point is that you didn't think about the consequences of your actions. You didn't think about how it would sound to me. I haven't made it this far in my life without having pride. Without working to maintain dignity. Some may say those things don't matter, but they matter to me. They mattered to your grandparents. They will matter to you.'

As she stands with her feet rooted on her earth, she has the strangest sense of time shifting. The time before her; the time after. The time in between, when she had everyone she loved here on this earth; and the time when all but Tom had gone. That time is no longer now, because now she feels her capacity for love expanding in the same measure it contracted. There are new friends in her life, and all the tentacles of connection they bring with them. Her world is not small any more. Neither is her heart.

She sighs, letting go of any resentment that's still lingering. 'And I didn't think about the consequences of my actions either. I reacted, and I continued to react. For too long I didn't stop and think. So that's why we're here now.'

'I'm so sorry, Mum,' Tom says. 'Honestly. I never meant to shut you out. I thought I was helping. Thought you'd be glad to be free of the place. I just didn't . . .' He shakes his head. 'I really didn't think. But I won't make that mistake again.'

'I know you won't. Most of us do the best we can. Sometimes I just have to remind myself of that.'

Tom puts his hands on his hips. He looks tired. Probably she does too, but at her age it's hard to tell.

'I love you, Tom,' she says. 'That has never changed. It never will.'

'I know, Mum.'

He smiles, but his face sort of collapses at the same time. That's her cue, as a mother. She walks to him and puts her arms around his waist. He hugs her back.

It's been years since they've held each other like this. It shouldn't take a blow-up and a reconciliation for them to embrace. Maybe if they'd hugged each other more regularly they wouldn't have blown up in the first place. Each would have felt more acknowledged by the other than they did.

She resolves to hug him more often. He may wonder why, or he may hug her back. It doesn't matter. It's her job, as his mother, to remind him that he is loved.

'Shall we go?' he says, putting his arm around her shoulder.

'Yes. A glass of red at the pub wouldn't go astray.'

'My thought exactly.'

As they walk towards the car Grace Maud glances back at the graves.

'Goodbye,' she whispers, and she turns her face towards the future.

CHAPTER FORTY-SIX

'I feel like a whale,' Dorothy says, putting her hands on her rounded belly and squinting up into the sky. The winter light is soft but still harsh enough to remind her that every time she sits in the garden she should wear sunglasses.

It's become an after-work ritual, this quiet time with Frederick in their garden, listening to the birds and insects around them. Even though they haven't said so to each other, it's almost as if they're both acknowledging that once the baby arrives their life won't be quiet any more, so they should enjoy this time while it lasts.

Dorothy's seven months into the pregnancy and already the baby seems to have taken up all the room she can give it. It seems impossible that she'll continue to grow larger. How can her skin expand that much? How can her uterus? She knows it's normal – as normal as the gestating of a whole human being inside another can be – but it feels like it's contrary to all the laws of science she ever half paid attention to in school.

Frederick kisses her. 'You are not a whale. You are a woman, and you're beautiful.'

She likes that he still kisses her on the lips instead of her forehead or somewhere that would suggest he's started thinking of her as a woman other than his wife.

When Ruth was pregnant, her husband used to pat her on the head like she was a dog. She'd laugh and pretend not to be bothered by it, but Dorothy has known Ruth longer than her husband has and she could see that her friend was offended.

'He hasn't kissed me in months,' she'd said to Dorothy not long after that. 'He says he can't while I'm pregnant. How does he think I got this way? It involved kissing! And other things!'

So Dorothy was half expecting that Frederick would behave similarly as her body expanded and she became less Dorothy and more incubator. She said that to him once, on a day when she was feeling vulnerable about the fact that her body – the body she's always had, the only one she knows – was morphing.

He'd frowned at her. 'Dorothy, why would I change how I feel about you? I did not marry you expecting you to always be the same. Did you marry me thinking I would always be the same?'

She shook her head.

'Exactly,' he said. 'I might lose my hair. Are you going to leave me?'

'No!'

'What if I develop a hump, hm? As I become an old man?'

She giggled. 'No.'

'Well, you have a bump now. What's the difference between your bump and my hump?'

She pretended to consider the question. 'You don't have the hump yet.'

'Ah, but I will.' He'd wagged a finger at her. 'Tall men get humps. It's gravity. We can't help it.'

'You can if you put your shoulders back,' she retorted.

He looked amused. 'Is that what you learn in that yoga class?'

She'd tried her best to look superior. 'Amongst other things.'

He smiled at her in that understanding, caring way he's always had. 'Your bump is part of you, and I love you, so I am not going to think differently of you.'

'Thank you,' she'd said, and hadn't again mentioned the fact that she's been feeling unattractive and bloated, until now.

'Are you still going to think I'm beautiful when my ankles disappear?' she moans. 'Because that's next.'

'I have to tell you, *Liebling*, that I am not making a list of all the things that are changing. I look into your eyes when I look at you. I am not looking at all the different parts of you.'

She's touched. Even if it's not true, he's trying to make her feel better.

'Now, I have brought home some food from the café so we do not have to cook dinner,' he says. 'And . . .' He turns his body towards hers. 'I have some news.' His eyebrows dance up and down.

'Do you want me to guess?' she asks, picking at the bread she brought into the garden. She knows she's not meant to eat more than she usually does but she craves bread most days, and Frederick keeps bringing it home.

'There's a café for sale in Port Douglas.'

'Mm?'

'The owner came to see me today. To tell me. He thinks it would be a good business for us.'

Dorothy chews the bread as she tries to comprehend why he's telling her this. 'But we have a business,' she says eventually.

'We could have another one.' He looks at her expectantly.

'We don't need another one.'

He looks slightly annoyed. He never looks annoyed with her and she feels contrite, like she's done something wrong. Except all she's done is state the truth.

‘If we don’t expand, we’ll never make much more money than we make now,’ he says steadily.

‘We might! More people may come.’

‘There are more people in Port.’

‘But there’s only one of you. How are you going to run another business? When it’s an hour away?’

The baby kicks her and she gasps. This always happens when she’s agitated, which makes her worry that the baby can tell when she’s upset and becomes upset too. Or maybe babies can’t get upset when they’re not yet born. But something goes on, that’s for sure.

‘Are you all right?’ Frederick says, his hand on her arm.

‘Yes.’ She puts a hand on her belly. ‘The baby wanted to take part in the conversation.’

They stare at each other, and she marvels – as she does, occasionally – that she can know Frederick so well yet sometimes not at all. They have so much in common, so many shared values, but he can still surprise her by saying something like this. Perhaps it’s a good thing: it stops her becoming complacent about him. Right now, though, it feels like the ground beneath her feet is turning to sand.

‘Another café would be such a risk,’ she says.

‘If we don’t take risks there won’t be rewards,’ he replies, and she feels irritated because the phrase doesn’t sound like him. It sounds like it’s come from the café owner from Port Douglas, trying to offload his problems onto someone else.

‘What about the café here?’

She hopes that reason will persuade him to drop the idea, because she knows they don’t have the money to buy a second business and she doesn’t want to have a quarrel about money.

‘You can run it,’ he says proudly, as if it’s a perfect idea.

‘Frederick, I’m about to have a baby. When am I running it?’

'Your mother is going to help with the baby, isn't she?'

'Not every day!'

Another kick from inside her, and this time she doubles over. 'Ouch.'

'Darling?' His hand is on her back, warm and comforting.

'That one was under my rib,' she explains.

'I think you should sit down inside,' he says softly, taking both of her hands and lifting her from the seat. 'We'll talk about this another time.'

She knows that means he's not going to let the idea go. She's voiced her objections but they haven't made him rethink anything. Still, she knows he's tenacious. That's how they got the café in the first place: he worked to save up the money, never losing sight of his goal. She admired it then. As far as he's concerned, it's no different now that he has a new goal.

'We'll need to,' she says, drawing on her own form of tenacity: the one that brought her to this pregnancy.

'Put your feet up,' he almost croons as he leads her inside. 'I'll get our dinner.'

'We can talk later tonight,' she calls after him as he goes back to the kitchen.

'Or tomorrow,' he calls back. 'It's worth considering, I promise.'

She's sure it is. But it also makes her feel exhausted.

To the sound of Frederick removing plates from the cupboard and opening the cutlery drawer repeatedly, Dorothy falls asleep.

CHAPTER FORTY-SEVEN

Patricia isn't one of those teachers who prefers the school when the students aren't there. As much as some of them can be challenging, on the whole she loves her job and the teenagers who come with it. For the five per cent who are difficult, there are five per cent who are focused and brilliant; and the ninety per cent in between are a changeable mixture of attention and disinterest. She knows that a lot of what she teaches them actually does penetrate their skulls because she can see the results in their exams and essays – and nothing, absolutely nothing, gives her more pleasure than seeing a student who wasn't doing very well turn into one who does. That change may be nothing to do with her, or maybe it is, but nontheless it's a thrill every time. She knows that success at school isn't the sole determinant of a successful life, but when you're fifteen it's usually the only benchmark you have, so improvement in marks, in attitude, tends to have a generally beneficial effect. If Patricia can play any part in that, she believes she's done her job well.

So now that school is over for the term and holidays have started, she's not on school grounds to relish the absence of students but to prepare for next term. She doesn't use the same class plan each year with little or no variation. It's more interesting for her if she can vary things, so in addition to the curriculum she adds some texts each year. Right now she's considering whether to reintroduce *The Catcher in the Rye* for her Year Elevens. It's been a couple of years since she's taught it, and while she's no fan of Holden Caulfield's self-indulgence the book is a classic and she would be remiss if she didn't teach it some of the time.

She picks it up and starts to read the first paragraph when a knock on her office door makes her jolt.

'Sorry! Sorry.' It's Dennis, with a mortified expression on his face. 'I should have made more noise when I walked up.'

He's looking quite out of character since he's wearing jeans and a long-sleeved top. He'd be almost staid if his hair and skin didn't advertise the fact that he spends part of each day in the ocean.

'What are you doing here?' she says, her heart still beating quickly, although she's not sure if it's from the adrenaline of the shock or something else.

'I check the equipment every holidays. Just to, y'know . . .' He shrugs. 'Make sure it's in order. I heard a bit of noise when I was walking past. Thought I'd see who it was.'

'Just little old me,' she says, smiling guardedly.

Ever since he made it clear he's still interested in her she's been feeling slightly off kilter around him and doesn't want him to know. Her solution, as always, is to keep her face in as neutral an expression as possible. Since he helped find her mother she's chatted to him more than usual, but not enough to make him think she might change her mind about going out with him. Even if she's been daydreaming about him – thinking about his face and his smile and his body. Thoughts she hasn't had about anyone for a long time. Thoughts that can't ever manifest in reality.

'So why are you here?' Dennis says, leaning against the door.

Patricia notices his long, lean torso and looks away.

She clears her throat. 'Preparing for next term. I want to set an extra book but I haven't decided which.'

Dennis gestures to the novel in her hands. 'Salinger's all right. And it's short. Students usually like that.'

She looks at him questioningly.

'What?' he says.

'I thought you didn't like English.'

He smiles. 'I liked it once I left school.'

'What was wrong with it at school?'

Maybe she's teaching the wrong way. For all she knows, there are Dennises in her class who will hate English until she's not teaching it to them any more.

'I dunno.' He looks more guarded. 'I just reckon . . . Books are meant to be enjoyed. Not pulled apart. It takes the fun out of them if you have to keep talking about them, trying to work out what the author meant.'

He surprises her again. She knows she shouldn't judge him just because he's the PE teacher. PE teachers read books too. But she's never met one, before now, who talks about them.

'So,' she says, 'maybe Salinger needs too much discussion. Would it be mean to set *The Lord of the Rings*?'

He laughs. 'Jeez – throw in a bit of Tolstoy while you're at it. Just to make sure no one has time to ever read anything ever again.'

'Don't give me ideas,' she says playfully.

He stands up straighter and folds then re-folds his arms.

'I, uh . . . I have some news,' he says, and she feels something grab at her solar plexus. Jealousy? She isn't sure and doesn't want to know.

'Oh?'

'Yeah.' He tugs at his sleeves. 'I'm leaving at the end of the year.'

Now it's her throat that feels grabbed.

'I'm going to India for a while,' he continues.

'India?'

'Yeah. My mum's always going on about it. She went for a trip when I was little – she, uh, kind of took off for a while.' He makes a goofy face. 'I can't remember it. She left me with her parents because Dad was a bit hopeless. I just thought I was on a holiday for a few months.'

'So you didn't see your father either?'

'No. My grandparents are on the Sunshine Coast. Dad stayed on the Gold Coast. They got back together when Mum returned.'

'And how did that turn out?'

Dennis laughs. 'She told him he had to learn how to cook and clean or she'd be off again. Whaddya know? Turned out he could use the oven after all.' His face changes. 'He liked to cook. I miss his spag bol.'

He makes more sense to Patricia now: this masculine man who – unlike many of the men she's encountered over the years – has no problem with women who assert themselves. Or girls who do, for that matter – she's seen him push the girls as hard as the boys in PE classes. Unlike previous teachers, who took the line that girls are too delicate to do anything strenuous.

'India was good for your mum, then?' she asks, wanting to know more about this woman who has clearly had such an influence on him.

He smiles in a dreamy way. 'She said it was life-changing.'

'Do you want to change your life?'

He leans against the door again. 'I reckon I do,' he says softly.

'What's there that you can't do here?'

'It's *there* – I think that's the main thing. I've never travelled, y'know.' He waves a hand. 'Didn't go to London – none of that usual Aussie stuff. I've got some money saved and I figure it'll last me a while in India.'

She can now identify what she's feeling: sadness.

'How long will you go for?' she asks.

'A year. That's the plan.' He stares at her. 'Will you miss me?'

The question is so direct, so intimate, that she has no idea what to say. Because he's not laughing, joking Dennis now – he's being serious; and she needs to take him seriously.

She needs to take herself seriously too. And that means giving him an honest answer.

'Yes,' she says, then she inhales and holds it as she waits for his response.

He nods. 'I'll miss you too.' Then he pushes off the door and walks away.

Patricia's heart is thudding as she watches the empty doorway, wishing he would return. That conversation isn't over – it can't be. There is more to say, if only she knew what it was. Inside her head is a swarm of competing thoughts and ideas; and her body is overrun by what she wants.

None of this is what she thought would happen when she sat down at her desk in the empty school and diligently tried to go about her work. Except if she has learnt anything since she moved home, it's that she can never expect things to turn out as planned.

She didn't think her mother would deteriorate the way she has, or that she would be prevented from seeking assistance for her mother when it was needed. She didn't think she would enjoy yoga so much to the point that she willingly puts herself on that mat every week and lets Sandrine tell her what to do.

She didn't think she would make new friends – especially not one who is around the age of her parents.

And she thought Dennis would always be around, so they could . . . what? Keep admiring each other from a distance? But now he's said he's leaving, she's very, very clear on one thing: she doesn't want him to go. She's feeling something about it, even if she can't yet name it. And she certainly didn't think she would feel anything for a man again. She's meant to be past all of that, isn't she?

Yet as she sits at her desk, clutching *The Catcher in the Rye*, wishing Dennis would return, wishing their conversation would continue not just now but for a long time, she realises – with the startling clarity she has come to recognise from moments when she is holding postures that once seemed beyond her, or opening herself up to the idea that the universe is limitless and so is her consciousness – that some feeling for him has come upon her without her deciding or willing it. It's not just that she finds him attractive – that doesn't take much effort at all. It's that she wants to be around him; wants to know what he's thinking, what he's doing.

Except she knows what he's doing: he's leaving. And that feels almost intolerable. Which suggests to her that whatever this feeling she has is, it's not just mild affection.

Sandrine has told them to listen to their bodies, because the body will give them information the rational mind doesn't yet know, or may never know. So Patricia sits, and breathes, and listens, and she hears this: what she feels is real, and not a mistake.

The question she doesn't ask – because she's not sure if she wants the answer – is whether this is love. Because that would be something she's never experienced before. Not with her high-school boyfriend. Not with anyone who tried to make a connection with her when she lived in Sydney. Falling in love hasn't been in her repertoire. Perhaps it will never be. Whatever she's feeling now may well fade once Dennis leaves.

There is something else her body is telling her, though, and she can't push it aside. It's a sensation in her heart centre. A lightness. Joy, even.

This is something else that Sandrine promised – or threatened – would happen if they stayed on the mat long enough: their hearts would open.

So she does what Sandrine would want her to do. She sits with the feeling, she breathes, she observes, and is thankful that she's learnt enough to not dismiss what's going on.

She almost feels like running to Sandrine to tell her, as if that will earn her a gold star. How pathetic to want approval at this age. How wonderful to care enough that it still matters.

She puts the Salinger down and makes a note to think about setting Tolkien for her Year Elevens.

CHAPTER FORTY-EIGHT

'Well, at least switching to the Saturday class means we can have coffee afterwards!' Dorothy says, smiling, her hands propped on her belly.

Grace Maud picks up the menu and peruses the options for cakes and biscuits. She isn't usually given to sweet treats but this morning she's in the mood.

'Thank you for changing,' Dorothy goes on. 'I'm just so tired by the end of the day that the evening class is becoming impossible. And now I've stopped working I can do every Saturday.'

Patricia smiles reassuringly. 'It's fine.'

'For me too,' Grace Maud says, deciding on a Devonshire tea. 'It's not as if my diary is so full that I couldn't fit this in.'

She looks around for someone to take their order and catches the eye of a loose-limbed youth slouching near the till. He pushes his hair out of his eyes, ambles in their direction and scribbles their order on a torn piece of paper.

'It's nice, this place, isn't it?' Dorothy glances around.

'Why aren't we at your café?' Grace Maud asks, and watches as Dorothy's face changes.

'I spend enough time there,' she replies, her words running together.

'You've not previously mentioned that that's a problem.' Grace Maud sits back. She's found that when trying to extract information from someone it's best to appear physically nonchalant. Not that she wishes Dorothy to say anything she doesn't want them to know. It's more that she believes Dorothy has been waiting all morning to tell them something, and now she's issuing the invitation.

Dorothy huffs a little, fiddles with her cutlery and tosses her head so that her plait almost whacks the window behind her. 'Frederick's talking about buying another business. In Port Douglas.' By the tone of her voice, this is the ultimate betrayal.

'Oh dear,' says Grace Maud. 'That sounds awful. Is it awful?'

'We can barely afford the business we have now! And we don't live in Port Douglas!' Dorothy says, the pitch of her voice rising.

'It's quite nice in Port Douglas,' Grace Maud says. 'I thought about moving there when I left the farm.'

'Why didn't you?' asks Patricia.

'I'm old,' Grace Maud says bluntly, 'and Cairns has a hospital.'

'I don't think you're old.' Patricia smiles and shrugs.

In return, Grace Maud frowns at her. 'Then you need your eyes checked. Dorothy, has Frederick told you why he wants to do this in Port Douglas?'

Dorothy huffs again. 'The business is cheap to buy.'

'What's wrong with it?' Grace Maud says, instantly sceptical.

'I asked that too. He said the owners are getting a divorce and they want to sell quickly for the settlement.' Dorothy's gaze flashes from Grace Maud to Patricia and her eyes fill with tears. 'Except I think *we'll* end up getting a divorce if he does this! He's going to be working all the time! And we're about to have a baby!'

'*You're* about to have a baby,' Grace Maud mutters. 'Let's not give him credit for work he's not going to do.'

Patricia's eyes widen.

'What?' says Grace Maud. 'He's not pushing out a small human being. I know he's a lovely man from the things Dorothy usually tells us, but this is a bit inconsiderate. Dorothy will have to recover from the birth, and by the sound of it Frederick will be in Port Douglas all day. An hour away. Not very helpful, wouldn't you say?'

'I'd suggest talking to him about it,' Patricia offers. 'But I can't say I've had much success at that so I really shouldn't be giving you advice. Apart from saying that when people get fixated on an idea they don't tend to let it go.'

'You don't have success talking to people?' Grace Maud says. 'I'm surprised to hear that.'

Patricia sighs. 'I guess I mean my brothers. Dad still hasn't talked to them about what we need to do to get Mum into a home, so I've tried to broach the subject a few times and they just keep saying they'll worry about it when they need to. But that time is now.' She slaps the table and Dorothy looks startled.

'Mum's brain is never going to fix itself,' Patricia continues. 'And I'm never going to have more time to look after her than I do now. My siblings won't help. And I don't have power of attorney or anything that means I can make decisions independent of them. Or of Dad. So . . .' She blinks rapidly. 'I'm stuck. Which means I understand how you feel, Dorothy. I just don't have any tips for how to become unstuck.'

Grace Maud looks at the two distressed younger women. Her dotage has come with experience, if not wisdom, and she thinks of all the times she had to negotiate people and their needs and wants that were different to her own. At least she can offer these two the benefit of her hindsight.

'One would think that family members should be the easiest to negotiate with,' she says. 'Sometimes, however, the only and best thing you can do is let them realise in their own time that they're being ridiculous.'

'Does that usually work?' Patricia asks.

'Surprisingly, yes. Quite often. Usually because their behaviour is unreasonable and it never gets them anywhere good. The world has a funny way of sorting things out for you so that people get their comeuppance. Eventually.'

She turns and takes Dorothy's hand. 'So, darling Dorothy, I recommend that you let Frederick go through all of this and he'll soon work out if it's doomed. But what you shouldn't do is let yourself become so upset about something you can't change. It's not good for you or,' her eyebrow arches, '*le bébé*.'

The other two giggle at her impression of Sandrine.

'So what other news do we have?' Grace Maud says. 'Patricia – what's going on at school?'

Patricia blushes, and Grace Maud wonders why.

'Oh, nothing major. My colleague Dennis told me that he's leaving at the end of the year to travel to India.'

'Who is this Dennis? Do we know him?'

'He helped me look for my mother when she went walkabout that last time.'

Grace Maud nods, remembering Patricia telling them about it after class. She also remembers thinking that this Dennis must be interested in Patricia to help her like that. Grace Maud has nothing against men, but she believes that most of them are not altruistic. There's usually another motivation for their actions, and if a man is willing to spend his time driving around a woman who is looking for her geriatric parent, it would suggest that he's keen on her. This doesn't nullify his kindness, of course – it merely adds a layer to the story.

'So he's a friend?' Dorothy asks, her eyes shining.

'Y-yes,' Patricia says. 'He is.' She blushes again. 'He asked me out once. Ages ago.'

Grace Maud and Dorothy exchange glances.

'I said no. He's too young.'

'How young?' Dorothy asks.

'Young. Younger.' Patricia shakes her head. 'I don't actually know.'

'Presumably he knows your approximate age?' Grace Maud says.

'He would know I'm in my forties. Beyond the realm of having children.' Patricia's voice catches on the last word. 'So I don't think he could really be interested in me.'

'You don't?' Grace Maud says incredulously. 'When you're intelligent and capable and – let's face it, my dear – beautiful?'

Patricia looks shocked. 'Beautiful?' she says.

Grace Maud looks at Dorothy, who starts laughing.

'You're the most beautiful woman I've ever seen,' Dorothy says.

'Maybe you haven't realised because your hairdresser keeps doing a number on you,' Grace Maud mutters.

Even though Patricia has been growing her hair out of the awful bob, it's now in something resembling a shag cut that would better suit Jane Fonda in her Vietnam War years.

'Grace Maud!' Dorothy says with a giggle.

'Well, it's true. It's almost as if she – I presume your hairdresser's a she? – is jealous of you and trying to make you less appealing. Sometimes it works.'

Patricia is looking like the proverbial stunned mullet, so Grace Maud decides to move the conversation along.

'So how do you feel about this Dennis going away?'

Patricia blinks. 'I, uh . . . I think I feel sad.'

Dorothy beams. 'You like him too, then?'

'I don't think he likes me any more,' Patricia says quickly.

'Of course he does,' Grace Maud says. 'That's why he told you. He wants you to react.'

A small frown shows on Patricia's face, then she releases it. 'How did you know that your husband was the right one for you?' she asks Grace Maud. 'I mean – I guess you must have loved him to want to marry him. Was that enough?'

Grace Maud remembers feeling a few things after she met Clark. Relief was the primary emotion, because she thought she could finally tick off the box she was meant to and become a wife, then a mother. That was the track laid down for her, and at the time she didn't realise that some tracks have sidings.

'No,' she says.

'No?' Dorothy looks slightly appalled.

'I thought I was in love with him,' Grace Maud says. 'But I'd talked myself into it. Or perhaps he talked me into it.'

She's only ever told Ellie Maud this – mainly because no one else has asked her. She knew that Ellie Maud would understand; that she wouldn't think her strange. They never had to explain such things to each other.

'Why did you marry him?' asks Dorothy, still somewhat aghast.

'Because I thought I loved him enough. And marriage was what a young lady did,' Grace Maud says truthfully.

She knew other girls who hadn't married for love. They had to be practical: without jobs of their own they didn't have money of their own, and that meant no home of their own, so the only way to have any kind of future that didn't mean living with their parents forever was to find a husband. It was a trap, and most of them knew it. But to remain unwed was a pitfall, so there wasn't much of a choice.

Grace Maud looks from Dorothy to Patricia and realises she could tell them not just *the* truth but *her* truth. She would be outrageously lucky to live another score years, and if she doesn't tell her story now she may not have another chance. And, really, doesn't every person want their story to be heard?

'I've never been interested in falling in love,' she admits. 'Because I had something most people never do.'

Two expectant faces look back at her.

'I had my twin, Ellie Maud. I grew up feeling intimately connected with another person at all times. It made it difficult to need other people.'

She smiles, thinking of the sister who would lie in the bed next to her, clutching her hand because Grace Maud was afraid of the ghosts their brothers told her were haunting the house. The sister who told her she was the prettiest girl in Atherton – 'And of course that means I am too!' – and the best, most perfect person ever. There were things between them that didn't need words, and would now never have them. It was ideal, their relationship. It was Grace Maud's ideal.

'I know Ellie Maud felt the same about me,' she says. 'But she moved away after she married so we didn't have that connection in person any more.'

'Did that hurt?' Dorothy asks, her voice tender.

'What do you mean?'

'That she didn't stay here with you?' Her eyes are big and round and deep with sympathy.

'Yes,' Grace Maud says. 'It hurt terribly. And it's probably one of the reasons why my marriage never stood a chance. I could never feel close to Clark. Not the way I did to her. In the end I couldn't bear him. And he was . . . unkind.' She huffs out a breath. 'Love isn't just the one thing. It's not only romantic. Or only maternal. I sometimes think of it as like plasticine.

We can pull it and mould it – it changes shape.' She makes a face. 'I don't know. There's no definition for it, really. There's what we feel, and I don't think we can help it.'

She turns to Patricia. 'What makes you think this Dennis isn't still keen on you? Why shouldn't someone be helplessly in love with you?'

Patricia blinks rapidly. 'Because I'm not lovable,' she whispers.

Seeing Patricia's distress, Grace Maud feels her own heart hurt. She observes it, as if it belongs to a stranger. Then she feels that hurt radiate towards her limbs, her cheeks, her eyes. It's how she used to feel whenever Tom was little and got upset. Before she left his father. Before she hardened her heart just so she could carry on each day. She recognises what the hurt is now: she loves Patricia like a daughter. Dorothy too.

Not that she will tell them – she wouldn't dream of imposing that on them. It's enough for her to know. But still, she thinks that Patricia might miss a trick with Dennis if she doesn't find out what might be between them.

'Don't you dare say that, Patricia,' Grace Maud tells her fiercely. 'You're the most lovable woman in the world. Apart from Dorothy.'

The hurt sensation in Grace Maud's body recedes as she sees Patricia smile, then laugh, wiping her tears from her cheeks.

'And I think you should give this young man a chance,' Grace Maud continues. 'He's an adult. He can decide for himself if your age difference is a problem. It's not your responsibility to do that. Just because you're looking after your parents, and you look after your students, doesn't mean you need to pick up all the strands of life for everyone else.'

'Thank you,' Patricia says.

'There's nothing to thank me for.' Grace Maud quickly squeezes her hand. 'Now, where's my Devonshire tea?'

CHAPTER FORTY-NINE

Y*our tummy is huge*, Cornelia says as she opens the door to Dorothy and Frederick.

I know, Dorothy says, her hands moving slower than usual. She groans as she steps into the hallway. *I don't think my skin can stretch any more.*

'Hello, Cornelia,' Frederick says, kissing her once on each cheek.

'Hi, Mama,' Dorothy says, kissing her mother on the cheek but not embracing her as she wants to, because the baby is getting in the way.

While they've never been a demonstrative family, Dorothy has found herself wanting hugs from her mother lately. She's tried to figure out if it's some sort of primal response to the fact that she's about to be a mother herself. Or perhaps she's simply scared of the pain and difficulty to come and wants reassurance from the person who used to make her problems disappear when she was younger.

'Hello, my Dorothea,' her father says as he appears, putting his arm around her from the side, then shaking Frederick's hand.

As they walk towards the living room Dorothy tries not to waddle. She's seen every pregnant woman do it and thought it looked undignified, until she found herself on that same small pendulum track.

When she asked Sandrine if there was anything she could do to stop the waddle, Sandrine merely said, 'Yes – give birth.'

Dorothy tried again, but Sandrine explained that when you're in your third trimester your body is doing its best to accommodate the baby and there's limited capacity for anything else.

'You have been doing enough postures that you have prepared the best you can,' she said. 'You could be stronger, this is true, but the time is past for that.'

Dorothy knew Sandrine was right: she hadn't done anything much to build her strength before she became pregnant. Not because she didn't believe it was important, but because she was working long hours, managing the hormone treatment along with everything else, and counting her week as a success if she made it to class. There was no scope to add anything, no matter how helpful it might be.

'So will yoga help me at all?' Dorothy had asked.

'The breathing,' Sandrine said, nodding enthusiastically. 'And it will help when you recover. You know your body better now, no? So you will take care of it better. I hope. Won't you?'

'I'll try,' Dorothy said meekly, although she wondered how she'd be able to do that. She'll be at home alone with the baby while Frederick goes to work. Her mother has a hundred tasks to do each day; her father is working; Ruth has a family of her own . . .

This is the part – where she's alone and not coping – that Dorothy tries not to think about, because remembering to breathe through it, as Sandrine would have her do, will be impossible.

There's also the part where she's not only alone but Frederick is working in Port Douglas instead of Cairns, and they have more debt and less time for each other than they do now, and the worries about money and the future and life and health and all the things that Dorothy can find to worry about have increased exponentially with no prospect of them decreasing before the two of them reach retirement. Then they'll be dead.

These are the sorts of things that crowd into her mind when she can't sleep because she's too bulbous. There is, she has found, no comfortable way to lie when you have an almost fully developed small human strapped to your insides. She's tried to breathe through that as well; and when she can't, she adds being bad at yoga to her worries too.

All these thoughts Dorothy keeps to herself, because Frederick doesn't need to hear them, nor do her parents, and her friends shouldn't be burdened with them. Besides, how can she explain that as she nears the moment she wants most – giving birth – she is so scared of everything that can go wrong in her life? They will think she's ungrateful for what she has, and they'll be right. They'll think she's not coping and can't look after the baby. Maybe they'll be right about that too. Something else to worry about.

As Dorothy lowers herself into a chair she hears her father asking Frederick about work while her mother goes to the kitchen.

Cornelia waves a hand to attract Dorothy's attention; once Dorothy has settled herself into position she nods and smiles.

I have a plan, says Cornelia, pushing her fringe out of her eyes.

For what?

To help you with the baby.

Dorothy hasn't said anything to her family about needing help with the baby so she's not sure why Cornelia is broaching the subject.

You don't have to worry about that, she replies.

Cornelia frowns. *Frederick will be working.*

I know, Dorothy says, laughing wryly.

'You'll need help.' Cornelia says this out loud. She only speaks when she's really trying to make a point.

All right, Dorothy says. *What's your plan?*

Cornelia looks pleased with herself as she starts to sign. *I could move in with you. Then I could help you all the time.*

Dorothy's mouth drops open and she knows that Cornelia will notice because she observes everything about people's faces. It's how she works out tone and meaning.

What she'll read on Dorothy's face is surprise, probably mixed with irritation. Because Dorothy's first thought is that she and Frederick will never be alone with their baby – or each other – and given how many extra hours he's going to spend working they will start to feel more like housemates than husband and wife.

You don't like the idea, Cornelia says.

It's a surprise, Dorothy says truthfully. *Can we talk about it once the baby arrives?*

She avoids Cornelia's eyes because she doesn't actually want to talk about it ever again, but she'll have to, because Cornelia will feel slighted if she doesn't.

Cornelia nods and turns towards the kitchen door, through which their mother emerges carrying a tray of cake and coffee.

'You've been quiet,' their mother says, looking meaningfully at her daughters.

'Just having a chat,' Dorothy says, then she changes position on the chair.

'How are things at the café?' Clara says to Frederick.

'They're good,' Frederick says quickly, then he catches Dorothy's eye. 'And we have something to tell you.'

We? Dorothy knows what he's going to say, but there was no discussion about this beforehand. She can't say anything, though, because she has to stand by her husband even if she doesn't agree with him. That's what her mother has always done with her father.

Not that it ever seems to work the other way – Dorothy can't think of a single instance when her father changed his view to align with her mother's. Not because he's not a good man, or because he's unsympathetic. No doubt it's because it's never occurred to him.

'*Was ist das?*' her father says.

'There's a place in Port Douglas,' Frederick says, sitting forwards. 'We have the chance to buy it. To run it.'

'As well as the one in Cairns?'

'Yes.'

Clara frowns as her eyes meet Dorothy's. 'But you're about to have a baby. How are you going to manage this?'

'It's too good an opportunity to refuse.'

Frederick's voice is alive with enthusiasm, and this is why Dorothy hasn't pushed back harder against him when they've gone over and over this subject. Frederick is so passionate about it, and made so happy by it, that she doesn't want to crush him. He has supported her these past few months and never complained. She knows what Grace Maud would say – that it's his baby too so he shouldn't complain. Yet Dorothy knows what Grace Maud doesn't: that Frederick's had to live with her mood swings and doubts and fears. He's held her in the night when she's been desolate about things she can't name because she's not sure what they are. So she doesn't want to tell him that he can't do something that excites him, no matter how much it scares her.

'So you will work in Port Douglas?' asks Dieter.

'Yes. At least to start with. And we'll put in a manager here.'

Dorothy's parents look at each other, then away, but they don't look at her or Frederick.

'We're not here to ask for money,' Frederick says. 'I should have made that clear. You've already been very generous. I'm going to take out a loan.'

'*We're* going to take out a loan,' Dorothy says. They're both in this, even if the new dream isn't hers.

Clara is still frowning. 'As long as you're sure,' she says to Dorothy.

Dorothy wants to say that she's not sure. That she'll never be sure. But she won't do that to her husband.

'It's a risk,' she says instead, 'but so is having a baby. If we don't take risks we won't achieve anything.' And she partly believes it's true.

'All right,' Clara says softly.

'Let us know when we can see this new place,' Dieter adds.

Frederick's smile is relaxed as he sits back into the couch. 'We will,' he says.

Cornelia taps Dorothy on the arm. *How do you really feel about this?* she says.

Dorothy widens her eyes. *I'll tell you later*, she replies. Then she glances at her parents to see if they've witnessed the exchange, but they're both looking at Frederick, who is now looking at her.

'What did Cornelia say?' he asks.

'She asked how I'm feeling,' Dorothy says quickly and smiles in a way that she hopes is reassuring. But she can sense Cornelia watching her. She's never been good at hiding her feelings, as her mother is fond of reminding her, and knows her sister will probably see them on her face.

'I forgot the sugar,' Clara says, standing up.

As her mother leaves the room again Dorothy avoids looking at her sister and cradles her belly, silently promising her child that whatever happens, they will be together and they will be okay.

SPRING 1994

Australian films *Muriel's Wedding* and *The Adventures of Priscilla, Queen of the Desert* are released.

A new Australian band called Silverchair tops the singles chart with their debut release, 'Tomorrow'.

Ossie Ostrich leaves *Hey Hey It's Saturday* after twenty-three years as co-host with Daryl Somers.

Forrest Gump, starring Tom Hanks, is released.

Quentin Tarantino's *Pulp Fiction* is released, reviving the career of John Travolta.

Nirvana releases the album *MTV Unplugged in New York*.

Mariah Carey releases the single 'All I Want for Christmas is You'.

CHAPTER FIFTY

Grace Maud is usually out of bed early. Lying around is for lazy people, or so her father used to say. If you were still asleep after the sun was up, you were wasting the day. It's training that has never left her, even if she no longer has any reason to be up with the sun. There are no crops to attend to; there's not even much housework to do since Cecilia has been around. Today, however, Grace Maud stays in bed for a while and reads a book. The house is quiet – Cecilia likes a lie-in on Sundays – so she has the luxury of being able to concentrate on the story.

She's always read for relaxation, and read eclectically. Her belief is that if you like to read, you'll read anything. She said that to Tom when he was growing up and finding it hard to read as fluently as his classmates. Comics were fine, as far as Grace Maud was concerned, if they held his interest. They weren't fine with his teachers, of course – comics weren't 'proper' reading, apparently. Except Ginger Meggs could make Tom laugh in a way his teachers never could, and who was to say that wasn't proper?

The two of them were a good team for a long time. Then Viv came along, and she fitted in seamlessly. She wasn't one of those daughters-in-law who is jealous of her husband's mother, and it didn't occur to Grace Maud to be jealous of Viv. Tom didn't belong to her, after all. Maybe living on the land gave her a different perspective about that: their joint enterprise was bigger than both of them, so they weren't possessive people.

Perhaps that's why she hasn't been able to empathise with Cecilia's mother, Eva, who seems simultaneously possessive of her daughter yet does everything possible to repel her. Several times Cecilia has asked Grace Maud for advice about her mother – often coming to her in tears after a phone call that's ended badly – but Grace Maud has never been able to adequately explain Eva's actions to her daughter. If Cecilia were her child, she would thank the heavens for the miracle of having such a lovely person in her life. Instead, Eva finds only faults.

It's no wonder Cecilia has latched onto Luca with his easy-going nature. The pair of them have been spending increasing amounts of time together – more than Grace Maud would probably advise, given they're still young. Although she married young, as did Ellie Maud, and Tom, so she's not really qualified to give that advice.

There is so much more for women to do these days, though; they have options that she and Ellie Maud could never have imagined. They can travel on their own; they can even keep their jobs after they marry. Feminism may be a dirty word for some women, but Grace Maud has the perspective of having lived decades on this earth and she sees the change it's wrought. Women have the vote; they have jobs and bank accounts, and they don't need permission to spend their own money. All this in under a century.

Cecilia is in the bloom of first love and doesn't think she needs to take the opportunities that her forebears fought for – possibly because she takes them for granted – but Grace Maud wishes she would at least consider travelling.

She tried to have that conversation with her just yesterday, suggesting that Cecilia might like to visit Sydney or Melbourne.

'Why?' she'd said. 'I have everything I want here.'

'Yes, for now,' Grace Maud said evenly.

'What do you mean, "for now"?'

'You're young. What you want will change.' Grace Maud smiled to soften the blow.

Cecilia shook her head with the vigour of youth and certainty. 'I don't think so,' she said, and Grace Maud knew enough to not press the point.

She puts her book down. It isn't holding her interest the way it did last night. Perhaps because she feels guilty about lying in bed while the sun is up. Her father has been dead a long time but the guilt he instilled is as alive as ever.

She hears noise in the kitchen, then the phone rings. Cecilia's singsong 'Hello', then silence, then her tone changes. Is she upset? No, she's cross. The phone slams down; now there are heavy footsteps coming closer.

A tentative knock on the door. 'Grace Maud?'

Cecilia would know she'd be awake because she's always awake by eight o'clock.

'Yes. Come in.'

'Sorry. I didn't think you'd still be in bed.'

'It's fine. What's wrong?'

Cecilia sits on the end of the bed. 'That was Mum. She says if I'm not at mass at nine o'clock she's never speaking to me again.'

'That sounds rather dramatic. I know you've missed a couple of Sundays, but that's to be expected. You have other things in your life.'

Cecilia sniffs and her eyes shift around the room. 'She saw me with Luca,' she says. 'At the marina. We were only holding hands!' She sucks in a breath.

'I take it she didn't know you have a boyfriend?' Grace Maud enquires gently.

'No. Why would I tell her? He's not Catholic so she'll say he's not suitable.'

'She probably only says that because she had to marry a Catholic boy, and her mother would have too,' Grace Maud says. 'But it's a hard thing to enforce in a country with people from as many different places as this one.'

'I know!' Cecilia huffs. 'And she's never even met Luca!'

Grace Maud carefully considers what she should say next. She doesn't think Cecilia wants to stay estranged from Eva, but she wants Eva to accept her on her terms, just as Eva wants Cecilia to submit to what she wants. There is love there – obviously, otherwise neither would care so much – but they don't have the mechanism to make their relationship work. It is a difficulty now, but it could become a heartbreak.

Grace Maud had ample time to think about this while she and Tom weren't speaking. She was stuck in the quagmire of wanting to have her own way, yet loving him so much she wanted him to have his way too. It's a problem that has existed, no doubt, for as long as there have been parents and children. Each wants what they want; each wants what the other wants so the other can be happy. Sometimes it seems easier to give up and leave each other alone. But it never is, because there is nothing left in this life if we give up on love. That love will always remain, even when you're not speaking to each other. You may not be conscious of it, but it will sit in your cells, so much a part of you that there is absolutely nothing you can do to be rid of it. Denying it may kill you – Grace Maud is convinced of that. When something is so fundamental to your person – to your actual physical being – it has the power of life and death over you. Those are the stakes. This is what it means to be alive. It has taken her almost four score years to realise it, and she doesn't want Cecilia to wait that long.

'Do you miss your mother?' Grace Maud asks.

Another huff from Cecilia, then she says, 'Yes.'

'Don't you think she misses you?'

'No, she just wants to control me!'

Grace Maud can't help a little smile escaping. 'I'm not sure that's true. I think perhaps Eva is talking in code. She wants you to go to mass so she can see you. She thinks that if she asks you to do something else – meet her for coffee, for example – you'll say no. But if she tries to make you feel guilty enough to go to church, that may work.'

Cecilia folds her arms tightly against her chest. 'That's silly. She should just say what she wants.'

'If only we were all so straightforward.' Grace Maud gazes towards her window, with its curtains slightly open to reveal the frangipani tree in the front garden. 'Some of us are brought up to never say what we want. Girls, in particular. It's not polite to say what you want. You have to learn what other people want and do that. Say that. We all think it's madness. Yet those are the rules.'

Cecilia looks less defiant.

'From what you've told me,' Grace Maud goes on, 'Eva was brought up in a very strict, traditional family.'

Cecilia nods.

'She didn't bring you up so strictly, did she?'

'No,' Cecilia admits softly.

'She changed. For you. But it might be too much to ask her to change everything.'

Grace Maud tries to find the words to say what needs to be said next. She thinks of something Sandrine says over and over in class, and laughs to herself. *Be open, ladies. Open your hips, open your hearts, open your minds. So many people are closed! It's no good for the health.*

'This may sound ridiculous,' Grace Maud says to Cecilia, 'but could you try being open-minded about your mother's real motivations? She may mean well and simply not be able to express it in a way you recognise. And it's also possible that you appear closed-minded to her. She may think you simply don't care about her.'

'That's not true!'

'I didn't say it was. I'm merely saying what she may be thinking.'

Cecilia relaxes her arms and shuffles around on the bed.

'Cecilia, my dear – we are a mystery to our own selves most of the time. How can we possibly know someone else well enough to know exactly what they want or what they feel? Wouldn't it be better to stay open to all the possibilities of what's in their minds, and in their hearts, the way we would like them to stay open to us?'

With her eyes wide, Cecilia nods slowly. 'I think I know what you mean,' she says.

Grace Maud smiles. 'That was a longwinded way of saying that I think your mother loves you and misses you, and I think you love her and miss her, and if you were both able to just say that to each other you'd solve a lot of your problems.' She reaches over and pats Cecilia's cheek. 'Go to mass. Kiss your mother hello. Tell her that you love her. You may be surprised by what happens next.'

Yet it is Grace Maud who is surprised when Cecilia suddenly hugs her.

'Thank you, GM,' she says, her arms tightening. 'I don't know what I'd do without you.'

Grace Maud slowly pats her back and thinks of the girl who came to help her with the housework, then moved in and stopped her from sitting in this house alone with her memories and ruminations. The girl who became a young woman who cheerfully takes care of things for her and never gets irritated when Grace Maud is being as curmudgeonly as she can be. And who, Grace Maud noticed, started calling her GM after she heard Luca doing it. Not that Grace Maud minds.

Cecilia opened her heart to Grace Maud, and while they have both benefited, Grace Maud knows she's had the best of the bargain.

'I feel the same about you,' she says.

CHAPTER FIFTY-ONE

Each year seems to pass more quickly than the last. Patricia is quite sure that before she knows it Christmas will arrive, then 1995 will have begun and she will start the same routine over. And over. And over. Until she retires. Or dies. Whichever happens first. Another year of trying to manage her parents with no help and no change. Stasis. The story of her life. Such a worn-out phrase, but it's the one that fits. The story of her life is that there is no story. She had nothing new to report when she bumped into her former student Rachel at the supermarket. Absolutely nothing to mark the years since she'd seen her last in Sydney. What sort of adult – what sort of person – doesn't change in all that time? A boring one. Or one who is stuck against her will.

If it really is against her will.

Rachel looked delighted to see her.

'I always meant to write to you,' she says. 'After I left school.'

'Really?' Patricia quickly searched her memory for anything she might have said or done to Rachel to prompt a letter.

'Yeah. I . . .' She looked shy for a second. 'I wanted to tell you that you changed my life.'

'I hope in a good way?' Patricia said, slightly taken aback.

'Oh, absolutely! You believed in me. You told me I could do better. You said you knew I was really bright and that I was capable of more. At the time I didn't really want to hear it. Guess I was too young. But when I got to uni I remembered it. And I pushed myself. Did really well too. I wouldn't have my job without that.'

Patricia felt the warmth of recognition and achievement, and smiled. 'That's lovely of you to say, but I think you did that all yourself.'

Rachel shook her head. 'My parents never thought I'd get anywhere. Mum used to tell me I was never going to get a good job. But I did!' She gave Patricia a curious look. 'Are you teaching up here?'

'Yes.'

'Lucky for them,' Rachel said, then looked thoughtful. 'I just always thought you'd have done something else. I don't mean that in a bad way! I thought you'd have moved to London or New York or something. Which makes it sound like I don't like Australia but . . . You're so smart, miss. I thought you'd become a professor at some fancy uni.'

Patricia considered what she said. 'It's not always easy to leave,' she replied, then wondered if that was true – or if she'd made it harder for herself to leave.

Since that conversation she's been wondering if she really has no options in her life or if she's just telling herself that she doesn't. It is safer, by far, to never change. Dull, and staid, but safer. And she's always been sensible.

She had thoughts years ago of travels she could undertake and things she could achieve if her world was broader. Cairns will always be home because it's baked into her skin, but she would have liked to see more of the world. Partly she's stopped herself because she didn't want to travel alone and she spent years waiting for that perfect travelling partner to materialise. Partly it's because there is safety in what's familiar and she isn't as brave as she would like to be.

Although Sandrine often exhorts them to 'have courage' on the mat – to attempt things they might not otherwise – and Patricia always takes her up on that. So maybe she's not so timid as she would have herself believe.

We tell ourselves neat stories: that's something else she's come to recognise thanks to Sandrine. We tell ourselves that our bodies won't do this, that and the other, then one posture can explode that belief. It's happened to her several times and each time it's confronting, because she has realised how much she's grasped onto those beliefs. If she's stuck in this life, she can say that it's circumstance holding her – that she has to take care of her parents, that it's too late for her to change careers – yet, truly, she's the one holding herself here. Holding herself back.

When she was young – Rachel's age – she imagined a much different life. She wanted classical music playing in her house on Sunday mornings; she wanted interesting, artistic acquaintances who told fabulous stories; she wanted nights at the cinema with a companion to whom she could talk for hours afterwards over a bottle of wine. She wanted croissants and flowers and books and paintings. Instead she has this suburb. This beach. This life. It's impossible to guess when she deviated from those dreams and arrived back where she started, yet it happened. She either omitted to do something, or didn't take chances as they came up.

That's how she finds herself on this beach again, walking before work. It's not a part of her routine that she resents, but it is another sign that her life never changes. She has been walking on this beach for . . . How long? She can't remember.

This time she's going to do something different, though: she's going to walk with her feet in the water. Usually she stays on the sand, not wanting to get her feet wet because that means sand will stick to them and – perversely for someone who loves the beach – she's no fan of sand lingering on her skin. Or so she's always thought because that's how she felt as a child. She's never actually attempted to discover if she's changed her mind.

The water is warm. Of course. It's always warm. In summer it's verging on hot, although she wouldn't put her feet in then. Stingers may not come that close to shore, but it isn't worth the risk.

She kicks her feet a little through the foam. How adventurous! First she gets her feet wet and now she's being playful.

'Patricia?'

She stops, suddenly feeling guilty, as if walking in the water is bad and she's been caught.

As she turns towards the voice, she feels something else: embarrassed. Because it's Dennis standing in front of her; Dennis who's seen her behaving like a child. Dennis, whose muscles are bulging out of his T-shirt. She really shouldn't notice these things.

'Dennis – hi.' She tucks her hair behind her ears in a pointless stalling gesture. 'What are you doing here? The surf's round the other side.'

He glances towards the knob that separates this beach from the surf beach. 'I'm not here to surf. I came to find you.'

'How did you know I'd be here?'

He smiles faintly. 'You told me you always walk on the beach before work.'

She can only barely remember telling him that. 'Right,' she says, stepping up the sand as the waves come in a little higher on her legs.

'I wanted to talk to you – outside of work.'

'Oh? That sounds . . .' She frowns and smiles at the same time. 'Serious. And a bit . . . strange?'

'Yeah. Maybe.' He shoves his hands in the pockets of his shorts and bites his bottom lip. 'This probably is going to sound strange but I'm going to say it anyway.'

Patricia's mind is packed with thoughts about what he could be about to tell her that required him finding her on the beach. Has she been mooning over him without realising it and he's going to ask her to stop? Has someone finally reported Gordon for being a creep and Dennis is going to take over as headmaster, right before he leaves?

'Okay,' she squeaks.

'You know how I said I'm going to India?'

'Yes.' Her brain starts to recalculate the possibilities, but doesn't come up with anything convincing.

He clears his throat then lifts his chin a little. 'I want you to come with me.'

This is an option that hadn't occurred to her – and threatens to turn her brain inside out.

'Um,' is all she can manage, and his expression falters.

'I've never stopped liking you. Only . . .' He looks down, then up at her again. 'It's a little bit more than like.' His face relaxes into a smile. 'I'm really going to put my foot in it, but I'm leaving anyway. So I'm going to say it. When I met you I thought you were gorgeous – I'd have to have been blind not to see that. Everyone can see that!'

He laughs as if he's been set free. 'Then I got to know you and you're really . . . wonderful. I think I'm going to have an incredible experience over there and I want to share it with you. I think you'd love it. And I'd love you to be there.' He stops and breathes. 'I could go on. But I've probably said enough for now. Anyway, I don't want to go without you. And I reckon . . . I reckon you may consider coming with me. Just a hunch.'

Patricia has heard the expression 'time stands still' and always thought it fanciful. Yet she understands it now. Or perhaps time isn't exactly standing still – it feels like it's reversing and forwarding all at once. She's inside this moment; the one just after she heard words she never thought she'd hear. Words that are said to other women who aren't her.

And yet . . . Just because he's said them doesn't mean anything in the world she lives in. Which isn't the same world Dennis lives in, because he has more options. He could marry someone when he's sixty and have children, like Cary Grant. For him this could be a fling. For her it could be everything.

It's not that she doesn't believe him – she can see that he's sincere – nor that what he's said is something she didn't even dream about. It's that this moment in time is reversing and forwarding because it's the only moment they'll have.

'I'm too old for you,' she says, knowing it's true.

'Patricia, I'm not as young as you think.' He looks amused. 'I'm thirty-nine. People just think I'm younger because I walk around in shorts all day.'

'I'm forty-seven.' Checkmate.

'I know.' He steps towards her. 'I really don't choose women based on their age.'

'So why did you choose me?'

'Well . . . I don't think I did actually.' He takes her hand and she lets him. 'It's just one of those things.'

'I'm too old for children.'

'I don't remember saying I want them. Hasn't working in a high school put you off them anyway?'

He takes her other hand and stands opposite her. His eyes

are hazel, with flecks of gold and green in them. She hasn't looked into his eyes for long enough to notice before.

'You haven't said you don't want to come with me,' he says softly.

His hands holding hers are warm and dry, and she makes herself remember this detail because years from now, when she's an old lady sitting in a sunroom with a blanket over her knees, looking back on her life and thinking about the few high points, she wants to remember this man standing in front of her, to recall the touch of his hands and the way he looks at her with acceptance and attention.

Maybe that old lady will regret what she's about to do. She'll just have to wait to find out.

'I don't want to,' she says firmly. She, who dislikes lies. But the stakes have never been as high as they are now.

Because she does want to go away with him – why wouldn't she let herself be swept up in this opportunity and what it might become? – but it would mean changing everything she knows. Leaving her parents behind, with no one to look after them. Abandoning the career she has tended like a pot plant for years. There would be yoga in India, but no Dorothy or Grace Maud. So yes, she has many reasons for not telling him the truth. None of them an obstacle in and of themselves, but added up they make a mountain.

'I don't believe you,' he says, but he lets her hands go and she feels the regret that she knew would come. 'But I'm not going to push you.'

He smiles faintly and takes a step back. 'Like I said, I'm not leaving until the end of the year. So you have time to reconsider.'

'I won't,' she says quickly and looks away, not wanting to meet his eyes.

He nods slowly. 'All right. Guess I'll see you at school.'

'You will,' she says, nodding so quickly she's worried she'll shake something loose. 'And I won't make it awkward. You know.' She gestures at nothing.

'I know. I won't either.' He starts to turn away. 'See you there.'

She doesn't say goodbye but she does watch him walk away, thinking about how she's so great a coward that she can't take what he's offering her with open hands and let the consequences happen as they may. Because that's not who she is.

She knows she is stuck; she knows she can't change. Because the price of change is embracing the unknown – and the most terrifying part of that is realising that she might like it.

CHAPTER FIFTY-TWO

'What on earth is wrong with you?' Grace Maud says more loudly than she normally would in the sanctuary of the yoga class.

Patricia looks up from rolling her mat, clearly sheepish. 'What . . . what do you mean?' She clears her throat and bends over her mat once more.

'You've rolled up that mat and unrolled it about three times. And during relaxation I could hear you breathing. Loudly.'

'Sorry,' Patricia says meekly.

'You're missing the point. I don't ever hear you breathing.' Grace Maud glances at Dorothy, who has folded her arms over her large belly and is shaking her head from side to side.

'Something's wrong,' Dorothy says.

'Or right,' Patricia mutters.

'Honestly, Patricia, if you're going to obfuscate,' Grace Maud says, slinging her handbag over her shoulder, 'I'll start to lose respect for you as an English teacher.'

'Grace Maud!' Patricia says with a look of horror.

'Not once, in all the time I have occupied a mat next to you – or been in your car, for that matter – have I known you to be so . . . so . . . scattered.' Grace Maud is used to Patricia being steady, measured – reliable. The person almost levitating out of her skin during the class was not the Patricia she knows at all. 'Are your parents all right? Has something happened at work?'

'Well—' Patricia stops and frowns. 'Yes. I guess it has.'

Grace Maud sighs. '*Obfuscating.*'

'All right!' Patricia makes a noise as if she's irritated – also not something she usually does. 'Dennis – I've mentioned Dennis . . .'

'Indeed you have.'

'He asked me to go to India with him.'

She turns as if she's going to walk away and Grace Maud grabs her arm.

'I don't know what possessed you to think you could simply get away with that declaration without further explanation,' Grace Maud says, digging in her fingers a little and arching an eyebrow.

She relaxes her grip when she sees Patricia's eyes: wide and full of uncertainty. Patricia, who always likes to seem in control, even though Grace Maud knows – as only a person who has been alive as long as she has can know – that control is an illusion, always. The only thing that can be controlled is the time we wake up each day; after that, every minute is at the whim of the fates. We just tell ourselves stories about how that's not the case so that life seems vaguely manageable.

'My dear,' Grace Maud says, moving her arm to take in Patricia's shoulders as Dorothy takes Patricia's other hand, 'whatever is going on?'

'Bloody yoga!' Patricia says with a ragged exhalation, wiping her eyes with the back of her free hand. 'Why do I cry in these classes more times than not?'

'Because it's a release,' says Dorothy, 'like Sandrine says. We don't get to release things anywhere else, do we?'

'I like to kick the occasional tree,' Grace Maud says, thinking of one particularly ugly palm on the nature strip outside her house.

She is rewarded with a muffled laugh from Patricia.

The other students are starting to walk slowly from the room and Grace Maud thinks that they should really move along too, so Sandrine can have her house back. But this isn't the right moment to rush anything. Patricia is vulnerable in a way that Grace Maud knows should be supported. The younger woman holds herself together – for her work, for her family – but she is not made of steel, and Grace Maud doesn't want her to think that she should be. So she won't move her out of this room. Sandrine can wait.

'I think I told you that Dennis is leaving his job,' Patricia says. 'At the end of this year. He's going to India for a while. He doesn't know how long.' She looks at Grace Maud and Dorothy in turn. 'He showed up on the beach and said he wants me to go with him.'

'That's amazing!' Dorothy almost squeals.

'Is it?' Patricia's face crumples.

'You like him! And he's asked you to travel with him? That's incredible!'

Grace Maud watches Patricia's face as a range of emotions cross it: confusion, joy, concern.

'He's too young for me,' Patricia says. 'It could never work.'

'Oh, that again. Well, if you're going to be defeated before you start,' says Grace Maud, seeing Patricia's fear and wanting to help her push past it.

'That's not it!' Patricia says heatedly.

'Ladies,' Sandrine says as she walks up to them, 'you seem to be having a little disagreement for the first time ev-errr. What is happening? I cannot have this discord with my favourite students!'

'Favourite?' Dorothy says.

'Of course. You are here regularly. You pay attention. You progress. This is the dream for a teacher.' Sandrine pats her cheek. 'And you are sweet, Doro-tee.'

She turns towards Patricia and puts a hand on her hip. 'Now – what is this all about?'

'Nothing,' Patricia says.

'So convincing, I do not think.' Sandrine raises an eyebrow in Grace Maud's direction.

'Patricia has a beau,' Grace Maud says.

'He's hardly that,' Patricia says.

'He wants to be that.' Grace Maud looks at Sandrine and realises that it's perfect she's joined their conversation at this exact moment. Sandrine, of all people, may be able to convince Patricia to abandon fixed ideas of what's acceptable and embrace what she really wants – just as Grace Maud did herself once upon a time. But Grace Maud did it to stay in place. Sandrine ran away and had adventures, which is exactly what Patricia needs to do.

'He's invited her to join him on a trip to India,' says Dorothy, looking like she's won a prize – because, as Grace Maud now knows, other people's happiness *is* Dorothy's prize.

'India!' Sandrine beams. 'How mar-vel-lous. So, Patricia, why have you not said yes already to this beau?'

Patricia sighs and her shoulders slump a little. 'Because he's a lot younger than me.'

Sandrine's brow furrows. 'Is he old enough to drink wine?'

'Yes. He's in his thirties.'

'Then what is the problem? This is legal, *non*?'

'Sandrine!' Patricia looks shocked. 'I'm in my forties!'

Sandrine looks at her as if she's said something profoundly odd. 'I do not understand.'

'I'm too old for him.'

'*Chérie*,' Sandrine says as she wags a finger in Patricia's direction, 'clearly he does not think so if he asks you to take a trip with him. So why do you think so?'

'Because . . .' Patricia looks at each of them in turn, her vulnerability so plainly visible that Grace Maud's heart aches for her. 'What happens if we're together for five years? Ten? He won't want me any more then.'

Sandrine steps towards Patricia and enfolds her into a hug. 'You are worrying about something that may never happen,' she says as she lets her go. 'I am older than you and my boyfriend is younger than you – do you think I am worried about him leaving me? Never! He is lucky to have me! And this man – his name, please?'

'Dennis,' Dorothy provides.

'This Dennis is lucky to have you.' Sandrine pinches Patricia's cheeks. 'You are afraid of being loved, beautiful Patricia, because your whole life you have been told you are not lovable.'

Patricia gasps. 'How do you know that?'

'It is written on the body, my dear. Plus I am a witch.'

Sandrine laughs but Grace Maud isn't sure she's joking.

'But I think you can see, Patricia,' Sandrine says as she takes her hand, 'that there are people here who find you *very* lovable. Grace Maud does not strike me as someone who loves easily. Am I correct, Grace Maud?'

'You are.' And Grace Maud, like Patricia, wonders how Sandrine could know that. Wonders what else she knows just by observing them. She feels exposed – but also seen and understood. It is an unusual combination.

'And she has chosen to love you,' Sandrine goes on. 'Dorothy has a big heart, does she not? But I think she only gives special attention to very few. So these two love you.' Sandrine lets go of Patricia's hand. 'Why is it so hard to believe that this Dennis could love you? That he will take care of you if you go with him?'

Patricia's bottom lip is trembling and she sniffs several times.

'I'm still scared,' she whispers.

'That is life, *chérie*!' Sandrine throws her hands up. 'It is scary! It is wonderful! It is strange! Just like this yoga practice, you see? That is why I have been doing it so many years. You do not know what will happen when you arrive on the mat. You do not know what will happen when you arrive in a new country or when you take a new lover. But you do know that it will be an adventure. And adventures are glorious. Do you not agree?'

Patricia's nods are small but certain.

'Thank you,' she says softly. 'All of you.'

'Now, if you are going to India you must tell me, because I will have some tips.' Sandrine smiles and pinches Patricia's cheeks again.

'I will.' Another nod.

'All right, ladies, enjoy your Saturday.'

'Are we being dismissed?' Grace Maud says, laughing.

'Yes. My lover is waiting for me.' Sandrine winks. 'We are going out on a boat.'

Grace Maud and Dorothy each take one of Patricia's arms as they leave the house and the three of them walk wordlessly to the street.

'Whatever you decide,' Dorothy says as they reach their cars, 'I will think it's great.' She kisses Patricia on the cheek.

'As shall I,' adds Grace Maud.

Patricia smiles. 'Thank you. I have some thinking to do.'

'Then we'll let you do it.'

Grace Maud opens the passenger door, waves Dorothy goodbye, then pulls her seatbelt across and straps herself in for the ride home.

CHAPTER FIFTY-THREE

The last thing Patricia feels like doing is having her brothers and sister to lunch. She's distracted – she has been ever since Sandrine gave her quite rational reasons for considering Dennis's suggestion. It's made her think about all the ideas she's held onto. Some of them are ideas others have foisted on her – that her life should turn out a certain way. If she examines herself, her past, she can see that she could have steered herself in the direction of marriage, children, house, garden. That might have been an enjoyable life – but she could never be sure that it would be. She had friends who weren't happy even though they did everything 'right'.

There was also the fact that Patricia never wanted to give up her work. It is her nature to work; at school she never shirked homework, never questioned the need to learn and improve. It's what she does. Who she is. She knew herself well enough to understand that and her choices have, whether conscious or unconscious, kept her on the path of work.

Except she has always castigated herself for not trying harder to have the other. To be the conventional woman sending her husband off to work instead. To be satisfied with a domestic life. She's never let go of the idea that what she wants for herself isn't as valid as what others told her she should want.

Until Sandrine basically gave her permission to be free of any and all preconceptions. The liberation has been heady. And preoccupying.

However, her mother is turning eighty years of age and, even though she probably doesn't even realise it, Patricia thinks they should celebrate. Or, rather, her father suggested they celebrate and Patricia didn't disagree, even though she knew what it would mean: John, Peter and Annette, along with their families, in the house together for the first time in a while.

There's another reason to gather. Her father finally spoke to his sons and informed them of his decision, so next week their mother will go into a nursing home. That means it's probably the last time they'll have a family meal with her present in this house. Patricia is trying hard not to feel like a hanging judge, but her guilt makes her breath catch every now and again.

So here they all are, crammed around the dining room table that was a good size when it was just the four children and two adults but isn't adequate when three of those children bring others. Elbows are clashing, along with opinions about the prime minister – Annette has pronounced him 'dishy' while John and Peter think he's a weasel and say they'd rather see the National Party running the country – and the movie *Priscilla, Queen of the Desert*, which, unsurprisingly, has moved Peter to a tirade about the outrageousness of 'blokes in frocks', poked by John, who says he found Guy Pearce half attractive. Their mother has sat, silent, at the head of the table throughout.

Patricia has taken her usual place in the kitchen, organising platters and realising they don't have enough cutlery so she has to keep washing up after each course. This time, however, her father helps her to clear plates and serve drinks.

By dessert time, her brothers have drunk a few cans of beer and Annette is several glasses into a cask of moselle.

'A *cask*?' she had almost shrieked when she saw it in John's hand. 'A CASK?'

'Yeah,' he'd said, nonplussed. 'That's all they had at the bottlo in town. Nothing stopping you bringing something else, Annette.'

Annette had sniffed and Patricia knew why: it isn't Annette's usual policy to bring anything to anyone at any time. So she's been drinking the cask wine at pace, and now her eyes are glazed and her tongue sharpened.

'You know,' she says, waving her hand so vigorously that it almost connects with Patricia's face as she deposits a piece of limp pavlova on the table. She should never have tried to make meringue at this time of year with the build-up thickening the air; even the strawberries on top are sagging.

'Know what, Nettie?' says Peter as he manoeuvres his rotund self around the table to remove a can of beer from his teenage son's hand.

'Don't call me that,' Annette spits.

'You never used to mind,' he says, although his facial expression shows that he knows she did.

'I was five when I didn't mind.' Annette goes back to hand-waving. 'You know, I really think it's *outrageous* that Mum is going into a home.'

'Oh yeah?' says John, examining a fingernail.

Patricia had asked him to help her with the arrangements to move their mother but he had said, predictably, that he was 'too busy with sport'. Now he's coaching cricket. Or so he says.

'She should be able to stay in her own home. She's not that bad!' Annette points at their mother, who looks bewildered.

'She's just been sitting quietly,' Peter adds. 'How is that a problem?'

Peter and Annette turn towards Patricia, who is now sitting down with her own sliver of pav. It was all that was left.

Patricia looks to her father, who isn't meeting her eyes. So the response is going to be on her, as if she's the only one involved.

'She's sitting quietly *now*,' she says calmly. 'But sometimes she is very distressed. And sometimes she wanders off.'

'You should be here watching her,' says Peter, who doesn't even seem to have noticed that his own wife has left the table with his daughter, who has spent most of lunch crying about some boy who doesn't like her.

'Should I, Peter?' Patricia says. 'I have a job to go to.'

'This is more important.'

'I can't afford to live on nothing.' Oh, it is so hard to keep her tone measured and she resents even having to try.

'If you'd just gotten married like you were supposed to,' he says, pressing his finger on a dob of cream on his plate, 'you wouldn't have to work.'

Patricia counts her breath: in for four, out for four. If anyone asks her why yoga is beneficial she's going to say, because it taught her how to keep her cool when she's surrounded by idiots who are related to her.

'And if I were married,' she says eventually, 'I wouldn't be available to look after Mum and Dad.'

'Yeah, but you're not, are ya?' says John, still looking at his hand. 'You're putting Mum in a home.'

'She needs professional care,' Patricia says. 'I've discussed this with you all in the past. Several times.'

'Or you're being lazy.' He smirks.

In for four, out for four.

'That's enough.' It's their father, his hands on the table, his eyes fixed on John.

'C'mon, Dad,' says Peter. 'He's not wrong.'

'He *is* wrong,' their father says, standing, almost reaching the height he used to command. 'You are all wrong. Patricia gave up her life to move in here to help us. She is the least lazy person I know. Certainly not as lazy as any of you, who rarely bother to visit or to call.' He glares at Annette. 'She works all day, she comes home and cooks and cleans and does a lot of things that your mother and I can no longer do easily. What's happening to your mother is breaking her heart.'

His eyes meet Patricia's and she wonders where he's been all this time, when she's felt like she's not coping with all the demands in this house. But better late than never, as he might say himself.

'It's breaking *my* heart,' he goes on, looking at his wife, whose expression is unchanged. 'I don't want her to leave here. But we must do what is best for Nora. We can't look after her the way they can.'

He picks up his plate, the dessert fork balancing on it, and walks towards the kitchen. Patricia, not wanting to be left alone with her siblings, follows him.

'I feel like I've failed,' he says, putting his plate on the bench.

'Why, Dad?' She places her plate next to his.

'Three ratbags.' He shakes his head. 'Ah well. I guess we got you right. One out of four ain't bad.' He smiles at her then, more sweetly than she's ever seen.

'Thanks, Dad,' she says, still not sure why he has chosen this time to stand up for her.

'No, my girl,' he says, coming closer. 'We're the ones who should thank you.' He looks down at the floor and slowly nods. 'I should have said it before. You've done a lot for me and your mother.'

'It's all right, Dad.' She pats his shoulder.

And it is all right. She's made her peace with her place in the world. If she can be of service to her parents, it's not so different to being of service to her students. It's karma yoga – the yoga of work. Work for its own sake, without expectation of reward. She doesn't expect rewards for taking care of her parents. It's work that needs doing, so she's been doing it.

She's tired, though. Holding herself tense all this time, worrying about what will happen to her mother, has exhausted her. It's only now that her father has acknowledged what's been going on that she really feels it.

'Maybe you should think about taking a break, love,' he says. 'Once we've settled her, things'll get easier. I can look after myself for a while. School holidays are coming up.'

He smiles reassuringly, as if he's giving her permission to go. Which, she supposes, he is.

'I'll think about it,' she fibs. Because she's already been thinking about it.

She now truly understands what the expression 'on your mind' means, because it feels like the idea of going away with Dennis has been draped over her brain for weeks.

Not that she'll tell her father that. He doesn't know Dennis, and the most he knows about India is that they field a national cricket team. Instead, she puts the plug into the sink for the third time that day and turns on the tap.

CHAPTER FIFTY-FOUR

'I'm still not sure this is a good idea,' Patricia says as she turns the car into Macrossan Street, the closest thing Port Douglas has to a main drag.

'I told you, I'm fine,' Dorothy says. She's looking out the window, watching for street numbers. 'The baby's not due for three weeks. There's plenty of time.'

'Not necessarily,' Grace Maud mutters from the passenger seat.

She wanted Dorothy to sit in the front, but Dorothy would never let Grace Maud sit in the back. It would be disrespectful. Besides, in the back seat Dorothy can sit with her legs apart and no one can see her and think she's being unladylike.

'Just because I'm not going to class any more doesn't mean I'm about to give birth,' she says. 'The baby's just . . .' She moves around to make herself more comfortable. 'Sitting so low that I can't even do downward dog. So what's the point?'

'I can't believe you love that posture so much,' Patricia says, putting on the blinker and pulling into a parking spot. 'I still don't feel I can hold myself up in it.'

'That's because you don't believe you can,' Grace Maud says authoritatively. 'Which surprises me, given how capable you are.'

Patricia looks at her as if she doesn't understand, then turns to look at Dorothy. 'This is the spot, isn't it?'

'Oh!' Dorothy sees a café next to the car. 'I didn't notice. Sorry – I was looking for the numbers and then . . .' She shrugs. 'I don't know what happened.'

'What happened is that you're tired because you're not sleeping properly, so your attention span is shorter. That's all.'

Grace Maud has been full of helpful hints and occasional instructions as the pregnancy has progressed. The visit to Port Douglas today was her idea: Dorothy's been fretting about the new business, and Grace Maud thought that if she actually saw the place she may feel more informed. Patricia said she'd drive them, and they decided to forgo their Saturday morning class to come today.

It took an hour from Dorothy's place because there's no road through the state forest, so they had to backtrack from Kuranda, down the hill as if they were going to town, then past Yorkeys Knob and onto the coast road. Dorothy felt almost ashamed as they drove along that road. She's been working so much and become so caught up with everything else in her life that it has been years since she's come along here. What a waste, to live in this beautiful part of the world and not take the time to properly see it. She hasn't been to the Daintree Rainforest since she was a teenager, although she thinks about it often. It's so easy to become locked into the patterns of your life and not see the adventures and beauty outside them. Not that she was alone there: Patricia also said she hadn't been to Port Douglas in ages.

'I can see why Frederick would want this drive to work,' she'd said as they headed north. 'Look at it.' Her head had flicked towards the window and the ocean view.

The sun was still climbing, glistening off the bluey-green of the sea. The road hugs the coast, sometimes next to sand, with the khakis and grey-greens of the trees climbing up the ridge on the western side, and sometimes close to the edge of rock that drops to the ocean.

The road reminded Dorothy of that scene in *To Catch a Thief* when Grace Kelly drives down the winding streets of Monaco that hug the escarpment. The same streets where, as Princess Grace, she would one day meet her death. Dorothy had swallowed and tried to forget about that.

'He says it will only be for a while,' she'd told the others. 'Once he finds a good manager he'll go back to the Cairns café. And this Port Douglas place will close earlier each day than we do.'

They'd all fallen silent then, Grace Maud and Dorothy transfixed by the ocean, and Patricia, thankfully, keeping her eyes on the road.

When they step out of the car to inspect the café, Dorothy feels a twinge low down in her abdomen. It's been happening since she got up this morning, and she rues the fact she can no longer manage her stretches on the yoga mat. Her muscles have been letting her know that they need attention, but it's just too hard for her to move. She can't do sitting postures or standing postures in any way that's beneficial, so her body will have to wait until after the baby has vacated the premises. That's when she'll stop feeling like a frigate listing at sea every time she walks.

She holds onto her lower back for support as she slowly approaches the café, which is closed. Frederick hadn't mentioned that the previous owner had already stopped trading. Although given the place was sold for a divorce, perhaps Dorothy should have assumed it.

'That's a shame,' she mutters as she peers in the window.

'What is?' Grace Maud asks.

'It's harder to pick up a business than to take it over. If there were still customers coming here it would give us a base to work from.' Another twinge causes her to suck in a breath. 'Ow!'

'What's happening?' Patricia is at her side, frowning.

'What's happening is that this baby is running out of room,' Dorothy says, trying to laugh it off. 'And protesting about it.'

She sees Patricia and Grace Maud exchange glances.

'Are you sure that's what it is?' Patricia says.

'What else would it be?' Dorothy says brightly. 'I'm not due for three weeks!'

'Dorothy, babies keep their own calendars,' Grace Maud says, taking hold of her arm with a grip that is surprisingly strong for a woman her age.

They peer through the café's windows and see tables without cloths, not enough chairs, a menu on the floor and hardly any natural light.

'Are you going to change the décor?' Patricia asks.

'Frederick didn't say he wanted to. He said the place would be ready to walk into.'

'Does that include those strands of garlic hanging from the ceiling?'

Grace Maud nods upwards and Dorothy sees evidence of what this place used to be: an Italian restaurant. That's when she notices the red-and-white checked curtains and the empty bottles of Chianti with candles in them. Terrific. None of that will be appropriate for their place. Frederick has never met a pasta sauce he likes.

Dorothy gasps as a stronger twinge – something that could be classified as closer to being pain – hits her. 'Oh. *Oh.*'

Grace Maud tugs on her arm. 'Right, back in the car. Port Douglas is lovely and I'm sure Frederick will make a success of it here. But there's no hospital so we're going to Cairns right now.'

'But it's only a little pain. We don't have to go back yet. We're going to have morning tea!' Dorothy wails, not ready to let go of her idea of a lovely morning despite the reality that is crashing into it.

'Don't be silly,' Grace Maud orders. 'You're in labour. Get in the car.'

'*Labour?*' That can't be right.

'What do you think is going on?' Grace Maud almost pushes her into the back seat.

'Really?' Patricia says, still standing on the footpath.

'Well, I'm not prepared to take the chance that it's not,' Grace Maud says. 'Are you? The hospital is an hour that way.' She nods to the south. 'I recommend we leave now.'

'Um . . . right. Yes. I see.' Patricia scurries to the driver's side and yanks open the door.

In the back seat Dorothy squirms as another pain arrives. 'I'm sure this is nothing,' she pants. 'Just muscular.'

'You're right – it *is* muscular,' Grace Maud says as Patricia makes a quick U-turn. 'It's your muscles getting ready to give birth.'

'But *I'm* not ready!' Dorothy wails.

'No one ever is, darling.' Grace Maud turns around to smile at her. 'You'll be fine.'

Dorothy tries to remember all the breathing they practised in class, more to distract herself than anything. Sandrine told her that focusing on her breathing could help her to not panic, and that panic is the thing to avoid because it delays the labour – something about primal responses and panic meaning the body believes there's a predator nearby and so will slow down the labour. Which is all very well in theory, but now the baby might actually be about to arrive, and it's three weeks early and she's not with Frederick, and she's never done this before – and what if it's really three weeks early and that means something's wrong? Maybe it will be too early for the baby to survive and she's going to lose another one. But she can't lose another one. She just can't. Not after having it inside her for so long, and talking to it and loving it and dreaming about it. And she's meant to be breathing slowly and not holding her breath, but she can't help it because her thoughts are racing now and she can't think about breathing and also think her thoughts and try to work out what's going on and—

'You're going to pass out if you keep hyperventilating like that,' Grace Maud says.

'*What?*' Dorothy shrieks. Not that it's reasonable to shriek, but she really can't help it.

'I can hear you panting.'

'I'm not! I'm doing the slow breathing like Sandrine said!'

Patricia laughs nervously. 'No, Dorothy, you're panting.'

'Just count your breathing.' Grace Maud swivels her head so she's looking her in the eye. 'Four counts in, four counts out. Don't try to breathe deeply because you can't – there's a baby in the way. Just count.'

Dorothy nods and closes her eyes. *In-two-three-four. Out-two-three-four. In-two—*

'Aaaaahhh!' she cries, pain shooting up her sides.

'Count,' Grace Maud orders, but Dorothy sees her glance at Patricia.

In-two-three—

Dorothy feels a ripple across her belly like a pod of dolphins are swimming inside her.

'This hurts!' she gasps. 'It's hurting!'

'Are you willing to go over the speed limit?' Grace Maud mutters to Patricia.

'Are you joking?' Patricia responds.

'No. That contraction was very close to the last one.' Grace Maud turns and smiles reassuringly at Dorothy. 'Count, Dorothy.'

The pain subsides but Dorothy feels something give way between her legs. Something warm and wet and . . .

'Oh nooo! The dolphins!' she says.

'What?' Patricia sounds worried.

'The dolphins have caused a wave!' Dorothy reaches down and feels her thighs, which are slick with whatever just emerged from her.

Patricia starts to laugh. 'What dolphins, Dorothy? What are you talking about?'

'Oh . . . that was in my head.' Dorothy starts sniffling, then crying. 'I've ruined your car.'

'It'll come out,' Patricia says.

'That's just your waters breaking, darling,' Grace Maud says cheerfully, as if she's talking about a couple of drops spilled. 'Natural part of the process.' Her head turns to Patricia again. 'We need to get there as quickly as we can.'

'Bugger it,' says Patricia, and Dorothy feels the car lurch as it accelerates. 'If the cops stop me they can take Dorothy to hospital with sirens on.'

'I'm terrible! I've ruined your car and you're going to get a speeding fine!' Dorothy tries to move position on the back seat, but finds herself sliding along it instead. Now she's not a beached whale – she's in the ocean.

'Stop feeling sorry for yourself,' Grace Maud commands and Dorothy immediately feels more alert.

'Now,' Grace Maud continues, 'if we had time to pull over and clean you up, we would, but we don't. This baby's coming soon. But I think we'll make it. You just keep counting those breaths and we'll be there before you know it.'

Dorothy tries to concentrate on her breathing, interrupted every few minutes by a contraction.

'Keep your legs together!' Grace Maud says at one point and Dorothy does what she's told. She doesn't want to ruin Patricia's car any more than she has by actually giving birth in it.

No police officer stops them on the road as they roar into Cairns, heading for the hospital, and Patricia comes to an abrupt stop at the entrance to Casualty.

'Could you take her in?' she says to Grace Maud. 'I'll move the car. And I'll call Frederick once I'm inside.'

Grace Maud exits and opens the back passenger door, holding out her hands for Dorothy to take.

Dorothy cringes as she feels her damp dress clinging to her legs and fluid running down her shins, and doubles over as another contraction – close, so close to the last one – overtakes her.

She's barely aware of Grace Maud holding her arm firmly as they walk through the doors, nor can she hear what Grace Maud is saying to the nurse who has appeared at their side. Then she is placed on a gurney and wheeled through swinging double doors.

All she can think of is the baby inside her and the pulse of life within her. The beating of her heart and the pain that tells her that all she has wanted, all she has suffered for, all of her hopes and dreams and yearnings, are coming into being. This time she's made it. This time her baby is real.

'You're going to be fine,' someone whispers in her ear and Dorothy doesn't know if it's a nurse or a doctor or a kindly spirit.

All she knows is that all the years behind her and all the years ahead have come to this one moment, and she is right here, right now, in pain and in love, waiting for her baby to be born.

CHAPTER FIFTY-FIVE

That drive from Port Douglas to Cairns to get Dorothy to hospital felt like a strange dream mixed with flashes of a nightmare. It wasn't until Patricia was home that she remembered that Dorothy's waters had broken all over the back seat and she spent the rest of the day cleaning them up, although she didn't mind, not for a second.

Then the call came from Frederick that the baby was born and he was fine, and Dorothy was dazed but all right.

This morning is the first time Patricia and Grace Maud are going to meet Nicholas. She picks up Grace Maud and they drive to Kuranda with presents of booties – probably not needed in the tropics, but all babies seem to be given booties – and rattles, and a bottle of Champagne for Frederick and flowers for Dorothy.

At the front door a frazzled-looking Frederick greets them with nods and kisses on each cheek, takes the Champagne with thanks and guides them to the sitting room.

Patricia smiles as she sees Dorothy with her hair out for the first time, spread over her shoulders and halfway down her back. She's gazing at her baby then she lifts her head and gives her visitors a wobbly smile.

'Hello,' she says, looking as if she might cry. 'It's so good to see you.'

'Are you all right?' Grace Maud says briskly, moving to stand over Dorothy like a sentinel.

'I'm a bit tired,' Dorothy sniffs.

'Of course you are,' says Grace Maud. 'That's what babies do to you. Here, let me give you a break.'

She holds out her arms but Dorothy gazes down at Nicholas as if she isn't sure what he's doing there.

'Is he real?' she says.

'As real as I am,' replies Grace Maud. 'Which is perhaps more real than most people would prefer.'

Dorothy laughs as if it's the funniest thing she's heard, and for a moment Patricia worries that she is slightly out of her mind. Then she stops laughing and says, 'I'm just so happy. I can't believe he's here and he's safe.'

'He is,' affirms Grace Maud. 'And he's the luckiest little boy in the world. I'd love a cuddle.'

'Oh,' says Dorothy as if the idea has just occurred to her. As Grace Maud carefully takes the baby, Dorothy appears not to want to let him go.

'He's lovely, Dorothy,' says Patricia, although she's no expert on babies. Teenagers she can comment on with authority, but it's been a while since she's seen a baby.

As they make small talk Frederick says hardly a word, looking as stunned as his wife that this small, perfect creature is theirs.

They don't stay long – Grace Maud saying that a quick visit is a good visit – and now Patricia is heading home to talk to her father. To have yet another discussion about the future, although this time with a twist.

She made a decision, after the shock of that drive from Port Douglas had worn off. Life is unpredictable, no matter how much she may wish to control it. She has been so dutiful, so ordered, so correct. The organised teacher; the attentive if slightly resentful daughter; the tolerant sister. This was meant to make her content. Fulfilled. That's the promise of doing all the right things. Except it isn't, because she isn't fulfilled. She has an adventurous mind trapped in a body that she has bound to one place for far too long, and in the process that mind has started to circle in on itself.

She isn't sure when she stopped seeking out newness: new art, new music, new books. New places. Yoga is the first new thing she has done for years, and it's shown her how closed she'd become. Patricia opened her body, as Sandrine commanded, and that has opened her mind to all the things she shut out.

So while she hasn't decided where to go, she does think she should leave Cairns. Just for the summer holidays and a couple of weeks extra at the start of term. She's already cleared it with Gordon. Because she's discovered there are things she doesn't want to change: where she lives, who her friends are, what she does for work. All those things are here, and she thinks she'll appreciate them more if she takes a break from them.

In order to do that, though, she has to take steps. She can't jump on a plane tomorrow. That's for younger people with fewer responsibilities. Or for someone who is willing to abandon those responsibilities. She knows herself well enough to be aware that abandoning her parents would make her unhappy. That's not freedom; it's cruelty.

'Hi, Dad,' she says as she enters the house through the back door.

'Hi, love. How was it?'

'Fine. The baby's cute.'

She knows he's asked because it's polite and she's responding for the same reason. He's not really interested in her life – hasn't ever been – and she accepted that a while ago, because she accepts that you can't change other people.

He nods and goes back to his newspaper.

'Dad, I need to talk to you.'

He lifts his head. 'Yes?'

He sounds wary, probably because she rarely says she needs to talk to him.

'I want to go away for a while. Two months.' She smiles quickly, reassuringly. 'You suggested I take a break. You were right. I need a break. I need to go somewhere different.'

Her father remains silent so she can only guess at what he's thinking. Maybe he's changed his mind, just as she has.

'I'm not sure I want you staying here alone while I'm gone,' she continues. 'Not with Mum just in the home. You'll be lonely. And I don't want you trying to manage the housework on your own. So I'm going to pay some professionals to come in and help you.'

He opens his mouth and she puts up her hand.

'I'm taking out a loan to pay for it. Annette can call to check on you every now and then – maybe she could even come and stay for a few days. But I really need this, Dad.'

What she wants to say is that if she's going to spend the remaining years of her parents' lives worrying about them – an indeterminate number of years – she has to take this break now, because the next opportunity will be after they are both dead, and then it will have a decidedly different hue.

'What will you do?' he croaks.

'I haven't decided. Maybe Europe. Although I'm going to leave after term ends so it will be cold there. I'm also thinking of Hawaii.'

She's also thinking of India, and of Dennis, because what Sandrine said has been revving at the back of her mind, the noise getting louder and louder. But India isn't a conventional holiday destination, especially if she tells her father that she wants to take yoga classes there. That she wants to take the time to just be, in one place, with herself. It's hard to explain to someone who hasn't been on the mat that sometimes the big adventures happen inside us. She knows Grace Maud and Dorothy will understand, and she knows that they will want to hear all about it when she returns. It would be unreasonable to ask her father to have the same interest.

'I hear that's nice,' he says, nodding. 'Hawaii.'

'Maybe I'm crazy to swap one place with beaches for another,' she says, shrugging.

'No, you're not,' he says firmly, looking her in the eyes. 'You deserve a holiday.'

'Thanks, Dad. So . . .' She looks at him enquiringly.

He nods slowly. 'I wouldn't mind a bit of company while you're gone.'

She feels relieved that it was so easy. 'Okay.'

'Perhaps your mother could come back for a few days while you're away?'

'Dad . . . she can't. She's in the home now. She can't leave for days at a time.'

She watches his face to try to figure out if he too is losing his memory, or if he's just trying on the idea.

'But . . .' He sniffs a couple of times. 'I miss her.' His voice is soft, broken.

'I do too.' It's true, even if unlikely. While she's never been her mother's favourite person, Patricia misses the woman she's known all her life. 'But she can't come back here, Dad. I think you know that. For such a little woman she can cause a lot of mischief.'

His laugh is knowing and regretful. 'She sure can.'

'But maybe someone can take you to visit her while I'm gone.'

'Good, love.'

'I'm about to make lunch. Are you hungry?'

He nods.

'You read for a bit. I'll let you know when it's ready.'

He nods again.

Heading for the kitchen, she feels the rush of knowing that she will be able to leave, and guilt at feeling so free. This seesaw of emotions will, she reasons, probably go on for the rest of her days.

CHAPTER FIFTY-SIX

For someone who grew up and lived on a property that had the same routines for years, Grace Maud likes to think of herself as being quite adaptable to change. Something about close observation of the seasons and knowing that nature is always changing, even as those same seasons have a clear structure that doesn't change. There are small adjustments, of course – it's not as if every single day's temperature is the same as on that day the year before. Yet wet season, dry season – what southerners would know as summer and winter – and the gaps in between, when the humidity builds up and seeps out, arrive pretty much as expected. They couldn't manage the cane if they didn't.

One change Grace Maud is sure she's been quite relaxed about is to do with people coming and going. She doesn't like it necessarily – although she was quite pleased to see the back of her husband – but she's managed it. It is, therefore, a surprise to her that she's not taking the news of Patricia's planned departure well, even if it's not to be permanent.

That morning Patricia picked her up to go to class – they have stuck to the Saturday class even though Dorothy is unable to attend – then drove them both to Kuranda so they could visit their friend and her baby – and that's where Patricia made her announcement.

Dorothy had looked as surprised by it as Grace Maud was. 'What do you mean – travelling?' she'd asked.

Patricia had laughed and Grace Maud noted that she seemed happier than she'd ever been. 'Not forever,' she said. 'Just for a few weeks. I've never been anywhere much outside Australia.'

'Nor have I,' said Grace Maud, because one of the prices you pay for a life on the land is not being able to leave it very often.

'But your life is more interesting,' Patricia said, to Grace Maud's surprise. She's never thought it that interesting.

'Mine's fairly staid,' Patricia went on. 'School, home, school, home. The best thing about it is yoga and seeing you two.' She smiled. 'Which will continue once I'm back.'

Then something had shifted in her face. 'Mum's going to keep getting worse, and even though she's in the home now I'll still be visiting her a lot. And I'll need to keep looking after Dad. That could be for years. Now's the time to . . .' She paused and sighed.

'Liberate yourself?' Grace Maud said, and Patricia looked at her knowingly.

'That sounds about right,' she said.

Grace Maud did not, of course, begrudge Patricia her decision, but she was surprised to find herself feeling sad after she arrived home.

Sadness is not, however, an emotion she indulges on a regular basis so she had plans to make a cup of tea, locate a chocolate biscuit and sit in the garden while she found herself a different mood. That was until Cecilia informed her of her own decision to change: she's moving back in with her mother.

Now Cecilia is looking at Grace Maud expectantly, and Grace Maud is wondering why this Saturday, of all the days in her life, is the one when two people she cares about so much have decided to make such announcements.

'Oh,' she says, holding onto the teacup in her lap and trying hard not to let it tremble as she feels disappointment surge through her.

'I love it here,' Cecilia says. 'And you've been so nice letting me stay. It's just time for me to go back. Mum and I are getting along much better now. Thanks to you.'

'To me?'

'What you said that day when I told you she wanted me to go to church . . . I realised I was only thinking about myself. Not seeing it from her point of view.'

Cecilia's eyes are bright, and while she doesn't have Patricia's air of liberation she does look as though something has been settled. It's not Grace Maud's place to destabilise that. So she has to put up and shut up, as the saying goes.

'I'm so pleased,' she says, not adding the next part: *pleased that I've been able to help you decide to leave me alone.*

'And I told her all about Luca.' Cecilia blushes, which is charming considering she and Luca have known each other for a while now. Their relationship is hardly anything to feel abashed about. 'She's still not happy that he's not Catholic, but she's not going to try to stop me seeing him.'

'So it seems, perhaps, that she's able to see things from your point of view?'

Cecilia nods. 'I'll still come here!' she says. 'To work.' Then she looks uncertain. 'If you want me to.'

'Of course I do,' Grace Maud says quickly, thinking of how those days will become highlights again. She has become so used to having company that she's unsure whether she wants to live without it now, but she has no choice.

'Are you all right?' Cecilia says gently, stepping closer.

'Hm?'

'You look upset.'

Grace Maud is annoyed with herself for having slipped. Cecilia doesn't need to know what she's thinking.

'It's nothing,' she says dismissively. 'I was simply thinking about how things change. Patricia is going overseas for a while. So . . .' She smiles with her lips pressed firmly together. 'I'll have no one to go to yoga with. Which shouldn't be a problem, I know. It's not as if I'm not a big girl.'

'I'll go with you,' Cecilia says without hesitation.

'That's very kind, but I'll be fine.'

'I want to go! You love it so much. And I didn't give it a chance. All those funny names for things . . . I felt a bit stupid when I couldn't understand what was going on.'

Grace Maud contemplates the vivacious young woman in front of her and wonders how she could ever think herself stupid. But she is also aware that none of us knows the catalogue of doubts and insecurities that others carry around in their heads.

'I couldn't either,' Grace Maud says. 'But I learnt. You will too.'

'I'll see if Luca wants to come.'

'Why would he want to come?'

She tries to picture her lanky great-nephew in that room with a mixed bag of women – then realises it's not her place to stop him trying something just because no other man is doing it.

'He gets sore muscles from work. He says you think it works really well for sore muscles. Plus he used to learn ballet. Did you know that?'

Grace Maud did not. But she thinks of Luca's embodied grace – which she noticed the first time she saw him walking around the farm – and now realises its source.

'He stopped when he started getting tall,' Cecilia continues. 'They told him he'd be too big to be a professional. How unfair is that?'

'He won't have that problem in Sandrine's class,' Grace Maud says. 'I'd love to have you both come with me. If Luca is allowed Saturday mornings off, that is.'

Cecilia frowns. 'That's true. Oh well, I'll ask.'

They smile at each other and Grace Maud realises she has a hard question to ask.

'So when are you planning to move home?'

Cecilia looks hesitant, then bites her lip, then smiles awkwardly. 'This weekend. I don't have much to move.'

That's true: she only brought a small amount of clothes and two pairs of shoes. In all the time she's been here she's rotated them like uniforms.

'I'll be frank,' Grace Maud says. 'This is sad news for me.'

Cecilia nods. 'I'm going to miss seeing you every day. But I won't be far away. And I'll see you twice a week here and on Saturdays at yoga.'

Grace Maud takes a sip of her tea, unsure what to say next.

'Thank you,' Cecilia adds. 'That's really inadequate, but thank you. You helped me so much.'

'No,' says Grace Maud, 'it's you who helped me.'

Cecilia makes a face which suggests she doesn't believe her.

'I'll go and pack,' she says, then turns away, leaving Grace Maud alone with the sunshine and the garden.

If Grace Maud thought that two imminent departures were a blow, she feels less assailed than she expected she would. Cecilia will still be around, and Patricia will eventually return. Life, for all its changes, will keep some of its structure.

She puts her teacup on the grass, sits back and closes her eyes, and lets the sun warm her face.

CHAPTER FIFTY-SEVEN

'Shh-shh-shh, it's all right,' Dorothy croons as she picks her son up and walks softly into the sitting room.

She loves this room because the glass doors let her see out to the garden – especially appealing now that she's breastfeeding. It's nice to have something to look at while Nicholas sucks away.

'I feel like a cow,' she told Patricia on one of their phone calls. Patricia and Grace Maud have both taken to phoning every day to see how she is, how the baby is, if there's anything they can do. 'I exist just to feed the baby.'

'If you were a cow you'd have extra udders,' Patricia replied. 'Maybe that would be useful.'

'Mine are getting a bit tired,' Dorothy said. 'But I don't really have a choice.'

No choice, but she doesn't mind. In between the curtailed sleep and the dead-of-night feedings and the occasional tear when she's at home alone with the baby while Frederick is at work, she doesn't mind. She could never mind. Her life has changed irrevocably and this is exactly what she wanted. She hasn't gone through years of loss, not to mention medical procedures, to worry about missed sleep and sore nipples.

She can be desperate for a nap and still think her son is the highlight of her life.

Nicholas is just latching on when she hears the front door open and footsteps coming towards her.

'*Liebling*, I have brought Nicholas's auntie to say hello,' Frederick calls as he closes the door.

Cornelia appears in front of her, grinning.

How's my nephew? she asks.

'He's fine,' Dorothy says out loud, knowing Cornelia will lip-read and realising that they can't have a proper conversation while ever either of them is holding the baby in her arms.

When their parents brought Cornelia here for the first visit Frederick was holding Nicholas and Dorothy could sign. Before now she hadn't contemplated how her son might compromise her communication with her sister, and she feels stupid. Inconsiderate. Nicholas is going to be in her arms for months, and there won't always be someone else around to take him so she can talk.

Can I hold him? Cornelia says.

Dorothy points to the breast Nicholas is attached to, hoping Cornelia will understand.

Frederick walks past and kisses the top of Dorothy's head. He always kisses her on the head, hello and goodbye. He hasn't kissed her on the lips since Nicholas was born. Sometimes Dorothy will catch him looking at her with confusion in his eyes, and she thinks she knows what it is: she spends so much time cooing to Nicholas that she doesn't have time to talk to him. That's why, whenever she sees that look, she says, 'I love you,' and the expression vanishes.

'Your mother says hello,' he says. 'She will come by later to pick up Cornelia.'

He keeps walking towards the kitchen.

'Oh – you're not taking her?' Dorothy swivels her head as much as she can, trying to make eye contact with her husband.

They never seem to have much time to really talk to each other any more. Again, she doesn't mind – she has a more pressing priority right now – but it does make her feel slightly disconnected from her own life.

'I'm going to Port Douglas,' he says, returning with a banana in his hand. 'We have a delivery today.'

'I thought you would be home today.' Dorothy smiles tightly, wanting to suggest she's not irritated even though she is. Not wanting to inconvenience him even though she feels inconvenienced.

Becoming a mother hasn't changed her fundamental desire to please people, although sometimes she wonders if there's anyone who is trying to please her.

'So did I.' Another kiss on her head. 'But the delivery is late and I want to be there when it arrives.'

Dorothy stands up, holding Nicholas against her as he continues to feed, and follows her husband to the door.

'I really need you to stay for a little while so I can talk to Cornelia,' she says. She's fairly sure Cornelia is about to remind her of her offer to move in and she can't respond to that with her hands full.

Frederick looks at her quizzically. 'Can't you talk while I'm not here?'

'Not while either one of us is holding Nicholas. We can't use our hands.' She wonders why this isn't as self-evident to him as it is to her, but he does have a lot on his mind.

'Then just wait until Nicky has a nap,' he says brightly.

'He's not due to have one for at least an hour. I don't want to wait.'

'It will be fine,' Frederick says, and she can see his mind is already out the door.

'Frederick – I need you here!' Dorothy says, trying to control the exasperation in her voice.

The truth is, she doesn't so much need him as want him here. They're both parents of this little boy, but at the moment it feels like she's the only one who is interested. In fact, Frederick even said he can't wait until Nicholas can talk so he'll be more interesting.

'I'll be back as soon as I can. *Auf wiedersehen, Liebling.*'

No kiss on the head or anywhere else as he goes, and Nicholas unlatches from her breast and starts to cry. Sometimes, when he does that, she wants to cry too, mainly because her life has become a stream of feeding and crying and putting him down for naps and washing his tiny clothes, and while she adores him she sometimes finds herself wondering if in reality she's lying in *savasana* in Orange Blossom House and daydreaming this whole thing. Except Sandrine has yet to appear and tell her to roll over to her right-hand side before she comes up to sit. And it would be wrong, Dorothy knows, to wish she would. This is the reality she wanted, and she has it, full force.

She walks back in and sees Cornelia looking at her questioningly.

'Where did he go?' Cornelia enunciates.

Dorothy shrugs. What more can she do? She knows that Frederick believes that all this running around to Port Douglas, back to Cairns, interviewing staff, taking deliveries, is for their long-term benefit. He wants to provide for her, for Nicholas. Even for Cornelia, if it comes to that. It's impossible to resent that motive, although Dorothy knows now that she has needs of her own. To reconnect with him, to communicate with her sister, to be able to see her friends. To be in the world, be present, be *her.*

Sandrine told her that when her baby arrived, her heart would expand so much that she wouldn't be able to believe it. 'There will be room for the baby along with everyone else you love,' she said. 'And if you have another baby, it will expand again. It is not a muscle, Doro-tee, so much as it is a universe inside your chest.'

It sounded esoteric at the time, because while Dorothy loves fiercely and expansively, this sounded like something different. Something she'd never known. And it was. It is. She feels that universe inside her chest each time she looks at her son. At her sister. At her husband. At her parents.

What Sandrine didn't mention is that her heart would also expand enough to take in herself. Dorothy has never really considered whether she loves herself or not, but now realises that the scale was tipped to not. These days, when she looks in the mirror, she sees a woman who is braver and more fierce than she ever thought she could be. Brave in her pursuit of her dream, in her willingness to embrace new paths, new friends, new worlds of understanding. Dorothy has been pleased to meet that woman. She's been waiting for her for quite a while. That woman, she knows, has love enough for everyone.

Sometimes she feels so overwhelmed by love that she could run into the garden at night and shout it to the sky, to the people around her, to this whole town, to this land. 'I love you!' she will yell, and mean it; and she will marvel at the fact that a tiny human being has changed her so much that she won't care what people think. Or maybe it's that she has changed herself, and was just looking for an excuse to do so.

This new version of her is trying to remember that she needs certain things as much as Frederick does. As much as Nicholas does. As much as Cornelia does. She has been, she realises, in service to others in her life for quite a while. That doesn't have to stop; she doesn't want it to stop, because it's one of her ways of expressing love. But in order to continue she needs to do it on her terms, which means she has to stand up for what she wants. That, in turn, will train her to stand up for her son.

Nicholas unlatches again, and Dorothy pulls her top down before settling him over her shoulder to burp him. Holding him in place with one forearm, she can have both hands free.

We have to talk, she says to Cornelia, and she begins to set the boundaries for the new version of her life.

SUMMER 1994/1995

Sheryl Crow releases 'All I Wanna Do'.

The Cranberries top the singles chart with 'Zombie'.

Fourteen-year-old American tennis player
Venus Williams turns pro; German player Steffi
Graf ends the year ranked number one.

HRH Diana, Princess of Wales, attends her last Christmas
service at Sandringham as a member of the Royal Family.

CHAPTER FIFTY-EIGHT

Patricia's final yoga class is harder than she thought it would be. Harder emotionally and physically. It's almost as if Sandrine wants to give her something memorable – that is, something her muscles are going to remember for days.

As Patricia rolls up her mat and tucks it under her arm, Sandrine appears by her side.

'So you have the name of the *shala* in Mysore?' she says. 'You may not be able to study with Desikachar himself but you will learn many things. Great things. I am a little jealous.' She draws out the 'little' and lightly pinches Patricia's cheeks. 'But not too much. I am happy here. And maybe you will have something to teach me when you return?'

'I doubt that!' Patricia says, knowing how far she has to go before she can know even half of what Sandrine knows about yoga, but thrilled that once she made the decision to actually go to India, Sandrine proved that she'd meant what she'd said and gave her lots of tips.

'I hope you have a wonderful time.' Sandrine arches an eyebrow. 'Whatever you are doing.'

Patricia hasn't told Sandrine that she's hoping to see Dennis in India – even though she hasn't yet shared that information with him – but by now she's no longer surprised that Sandrine guesses – or knows – so much about her life. She has always detected when Patricia is feeling tired or overburdened or stressed.

Not long ago she sidled up to her before class and said, 'You have changed, Patricia. You are thinking of someone. Perhaps a certain someone, hm? Keep doing this thinking. It is good for you.' She'd winked and walked away, but not before Patricia's cheeks had turned to flame, and she'd looked around quickly to check Grace Maud hadn't heard.

Patricia hasn't confessed all to Grace Maud either. Because she's sitting on that proverbial fence: half wanting the grand adventure of going abroad with a man who's invited her, and half scared about what might happen if she does.

When school ended for the year, just before Christmas, she and Dennis had exchanged farewells.

'I'm not leaving until January fifteenth,' he said. 'In case you change your mind.'

The way he smiled at her – as if he was sad and adoring all at once – made the flighty, romantic part of her want to tell him. She wanted to say she'd see him by the Ganges or something equally fanciful, because she'd been inspired by his trip and decided to take her own.

But she hadn't told him yet because part of her believed her mother would deteriorate quickly and she wouldn't be able to go. Patricia didn't like to let him down. She didn't *want* to let him down.

Later that day, however, she'd called Dorothy to see how she was and ended up receiving some unsolicited advice.

'You need to tell him,' Dorothy said, quite forcefully for her. 'Even if something happens to your mum, you can't not go, okay?'

'Why not?'

'Because you're not going for that long anyway, and you deserve a holiday!'

Dorothy almost squeaked the last part out and Patricia could imagine her exasperation. Dorothy had given her a similar lecture when she was still tossing up whether or not to go at all.

'We're both too responsible for our own good,' she'd told Patricia. 'So please go and be irresponsible for both of us.'

'Sandrine was in a mood, wasn't she?' Grace Maud says, snapping Patricia back to the room.

The other students are packing up their belongings and gliding out quietly, as so often happens because they've all just emerged from lying on the floor in relaxation and no one wants to break the spell.

'It was tough,' Patricia says, bending down to pick up Grace Maud's mat.

'She'll miss you,' Grace Maud says. 'As will I.'

'I'll miss you too.'

'I doubt it. You'll be too busy. Then you'll be back. You won't have time to miss us. And that's just fine.'

Grace Maud puts her handbag over her shoulder and they walk together to Patricia's car.

'Who's going to carry my mat for me?' Grace Maud says.

'I thought you said Cecilia would be coming along?'

'She's coming to the Thursday night class because Luca can come with her then. She may or may not decide to come on Saturdays as well. I'm going to try doing both for a while.'

Patricia feels slightly hurt. Not that she has ownership over Grace Maud, but she does feel like the classes are their time. Grace Maud didn't tell her that she's gone back to Thursday nights. It means their experiences have diverged, and . . .

And she's being ridiculous. She's about to travel to another hemisphere to practise yoga with some expert she knows nothing about but whom Sandrine swears is 'amazing, *chérie*, really'. When she returns she may not think Sandrine's class is right for her any more.

Now that is a thought to almost make her stop in her tracks. She considers Sandrine to be not just her yoga teacher but her guide. This class has led Patricia to paths in her life that she would never have found otherwise. Yet what had Sandrine said to her in the café that day?

'The guru says to the student, "You have three jobs: the first is to find me, the second is to love me, the third is to leave me."'

Patricia hadn't understood it at the time because it's so different to her own experience of being a teacher. Yet she appreciates it now. She found Sandrine and her class right when she needed them both. She loved Sandrine even when she'd wanted to scream to the heavens because what Sandrine was putting her through hurt so much. Now, in making the decision to leave, she is declaring that she's ready to stand alone. This doesn't mean that she won't return to Sandrine – but it may mean she doesn't return as the Patricia she was before. Because she knows now that it's not necessarily Sandrine she is leaving. It's the version of herself that she no longer has any use for.

Another time, after one of the students complained that Sandrine wasn't 'nice' to them and wasn't yoga meant to make people nicer, Sandrine had said: 'Yoga does not make you nice. It reveals more of who you are. It helps you shed the layers, my darling. Why should that mean you become nice? Nice only serves other people, not yourself.'

It was the line about yoga revealing more of who we are that stuck with Patricia. She opened herself up to the practice and, week after week, she sloughed off her skin. Soon she will leave it behind. The person who emerges will still be her, but newer, shinier – and more vulnerable. But she is ready for it.

She can almost hear the crinkling of that old skin as she and Grace Maud get into the car.

'You're quiet,' says Grace Maud. 'I hope it's not because you're moping about that being the last class.'

'No,' Patricia says with a laugh. 'It's because I'm thinking about what that class has meant to me. I wouldn't be able to do what I'm about to do without it.'

'I don't know that that's right,' says Grace Maud as Patricia drives the familiar route to her house. 'I think you're very able to do many things. But if this class has helped you find that out, it's served a good purpose.'

They drive in silence for a few seconds.

'What has it helped you find out?' Patricia asks boldly.

'That you can teach an old dog new tricks,' Grace Maud says wryly. 'And . . . well, I found you and Dorothy. I didn't expect at my age to meet anyone who could intrigue me. It's so much easier to not even attempt to find out.'

'I don't think that has anything to do with age. People are difficult to get to know no matter how old you are.'

'You're not difficult,' Grace Maud says with something that sounds like pride in her voice. 'You're very easy to love, Patricia. And I count myself fortunate to have the chance to love you.'

Patricia's breath catches in her chest and she wants to stop the car because her eyes have filled with tears. But she blinks and keeps going.

All her life she has waited to hear her mother say she loves her, and has known for a while now that those words will never come. What she hasn't known – until now – is that she has unconsciously sought out another mother. It wasn't, after all, only her teacher she had to find and love. And whom she is now going to leave.

'I love you too, Grace Maud,' she says as she pulls up outside the little house.

'And I'll still love you when you're back from your trip,' Grace Maud says. 'So we'll have no tears.'

Patricia nods quickly. 'I'll pick you up tomorrow at eleven.'

They're going to Dorothy's so Patricia can say goodbye.

'I look forward to it.'

Grace Maud shuts the car door, and Patricia waits, as she always does, for her friend to walk into her house. This time, Grace Maud gives her a wave goodbye.

When she arrives home she pours her father a cup of tea but she's too nervous to drink one herself. She has a call to make, and it feels momentous yet practical at the same time.

To manage her nerves she's tried telling herself that Dennis can be her insurance policy in India – it would be silly to not stay in touch with someone from home if they're in the same country. But she knows why she's really calling him: she wants him to say the offer is still open. That they can travel together.

'Hi, Patricia,' he says when he answers, sounding surprised.

'Um . . . hi. Hi. How are you?'

She thinks she hears him laugh. 'Fine. How are you?'

'I like the idea of your trip to India so much I've decided to take my own,' she blurts, then hears him inhale sharply. 'Just for a few weeks. Not for the whole year.'

'That's amazing!' he says. 'When did you decide this?'

'The other day,' she says, not wanting to say she's been almost obsessing over the idea. 'Whereabouts are you going?'

'Kerala. You?'

'Mysore.'

'I'll change my flights,' he says without hesitation.

She is so taken aback that exactly what she wants to happen is happening that she takes a few seconds to respond.

'You can't do that!'

'Why not?' Dennis says. 'If you're going to be in India, there's no way I'm going to a different part of it.'

'Dennis, honestly – I just thought it would be good if we knew the other was there. In case.'

Now it's his turn to be silent.

'And how are we meant to find each other if we're not together?' he says at last, and she can hear the amusement in his voice.

'Um . . .' She knows it's a reasonable question. 'Carrier pigeon?'

He laughs. 'My dream girl is going on my dream trip and you're telling me I can't go with her? I'm changing my flights.'

'I'm hardly a girl,' she says, because she can't help herself. She has to push him on this point: their unsuitability for each other. Or, rather, her belief in it.

'No, you're not,' he says, and her heart sinks a little. 'You're a woman. Which is great, because I'm only interested in women.'

'Oh,' is the only thing she can manage to say.

'Why don't you tell me which flight you're on?' he says softly. 'And which flight you're coming back on?'

'But I'll have to leave you there,' she says. 'You're going for ages.'

'It looks like I've changed my plans,' he says. 'There's a bit of that going around.'

She smiles into the phone. 'Yes, there is.' She keeps smiling even though she knows full well that he can't see her. 'I'll just get my diary. I have everything in that.'

'I don't mind waiting,' he says. And she knows, with absolute certainty, that he has demonstrated this to be true.

CHAPTER FIFTY-NINE

'How is it possible that he's grown so much?' Patricia says as she passes Nicholas to Grace Maud.

'I suppose I don't notice as much because I see him all the time,' Dorothy says.

Her arms feel empty as she watches Grace Maud settle her son into the crook of her arm. She had no precedent for 'skin hunger', as she's come to think of it – the feeling she gets when she's had Nicholas in her arms, holding him or feeding him or bathing him, and then she doesn't. When she puts him down for a nap, for instance, she'll spend several minutes feeling like something is wrong, then she'll realise it's because her skin is singing out for him. It's an odd, overwhelming feeling and one of the best parts of motherhood. So good that it almost offsets the mastitis that has been plaguing her the last few days and makes her flinch each time she moves.

'How are you feeling?' Grace Maud asks.

'Yes.' Dorothy beams, trying to avoid the question. Her body doesn't feel like it belongs to her any more, but it's worth it – she has her son.

'"Yes" is not an answer to "How are you feeling?",' Grace Maud says with a narrowing of her eyes.

'Honestly, I'm fine. There's the odd thing. You know what it's like.' She smiles quickly, then remembers that while Grace Maud does know what it's like, Patricia doesn't, and she doesn't like being so thoughtless.

'I do,' says Grace Maud. 'And I don't remember thinking I was fine in the first few weeks. I had terrible mastitis, for one thing.' She looks pointedly at Dorothy while she jigs Nicholas up and down.

Dorothy opens her mouth, then closes it. She really doesn't want to bore the others with her niggles.

'Dorothy, you have a bad poker face,' Grace Maud says.

'I have mastitis too,' she admits. 'I've tried giving him formula to give my nipples a rest, but it seems to be worse.'

'That's because the only solution is to keep nursing.' Grace Maud raises her eyebrows. 'Perverse, but true.'

'What?' Dorothy shudders. 'How?'

'You need to clear those milk ducts. That's the only way to fix it. So just grit your teeth and do it.'

Grace Maud looks towards Patricia. 'I'm sure you're thrilled by this conversation.'

'I just wish I could contribute,' Patricia says.

'If you're going to launch into some I'm-worthless-because-I-don't-have-a-baby self-pity extravaganza, I'd advise against it,' Grace Maud says. 'Babies are lovely but they're not everything.' She looks down at Nicholas. 'Although this little one could just about be everything. Isn't he a treasure, Dorothy? What a handsome fellow.'

Dorothy feels the flush of maternal pride even though she knows she had no control over how her baby turned out. She also loves the fact that someone else thinks Nicholas is as gorgeous as she does.

'How's Frederick going with the new place?' Patricia asks.

Dorothy's smile falters. 'Good. Busy. I barely see him. But we knew that would happen.'

Grace Maud glances up sharply.

'And how's the Cairns café going?' Patricia presses on.

'Um . . .' Dorothy tries on a fake-cheerful smile.

'Poker face,' Grace Maud says.

Dorothy sighs. 'The manager isn't working out. So, um . . . I think I have to go back earlier than I thought.'

'Like when?' Patricia asks, leaning closer.

Dorothy gestures to her son. 'As soon as I can figure out what to do with him.'

When she and Frederick discussed the situation, she wanted to rail and rant about how unfair it is: she's waited years for this baby and now she's going to have to leave him with someone else while he's still tiny. She should have known nothing would be easy, because nothing ever has been.

'Can your mother help?' Patricia asks.

'A couple of days a week. But she has other things to do and I don't want to ask for more time than that.' Dorothy sighs as she looks at Nicholas. 'I guess I'll have to take him with me and park him in the kitchen.' She hears her voice become high pitched, reflecting her unease with the suggestion. She used to love the idea and now all she can think about is how unsafe it will be.

Her response earns her another sharp glance from Grace Maud. 'That's not ideal,' she says.

'No. But we can't afford a babysitter.' Dorothy squeezes her eyes shut as she thinks of the debt they've taken on to buy the new café and Frederick's confidence that they'll be able to pay it all back quickly. 'My friend Ruth said she can take him two days a week, but I don't know what to do about the rest. The café is open seven days a week.'

The three of them sit and listen as Nicholas burbles.

'It's been a long time since I've held a baby,' Grace Maud says, her face softening. 'I've missed it. They're easier when they're small.'

Dorothy thinks about the middle-of-the-night feeds and the constant churn of washing clothes and nappies, of never finding enough time to take care of herself and the house as well as the baby. If this is the easy part, she isn't sure she's prepared for the rest.

Grace Maud looks up and her eyes meet Dorothy's. 'I have a fair amount of free time,' she says.

'Hm?' Dorothy is thinking of the muslin wraps hanging on the line.

'I have time, Dorothy,' Grace Maud says more firmly. 'If you'd like help with Nicholas, I have time.'

Dorothy feels a flash of excitement, tempered by a rationalisation that this might be too good to be true. She glances at Patricia, who is beaming.

'That's such a good idea,' Patricia says.

'I wouldn't expect . . .' Dorothy says quickly. 'You wouldn't have to . . .'

'We'll sort it out,' Grace Maud says. 'You just let me know when you're thinking of going back and we'll come up with a schedule.' She gazes at Nicholas and chucks him under the chin. 'He's such a beauty. I'll take good care of him.'

'I know you will,' Dorothy says, and feels the weeks of tiredness and worry collapse on top of her. She puts her head in her hands and lets out a loud exhalation.

'Oh, Dorothy!' Patricia is next to her, a hand on her back.

'This is relief!' Dorothy says, lifting her head. 'I'm relieved! Thank you, Grace Maud.'

'I think we're both getting something out of this,' Grace Maud says, then she turns to Patricia. 'Why don't you take him for a little while? I'm going to help Dorothy with lunch.'

Patricia nods and somewhat awkwardly manoeuvres Nicholas into her arms, trying so hard to support his head that she almost fails to extract him completely.

'Come on,' Grace Maud says, offering her hands to Dorothy as she stands up. 'Let's give Patricia some time to figure out that she's going to miss a few weeks of that little boy's life.'

Dorothy leads her into the kitchen and starts pulling out everything they need for sandwiches. Being a mother has taught her that she can never know what each day will bring, and today it has brought her the generosity of others.

Grace Maud will never know how much her offer has meant, but Dorothy will try her very best to tell her.

CHAPTER SIXTY

Sydney's Kingsford Smith Airport is a microcosm of the city: packed with people speaking lots of different languages, all in the process of coming or going, making plans, doing things, talking, laughing, *being*.

Once Patricia knew her flight to India would leave from Sydney she decided to spend a day in the city, trying to catch up with friends she hasn't seen since she left, and reminding herself of the beauty of the harbour and how much Sydney has to offer: restaurants, art galleries, so many places to visit. Her time living at home, though, has made this city too busy for her. Or perhaps she's simply past the point in life of finding bustle exciting. Or Cairns is just the right place for her. So when she returns from her adventure, she will fly back into Sydney and take the first available flight north. She will wave to the harbour as the plane goes overhead, but won't regret not leaving the airport.

She pushes her luggage trolley past the check-in counters for other airlines, searching for the one she needs. Her suitcase is compact, and new: her father insisted on buying it for her, even though she knows he doesn't have much spare cash.

'You've never been on a big trip before, love,' he said. 'Please – let me.'

He'd even accompanied her to the airport in Cairns and waved as she went through the security checkpoint. This from the man who didn't say goodbye when she moved to Sydney.

Grace Maud said that yoga has taught her that old dogs can learn new tricks, but Patricia's father has learnt them all on his own. She will miss him, and she'll come back to him.

Her father's behaviour was quite at odds with that of her sister; given Annette's fondness for overseas travel Patricia had hoped she would be interested, at the very least, in the trip, but when Patricia called to tell her, and to ask her to call their father every couple of days, she was met with a lukewarm response.

'India?' Annette said. 'Why would you want to go there? It's not very relaxing. There are people everywhere. And cows.'

'I'm not going to relax, necessarily,' Patricia said. 'I'm going to do some yoga.'

'Yoga?' Annette sniffed. 'You'll break something. You're not very flexible, Patricia, remember? You weren't very good at ballet.'

At that moment Patricia was tempted to extend her trip indefinitely, but she has found that, somewhat paradoxically, there's a lot of freedom in knowing she's travelling with an ending in mind. She'd feel far more pressure if she were simply taking off with no idea of when she might return. This way she has a date and a plan, and therefore she can immerse herself in what's to come with no expectation that it's to propel her onto something greater or further. The karma yoga of travel, perhaps.

'There you are.' Dennis smiles as she approaches him, then kisses her before she can reply.

It's the sort of kiss she might once have felt self-conscious about when performed in public, but that's the other thing about liberating herself from expectations: she's also liberated from caring about what other people think.

After Dennis had changed his flights to match hers he'd tried to book into the same hotel as her, without luck. So they'd met for dinner last night, and at the end of it he'd taken her back to her hotel and walked her to the foyer. That's where he'd taken her hand and kissed her.

'I figure if we're travelling together that might be allowed,' he'd said.

'It is,' she'd breathed, and he'd kissed her again.

As he kisses her in the airport now, she no longer notices the swirl of people around him. Not until the kiss ends and he takes the handle of her trolley.

'Come on, let's get checked in,' he says, then grabs her around the waist and kisses her cheek.

She expected him to be in shorts, as he usually is; instead he's wearing long pants and a shirt with the sleeves buttoned up.

'I like your outfit,' she says.

'I could hardly take you away looking like a beach bum.'

His hand is still on her waist and she has to admit to herself that she likes it. May even love it.

'You deserve more than that,' he says. 'Love your dress.'

He pinches some of the material of the broderie anglaise number she bought at Grace Brothers yesterday.

'Thank you.' She rests her head on his shoulder as they come to a stop in the queue. There are a couple of dozen people ahead of them, but plenty of time before their flight.

'I'm glad you changed your mind,' he murmurs into her hair.

'So am I,' she says. 'About a lot of things.'

Patricia lets herself relax into Dennis's side, closes her eyes and daydreams about tomorrow and the day after and all the days after that.

CHAPTER SIXTY-ONE

Although it's been decades since Grace Maud had a baby to look after, she finds Nicholas to be considerably easier than Tom – perhaps because she raised Tom while also helping to run the farm. Her days started before dawn after a night of little sleep, and she hauled Tom around in a bassinet wherever she needed to go. He was a good baby – content to go along with her and interested in everything happening around him – so it didn't seem too onerous at the time. But she looks back now and wonders how on earth she coped. It wasn't just youth – it was the lack of option to do anything else.

She doesn't want that situation for Dorothy, which is why she has Nicholas in a pram in her kitchen and a bottle of expressed breast milk warming in a saucepan.

Dorothy drops off Nicholas on the way to work in the early morning and returns mid-afternoon. By then Grace Maud is usually spent but content, although with the intensity of her new activities her life has changed in a way she sometimes finds hard to believe.

Those new activities include a puppy that Tom insisted she must have because he thought she might be lonely without Cecilia living with her. Cecilia had been gone for several weeks by the time the idea occurred to him.

The puppy, a blue heeler named Birdy by the breeder's daughter because she liked budgerigars, turned up at the same time as the baby, but luckily Cecilia still works for her two days a week so Grace Maud has delegated some of the puppy raising to her.

'My life is a madhouse,' Grace Maud said to Cecilia one day as she held a grizzly Nicholas and Birdy did a wee on the kitchen floor.

'Didn't you volunteer for this?' Cecilia said, laughing as she put newspaper over the wee.

'Not the puppy-wee part.'

Sandrine was delighted when Grace Maud told her what she was doing, after she'd noted that Grace Maud was more enthusiastic than usual for relaxation.

'I'm exhausted,' Grace Maud had muttered, then listed her duties.

'How wonderful!' Sandrine clapped her hands. 'All that love, Grace Maud, and it was just stuck.' She poked Grace Maud between the shoulder blades. 'You kept it all in here, you see? Trapped inside your shell. Now you have let it out – marvellous!'

Grace Maud has never thought of herself as having a shell but had noticed herself hunching over more as the years went on. She used to have such a straight back; she didn't notice when the change began but always thought it was old age.

She'd pondered Sandrine's words for a while afterwards. What did she mean by 'all that love'? Grace Maud has never thought of herself as an especially loving person. Yet there is something that caught her by surprise recently: she doesn't think of Ellie Maud so often these days. She knows it isn't because she loves her less, but perhaps her heart is not as broken as it was. If she developed a shell it may have been to protect that heart, and now she doesn't need that protection any more.

Because the truth of her life – if she has time to think about it – is that she may have thought of herself as difficult and solitary all these years, but she's really not. That was a version of herself that suited her at the time; in fact, it was the only way she could function. She never believed she could rely on others as much as she could rely on herself, so it was easier to never try. Yet she lives in the world. She hasn't chosen to be a hermit. She is here, in this town, on this street, in this house that now has people coming and going, noise and laughter and a yapping dog.

Grace Maud thinks Ellie Maud would approve of this. So, at last, she feels she can let her go. The love they shared has sustained her through hard times and good. It has been the one true thing she has known.

Now she has another truth: that love was preparing her for this new phase of her life. Her heart could not expand to allow these other people in if she hadn't loved her sister so voluminously first.

A knock at the door is answered by Cecilia's shout from the back of the house. 'I'll get it!'

It will be Dorothy at the door; it's her time to arrive to take Nicholas home.

'Hello, hello!' she says, hurrying past Cecilia to Grace Maud and kissing her on the cheek before she kisses Nicholas softly on the head. His little face responds with a burbling smile.

'I brought in your mail,' she says to Grace Maud, handing it over.

On top is a postcard showing a temple and Grace Maud immediately turns it over. In Patricia's neat, schoolteacher handwriting is a short message that says she and Dennis are heading for Kashmir and that she sends her love.

'I still can't believe she didn't tell us she was going with him!' Dorothy says as she hugs Nicholas to her chest.

'I don't think she knew herself until the very end.'

Grace Maud looks at the front of the card again. Once upon a time she'd minded that she had never travelled; now, she doesn't. There are riches to be found everywhere, and she knows what she has right here.

'She'll be back before we know it,' she murmurs as she puts the card on the coffee table in front of her.

'I miss her,' Dorothy says, patting Nicholas's back.

'I'm sure she isn't really missing us,' Grace Maud says. 'But I know Sandrine misses you. She asks after you every week.'

'I'll get back one day.' Dorothy lifts Nicholas in the air and makes a silly face at him.

'She also says that yoga will always be there for you whenever you're ready,' Grace Maud adds.

Dorothy nods. 'I do practise the breathing, you know. Sometimes if it's been a hectic day. It helps.'

'I'll let her know.'

'I'd better take Nicholas home before he's hungry again,' Dorothy says. 'Thanks so much, Grace Maud. Again. I don't actually know how I'll ever pay you back.'

'I don't recall asking you to.'

Grace Maud stands, a little stiffly. Sandrine has told her that she needs to stretch throughout the week and lately Grace Maud has been forgetting.

'Have a lovely evening,' she says as she walks Dorothy to the door. 'See you on Thursday. And say hello to Ruth for me.'

'Thank you!' A kiss goodbye, then Dorothy is gone.

The telephone rings and Grace Maud hears Cecilia answer it.

'It's Tom!' she calls.

'Hello, love,' she says as she picks up the phone, watching as Birdy scampers around the garden before disappearing from sight.

She listens to Tom telling her about the progress of the new house, and about the fact that his daughters have decided to move home to the farm but he doesn't really want them there, so he's coming into town to look for a place for them to live.

The sun holds its hard, yellow light well into the late afternoon, and Grace Maud hears Cecilia opening and closing the linen cupboard, and Birdy's paws on the lino in the laundry.

A car goes by on the street and the teenage boy next door has started his trumpet practice, and Tom is now telling her that Luca wants to go to TAFE to study something related to agriculture and wants to talk to her about staying with her for a while.

The sounds of life. The sounds of *her* life.

She feels her heart beating in her chest. The same heart that once beat, seventy-six years ago, right next to that of the girl who looked exactly like her. They were together, now they are apart, and while Grace Maud will never quite recover she knows that it's no longer her destiny to mourn forever.

She has too much to do. Too many people to hold in her heart.

She is still alive. She is still here. All is well.

ACKNOWLEDGEMENTS

Thank you to Fiona Hazard, Louise Sherwin-Stark, Daniel Pilkington, Jemma Ferreira-Rowe and all at Hachette for their support.

I was very lucky to again work with Karen Ward, in-house editor extraordinaire. Thank you to editors Celine Kelly and Nicola O'Shea, and proofreader Pam Dunne.

Christa Moffitt has created such a beautiful cover – I didn't think it was possible to make a cover even more lovely than the last one! Thank you, Christa.

Thank you to my agent, Melanie Ostell, for her reassuring counsel.

Jen Bradley – not only are you my beloved friend but you provided integral assistance to this novel (and took the author photo!). Thank you.

For their support and encouragement, thank you to Ashleigh Barton, Isabelle Benton, Anna Egelstaff, Kate Farquharson, Jackie and Ben Gillies, Robbie and Richard Hille, Chris Kunz, Amelia Levido, Neralyn and Col Porter, Kate Sampson, Veronica Sywak and Jill Wunderlich.

Thanks and much love to my parents, Robbie and David, and my brother, Nicholas. Especially to my mother, who not only reads my drafts but puts up with my author tantrums and still loves me anyway.

I went to my first yoga class in early 1993 in a church hall on Sydney's north shore. The teacher was Judy Krupp, and Judy would be my teacher for over twenty years. Since the mid 2000s I have been following the teaching of Shiva Rea, and I owe her more than I can say. I began teaching yoga in 2002 – thank you to all those students who have been in my classes over the years.

On problem-solving long walks the following albums provided inspiration and fog-clearing:

Fanny Lumsden – *Fallow*

Jasmine Rae – *Lion Side*

Luke O'Shea – *There in the Ochre*

Max Jackson – *Life of the Party*

The McClymonts – *Mayhem to Madness*

Troy Cassar-Daley – *The World Today*

The first chapter of this novel was partly inspired by the song 'Well Dressed Man' by Brad Butcher.

During the redrafting process the *Return to Sound* collection by Shivarasa was an invaluable aid to concentration.

This book was written and rewritten on Borogegal and Darramuragal lands. I acknowledge the Traditional Owners of those lands and pay my respects to Elders past, present and future.